by Harry Connolly

"Redemption comes wrapped in a package of mystery and horror that hammers home the old saying 'Don't do the crime if you can't do the time' . . . and even then you'd better check the yellow pages for one bad-ass exterminator first."
—ROB THURMAN, author of *Nightlife*

"A fine novel with some genuinely creepy moments. I enjoyed it immensely, and hope we'll see more of Ray Lilly."
—LAWRENCE WATT-EVANS,
author of the *Obsidian Chronicles*

"With an engaging protagonist, an unusual setting, fascinating magics, dark mysteries, and edge-of-your-seat action . . . everything you could want in a supernatural thriller. An exciting and original start to a great new series that will leave readers hungry for more."
—VICTORIA STRAUSS,
author of *The Burning Land*

CHILD OF FIRE

HARRY CONNOLLY

BALLANTINE BOOKS • NEW YORK

Child of Fire is a work of fiction. Names, characters, places, and incidents are the products of the author's imagination or are used fictitiously. Any resemblance to actual events, locales, or persons, living or dead, is entirely coincidental.

A Del Rey Mass Market Original

Copyright © 2009 by Harry Connolly
Excerpt from *Game of Cages* by Harry Connolly copyright © 2009 by Harry Connolly

Published in the United States by Del Rey, an imprint of The Random House Publishing Group, a division of Random House, Inc., New York.

DEL REY is a registered trademark and the Del Rey colophon is a trademark of Random House, Inc.

This book contains an excerpt from the forthcoming novel *Game of Cages* by Harry Connolly. This excerpt has been set for this edition only and may not reflect the final content of the forthcoming edition.

ISBN 978-0-345-50889-8

Printed in the United States of America

www.delreybooks.com

9 8 7 6 5 4 3 2 1

CHILD OF FIRE

CHAPTER ONE

It felt good to sit behind the wheel again, even the wheel of a battered Dodge Sprinter. Even with this passenger beside me.

The van rumbled like a garbage truck, handled like a refrigerator box, and needed a full minute to reach highway speeds. I'd driven better, but I'm a guy who has to take what I can get while I'm still alive to get it.

The passenger beside me was Annalise Powliss. She stood about five foot nothing, was as thin as a mop handle, and was covered with tattoos from the neck down. Her hair was the same dark red as the circled *F*'s I used to get on my book reports, and she wore it cropped close to her scalp. It was an ugly cut, but she never seemed to care how she looked. I suspected she cut it herself.

She was my boss, and she had been forbidden to kill me, although that's what she most wanted to do.

"Where are we going?" I asked for the fourth time.

She didn't answer. She wasn't talking to me except to tell me where to drive. To be honest, I didn't blame her. She had good reason to hate me.

At the moment, though, she and I had a job to do and all I knew about it was this: Annalise was on her way to kill someone. Maybe several someones. I was supposed to help.

Because she wouldn't talk to me, I was not entirely clear who had ordered her not to kill me or why they would bother. I was just the driver, and I didn't even know where we were going.

"Quarter tank," I said as we approached a gas station. I hated to drive on less than a half tank of gas, but so far the boss had refused to let me fill up. Since she had the money, the title, and the physical strength to tear my arm off, she made the decisions.

She glanced down at the scrap of wood in her hand—unpainted and unfinished except for the twisted nonsense shape made of several colors on one side—and said nothing. I stifled my irritation and drove past the pumps.

We were westbound somewhere on the Olympic Peninsula. There were no other cars on the road. The streets were slick with misting rain, and the sky was growing dark as evening approached. After my years in Southern California, I'd forgotten how long it could take for night to fall in this part of the world.

The road was one of those rural highways with one lane in each direction and a speed limit of fifty-five. I was staying below the limit because the van, with its balding tires, whining brakes, and load of equipment in the back, wasn't equipped for the twists and turns of backwoods driving.

I was enjoying the drive anyway. I had a key to the door and I could see the sky. It felt good to be a free man again.

Up ahead, I saw a big cedar right up close to the road. Annalise was not wearing her seat belt. I was wearing mine. The speedometer on the Sprinter shuddered at the fifty-miles-per-hour mark. All I had to do was swerve. She and her little scrap of lumber would fly through the windshield and slam against the tree, while I would be safe in the arms of the shoulder harness and air bag.

I didn't try it. It wasn't just the motorcycle Annalise kept on flimsy mounts in the cargo area behind me. In truth, I doubted that slamming face-first into a tree trunk would do more than muss her thrift-shop clothes. And piss her off. She'd survived worse. I'd seen it.

I was pretty sure Annalise wasn't a human being. She had been, once, I thought, but I wasn't sure what she was now.

A Volvo station wagon with luggage strapped to the roof drove eastbound toward us. As it passed, the painted scrap wood in Annalise's hand flashed like a camera flashbulb. The design painted on the face of the wood began to twist like a nest full of snakes.

Annalise lunged toward me. "Turn around!" she yelled. She had a high, funny voice more suited to a cartoon squirrel than a grown woman. "Turn around and follow that station wagon!"

I was already doing it. I hit the brakes and twisted the wheel, letting the clumsy van fishtail as much as I dared. I heard crashing noises from behind me as Annalise's things toppled over. We came to a rest, and I threw it in reverse.

"Let's go! Goddammit, hurry up!"

"Keep your shirt on."

I backed up onto the shoulder, swung the wheel all the way around, and stomped on the gas. We crept after the station wagon.

"Goddammit, Ray," Annalise growled. She was very close to my ear, and I could hear the hate in her voice. "If you let them get away, I'm going to tear you apart."

"Oh yeah? Who are you going to find who can reach the gas pedal?" I said. My voice betrayed too much fear. When Annalise threatened to tear someone apart, she meant it literally. "This is your broken-down van. If we don't catch them, you can blame yourself for not buying better wheels."

She settled back into her seat and glared through the windshield at the empty road ahead.

I forced myself to smile at her. "Isn't this nice? Our

first job together and we're getting along so well." It was stupid and dangerous to taunt her, but I was afraid of her and I hated to show my fear.

She ignored me, for which I was secretly grateful.

We picked up speed, rounding curves and topping hills the van could barely handle. Night was coming and the forest around us was filling with shadows. I switched on the headlights, but Annalise snarled at me to turn them off.

A red light flashed from between the trees on the right. I slowed. Annalise started to protest, but I shushed her. She didn't look pleased about that.

We came to a break in the forest—a gravel parking lot with a row of abandoned wooden stalls at the back. It looked like it had once been a roadside farmer's stand. The station wagon was parked at the far end, red brake lights glowing.

I parked a couple of car lengths away from the vehicle and jumped from the van as quickly as I could. Annalise was a little faster. She walked toward them, holding the fist-sized scrap of wood in her hand like a Geiger counter. The design on it writhed wildly; something about the car or the people in it was setting it off.

All the wagon's side doors stood open. A man and woman had their head and shoulders in the back doors, and they were working frantically at something. I checked their stuff. Among the things strapped to their roof was a vacuum cleaner in a clear plastic trash bag beaded with rain. These people weren't on a camping trip. They were skipping town.

All I could see of the man was a pair of extra-wide Dockers and the pale skin that peeked above his sagging waistband. *Office worker,* I thought. He must have heard us approach, but he didn't turn to look at us. Was he completely engrossed, or did he have a weak survival instinct? Out of unshakable habit, my next thought was: *Victim.*

No, no. I pushed the thought away. That was not part of my life anymore.

From what I could see through the car windows, the woman was also wider than strictly necessary and also dressed for casual day at the office. They continued to struggle with something in the backseat.

I felt a pressure against my chest, just below my right collarbone. Strange. I tried to ignore it and said, "Do you folks need any help?"

The woman glanced up, noticing us for the first time. She had a terrified look on her face, but I knew it had nothing to do with Annalise or me. Her husband glanced back as he came out of the backseat. His glasses were smeary from the drizzle. "No," he said too quickly. "We're fine."

The pressure against my chest increased.

Then their little boy climbed out of the car.

He was a good-looking kid, maybe eight or nine years old, although I'm no judge. His hair stuck up in the back, and he had scrapes on both elbows. "I feel funny, Dad," he said. He laid his hands on his chest and pressed. "I feel squishy."

Flames erupted around his head.

I felt light-headed suddenly, and the pressure against my chest vanished. Before I could think about it, I ran toward them, stripping off my jacket.

The woman screamed. The flames around the boy's head spread downward past his crotch. In an instant, his whole body was ablaze.

The father fumbled for a jacket draped over the driver's seat. I heard Annalise's footsteps behind me.

"Wow!" the boy said. "It doesn't hurt, Daddy. It doesn't hurt at all."

The father lunged at his boy with the jacket, knocking him to the gravel, then beating at the flames. I got there a half second later and slapped my jacket over the boy's face and head.

Rain steamed off the burning body. Beside me, the father made a noise like a strangled dog. I tried not to think about that. I tried not to notice the black scorch marks where the flames touched the ground. I tried not to think about what was happening. I just worked at the flames. I slapped at them, smothered them, wrapped them in my jacket.

It was no good. The fire flared up and my jacket erupted in flames. I threw it aside and started to drag my shirt over my head.

The kid laughed as though we were tickling him. Then his skin turned silver-gray and his whole head came apart.

The flames roared. A wave of heat forced me back. The father rolled back onto his padded behind, almost bowling over his wife as she rushed around the car toward us.

I let my backward momentum roll me onto my feet. Annalise stood nearby. She had unbuttoned the fireman's jacket she always wore, revealing colored ribbons alligator-clipped to her clothes. She pulled a green one free. The small sigil drawn on the bottom glowed with silvery light.

I turned back to the family. The boy's head, arms, and chest had come apart and been transformed into a mass of fat, wriggling, silver-gray worms, each about the size of my pinkie. Then his stomach came apart, then his hips. It happened so fast I had no chance to think about it. I saw the worms twisting themselves against the packed gravel, trying to burrow into the earth. They swarmed over one another, heading west. Everything they touched turned black with scorched, greasy soot.

I felt a tightness in my throat that might have been the

urge to vomit, but there was nothing to bring up. I was completely hollow inside.

The father struggled to his feet, and his wife tried to move around him to her son. The expression on her face told me she already knew the truth, already knew her son was gone, but she could no more stay away from his disintegrating body than she could leap up into the clouds.

I tackled them. My shoulder sank into the father's broad, soft belly, and I grabbed the mother around the waist. With all my strength, I pushed them away from the car.

I didn't look back at Annalise. I didn't have to. I knew very well what those green ribbons did and how little she cared about collateral damage.

The father and mother stumbled backward and fell over each other, hitting the gravel hard. I landed on their legs.

I heard a *whoosh* of fire behind me. Annalise's green ribbon had hit its target. I glanced back and saw flames, green ones this time, roar up around the wriggling mass that had once been a boy's body. Where the flames touched them, the gray worms burst apart.

The sphere of green fire expanded. I pulled in my legs, trying to get away, but I was too late. The cold green fire washed over me.

I sucked in a lungful of air to scream my life away. It was too soon. Too soon. I looked down at my legs, expecting them to burn away to blackened, smoking bones.

It didn't happen. There was no pain, no damage to my legs, nothing. My clothes didn't even burn. I felt nothing more than a slight pressure below my collarbone—a place the flames did not even reach.

The flames receded. I was undamaged. So were the parents. I had pushed them out of range just in time.

The worms had not fared so well. There was nothing left of them but gray slime.

"Holy God," the mother said, her voice thin and strained. Her face was slack and her eyes were glassy. If I hadn't pushed her away, she would have been killed along with her son—another person struck down for no other reason than she was next to someone Annalise wanted to kill.

Annalise took another ribbon from beneath her jacket. This one was blue. I had no idea what the blue ones did, but I knew it wouldn't be good.

Before she could use it, a *force* passed through me. It wasn't a physical push. It struck my mind, my consciousness, whatever you want to call it, and it felt as though I was standing in heavy surf. It almost toppled me.

At the same moment, I felt a twinge high on the right side of my chest again.

Annalise staggered and winced; her blue ribbon fell from her hand. She felt it, too. The mother and father didn't stagger. Their expressions went blank.

Then it was gone.

The couple stood and began to straighten their clothes. "You didn't have to knock me over," the man said. "I was only trying to help."

"What?"

"We pulled over to help—oh, forget it." He slapped at the dust on his pants.

His wife clutched at his shirt and looked at me worriedly. "Douglas, let's just go."

They started walking toward the car, glancing back at me as if I was a stray dog that might bite.

They did not look the least bit upset by what had just happened to their son.

After they got into their car and slammed the doors, Douglas started the engine. His wife leaned into the backseat and fussed with a baby sleeping in an infant seat. I hadn't noticed the baby until then. Douglas turned on the music. Bobby McFerrin. Gravel crunched under the tires as they began to drive away, as though they were leaving behind nothing more important than some old fast-food wrappers.

Annalise charged past me, lowered her shoulder, and slammed into the car's front panel, just above the wheel. Her legs pumped. The fender crumpled and the car slid sideways like a tackling dummy until it tipped into a ditch.

She stood and straightened her jacket, a scowl on her delicate little face. I had seen her strength before, of course. She could have flipped the car onto its roof or torn the door off and pinched off Douglas's head. I assumed the only reason she hadn't done either was that she hadn't finished with them yet.

Douglas jumped out of the car to inspect the damage. He looked at the crumpled metal, then at Annalise, then all around.

"What . . ." he started. He couldn't finish the question. He ran his hand over the ruined fender, reassuring himself that it was really bent metal. He looked at Annalise again. "What hit my car?"

"I'm not done with you," Annalise said. She stepped toward him.

The wife leaned toward his window. "Douglas, get back in the car," she said. She leaned into the backseat to check the baby. Still sleeping.

Douglas let the keys in his hand jangle and backed toward the driver's door. My own hands were shaking. I felt hysteria building in me. That little boy had called him Daddy, and now he was going to drive away as though he'd just stopped for a piss? They'd shrugged that kid off as if he was roadkill. I had never even met the kid before two minutes ago, and what I'd seen made me want to weep and puke my guts out at the same time.

I didn't do either. Instead, I got angry.

"You're just going to drive away?"

The woman's eyes widened. "Douglas . . ."

"What about your kid?" I stalked after them, determined to see some sign of grief from them. I needed my anger. Without it, I thought I might shake myself apart. "He called you Mommy and Daddy! Don't you care what happened to him?"

Douglas would have to turn his back on me to climb into his car. He wasn't going to risk that. "Sir," he said, "I don't know what you're talking about."

"He called you Daddy! And he just . . . your own son!"

My anger was growing too large for me, but I couldn't stop myself. I needed to see a reaction from them. These people were going to show some grief if I had to wring it out of them with my bare hands.

The man rounded on me. "My son didn't call me anything! He's only three months old!" he shouted.

"Ray," Annalise said.

I ignored her. I just stared at Douglas, stunned and horrified. "You don't care at all, do you?" There was no more anger in my voice, no accusation, only amazement. I was building toward something terrible, and I had no idea how to stop myself.

If I had Annalise's strength, I would have stripped the flesh from his bones. If I had her arsenal of spells, I would have burned him alive.

"Ray."

I turned toward Annalise. Her thin, girlish voice sounded pinched. Even she had been rattled by the boy's death. "Settle down," she said. "They can't remember. Something took their memory away."

It took a couple of seconds for that to sink in. The wave. The wave I'd felt after the boy fell apart must have hit them, too. It must have erased their memories.

Why hadn't it erased mine?

Douglas was leaning back, one arm reaching toward

his wife. There was a smack of metal slapping into a soft hand, and he came at me.

I was distracted and off-balance; if he'd been faster, he would have killed me. But he wasn't fast—he was an overweight office drone. A victim. I instinctively raised my arm to protect my head, and he slammed a tire iron onto my tattooed forearm.

I felt no pain and barely even any pressure. Annalise was not the only one with tattoos. Like hers, mine were magic. Hers covered her entire body, but mine covered just a couple of spots, including the outside of my forearms and hands.

Douglas thought he'd scored a winning blow. He smirked and waited for me to cringe and clutch my arm. Instead, I snatched the tire iron away from him and racked him up against the car.

Annalise stepped up to him. "Wallet," she said.

He barely glanced at her. Annalise was a far greater danger to him than I was, but all of his attention was on the big, tattooed man, not the tiny woman. She had to repeat herself.

His wife called out. "Douglas! For God's sake, give her your wallet!"

He produced the wallet and Annalise took it. " 'Douglas Benton,' " she read. " '144 Acorn Road, Hammer Bay, Washington.' "

"We don't live there anymore." Douglas sounded a little frantic. "We're leaving town."

I shook him. "Why?"

His mouth opened and closed several times. He couldn't think of an answer.

"He's forgotten that, too," Annalise said. She pulled a card from his wallet. It was white with a magnetic strip across the back. "Hammer Bay Toys," she read. "This where you work?"

"Yes," Douglas said.

"But you're not going back."

"No. Not planning to."

"You didn't return your security card?"

"I—I forgot." Sweat beaded on his lip. He glanced at each of us, trying to think of a phrase that would placate us and let him drive away. He thought we were crazy, and the way I felt at that moment, he wasn't far wrong.

"Hmm," Annalise said, as though she was unsatisfied with his answer. There was a moment of silence. Douglas couldn't bear to leave it unfilled.

"Look, I don't know what the problem is," he said. "I'm sure we can do something to work all this out. Right? I'm sure it's just been a misunderstanding or something."

Annalise seemed thoughtful. "Maybe you're right, Douglas."

I wondered if this was the moment she would kill them both.

That made him a little bolder. "Sure, sure, I understand. We're just a little confused. All of us. The baby didn't call me Daddy, right, Meg? He's too young for that.

"Meg and I have always wanted a son, but we were never blessed until just this winter. See? We're all just a little mixed up."

"One of us is," Annalise said. "Because you have a front-facing car seat in there."

We all looked into the backseat. A plastic car seat was buckled onto the far side of the infant's seat. A small one. The boy who had just . . . I wasn't ready to approach that thought yet, but he was too big to be sitting in such a small car seat.

Had they lost more than one? Had they forgotten that, too?

Douglas and Meg looked to each other for an explanation. Silence. Douglas turned to us and said: "We're bringing it to my sister?" As if he was guessing.

"There are scorch marks on it," I said. They were the same sort of marks on the ground where the boy had . . .

The Bentons didn't seem to know what to make of that. The blank confusion on their faces was fascinating. They really were enchanted. My anger was still going strong, but it wasn't directed at them anymore. I was beginning to pity them.

Meg went to the backseat, unbuckled the car seat, and heaved it toward the woods. It bounced once on the gravel and disappeared into a patch of nettles.

Douglas glanced at me nervously. "I don't know who put that there. Really." Then he turned toward Annalise. "Do you want money? Is that it?"

Annalise gave him a sour smile. She took the scrap wood from her pocket and laid it against the station wagon, then against Douglas's ample belly. The designs twisted, but more slowly than before.

"Does this hurt?" Annalise asked.

"No," Douglas replied.

"Tell your wife, because I'm going to do this to her, too."

She walked around the car and laid the scrap of wood on Meg's palm. Douglas stared at something fascinating in the gravel at his feet.

That's when I noticed his hands. They were red, swollen, and shiny wet. Burned. He didn't seem to be in pain. If I pointed them out to him the way we had pointed out the car seat, would he suddenly "remember" them? Would he suddenly be in terrible pain?

Annalise leaned into the Volvo and yanked on the gearshift. Then she walked to the front of the car, laid her tiny hand on the bumper, and shoved it. It rolled out of the ditch onto level ground. She started toward the van. "Ray, let's go."

"Get out of here, Douglas," I said.

"Yeah, Douglas," Annalise said. "Get far away from Hammer Bay, and don't come back."

We didn't need to tell him twice. Douglas jumped into his car and peeled out of the lot.

I watched them go, feeling my adrenaline ebb. I couldn't stop thinking about that little boy, or how fiercely hot the flames had been. I looked down at my own undamaged hands. I felt woozy and sick.

Annalise called my name again. I turned away, ran to the edge of the lot, and puked into the bushes.

When that was over, I had tears in my eyes from the strain of it. They were the only tears that little boy was ever going to get. I tried to spit the acid taste out of my mouth, but it wouldn't go away.

I wiped my eyes dry. My hands were shaking and my stomach was in knots. That kid had no one to mourn for him except me, and I didn't have that much longer in this world, either. Something had to be done for him. I didn't know what it was, but as I wiped at my eyes again, I knew there had to be *something*.

I heard footsteps behind me. "Don't get maudlin," Annalise said.

I told her what she could do with herself.

"Enough with this weepy Girl Scout routine. Drink this." She shoved a water bottle into my hands.

I rinsed my mouth and spat. As long as I did what she told me to do, she wasn't allowed to kill me. I did it again. "Thanks."

"Don't thank me," she said. "I just didn't want you to stink up the van with your puke breath."

We walked toward the van. I wondered how many dead kids Annalise had seen. Maybe the number was so high they barely registered anymore.

I climbed behind the wheel and buckled in. Annalise never wore her seat belt. She had other, less mundane protections.

"When the boy burned, he turned into something," I said. "It was, like, gray maggots or something, and they started burrowing into the ground. What were they?"

"Start the van."

"Why weren't my hands damaged by the flames? I don't have tattoos over my fingers. Why wasn't I hurt like Douglas?"

She didn't answer.

"What was that wave I felt? I know you felt it, too. It was like something pushed against my mind." The words coming out of my mouth sounded ridiculous, but Annalise had just seen me crying like a baby. It's not like I had any pride left. "And I felt this twinge on my chest—"

"Start the van," she interrupted.

I did. Once we hit the road, Annalise took a cell phone from the glove compartment. She hit speed dial. After a few seconds, she said: "It's Annalise." She told the person at the other end of the line Douglas's name, address, and license number. "Check him out," she said. "And I'm still waiting for a current report." She snapped the phone shut without waiting for a response.

At least I wasn't the only one she was rude to.

I focused on the road. The long, slow descent into an overcast northwest night was well under way. I turned on the headlights just in time to light up a sign that said HAMMER BAY 22 MILES. This time, Annalise didn't protest. Aside from the rumble of the van, it was quiet. Suddenly, I didn't like the quiet.

"Who did you call?" She didn't answer. "Your mom?" She shot a deadly look at me. Oops. Sore spot.

"Why didn't you kill Douglas?" I asked. "Isn't that our job? To kill people who have magic?"

Her response was irritated and defensive. "The Bentons didn't *have* magic. Were they carrying a spell book? Had they cast a spell on themselves? Were they hiding a predator?"

"Guess not."

"Someone cast a spell on them. That's who we want. Those people were no threat. They're victims."

I didn't say, *That's what I thought, too.* I didn't think the word meant the same thing to her as it did to me.

We were silent for a couple of minutes. I kept seeing the boy's face as the flames erupted around it. I kept hearing him say it didn't hurt. I needed to keep talking, or I was going to start weeping again.

"Why are we going to Hammer Bay?" I asked. "Not for Douglas. What's going on there?" She didn't answer again. "Come on," I persisted. "We're supposed to be doing this job and I don't know anything about it. Tell me what's going on. Or don't you know? Flames that don't hurt. Boys that turn into maggots. People who forget their dead kids. Something that pushed against our minds." She was silent. "Aren't you going to explain any of this?"

"No reason to."

"Why not?"

"Because you'll be dead very, very soon."

We drove the rest of the way in silence.

We passed over the crest of a hill, and the Pacific Ocean suddenly appeared below us. Then I saw the town of Hammer Bay. We drove down the hill, straight toward the heart of it.

CHAPTER TWO

Annalise wanted to visit Acorn Road immediately. Rather than drive aimlessly around reading street signs, I insisted we fill the tank and ask directions. The middle-aged clerk behind the counter tried to help, but when he told me to take a right turn where the bowling alley used to be, I snatched a map off the display rack and added it to our bill.

As I filled the tank, I noticed a young mother pull in next to us, with a little girl and a little boy in the front seat beside her. Her car was full of groceries. "For God's sake," she said, exasperated. "Sit still for five minutes! Please? Five minutes?" I finished refueling, trying not to look at the kids. Every time I did I imagined them crowned with flames.

The streets were sprinkled with potholes and dark from burned-out streetlights. We passed a lot of battered, run-down pickups and rattletrap station wagons.

We drove by three houses having their roofs repaired and two that were being landscaped. The town looked like it had just started to pull itself out of a long decline.

It turned out that Annalise was not good with maps. She sent me in the wrong direction twice. We had a lovely but useless tour of Hammer Bay's downtown. We drove past antique shops and small, family-owned hardware stores. There was a sign above a storefront that read THE MALLET. The newspaper box at the curb had the same name across the front.

We drove uphill. The waterfront road was on the top of a cliff that grew higher the farther south we went. There were several restaurants: pizza, diner, Mexican, Italian, Chinese, brew pub, and a couple of high-end places that had prime cliffside locations. Sadly, the sports bar was the only place that showed signs of life. A glance through the window at the big screen inside was all I needed to see that the Mariners game was on.

I had the sudden urge to pull over, but I ignored it. Baseball wasn't part of my life anymore, and it hadn't been for a long time. Just thinking about it reminded me of friends I'd lost and times when life seemed much simpler.

Maybe Annalise was right. Maybe I was being maudlin. What the hell, I was going to die soon, wasn't I? I had a right.

By this time my hunger had returned with a vengeance. I slowed as we passed a Thai restaurant.

"Are you buying dinner?" I asked. I didn't have any money. I didn't even have a change of underwear or a toothbrush. If she was going to kill me, she could at least buy me a meal first.

"Not right now, I'm not."

That made me hopeful.

I took the map from her. It was a cheap tourist map, covered with little icons showing the locations of local landmarks and restaurants that had paid for the privilege. Crude squiggles represented the cliff. Behind us, to the north, was the bay the town was named for. Ahead of us in the dark at the south end of town was some sort of lighthouse, supposedly, although I couldn't see any lights.

Acorn Road was at the northeastern end of town. We were at the southwestern end. I made note of the route we needed and started off.

So far I had not seen a single cop. That struck me as

a little strange. Most small towns station at least one car near the bars. I didn't know if they were busy with an emergency or were kicking back at a doughnut shop somewhere.

Now that she was not burdened with the map, Annalise picked up the scrap wood again and stared at it. The design churned slowly. It didn't slow down or speed up. It didn't change much at all. It just kept moving and moving.

Whatever this meant, Annalise didn't like it.

As I drove through the neighborhood, streetlights lit up three more black marks just like the one the gray worms had left in the gravel lot. One started at the top of a bright yellow plastic slide. Another lay across an asphalt driveway beside a skateboard and helmet. The last began next to a pile of windblown, rain-warped schoolbooks.

Not beside a riding mower. Not a Harley or a pickup. Only kids' things.

I found the Bentons' house and parked on the street. There were only five or six other cars on the block, and Annalise's Sprinter stuck out like a sore thumb. I didn't see any lights switch on or any curtains draw back. No one peeked at us. It seemed we had come to a small town where the neighbors were not particularly nosy. In other words, the Twilight Zone.

Annalise strolled up to the front door and rang the bell. When there was no answer, she rang it again. No answer. She lifted her foot to kick the door down.

"Wait," I said. I took the ghost knife from my pocket.

The ghost knife was nothing more than a small sheet of notepaper covered first by mailing tape, then actual laminate. On one side of the paper was a sigil like the ones on Annalise's ribbons or our tattoos. This one I had drawn myself.

It was a spell. My only one.

The ghost knife slid into the door as if the wood was

only smoke. I drew the mark down through the deadbolt latch and pushed the door open. The dark house lay waiting for me.

The first time I went to jail, it was a trip to juvie for a handgun accident that had crippled my best friend. There hadn't been any formal charges over that, but it set a sort of precedent.

The second time was when I lived in Los Angeles. I'd been working as a car thief, stealing popular models and driving them either to a chop shop or else down to the docks at Long Beach to be shipped and sold overseas. It was fun, sort of. I was in a crew of jack-offs and morons I could almost rely on, and I didn't have to carry a gun, which was a big plus considering my history. When I was busted for a bar fight, and wouldn't testify against the jack-offs and morons, the cops made sure I did a couple of years.

The third time was last year. That didn't go well, in part because it was how I met and made enemies with Annalise. The cops arrested me following that fiasco, too, but after a couple of months the charges were dropped. I had a lawyer hired by the society to thank for that, along with a lot of forensic evidence that appeared to have been tampered with and/or incompetently handled.

It hadn't been, of course, but no one in the legal system was ready to recognize the aftermath of supernatural murder. Even the lawyer the Twenty Palace Society hired thought I was being framed and tried to convince me to sue the Seattle PD.

I didn't bother. When I'd walked out of the courthouse just this afternoon, Annalise was waiting for me. Now I was here in this town, and I wasn't expecting to see the end of the week. What was the point of filing a bunch of legal papers?

The point of this digression into the not-so-distant past

is that I had a history with cops and jails. I didn't want to go back. Also, I'd never broken into someone's house before. Not a stranger's house, at least.

So I felt an unfamiliar chill as I pushed the Bentons' front door open. The house was quiet. I hesitated before entering.

There's a feeling of power that comes from invading someone's space. I'd felt it when I'd stolen cars as part of Arne's crew. I'd sit behind a steering wheel, beside their fast-food wrappers or whatever, and know I was taking something very personal. A simple action like readjusting the seat—

"Would you hurry up?" Annalise snapped. "I don't want to stand here all night."

"Sorry," I said. "I've never done this before."

"Well, don't step in that," she said, pointing.

There was a long black streak on the carpet that led to the door. I hopped over it into the living room. The streak led out the door and turned left toward the sea. I was glad I hadn't stepped in it.

Annalise shut the door and surveyed the room. She laid the scrap wood against the wall. The design continued to churn.

I looked around the empty house. Could there be a predator somewhere here?

"What do we look for?" I asked.

"Start by following this snail trail to its source. I want to know what happened here and why. Look around. Be thorough. Don't turn on the lights. And keep your ghost knife handy."

That seemed straightforward. Annalise went into the kitchen while I knelt beside the streak.

An opening in the curtain allowed light from the streetlamps outside to shine on the carpet. I got down on my hands and knees beside it. The carpet fibers appeared to have been scorched, and although I couldn't smell smoke, I could smell the nasty, sterile tang I'd smelled in the gravel lot.

The streak went up the stairs. So did I. There were three bedrooms and a bathroom on the upper floor. The streak led to the back room, where it ended in the middle of the floor, surrounded by a heap of scorched blankets.

There were Kim Possible posters on the wall and little pink ponies on the dresser. A third child for the Bentons. A daughter.

There was a certificate on the wall that said she'd won her sixth-grade math bee. I didn't read it. I didn't want to know her name.

The room was cluttered and disorganized—she wasn't a tidy kid—but there were a couple of blank spaces. One was on the wall beside her certificates and awards. Another was a rectangular space in the center of her bureau, among the piled clothes and school papers. Everything had two or three months' worth of dust on it.

The nightstand beside her bed was a nest of photos in cheap frames, except for a blank space at the front edge. Four or five more photos lay on the carpet beside the bed. I picked them up, wishing that Annalise had given me gloves.

Most of them featured a dark-haired girl on the verge of puberty. She was small-boned, like Meg, but she carried a lot of flab, like Douglas. She wasn't a kid I would have noticed, but standing in her bedroom, knowing that the scorch marks on the floor probably marked the spot where she died, I felt a profound sense of loss.

The pictures showed her smiling with a group of friends. She was, if you believed the photos, a happy kid. I saw the cowlicked boy in one of the pictures and looked away.

There was a second dresser in a corner of the room. Beside it, a mattress and box spring stood against the wall. This dresser was older and held fewer mementos. A photo on the back corner showed the same younger daughter with an older girl with the same narrow glasses and pointy chin. A sister? I liked the challenging, mischievous expression on her face.

I noticed that there was no dust on this dresser or any of the knickknacks. Someone had been cleaning it. Could Meg have been walking past the younger daughter's things to clean the older one's? It seemed so. Obviously, they still remembered the older sister.

The middle room was larger and had two beds. There was a definite clash of styles in here—the Wiggles versus Giant Japanese Robots.

On the younger side of the room, I noticed several more empty spaces amid the clutter. The older boy's things, however, had been torn apart. Drawers had been yanked out of the dresser and dumped on the floor. The closet had been ransacked, toys and books scattered.

Someone had packed in a panic.

I went back into the hall. The scorched black mark was still there. I noticed something funny about it and crouched down on the floor.

At the edge of the streaks were a couple of smaller burns. It was like a river that had one main channel and some small channels that separated for a short while and then rejoined the main flow.

The silver worms had made this trail. I'd suspected it, of course, from the moment I saw the trail leading out the door, but now I was sure.

I hopped over the scorched carpet and checked out the bathroom. It was also in disarray. Toothbrushes had been scattered across the sink and floor. There were a lot of personal effects in here, from expensive salon conditioners to a paperback beside the toilet.

The hall closet was filled with towels and cleaning supplies. Everything was neatly folded and arranged.

This had obviously been passed over during the frantic packing.

Last was the master bedroom, which looked like it had been tossed by the cops. I walked on the clothes on the floor because there was nowhere else to step. An abandoned crib at the foot of the bed was loaded with winter clothes. The end table had a pair of cheap paperbacks on it, along with a pair of alarm clocks and a pair of eyeglass cases. Behind the clocks sat a little box coated with a thin film of dust. I disturbed the dust opening the box. Inside was a pile of unused condoms.

The Bentons had skipped town like a drug mule who had been caught dipping into the product.

At this point, I started to feel dirty. This was too private, and there was too much grief and tragedy here. I was ashamed of the tingle of excitement I'd felt at the door.

And yes, it made me angry. Angry at Annalise for forcing me to come on this job. Angry at Meg and Douglas for having these problems. Angry at whoever had cast the spell that had burned these three kids.

I kicked the clothes on the floor into a pile in the corner but found only ordinary carpet underneath. No circles, sigils, or other signs of summoning magic.

I opened the bedroom closet and dug around. If I was going to do something I hated, I was going to do it quickly. I pulled stacks of clothes out of the back of the closet and uncovered a small safe. It was locked.

Annalise could probably tear it open, but I didn't need her help. I took out my ghost knife and sliced off the steel hinges and the lock. The safe door fell onto the floor.

Inside I found a long, slender box and a folder full of papers. I opened the box, revealing a diamond necklace.

I don't know much about jewelry, but it looked old, like necklaces I'd seen in old movies. It was probably an heirloom, and it was probably worth a lot of money, yet the Bentons had abandoned it in their rush for the county line.

I held on to the necklace longer than was strictly necessary. I had no job and no food in my belly. My bed and board were in the hands of a woman who hated my guts and wanted me dead. It would have been easy to slip this jewelry into my pocket. I needed money of my own if I was ever going to be free, and it wasn't like the Bentons were coming back for it.

I put the necklace back into the box and put the box back into the safe. I didn't think about it or try to reason it out. I just closed the box and moved on.

The folder was full of investment papers. Douglas had a 401(k), some stocks, and a house in Poulsbo that he rented out. There was a lot of money tied up in these papers, but they'd been abandoned, too. It looked like the Bentons were too busy saving their kid to worry about their investments. I was starting to like Douglas and Meg, tire iron or not.

Considering the find I'd made in the closet, I decided to check the closets in the bathroom and the rest of the bedrooms, too. None of them held anything of importance, and nothing otherworldly bit my arm off. I supposed I shouldn't have worried about the danger. If there was a predator in the house, Annalise's piece of scrap wood would have detected it.

Whether she would have told me about it is another matter, of course.

Once, not too long ago, I'd cast a spell from a stolen spell book to give myself a vision of a vast expanse of mist and darkness. The Empty Spaces. The Deeps.

There I'd seen predators moving through the void: colossal serpents, huge wheels of fire, groups of tumbling boulders that sang to one another and changed direction like a flock of birds. All of them were searching for living worlds to devour.

Then I came face-to-face with a predator that had come here, to our world. It was a parasitic bug the size of a house cat, and it had a hunger for human flesh. If I hadn't stopped it, it would have brought the rest of the swarm here to feed like locusts.

Before she'd discovered the truth about me, Annalise had told me a little about them. They were not demons or devils, with pitchforks and horns and contracts you sign in blood. They were simply creatures hunting for food—predators—and we were the food.

They were drawn to certain kinds of magic the way sharks were drawn to blood. People summoned and tried to control them for all sorts of reasons—to destroy enemies, to grant power, to guard, or even just to learn the secrets of the world behind the world. That house-cat-sized predator I'd destroyed had been brought here for its supposed healing powers.

The only thing the predators wanted was to be brought to a world where they could feed. *They love to be summoned,* Annalise had said, *but they hate to be held in place.*

She had told me that the second predator she'd ever seen was a strange, spongy lattice that was difficult to see even under bright light. The creature was only clearly visible when it was filled with the blood it fed on.

The man who had summoned it had killed derelicts and petty criminals for years to sustain it, prompting the press to call him "the Mad Butcher of Kingsbury Run" and "the Torso Killer." Annalise said she had no idea what that weird predator had done for him in return for all that blood, but she had personally burned them both to ash.

She wouldn't talk about the first predator she had seen.

Any of those predators, summoned to Earth and allowed to run loose, could scour the planet of life. That was why we had come to Hammer Bay—to make sure that, whatever was happening here, it was stopped.

I thought about that old friend of mine again, the one I'd crippled and who'd loved the Mariners. I had loved him like a brother and I'd nearly helped him—and the predator inside him—destroy the world.

My hand fell against my jacket pocket, feeling the laminated paper inside. Of the three spells I'd cast from that stolen book, the ghost knife was the only one I still had. I had a copy of that stolen spell book hidden away, but I hadn't decided what to do with it. There was power in it, absolutely, but spell casting was painful and dangerous, and if Annalise or one of the other peers found out that I still had it, they'd execute me on the spot. For the Twenty Palace Society, stealing magic was a capital crime.

I couldn't think of anything else to do on the second floor and went downstairs, stepping carefully around the marks on the carpet.

There was a message on the answering machine. Since Doug and Meg didn't seem likely to be coming back, I pushed Play. It was only thirty minutes old and was from someone named Jennifer. She sounded about fifteen. The message was for "Mom and Dad" and made clear her outrage that her parents were planning to pull her out of school—and away from all her friends in the dorm now that she'd finally made some—with only three weeks until finals. This, apparently, would ruin her chance to get into a decent college. Can anyone express contemptuous disbelief as purely and cleanly as a teenage girl? I pressed the Save button on the machine; I liked Doug and Meg too much to erase a message from their daughter.

Annalise stood in the dark kitchen, staring out the window. Her face was utterly blank. Something about her made me give her some space.

I looked away and noticed a crumpled sheet of paper in the corner. I picked it up but there wasn't enough light to read it.

Annalise glanced at me, her expression still inscrutable. I approached her and looked out the window, too.

In the next house over, a woman sat at her kitchen table, crying over a small, framed photo. I wondered how long she'd been sitting there, and how long Annalise had stood silently in the darkness, watching.

"What did you find?" she finally asked.

"Douglas and Meg, who think they hadn't been blessed with a boy until last whenever, have actually had five kids. Three boys and two girls. It sounds as if the older girl is at a boarding school somewhere. The younger girl died upstairs in her room, and the worms marked up this carpet as they made a run for the soil outside. I suspect the middle boy died in his car seat a while ago. They packed in a frantic rush, but only for the middle child. We saw what happened to him.

"They rushed off in such a hurry that they left jewelry and financial documents in the safe upstairs. It looks like they threw a bunch of clothes and crap into their car and took off.

"I didn't find any evidence of a spell, or a spell book, or predators. Nothing except that scorched streak in the carpet. That . . ." I wasn't sure how to continue. "Those worms that came out of the boy . . . those were predators, weren't they?"

Annalise didn't look at me. "Did you take the jewelry?"

"No," I said.

She started to pat me down. Without thinking, I drew away from her. That was a mistake.

Annalise grabbed my upper arm and squeezed—not hard enough to break the bone, but enough to remind me she could. I held myself very still.

I still had the ghost knife, of course, but I wasn't confident enough to try it against her. Maybe later, though. Maybe soon.

She searched me and I didn't do a damn thing about it. When she was done, she went back to the window without a word. I moved next to her and stared at the woman, too. Whatever Annalise was seeing, it didn't entrance me the way it did her.

Eventually, Annalise went upstairs to the master bedroom. I followed. She took the jewelry from the safe and laid the wood scrap against it. The sigil twisted at the same steady pace. The necklace was no more magic than anything else in the house. Annalise didn't seem surprised.

"So, boss," I finally said, "do you want to see what picture she's crying over?"

"Yes," she answered. Her funny little voice sounded small.

"Does it have anything to do with the job?"

She looked up at me. Her tiny eyes were shadowed and impossible to read. "I'll know soon enough, won't I?"

I walked out the front door, up the Bentons' walk, and down the sidewalk to the next house. The mailbox had the name FINKLER on it in gold stickers.

I rang the front doorbell. After about three minutes—a long wait, but I knew she had to wipe away tears and check herself in a mirror—I heard her turn the knob. I stepped down her front step, giving her space and putting myself below her. I wanted to be as nonthreatening as I could.

She opened the door without undoing a lock. I'd have placed her in her mid-forties, although she could have been older. She had grim lines around her mouth and eyes, and her face was puffy.

As I looked at her, her expression changed. The traces of sorrow vanished. Within a few seconds, she was as pleasant as if she had just been watching a dull sitcom. "Yes?" she said.

I wanted to tell her to lock her doors. What if some ex-con came by with some song-and-dance story? Instead I said: "I've been trying to reach the Benton family next door? I'm a day early? No one seems to be answering, though?" I let my voice rise at the end of each sentence, turning everything I said into a question.

"I saw them loading up their car. It looked like they were taking a trip."

"Really? They were expecting me. Aunt Meg was going to help me find a job."

"At the toy plant?"

"She didn't say. I guess so."

"And she's your aunt?" She looked at me carefully, measuring me.

"We haven't met. Our family is pretty spread out. I'm still not sure what I should call her. 'Mrs. Benton' sounds so formal, but I'm not comfortable yet calling her 'aunt' when we haven't even met." I kept vamping, wondering how much time Annalise would need.

"When you see her," Ms. Finkler interrupted, "ask her what she wants to be called. People should let people pick their own names."

"Welp, that makes a lot of sense."

"But they went on some kind of trip. You say you're early?"

"Only by a day."

"They looked like they were going to be gone longer than that. I don't know what to tell you. But if you want a job, you should go to the toy plant tomorrow. They're always hiring lately." She looked me up and down. "Wear something decent."

I smiled at her. It took an effort. "Thanks. I appreciate the advice."

"You're welcome." She closed the door.

I walked back to the van and climbed behind the wheel. Annalise hadn't told me where to meet her, but I hoped she knew better than to think I was going back to the

Bentons' house. I drove around the corner, parked beside the alley, and waited.

The streetlight was overhead. I took the piece of paper I'd found on the floor of the living room and held it up to the light. It read:

> I'm putting this where you will find it. This is the only way we can talk about the truth. Every time I try to talk to you . . .
>
> We need to get away from here before we lose Justin and Sammy, too. I sent a postcard to my sister asking her to invite us for a visit. I told her to make it seem like an emergency. When she calls, let's run and never come back.
>
> I'm terrified and I don't know what to do. When I'm alone, I remember them just for a couple of minutes at a time. Do you remember them, too, in the middle of the night when no one else is around?
>
> I miss them terribly. I don't know what's happening. I just want to get away. I don't think I'm crazy. Am I crazy?
>
> I love you.

That was it. The note was unsigned, but it looked like a woman's handwriting.

They'd lost three of their kids, and while I didn't have kids of my own, a lifetime of Hollywood movies had convinced me it was the worst thing that could happen. Except they only knew it had happened in odd, lonely moments.

Why the Bentons? Who had targeted their kids, and why?

The passenger door swung open. Annalise climbed in.

"Everything go okay?" I asked.

"I'm hungry. Let's find someplace to eat."

I started the van. "What did you find out?" She didn't answer. I drove toward downtown.

Her silence annoyed me, but then I had a scary thought. What if I hadn't distracted Ms. Finkler for long enough? What if she'd caught Annalise in her kitchen?

Annalise had spells that could deal with people without taking their lives—I'd seen them in action—but she didn't always use them. She hadn't been all that concerned about catching Meg and Douglas in her green flame. They had survived only because I had knocked them back.

Annalise only cared about one thing: she searched for people who cast magic spells, especially those that summoned predators, and she killed them. Nothing else mattered to her. Certainly not innocent bystanders. They were expendable.

And, to tell the truth, I'd seen a little bit of her world, and I understood her. I'd seen what predators could do. With their appetites, they could devour every living thing on the planet.

Maybe we needed people like Annalise—people who were willing to do whatever it took to protect us. Without her, and others like her, maybe we wouldn't even be here now.

But I really hoped she hadn't killed that sad woman.

Annalise held the scrap wood in her hands, staring at the designs as if they were tea leaves. Whatever she could read there, it was pissing her off.

I turned into the business district and pulled into the parking lot of a Thai restaurant. I didn't know how good it would be, but pad thai wasn't rocket science and I'd been craving it for months. They didn't exactly let you order in from a jail cell.

"What are we doing here?" Annalise asked.

"Grub."

"I don't eat this. Find a place that serves burgers or steaks."

I sighed to let her know how disappointed I was and found a diner just a block farther down the road. As we entered, Annalise placed the scrap wood on the doorjamb. As far as I could tell, the designs continued to churn slowly, without any change. We went inside and found a booth.

By the clock above the counter it was nearly eleven. We'd had a busy day.

There were three or four other customers. All of them thought we were worth a good, long look. I couldn't blame them. Annalise was quite a sight in her oversized firefighter's jacket, tattoos, and clipped red hair. Standing next to her, I looked almost reputable.

The waitress came to our table. "New in town?" she asked. Annalise grunted.

"Just drove in," I said. I smiled politely, knowing what some waitstaff do to the food when they don't like a customer.

"Looking for work at the plant, I guess?"

"They really need people, huh?"

"Sure do," she said. She took our order. Annalise asked for iced tea and a grilled steak. When she was told they were out, she ordered a cheeseburger with bacon. It sounded so good I ordered the same thing but with a cola. Maybe the sugar would keep me awake.

As the waitress started to turn away, Annalise grabbed her hand. The waitress tried to wrench herself free but couldn't break Annalise's grip.

Annalise laid the scrap wood on the woman's wrist, then let her go. The waitress quickly retreated behind the counter.

Great. I hoped I wouldn't be eating her spit later.

Annalise stared out the window. She looked distinctly unhappy.

I smiled. "Nice little town, huh?"

"I've been to some that were nicer. Smaller, too."

"So what's be—"

Annalise abruptly stood and moved toward the counter. The other customers had turned back to their own conversations, but one of the men at the counter tapped his companion. They watched her approach. Both were in their fifties and wore blue overalls smeared with machine oil.

"Excuse me," she said to them. She laid the wood against the first man's arm, then the second's. She moved to a booth in the corner and the last of the diner's customers: a pair of ladies who must have been in their seventies.

"Excuse me," Annalise said again. She laid the block against one woman's shoulder. After a second, she moved to the next.

The second woman flinched. "I don't—"

"It's all right," Annalise said, and laid the wood against the woman's arm. After a moment, she started back toward our table.

The first mechanic caught her eye as she passed. "If you're looking for something radioactive, honey, you put your hand on the wrong body part."

His buddy chuckled. Annalise walked by without comment. As she settled back into her seat, the waitress returned. She didn't seem terribly happy with us. "If you keep bothering other customers, I'm going to have to ask you to leave."

Annalise didn't acknowledge her. "Understood," I said.

The woman moved away from the table while keeping a wary eye on us. I wondered how long it would take for word about us to spread around town.

"I expected you to keep a lower profile," I said.

Again Annalise didn't acknowledge the remark.

"What's the matter? Turn off your emotion chip?"

She stared at me as though she was imagining me dead.

I've seen that look before, but it's not something I've ever gotten used to.

I settled back in my seat and was silent. Annalise didn't need to talk to me. I was going to be dead soon.

I remembered the way the boy had split apart into a mass of worms and my stomach flip-flopped. Why had I ordered a cheeseburger with the works?

I didn't have the guts to keep pestering her. The peers of the Twenty Palace Society might have forbidden her to kill me, but I had no idea how or if they would enforce that rule. I knew very little about her society except that, like Annalise, they were sorcerers. Like Annalise, they killed predators and people who toyed with magic. Like Annalise, they hunted for copies of spell books.

One thing I did know: as powerful as Annalise was, she was one of the weaker peers in her society. It was a scary thought.

Our drinks arrived, then our burgers. Despite my queasiness, I tore into my food, my body's needs taking over. All my concerns about dead children and murderous sorcerers receded just far enough for me to fuel up.

Spit or no spit, the eating was good. I could see that Annalise was enjoying it, too.

"So," I said between bites, "do you think the Benton family was targeted specifically?"

Annalise looked at me like I was a bug that needed squashing. She took another bite of her burger and kept chewing.

"I found a slip of paper on the floor of their living room," I said. I took another bite of food, making her wait for the rest. Eventually, I said: "They could remember their kids when they were alone. They could see their kids' things and remember what happened to them. It was only when they were with other people that the memories were wiped away."

Annalise took another bite. I set my burger on the plate and leaned toward her.

"Is that what you found in Finklers' kitchen? A photo of her with her kids? Or maybe her grandkids? Was that why you were so entranced by her? A mother all alone, grieving over her children?"

Annalise became very still. She stared at me with all the warm gentility of a shark.

"I'm not trying to push your buttons," I lied, "but I can be useful. I want to help."

"I don't need your help," she said.

"If I'm going to be dead soon, it won't matter if you answer my questions."

"I don't want your help."

"I work for you," I said. "Your peers in the society, whoever they are and whatever that is, put me here to help you."

"You agreed to be my wooden man," she said. Her tone was even and low. "You lied to me and betrayed me. I attacked a peer because of you, and the closest friend I have ever had in my long life is dead. Because of you."

"I'm sorry about Irena," I said. "I liked—"

"I don't want to hear you talk about her. At all. If you say her name to me again, I will splinter every bone in your body, peers or no peers. Am I clear?"

At that moment, before I even realized it was possible, I stopped caring what she would do.

I'd spent the whole day in the van with Annalise, knowing she would eventually kill me. Before that, I'd sat in a jail cell for months waiting for someone in the society to collect my head.

People become accustomed to their circumstances. It was one of the many unpleasant truths I learned in prison. We can't be afraid all the time; our bodies can't sustain it.

I was getting used to Annalise's hatred and to my quite

sensible fear of her. What I was not getting used to was my own ignorance. I didn't like stumbling around in the dark. I didn't even know what a "wooden man" was. I was pretty sure it involved more than just driving around.

So, against all common sense, I pressed on. "The way you've been frowning at your scrap of wood makes me think the Bentons were not specifically targeted. The design on that scrap moves when magic is nearby, right? And does other stuff when predators are close, right?

"But you've been frowning at it wherever we go. I think it's telling you the whole town is enchanted. It's picking up a lot of background static but not directing you to the source. Maybe those two mechanics have lost their kids, too. Maybe that waitress cries herself to sleep at night, thinking about the son who never came home from school."

Annalise sighed. "I usually drive around until the spell registers magic, then I home in on foot."

"What does it mean that the magic is so spread out?" I tried to keep my voice reasonable and calm. Professionalism breeds professionalism.

Annalise sopped up some ketchup with a fry. "It means I don't know what to do next."

The window beside us shattered. I covered my head as shards of glass rained over me. Annalise turned toward the window, her hand reaching under her jacket.

Broken glass covered my half-eaten burger. Ruined.

I turned my attention to Annalise. She was standing beside the broken window, staring into the street.

"What happened?" I asked.

"Him," she said.

I looked into the dark street. I couldn't see anyone, but I heard a voice.

"Where are my daughters?" a man shouted. "Who stole my little girls from me?"

Then I saw him. He was tall and stooped, with lank

hair hanging past his shoulders and a bare scalp on top. He was so skinny he looked like his skin had been shrink-wrapped around his bones.

And he was carrying a rifle.

It looked like a bolt-action hunting rifle, but he was all the way across the street just beyond the glow of a street-light, so I couldn't be sure.

"Who took my daughters?" he shouted. A man and woman bolted from the cover of a parked car, sprinting for the corner. I clenched my teeth as the tall man noticed them. He aimed the rifle at them but didn't fire. The couple reached the corner and safety.

"Where are they?" he shouted again. "Who stole my little girls from me?"

"He remembers," I said to Annalise. "Just like we do. How can he remember his kids?"

"I don't know," she said. "Go ask him."

CHAPTER THREE

She wasn't joking. She wasn't smiling. She just looked at me, waiting to see if I'd flinch.

I did. Hell, who wouldn't?

But I still made my way toward the front door. When it came down to a choice of facing a gunman or my boss, it would be the gunman every time.

One of the two mechanics had ushered the old ladies out of their booth and led them into the kitchen. The other mechanic and the waitress crouched beside the door, peering out into the street from the dubious cover of a foam-padded wooden bench. The cook left the relative safety of the kitchen and joined them.

The waitress swore under her breath. "Old Harlan has finally gone round the bend."

The mechanic dared a glance into the street. "I thought Emmett Dubois confiscated his guns."

The waitress let out a contemptuous grunt. She didn't think much of Emmett Dubois.

"Whose guns?" I asked as I crouched beside them. We were all keeping our voices low.

"Harlan's," the waitress said. I glanced out the window. Harlan sighted along his rifle, slowly turning toward us. I ducked back down before he saw me.

"This Harlan guy," I said. "I take it he's local color?"

The mechanic snorted. "You could put it that way."

The cook came up behind me. "He fell off a ladder in

'97 putting up Christmas lights. Hit his head. He ain't been right since."

"He was never a bad guy, though," the mechanic said.

The cook scowled at him. "Tell that to my window, and these customers he nearly killed."

"What was he shouting about?" the waitress asked.

"His daughters," I answered her. "He wants to know who took his daughters away."

"Why, that's just crazy," she said. "He doesn't have any little girls. He never has."

"What the hell?" the cook said. His sour breath was right next to my ear. "Your girlfriend is just sitting in her booth like a duck in a shooting range. Don't she care about her own life?" He scrambled across the dirty floor toward her.

"Care about her own life?" I said. "Where's the fun in that?" Before anyone could stop me, I opened the front door and bolted into the street.

I didn't look at Harlan. I looked at the Corolla I was planning to use as cover.

I hit the pavement and rolled behind the wheel. I heard a shot and more glass breaking in the diner behind me. Someone cursed up a storm, which I'm sure was directed as much at me as at old Harlan.

I scuttled across a patch of grass and put my head right against the hubcap. There was a tree beside me, but the trunk was no wider than my hand. I wasn't counting on it for protection. "Stop shooting!" I shouted. "I'm trying to help you!"

"Can you tell me where my girls are?" There was a dangerous edge to his voice.

"No," I said. "I'm—"

"Then butt the hell out!"

I heard another rifle shot. The bullet punched a hole

through the car door beside me and tore bark off the skinny tree. I hunkered down lower.

"I can help you," I shouted. I looked back at the diner and saw Annalise sitting by the window. She stared at me blankly. My situation meant no more to her than a dull television show. I saw the top of the cook's head as he beckoned her to safety.

"I can help you!" I shouted again, louder this time. If Harlan came toward me, I'd be screwed. My tattoos only protected part of me. I wasn't sure how well they'd hold up against a rifle.

"How?" he answered.

"Look, let me stand up and talk to you. My name is Ray. I came here to find out what's happening to the kids in this town."

"You did?"

"I'm standing up now. Hear me out before you shoot me, okay?"

I stood. Harlan had moved toward me into the street. He aimed his rifle at me.

No matter how hard you try, there's really no steeling yourself to see a brain-damaged redneck point a gun at your face.

He saw my hands were empty, and he started glancing from side to side as if he suspected I was a decoy.

"Harlan, my name is Ray."

"You said that already."

I had, but I hoped he would be reluctant to shoot me if he had a name to go with my face.

Harlan was younger than I expected, barely into his mid-thirties. His face was narrow and gleaming with sweat. His long nose curved over a thin, unhappy mouth. His clothes looked like they hadn't been washed in weeks. He'd have been scary without a gun.

"Harlan, do you know who Justin Benton is?"

"Nope," he answered. He shifted his grip on his rifle and looked up the street. He was getting antsy. Where were the police sirens? It had been more than two minutes since that first shot.

"He was a little boy who lived in this town. Earlier today, I saw him burn up."

Harlan burst into tears. The barrel of his gun wavered, then angled toward the asphalt. "My girls," he said, his voice small and broken with pain. "My girls."

"Is that what happened to them?" I asked.

"I don't know. The Monday after Thanksgiving, Lorelei didn't come home from school. I went nuts looking for her. But . . . but . . ."

"But the people in this town acted as though they'd never heard of her. They acted as though she didn't exist."

"They're liars!" he shouted, his grief flaring into anger. He didn't point his gun at me. "And the next week, my little Marie disappeared from her bed. Right in the middle of the night. And . . ."

He couldn't go on. I helped. "And there was a black mark on the floor. A long, scary mark. It led to the door—"

"The window." He approached me slowly. There was no threat in the way he moved.

"And it disappeared into the dirt. Now no one in town remembers either of your girls."

"They don't remember any of the kids! Not even their own!" His face was slack with astonishment. He'd apparently forgotten that he'd just accused the whole town of lying to him. Maybe he'd never really believed it. "Even after they saw it happen with their own two eyes! They still have tricycles sitting in their front yards and Happy Meal wrappers on their dashboards, but it's like they can't see them!"

"*You* saw it, though, didn't you? You saw it happen right here in town."

"Five times."

"Is it always kids? Does it happen to adults, too?"

"Only kids. Never adults. My God, every single person in this town must have seen it, but I'm the only one who remembers." His eyes welled up with tears. The rifle hung loose in his hand. "Why am I the only one who remembers? And why do I feel this pressure in my head! It's been there for months, since before my Lorelei vanished. It's driving me wild!"

"Harlan, I'm new in town but I came here to find out what's happening in Hammer Bay. I can't promise that I can get your girls back, but I'm going to find out what's going on."

I saw hope in his expression. He was a tired man, with a heavy load of grief. He'd been carrying it for nearly half a year, but he wasn't so far gone that he couldn't recognize a helping hand when it was offered.

"Can you do that?"

"Man, I don't know," I told him. "But I intend to try. I have some questions for you, and I'm going to want to check out the black mark in your house, but I'm not going to be able to do any of that if you shoot me."

Harlan looked down at the gun in his hand and blinked.

I kept my voice low. "Can I have that gun, please?" That was when we heard the sirens.

Harlan backed away and lifted the rifle. "I'm not crazy," he yelled. "I was married. I had two little kids!"

Goose bumps prickled on my neck. "I know, Harlan. I believe you."

"Someone in this town is going to tell me where they are. Someone knows what's happened to them."

"Harlan," I said. His expression had become hard and

distant. "You're that someone. None of these people can remember. Only you."

A police car turned the corner and stopped in the road, lights flashing.

Harlan looked at it like a man nearing the end of a big job. Suddenly, I understood. He was done. His kids were gone, and he was going to commit suicide by cop.

"Harlan, don't do it. There are other kids in town," I said, thinking of the two kids at the gas station. "You could help me put a stop to this. You might be the only one who—"

He leveled the gun at my chest. His face was calm. "Why don't you go back into the diner now," he said in a resigned voice. "Before something bad happens to you."

He was aiming at my chest. Would the tattoos there protect me if he squeezed the trigger?

I had no idea how to talk him down. I imagine cops and paramedics are trained in that sort of thing, but I was just an ex–car thief.

I laid my hand against the pocket containing my ghost knife. I could feel it there, thrumming with life. If talking wouldn't work . . .

Harlan turned away from the flashing lights on the patrol car and looked up the street. His eyes narrowed. I followed his gaze.

A wolf stood in the road. I'd never seen one outside a zoo before, but I recognized it immediately. The fur along its back was tinged with red, and it stared at us, standing sideways as though it wanted to present the largest possible target.

It was big. I don't know much about wolves, but it looked much bigger than I'd have expected. Then again, when Harlan had pointed his rifle at me, it looked like a .90 caliber. Fear can do that.

Harlan swung the rifle to his shoulder and fired. I saw

the bullet chip the asphalt between the animal's legs. The wolf bolted, running down the street and out of sight.

Harlan worked the bolt of his rifle. I slid my hand into my pocket and took out my ghost knife.

Harlan saw me out of the corner of his eye. He spun and slammed the butt of his rifle against my hand, smashing it against my hip. The ghost knife fell onto the street, and I staggered a few feet away from it.

He aimed the rifle at my face. I didn't have any tattoos to protect me there.

"It was just a piece of paper," I said.

Harlan glanced at the ghost knife and confirmed that what I was saying was true. Without a word, he swung his weapon around and sighted down the street, looking for the wolf.

I had cast the spell that created the ghost knife, and I could sense it there on the asphalt. I opened my hand and *reached* for it. The laminated paper flew into my hand, and in one motion, I threw it at Harlan like an oversized playing card.

According to the spell book I'd copied it from, a ghost knife cuts "ghosts, magic, and dead things." The wood and metal locks of the Bentons' front door were dead things, and the ghost knife cut through them easily. It could also destroy magic spells like my tattoos or the sigil on Annalise's scrap of wood; the results weren't always pretty.

But every living person has a ghost in them. At least, the spell thinks so, because when I use it on people, it passes through their bodies as though they aren't there and cuts at their "spirit."

And that's all I know about it. Even though I cast the spell myself from an old book I'd acquired under less-than-honest circumstances, and even though I'd used it a few times against people who were trying to kill me, I had no idea how it worked or what it truly did. As with so much else having to do with magic, Annalise, and her society, I was in the dark.

The ghost knife zipped across the few feet separating us and entered Harlan's body just below his armpit. His shirt fell open where the ghost knife sliced through it, but the laminated paper plunged into his body without leaving a visible mark. A moment later, the spell exited through the other side as if he wasn't even there.

Harlan sagged. His eyes dulled, and whatever was driving him to shoot up the town dwindled away. That's what the ghost knife did; it stole away aggression and vitality for a while. The effects of the spell were temporary—at least, they seemed to be.

Harlan lowered his rifle. I stepped toward him, ready to take the weapon away. The left side of Harlan's rib cage burst open. I never heard the gunshot. I only saw the exit wound. Blood splattered my left hand, and I felt the bullet whiz past me.

Harlan collapsed, falling onto his face on the street.

I looked up and saw a cop moving toward us, his revolver pointed at Harlan. "Move away!" the cop yelled. "Move away from the body!"

I was frozen in place. The cop pointed the gun at my face. He asked me who I was, and I told him.

He told me to move back again. I took a step back. The cop kicked the rifle just like they do on TV. It slid away up the street.

I heard a faint sucking noise and looked down.

"He's alive," I said.

"An ambulance is coming," the cop said. "Don't move."

The cop was in his mid-fifties, with a good bit of muscle and a little paunch. He had long, slightly graying hair, which he combed back like a European movie star. His face, though, was scarred and rounded as though it had been punched too many times. His jaw was long and heavy, and the look in his eyes was slightly feral.

He looked down at Harlan and smiled slightly, as though the dying man was a nifty bit of entertainment.

"Where's that ambulance?" I asked. I couldn't hear sirens.

He looked at me as though he thought I might be his next fun project. "*On its way,* I said. Who are you again?"

"Raymond Lilly," I said again. "Harlan has a punctured lung. He needs help right now."

Someone said: "Did you get him?" I looked up and saw two more officers approaching. One bore a close resemblance to the first cop—a younger brother, I assumed. Except this new arrival hadn't shaved in about a week and was chewing the ragged end of a burning cigar. The other cop had too much flab pressing down on his belt, and his face was red and shiny with exertion.

"I surely did," the older cop said.

They stood around Harlan's body, looking down at him as if he was about to turn into candy. I still couldn't hear ambulance sirens. The fat one licked his lips in a way that gave me chills. None of them moved to help him.

So I did. The three cops jumped back and trained their weapons on me, but I didn't look at them. I laid my hand over the wound on Harlan's back, then slid my other hand under him, searching for the exit. When I found it, I covered it with my palm. I tried to seal the wounds with my hands. Harlan seemed to be breathing a little better. Maybe it was my imagination.

"What are you doing there, son?"

I wasn't sure which of them was talking to me. "Trying to save his life."

"Why?"

"I thought you might want to shoot him again later."

I heard chuckling behind me. Someone thought that was funny. Ambulance sirens came next, finally.

Harlan tried to say something but couldn't manage it. Kneeling in the street, I tried not to think about what I was doing. A crazy man who hadn't bathed in weeks was bleeding all over my hands, and three cops were pointing their guns at me.

I heard more voices. The folks in the diner had come out into the street to gawk, and the sports bar up the street was emptying, too.

Annalise came near. "Boss," I said, catching her attention. "I think I dropped a piece of paper around here somewhere. Would you find it? It might be our map."

She understood immediately. We couldn't leave a spell lying out on the street for anyone to pick up. I could have called it to me again, but an awful lot of people were watching.

She moved off toward the far side of the street. The older cop followed her. They talked, but I couldn't hear them. The waitress and the mechanic were loudly telling the fat cop what I had done, and how I had almost talked Harlan into giving up his rifle. They were split over whether that meant I was brave, stupid, or both; their voices drowned out whatever the older officer was saying to Annalise.

The ambulance finally arrived and the EMTs gently shouldered me out of the way. I scuttled toward the curb, happy to sit and watch professionals at work. A chubby little guy with too much beard taped plastic over the gunshot wound. Beside him, his lean and hairless partner snipped the finger from a latex glove and then slid a long needle through the fingertip. They rolled Harlan onto his back. The bearded guy covered the exit wound with more plastic while his partner searched Harlan's ribs for a place to insert the needle.

I didn't watch. Weariness washed over me as my

adrenaline ebbed. I was tempted to lie back in the street and go to sleep.

I wondered if I was going to be sleeping in jail tonight. I hoped not. It was too soon.

The older cop with the movie-star hair and the road-house face crouched beside me. "Your, uh, companion there tells me you came out to talk old Harlan out of shooting up the town."

"That's right," I said. I wanted to stand, but I didn't want to smear my bloody hands against the street. It was a weird impulse, but it was a day for weird.

I glanced at the man's badge. He was the chief of police. The name tag beneath read E. DUBOIS. This was Emmett, I guessed, who hadn't confiscated all of Harlan's guns.

"Hold on there a moment," the cop said. He stepped over and conferred with the fat cop standing just a few feet away. The fat cop walked away, and the older one came back. "That wasn't the smartest thing in the world to do," he said. "Why did you do it?"

"I didn't think about it, really," I lied.

"Good Samaritan?"

I didn't respond to that. The fat cop returned with a plastic squeeze bottle and a wad of paper towels. The bottle was labeled "waterless cleaner." I thanked him, squeezed the bottle over my hands, and started washing the blood away. The cleaner felt like jelly and smelled like rubbing alcohol.

"Witnesses said you'd just about talked him down when we showed up."

I understood where this was going. He didn't want people saying that I'd almost handled the situation diplomatically when he'd come in with guns blazing.

"I hadn't talked him down from anything," I said. "I had the impression that he was planning a suicide by cop."

"That's better. Much better than a smart mouth. I didn't much care for your remark about shooting Harlan again. I didn't like having to shoot him."

I remembered the way he'd smiled at Harlan's bleeding body and knew he was lying. "Sorry about that," I told him. "I was all worked up with adrenaline."

He smiled that same smile. "Fine," he said. "That's just fine."

He asked where I was from and why I was in town, but he seemed distracted and his questions were careless. I managed to avoid saying that I'd been in jail that morning. He didn't seem to care about me, now that I'd apologized.

I watched the ambulance drive away. "Where are they taking him?"

The cop eyeballed me, as if trying to decide whether answering my question would undermine his authority.

"County hospital," he said. "You planning to visit?"

"Yep. I'm a Good Samaritan."

"Fine. That's fine." A brown, rusted Dodge Dart parked at the intersection, a little too close to the police car already there. A fourth cop, this one tall and slender, moved out of the shadows to intercept the driver. As he stepped into the light, I saw bright red hair on the top of his head.

"That's our local paperboy," the cop said. "You better go now if you don't want to be here all night answering his questions. But stay in Hammer Bay for a couple days, understand?"

"I intend to."

Annalise stood on the sidewalk a few yards away, the broken windows of the diner behind her. Her eyes were hooded and her face expressionless.

As I approached her, the cook stepped up to me. "You cost me a door," he said. "Harlan busted my glass door because you wanted to be a hero. What if one of my customers had been shot, huh? What then?"

"Don't you pay any attention to him," the waitress said. "Anytime you want, you come back and have another burger. On me."

The cook turned on her. "What about my window?"

She told him that's what insurance was for, and the cook grumbled that all the different kinds of insurance in this town were going to put him in the gutter.

I edged away from them and stepped up to Annalise. I could feel the ghost knife on her somewhere. Good. I didn't want it to fall into just anyone's hands, and I didn't want to stick around here any longer.

She held out her hand. "Keys," she said. "You're not driving my van until you wash your hands."

I hesitated, hoping she would offer me the ghost knife. She didn't. I could feel that it was nearby, probably right in her pocket. I wondered how long she was going to keep it, because I sure couldn't take it from her. I dug the keys from my pocket and gave them to her.

There was a change in the noise behind me. I turned back toward the crime scene.

New people had arrived, and Emmett Dubois was speaking with them. They were four men: one was very tall, very lean, and somewhere in his late fifties; beside him was a younger man, also tall, also lean, with a thick head of dark hair. Another was a short man with a shaved head, and the last was a fat man with long, graying hair. Dubois's body language had altered. He didn't look imposing. I only caught a glimpse of them before they moved out of view behind a parked van.

Then I felt a twinge under my right collarbone. There was no wave of force this time, but I knew what that twinge meant. Another kid had caught fire somewhere.

One of the men talking to Emmett Dubois fell to the

ground and flailed around. My view was partly blocked
by the wheels and fender of the van, but I could see he
was having a seizure. It was the tall young one with the
dark hair.

Dubois bent down to him. "Medic!" he shouted, his
voice worried.

"Let's go," Annalise said.

"Look," I told her. "At the same time that I felt the—"

"I know. Let's move."

She dragged me toward the van and drove away from
the scene. I glanced back and saw the little reporter trying
to climb back into the Dart. The officer was blocking his
way.

"Well?" Annalise said as we pulled into the street. There
was very little traffic. Men walked down the street, guns in
their hands. They didn't look like citizens protecting their
own. They swaggered and looked bored.

I told Annalise what I'd learned from Harlan. I mentioned that he had a black mark on the floor of his
home, too. Annalise asked a lot of questions I couldn't
answer, like where he lived and how old his kids had
been. She didn't like that I hadn't gotten those answers,
and his punctured lung wasn't a good enough excuse.

I knew she was just riding me, so I let it pass. I was too
tired to be angry anyway.

I said: "Sorry I didn't get killed."

"There's always next time," she said.

CHAPTER FOUR

Annalise drove around until we found a motel. She had to circle the block twice before she turned down the right street, but we got there eventually.

It was a small place, one story, just a parking lot ringed by rooms, all their doors facing inward.

My shirt was speckled with blood and my jacket had greasy black smears down the back. Annalise made me wait in the van while she rented our rooms. While I sat, I saw that one of the rooms had a black streak on the front walk. It came from under the door, turned forty-five degrees to cross the pavement, and disappeared at the muddy lot.

That was interesting. Going that direction, the worms had to travel farther before they could tunnel into the earth than if they'd gone straight—at least ten feet farther. Were they being drawn toward something in the west? Maybe it was the Pacific.

Annalise emerged with the room keys. Thankfully, I didn't have the room with the black streak. "Clean up," she said. "We're getting an early start tomorrow."

She went into her room and I went into mine next door. I stripped off my clothes in the bathroom and examined them in the bright lights by the sink. My jacket, shirt, and pants were nasty. I needed a laundromat and some industrial detergent. I wasn't going to get them. I took the clothes into the shower, washed off the waterless cleaner and blood, then scrubbed at every spot of blood on my clothes I could find. The blood was still wet, and the clothes came clean fairly well. I tried not to think about what sort of diseases Harlan might have had. I just wanted to be clean.

Eventually, I ran out of steam. I hung the clothes on chairs by the heater and turned it on low. Then I fell onto the polyester bedcovers and disappeared into dreamless slumber.

It seemed like an instant later that Annalise thumped on my door, hitting it hard enough to rattle it in the jamb. I climbed out of bed, wrapped a blanket around me, and opened the door.

She had changed her clothes, switching her fireman's jacket for simple brown leather. Her pants were black and her shirt a white button-down that looked a size too big for her. Her boots had been exchanged for simple black leather walking shoes.

She barely glanced at me. "Get dressed. We have a lot to do today." She tossed the keys to me.

My clothes were still wet, but they were all I had. There were traces of Harlan's blood that I had missed the night before. Damn. I put the nasty clothes on my clean body and went out to the van. I left the jacket in the garbage.

It was just after 7 A.M. The sky was gray, and there was a steady drizzle. I was hungry but I couldn't picture myself sitting at a restaurant with wet, bloody clothes. I just drove, hoping to find a drive-through somewhere.

Instead, Annalise had me turn into a side street beside an outdoorsman's store. Aside from the diner, which had cardboard taped over the broken windows, it was the only place open at this hour.

Annalise led me inside and bought me new clothes. They weren't fancy—four pairs of jeans, four black long-sleeved pullover shirts, four pairs of white socks, one pair of black hiking boots, one windbreaker with a zip-out lining.

The clerk held open a trash bag and I threw in all my old things, including my sneakers, which were rimmed with Harlan's blood. I hadn't even noticed. He threw all that old stuff away, and I walked out in new clean clothes.

It felt good. I wondered if the four pairs of clothes meant she expected me to live another four days.

Next, we stopped off for breakfast. We chose a different diner this time. Annalise ordered very rare steak with eggs and a side of ham. The waitress looked dubious, but Annalise packed all of it away.

Her tattoos were visible above the open collar of her shirt and at the edges of her sleeves. They looked like mine, which meant they were made with a paintbrush and a spell, not a needle and ink. They were just as permanent, though.

I didn't know who had given them to Annalise, but I wondered if she'd been conscious for it. I'd been awake for part of my own tattooing, and the pain had been worse than anything I'd ever experienced in my life, with the exception of casting my ghost knife spell.

I absentmindedly touched the spot below my right collarbone where I'd been feeling twinges for the last few hours. My fingertips registered the touch of normal flesh, but my chest registered nothing at all. The parts of my body marked with spells couldn't feel a thing.

And those spells had come from Annalise. I wondered if she could sense them—and me—the way I could sense the ghost knife. I also wondered if my tattoos had been as painful for her to cast as my ghost knife had been for me. When I'd created the ghost knife, channeling all the energy needed to power it had been like dousing myself with gasoline and setting myself on fire.

It was possible that I'd cast the spell incorrectly, but what if I hadn't? Annalise might have had to go through that same pain when she'd put these marks on me, and when she created each of the ribbons she carried. I didn't want to think about that.

Her abilities went beyond the marks though. Her strength was incredible, and she could heal herself by eating meat, the more raw the better. She also wore that vest full of spells, which was probably back in her room with the fireman's jacket.

I wondered what effect all those spells had on her. Was she still human? Would she still be human even if her body changed into something monstrous, as long as she thought like a human? I wondered how much her quest to hunt down and destroy dangerous magic had changed her. I wondered how it would change me, before she put an end to me.

Of course, the only reason my mind was wandering this way was because I had no one to talk to. Annalise sawed at her food and shoveled it into her mouth, one bite after the other.

The silence became annoying. I asked Annalise why Harlan was the only one who remembered his kids. She didn't answer. She didn't even look up from her plate. I asked her if she thought we'd find someone else like Harlan in town. No answer. I asked her where she grew up.

She stopped eating and looked up at me. It was not a friendly look. Fine. I dropped the subject. I got a Seattle newspaper off the rack and began to read it.

Hammer Bay was too far away from the city for Harlan's shooting to make the paper, but surprise surprise, I found a small mention of me in the local news section.

It was strange to read about myself in the newspaper. It was like being in a crowded room where everyone else suddenly sat down but I didn't have a chair. I felt exposed. Maybe that was absurd, but that's how it felt.

The article was on the fourth page, and it was barely one and a half column inches. It said, simply and quickly, that Raymond Lilly, convicted felon, had been released from police custody in the matter of the several slayings, followed by a list of the dead. It was quite a laundry list of names. The official reason given for my release was insufficient evidence to charge me with murder, attempted murder, kidnapping, drug trafficking, assault and battery, and breaking and entering. They left out grand theft auto and discharging a weapon within city limits. Maybe they'd been short on space.

What the article didn't mention was that certain prominent local citizens claimed that I had saved their lives while those crimes were being committed. It also glossed over the forensics reports that stated the people I had supposedly killed seemed to have been dead for days or weeks before they met me.

I looked over the list of names again. Some were strangers to me, but there were several I had known all too well. It still made me heartsick to think about them, even after all these months.

Irena's name wasn't on the list. I wondered if her body had been tidied away by the society, and I wondered if they would do that for me when my time came. Would people think I'd left the country or changed my identity? I didn't have much in the way of family or friends anymore, but I had an aunt who'd opened her home to me when no one else would. I'd hate for her to think I wasn't grateful or wanted nothing to do with her.

Annalise finished her meal. I showed her the article, but she didn't care. I finished my breakfast while she paid the bill. I didn't feel like eating anymore, but I'd need the fuel later.

We got back into the van, and Annalise handed me a slip of paper with an address on it. I consulted the ridiculous tourist map and saw that it was near the toy factory.

We drove there through the mist and drizzle, and I realized that it *was* the toy factory.

The factory was actually two buildings. The first was

a glass office building, four stories high, with curves instead of corners. If it had been in a corporate campus or an urban downtown, and if it had been ten stories taller, it might have seemed sleek and prosperous. Here it looked rinky-dink.

The second building was an old warehouse. It stretched from the edge of the office building toward a thick stand of pines and a steep slope that could have been the outer reaches of the Olympic Mountains. The warehouse was three stories tall, although I doubted there were actually floors inside. It was ringed with cars, mostly new, inexpensive models—Kias, Hyundais, that sort of thing.

There was no guard at the entrance to the campus. I pulled in and found a space at the west end of the lot.

I climbed out. The ocean lay before me, just within the limits of visibility in the misty weather. It had been a while. To the south I saw the shape of the lighthouse marked on the tourist map. It was also obscured by fog, so I couldn't see much detail, but it was certainly picturesque.

Annalise and I walked to the front of the office building. The two spaces closest to the building were reserved. There was a Prius parked in Charles Hammer's parking spot. He was a man who drove with a conscience. A black S-class Mercedes was parked beside it.

I opened the door and held it for her. She carried a worn leather satchel like she knew what we were doing; I followed along.

The lobby was simple and elegant, if a little low-budget. Annalise stalked up to the receptionist, told the woman her name, and said she had a meeting with Charles Hammer.

The receptionist wore a name tag that read CAROL and had a burning hoop with a squiggle of black lines inside that, at first glance, looked like the sigil on my ghost knife or on Annalise's ribbons. After a second, I realized it was a stylized HBT, for Hammer Bay Toys. Carol looked at her schedule, then picked up her phone and told the person at the other end of the line that Mr. Hammer's ten o'clock had arrived. She hung up, smiled at us, and told us it would be just a moment.

The lobby had a slate floor and walls lined with something stained to look like unweathered cedar. A wide flight of concrete stairs swept up to the next floor. I toyed with the idea of asking the receptionist for a job application. Everyone in town seemed to think I should, so why not? It would certainly annoy Annalise. I was wearing clothes she'd bought, had a belly full of food she'd paid for, and had slept in a room she'd rented. I felt like her personal toy, one she would break at her whim. The urge to annoy her was strong.

The elevator dinged, interrupting that dangerous train of thought. A man of about sixty walked out. He wore a six-hundred-dollar suit, three-hundred-dollar shoes, and a twelve-dollar haircut. He had a wide, playful smile on his face. His eyes reminded me of twinkling plastic.

"Ms. Powliss," he said, extending his hand. There was a little hitch in his smile as he took in Annalise, then his grin redoubled. "I'm Able Katz, vice president of operations. How was your flight?"

"I drove. I don't like to have my head in the clouds. It's nice to meet you, Mr. Katz."

Able turned to me, waiting for Annalise to introduce us. She didn't. "I'm Ray Lilly," I said, to end his discomfort.

"That's a familiar name. Have you been to New York?"

"I haven't," I confessed. He shrugged, smile still in place.

"Shall we?" He stepped toward the elevator. Annalise didn't order me back to the car, so I followed them.

We rode to the top floor in the tiny elevator. The

cramped space made us all stand slightly too close together, so we said nothing. The elevator dinged again
and Able led us out.

I looked around the office as we walked through it.
There were desks everywhere but no cubicle walls. Carts
and shelves were packed with stacks of papers, disorganized jumbles of folders, and assorted toys. Many of the
toys were posed in various positions of everyday life.
Heroic action figures sat around a tiny table holding
flowery teacups. Barbie-type dolls dressed as Marie Antoinette posed like country-western line dancers. A tiny
soldier seemed to be pondering a spreadsheet of sales
figures, and another passionately embraced a coffee cup.

The toys made me smile. In fact, they made me feel
damn good. I suppressed the urge to pick one up and put
it in my pocket.

All the employees were middle-aged women. Every
few seconds one of them would stop typing or whatever
and touch one of the toys—just lay a finger on it or ad-
just its position slightly—with an absent expression that
suggested it was an old habit.

An action figure dressed as an ancient Greek warrior
but mounted on a huge eagle sat on the edge of a file cabinet. I ran my finger along the front edge of its wing and
felt a sudden contentment. I could have played with that
toy all day.

Three of the office workers were watching me closely.
I left it where it was.

"I'm afraid my office is a little cluttered right now,"
Able said. "But we have a conference room set up."

"That's fine," Annalise answered.

I tried to study her face to see if she was drawn to the
toys, too, but I couldn't get enough of a glimpse to tell.
Able Katz seemed to be perfectly fine, and the workers
around us seemed basically normal. One woman burst
out laughing as we walked past. Able glanced over and

saw that she was looking at a toy train with hands that were holding a jump rope. Suddenly, all the women began to handle the toys and smile.

Able grinned. That was just what he wanted to see.

He opened a glass door and stepped aside to let Annalise and me into the conference room. The windows were large and scrupulously clean. I couldn't see the ocean from here, but I could see the town. Hammer Bay spread out before me, stretching north toward the hills.

"I was surprised to hear from Jimmy Larson," Able said. "I haven't spoken to him since we were at Mattel. How do you know him?"

"Excuse me for one moment," Annalise said. She drew the scrap wood out of her satchel and held it so that only she and I could see the moving design. The lines seemed to be moving more quickly than usual. It wasn't a big difference, but it was there. She turned to Able Katz and said: "Will Charles Hammer be joining us? My meeting was with him."

"Mr. Hammer was unavoidably detained," Able responded. For an absurd moment, I thought he meant that he'd been arrested. "When one of his creative jags comes on, he goes into seclusion to work out the new toy."

"I'm disappointed," Annalise said.

"I understand. I'm sorry. However, I can pass to him any information you give me here."

"Before we do that," Annalise said. "I'd like you to indulge me in one favor. Hold your hand out, as if you were stopping traffic."

"And why would I do that?"

"Because I'm rich and eccentric and I'm asking you to."

Able looked at us for a moment, then shrugged. He held out his hand, fingers pointing toward the ceiling and palm facing us. Annalise laid the scrap wood against him. The moving design didn't change. She scowled and returned the scrap to her satchel. "Thank you."

Able laughed. "Jimmy warned me you would be a creative type. In this business, you get used to odd things."

"It's funny Jimmy would say that about me. He's never met me. And I'm not creative at all. What I am is an activist."

"Okay. What cause?"

"Human survival."

"I can get behind that," Able said. He snuck a glance at his watch. "But I don't know why you've come to me."

Annalise began her pitch then. It was about the clothes they made and sold for some of their fashion dolls. Annalise knew they made them locally, and she had a company in Africa that could do the work cheaper and where the people needed the wages more. She was calm and articulate, and I'd had no idea she could string so many words together at once.

"I wish I'd known this was what our meeting would be about. I could have saved you the trouble. Mr. Hammer is adamant about sending work overseas. He won't do it under any circumstances. He started this company, in part, to revitalize Hammer Bay. See, he's also an activist, but his sole cause is the survival of the town his great-grandfather founded."

Annalise pressed him. She knew he had more orders than he could fill, and that he'd turned buyers away at the last toy fair. The company—

Able interrupted her. He understood and respected her passion for her cause. He'd had her checked out before the meeting, but if he'd known *this* was what she wanted, he would have saved her the trip. Mr. Hammer would rather burn the company to the ground than outsource the work.

Able looked at his watch again. I could see it was a lost cause. The absent Mr. Hammer had made his feelings known, and Able Katz didn't have the authority to make this decision and didn't want it. He just wanted to get on with his workday.

"I'm sorry," he said. "I have another meeting to prepare for. I sympathize with you, I really do, but I can't help. Here." He took a pen from inside his jacket and wrote on the back of a business card. Then he passed the card to Annalise. "Chuck is an old friend from New York. Talk to him about the problems he's been having with the clothes for his snow ninja line. Okay?"

Annalise took the card from him. "I still want to talk to Charles Hammer."

Able's smile faltered. Not even a thank-you from her. "He's in seclusion working on a new line. He can't be disturbed." He stood to show us out.

We stood, too. "You're protective of him," I said.

Able turned toward me. His smile was a little strained. "Absolutely," he said. "He's earned it."

"How?" I asked. "I don't mean to pry, but I'm really curious. Why did you leave New York to come to Hammer Bay, Washington?"

Able shrugged. "Four years ago I was bringing down six figures with my own marketing-and-consulting firm. We designed ad campaigns for promo toys and ran the best focus groups in the business. When I saw the Hammer Bay Toys exhibit at the toy fair, I thought they were a joke. Everything about them was wrong, according to the conventional thinking."

Able opened the door and led us back into the main office. "I mean, fashion dolls from the seventeenth century? What little girl would buy Marie Antoinette outfits? Every toy fair has a couple of exhibitors that seem a little wacky. We were all snickering at Charles behind his back."

We slowly walked across the office toward the elevator. Able was on a roll. There was a light in his eye and a note of desperation in his voice. He sounded like a convict who'd found Jesus and wanted you to understand why.

"But we were wrong and he was right. Those old-fashioned dolls flew off the shelves as fast as he could make them, even though the price point was too high, and the profit margin was nearly nonexistent. I was supposed to be the expert, and as far as I knew, kids just *didn't want* that sort of thing.

"By the next year, when he came out with the Eagle Riders, Robo-Zombies, and Helping Hand Trains, I didn't know what to think. The toys were still all wrong and they were priced too high, but this time I was *drawn* to them. I *wanted* them, just like all those kids did."

I noticed a woman walking the length of the office toward us.

"So I left New York and my six-figure job to work for someone who believes in ideas instead of focus groups. With every new line we release, I expect the company to come apart. But it doesn't happen. Every knockoff line out of Mattel or Hasbro flops, even though their prices are lower and they can fill the shelves. I can't explain it, but it's been an amazing ride. And this year we're releasing more toy lines than ever."

He pushed the elevator button. The woman reached us. "Excuse me, Able," she said. "Charles is ready to meet with you now." We looked across the office. A tall, angular young man with a thick head of dark hair stood at the far end of the row of desks. He watched us, apparently waiting for Able.

It only took me a moment to recognize him as one of the four who had met with Emmett Dubois beside the van. He was the one who'd had the seizure.

Annalise turned and looked at me. Her face was blank. It was the same expression I'd seen on her face dozens of times, but at that moment goose bumps ran down my back. The elevator dinged and the door opened.

Annalise casually pushed Able and the woman aside. "Stay," she said, and walked toward the dark-haired man.

I guessed she'd found the person she'd come to kill.

Able didn't stay. "Excuse me," he said. There was anger in his voice. "Excuse me, but that area is off-limits."

He started after her. I grabbed his arms from behind. He tried to shake me off. I shoved him at a desk, and he fell into the lap of a woman with a stack of files in her hands.

"She told us to stay," I told him. Able didn't understand how dangerous it was to cross Annalise. The woman dropped the papers she was holding and grabbed on to him to keep him between her and me.

Annalise was halfway down the rows of desks. "Charles Hammer?" she asked.

"Yes?" he said. I couldn't see Annalise's face, but I guessed that something in her expression made him uneasy.

A woman at the desk at the end of the row stood and stepped in Annalise's path. She was a big woman and she looked like she was used to getting her way. She grabbed Annalise's shoulder. Annalise smacked the woman's arm away. The woman gasped and grabbed her elbow, holding it as though her arm was broken.

Annalise grabbed Charles Hammer's left hand and laid the scrap wood on his palm. A shower of dull gray sparks and a jet of black steam blasted from the design toward the ceiling.

Everyone gasped. Hammer tried to pull away, but Annalise didn't release him. She tucked the scrap under her arm. "Your spell book," she said. "Give it to me."

"I'm sorry, what was that?"

Annalise sighed, then tore off his index finger with as much effort as it would take me to break a stalk of celery. She tossed the bloody digit over her shoulder.

Hammer screamed in pain. The women working in the office screamed and cringed against their desks. Hammer tried to yank his hand away, but Annalise held him as tightly as an iron vise.

She spoke to him in a clear, quiet voice. "I can ask you that question nine more times." Hammer drew his right fist back and threw a haymaker at the side of Annalise's face. He screamed again when he connected, then cradled his hand against his chest as though it was broken. Annalise's face was unmarked, and she kept talking as though nothing had happened. "You're not going to like it if I have to ask again after that. Spell book. Where?"

The sigil below my collarbone twinged. Again, there was no wave of force, but maybe that only come the first time. The room grew slightly dark, and the HBT name tags the women wore flared with yellow flames. Then the office workers dropped their arms to their sides and stood up in perfect unison.

They moved toward Annalise and Hammer like automatons. Annalise didn't see them.

"Boss!" I called.

Annalise turned, and just as one of the women drew in a huge breath as though she was about to scream, Annalise grabbed the front of her sweater and kicked her legs out from under her. I could hear bones break from where I stood. Annalise tossed the woman over the row of desks.

I didn't see her hit the floor, but I thought she'd survive. I hoped to God she would survive.

"Enough of this," Annalise said. She struck Charles Hammer with the back of her hand. His head tore away from his body and bounced into the corner.

I brought her here, I thought. *I helped her kill these people.* The thought made me sick.

A flat-faced woman stepped forward and took a deep breath. Annalise looked at her, obviously surprised that

Hammer's death had not restored the women to normal.

With both hands, Annalise slammed the scrap wood over the woman's mouth just as a jet of flame blasted out of it. The fire engulfed the enchanted wood and Annalise's hands, billowing over her wrists and setting her jacket alight.

Annalise screamed.

The scrap of wood exploded. Annalise fell backward, holding her burning hands in front of her face. As for the flat-faced woman, her head was gone. The stump of her neck was still ablaze as her body collapsed onto the carpet.

The women glided toward Annalise like ghosts. A tall redhead took a deep breath, and Annalise dove toward me and rolled. The jet of fire missed her and struck another woman, who went up like she was covered in gasoline.

The jet of fire stopped flowing from the redhead's mouth. Her lips and tongue were charred black. She clutched at her throat and collapsed.

Annalise curled up beside the top of the stairs. Her hands were still on fire and were blackened and shriveled. Her face was pale and her whole body trembled. I grabbed a jacket off the back of a chair and charged toward her.

The women surrounded her. A gray-haired woman took a deep breath. I shoved a woman aside to get to Annalise and was startled to realize it was Ms. Finkler.

Finkler knocked the gray-haired woman aside. The woman turned toward me.

I ducked low, grabbed her leg, and spun her.

I didn't have much leverage, but I managed to topple her just as the fire blasted from her open mouth. I felt the same scorching heat that had burned Justin Benton as the jet of flame passed over my head. I also had the strange feeling that it had somehow already happened. It was as though I was remembering the fire at the same time I was experiencing it.

The woman fell against a desk, blasting a jet of flame against her computer.

I threw the stolen jacket over Annalise's hands and hauled her into my arms. For all her power, she was tiny, barely a hundred pounds, and while I didn't have her strength, I did have adrenaline. A lot of it.

Then I saw Charles Hammer standing at the far end of the room. His clothes were bloody, but he was whole and healthy. His expression was one of pure, innocent astonishment.

Someone nearby took another breath. I carried Annalise to the stairs and leaped for the lower landing. I heard flames cut loose behind me. I felt the heat but no pain.

I hit the stairs about two-thirds of the way down. By some miracle, I didn't twist my ankle or crack open my head.

Annalise slipped from my grasp and bounced against the concrete steps. I jumped down beside her and yanked her off the floor. I glanced back and saw a column of flame scour the steps. I threw her over my shoulder and ran for the second flight down.

The fire trailed me, always striking where I'd been. If one of those women—and I knew very well they weren't in control of themselves, but I had no idea what was— had led me a little, she would have burned me to a cinder. That didn't happen.

I ran like hell to the next floor down, where the jet of fire couldn't reach me.

Figures moved down the hallway toward me. Cradling Annalise in my arms. I ran down the next flight of stairs. I reached the next landing, then the second floor. It took just a few seconds, but that was long enough for my adrenaline to ebb. It was also enough time for me to wonder why I'd gone to so much trouble to save a woman who wanted to kill me.

Too late to turn back now.

I ran down the last flight of stairs into the lobby. There, blocking the only exit, stood Carol, the receptionist. Her name tag was ablaze, and she stood stiffly, with her hands curled into claws at her side.

She was too far away. I could never knock her aside before she burned me alive.

She took a deep breath.

CHAPTER FIVE

I willed the ghost knife into my hand. It flew out of the inside breast pocket of Annalise's jacket. In one motion, I caught it and flung it.

Carol had just finished inhaling when the spell entered her throat, passed through, and exited the back of her neck.

I darted to the left. Although the ghost knife had left no mark, a jet of flame spurted out the front of Carol's neck, then a second shot out the back. Fire curled out of her mouth, but the pressure behind it was gone. The flames touched off her face and hair. She buckled. Fire blasted down the front of her clothes, the flames spreading. She didn't make any sound at all as the fire engulfed her.

I ran around the flames and pushed through the front door into the morning drizzle. The ghost knife lay on the sidewalk as though waiting for me. I hoisted Annalise higher on my shoulder and *reached* out to my spell. It flew into my hand.

Sprinting across the lot toward the van, I did my best not to jostle Annalise, but I doubted she could feel my shoulder bouncing against her stomach. But her hands . . . She let out a tiny whimper and pulled her knees closer to her chest. Unfortunately, my rib cage was between them.

"Ease up on me," I said gently. I had to gasp for air between every word, and I wasn't sure she could hear me through her pain. "Ease up."

She did. We reached the van. I unlocked the passenger

door and lifted her into the seat. I pulled the shoulder strap of her satchel over her head and threw it onto the floor, then clicked her seat belt over her.

At the same moment, I felt the now-familiar twinge against my chest. Memories were being erased. Was it because of the fight we'd just lost, or was another kid being killed across town?

I ran around the front of the van, got in, and started it up. Within seconds we were on the street.

"Annalise," I said. She didn't respond. Her hands were blackened and shriveled. Her face was pale and covered with sweat. I touched her cheek. Her skin was cold. She was going into shock.

I pulled over. We were only a block and a half from the plant, but I needed to get her feet elevated or she was going to die on me.

"What are you doing?" she said. She didn't look at me. "Remember the supermarket we passed on the way into town? Go there."

I did remember it, but only vaguely. I pulled back into the street and drove north until I hit Main Street, then turned right. It was only another half mile or so to the gas station where I'd bought the map, then another few hundred yards to the market.

I parked as close to the entrance as I could and took the plastic from Annalise's glove compartment. She told me the PIN and said to buy lean beef for her. Lots of it. I laid her down between the seats and wadded my sweaty windbreaker under her feet. "Hold on," I told her. "I'm going to be back as soon as I can."

"We can find you," she said, "if you don't come back. I put those spells on you and they don't come off. Any peer in the society can find them, and you."

I closed the door.

With a couple bucks' worth of items from the housewares aisle, I could have stolen any of the cars in the lot in less than twenty seconds. I'd done it hundreds of times before. I could have been halfway to Oregon in an hour. Leaving Annalise to die—and I had no doubt that without help, she would die, and very soon—would solve many of my immediate problems, whatever her threats. But I wasn't going to do it. It wasn't just that I had no idea what would happen to the spells she had put on me, and it wasn't just that the peers would hunt me down and tear me apart, although both of these were damn solid reasons. And it wasn't just the power Annalise had, although power like hers was irresistible to me.

It was also Justin Benton. Someone had to stand up for Justin Benton.

I followed signs to the meat department, then started loading beef into my basket. I didn't know much about choosing cuts, but I knew the white stuff was fat, the hard stuff was bone, and the red stuff was meat. I picked packages that were mostly red. I selected about ten pounds' worth, then grabbed a wide plastic cutting board from a hook above the case and hurried to the checkout line.

There were two people ahead of me. I had a little too much time to think.

Hammer knew we were coming after him now. He would either move against us right away or withdraw to somewhere safe, maybe somewhere out of town. If I were him, I'd be trying to figure out a way to kill us before the hour was up, but judging by the way Hammer had looked as Annalise had done her thing, I didn't think he'd be that together. I figured he'd run.

It was my turn at the register. "Nice town you have here," I said to the middle-aged cashier.

"Thanks!" she said.

"Isn't there a family somewhere still around here, the one who founded this town? The Hammer family?"

She looked immediately suspicious. "Maybe."

"They live in town? Where would I find them?" I

asked, figuring that the town wasn't small enough for everyone to know everyone, but it would be small enough for everyone to know their first family.

"What do you want with the Hammers?" the man behind me said. He was about forty, with a thick biker's beard and heavy muscles in his arms and shoulders.

I hadn't thought this through, and it was turning sour. I swiped Annalise's card and punched in her PIN. "I just wanted—"

"Don't bother," the cashier said. "I know exactly what you want."

"And you ain't gonna get it." Biker Beard stepped up very, very close to me. "Ain't nobody in this whole town gonna answer a question like that for you."

The cashier glared at me. "Time for you to go." She held the bag out to me, then dropped it on the floor.

I turned back to the big guy. My adrenaline was too high and I'd spent too many years behind bars to back down from him. Annalise was dying out in the van, and her medicine was lying on the floor beside me, all spilled out of its flimsy plastic bag, but I couldn't turn away. I was risking everything, but I couldn't turn away.

A little old lady came around the end of the counter and picked up my groceries. "Oh, enough of that, you two," she said, and took hold of my elbow.

Her grip was strong, but she couldn't have pulled me away unless I let her. I did. There were half a dozen good reasons for me to back down from Biker Beard, but the one that really mattered was that I didn't want to be the guy I was in jail. I wanted to be someone better.

The old woman had tiny half-glasses perched on the end of her nose and a thin, pinched mouth like a snapping turtle. I took the grocery bag from her when she handed it to me and I followed her outside. "You must be having a barbecue or something?" she asked.

"Thank you," I said.

"Of course, dear. Which one is yours?" I waved in the direction of Annalise's big white van. "Wonderful. You just get in that van and drive right out of town, understand, dear? There's no reason for you to stay here. We protect our own, and we don't want you here."

I glanced at her and back at the cashier and the small crowd that had gathered by the door. So much for small-town hospitality. At least I knew how to pick a fight, if I needed to. I nodded to the old woman and rushed back to the van.

Annalise was still alive. I pulled out of the supermarket parking lot with them still watching me. I drove a block toward town and parked beside a dry cleaners. Then I crouched behind the passenger seat with the front wheel of her motorcycle poking me in the back. I laid a hunk of meat on the cutting board and shaved off a slice with my ghost knife. Ghosts, magic, and dead things. Then I cut crisscrosses through the meat, being careful not to touch the cutting board. The ghost knife could cut straight through the bottom of the van and I wouldn't even feel it. The board was only there to keep the raw beef off the metal deck of the van.

I had to feed the bits of meat to her, of course. She took them almost blindly, like a baby bird. After she had eaten a pound or so, the color started to come back into her face. After three, her face no longer felt cold.

She rolled onto her side. She was more alert but also wary. I kept cutting meat, kept feeding her piece by piece. She watched every morsel move from the board to her mouth as if watching for some trick.

After she'd eaten half the meat I'd bought, Annalise said: "Help me up."

I did, lifting her by her elbows so she wouldn't have to lean on her injured hands, then opened the side door and supported her as she climbed down. She let me.

She turned toward the van, putting her back to the

parking lot, hunched over, and held her hands out of sight. She flexed them slightly. Flakes of black skin broke off her fingers and fell to the pavement.

My whole body tingled and I closed my eyes. Of all the things in the world I didn't need to see, that ranked pretty high.

With my eyes closed, I suddenly remembered Carol the receptionist. I remembered the way my ghost knife had cut through her neck, and the way she had burned away because of it.

I opened my eyes. The blackened skin of Annalise's hands had peeled off like burned paper, mostly. Beneath was raw, wet red flesh, and not much of it, either. Her hands looked scarily reduced. She touched her fingers together and gasped.

"Go back in," she said, not looking up. "Get more meat. Then we'll get out of here."

I did. I drove back to the supermarket and bought most of the lean meat remaining in the case, along with a box of plastic forks. I didn't speak to anyone and stood in a different cashier's line. No one threw me out. When I got back to the parking lot, Annalise had returned to her seat.

I put the groceries in the back, closed the passenger door, and buckled Annalise in, taking care not to touch the seat belt to her raw hands. She looked at me strangely, but I didn't think about that.

We pulled out of the lot.

"What happened back there?" I asked.

Annalise didn't answer at first. Finally, she said, "I don't know. Charles Hammer was the source of the magic in Hammer Bay, but I don't think he knew what was going on." She was quiet for a moment, as though the effort of speaking exhausted her. "Did you see the look on his face when those women all stood up at once?"

"I didn't."

"He was surprised. Bewildered. He was the source of the magic, but he didn't control it."

"You mean he doesn't control it."

"What do you mean?"

"He's alive. I saw—"

"Bullshit. I took his head off."

I shook my head. "Just before we got out of there," I said, "I saw him standing by the desk. His clothes were soaked in blood, but he was whole and alive."

"Shit. It fits, I guess. I just hate it when they won't stay down."

"Do you think Charles Hammer has someone behind him, pulling his strings?" I tried to imagine him with his own Annalise sending him out to fight and die.

"It's possible, but the spell I touched to him shot sparks. That means predator, and a powerful one." After that she was quiet.

I thought about that column of fire on the stairway, always striking where I had just been, never anticipating me. I mentioned it to Annalise.

"Some of the predators don't have concrete understanding of time, or three-dimensional space. It can be a weakness for them sometimes."

She fell silent again. I didn't press her for more information. I didn't want to push my luck.

We arrived at the motel. I fished Annalise's key out of her jacket pocket and opened her door. She collapsed onto the bed, exhausted from the effort of walking into the room.

I fetched the meat and cutting board from the van. The room had a small, round table, where I put the supplies down. I locked and barred the front door, then made sure the curtains were fully closed and began cutting the meat.

This time I fed Annalise with a plastic fork. It was more dignified than using my fingers. She watched me the whole time, her gaze wary and measuring. Obviously, she expected me to betray her again.

"Will this be enough?" I asked after she had eaten the first ten pounds I'd bought. I couldn't believe she'd eaten so much. Her stomach should have been swollen, but it wasn't. I assumed her body was using the meat to heal her injuries. I glanced down at her hands. It was a slow process.

"It should be," she said. "It had better be."

"What do you mean?"

"I've never . . . this should have been enough already. My hands should have been back to normal by now. Hell, a couple of years ago I only needed eight pounds to regrow an entirely new left foot. But we're past that now and I can still barely use them. Something's wrong."

I didn't like the sound of that. I kept cutting. "That was the same kind of fire that burned the little boy. I'm sure of it."

"I know what kind of fire it was," she snapped. "And we should have been protected. That spirit fire should not have been able to get past our iron gates."

We. I had run into Annalise's iron-gate spell before. It had once protected me from her green fire. I put my hand on my chest, just below my collarbone. That twinge I'd felt . . .

"That's right," she said. "I put an iron gate in the tattoos on your chest. It's supposed to protect against certain kinds of spirit attacks."

"Like the pressure waves that make people forget the dead kids?"

"Yes," she said. "Or fires channeled from the Empty Spaces."

"So why didn't it work?" I speared a piece of meat on a fork and offered it to her. She glared at me, then accepted the food without answering my question.

I kept cutting meat and offering it to her. I didn't ask

any more questions. Eventually, she was able to flex her hands into claws, then into fists. I could see that they still hurt, but she could move them. After I'd fed her eighteen pounds of beef, her skin looked healthy but still pale. That's when she took the fork from me and began to feed herself. She didn't ask me to stop cutting the meat, and I didn't.

She ate all of it. It was a little more than twenty pounds of beef, and she'd eaten it in a little less than three hours. She sat on the edge of the bed and flexed her hands. Her face was stoic, but I knew something was wrong. She kept testing them, moving them, staring at them. I suspected they still hurt her, and that she had expected them to be fully healed by now.

"I need to sleep now. And I need time to figure out what's happened to me."

She looked like she was about to say more, but she hesitated. I didn't care. "No problem," I told her, and started toward the door.

"Thank you," she said.

I knew it wasn't easy for her to say, and that it didn't mean she was ready to trust me. I didn't care. "You're welcome."

"Before you go," she said, "there's something I want you to leave behind."

I stopped and turned around. "Is that right?"

"Leave it, Ray. Give it to me."

"It's the only weapon I have."

"Do you think I can't take it? Right here and now?"

"I know you can," I said. "I just don't understand—"

"Give it to me," she said. She lifted the corner of her pillow.

I took my ghost knife from my pocket, crossed the room, and slid it under her pillow. Annalise watched me closely, her whole body tense. I got the message. I should have left her in the parking lot.

I went to my own room. There was next to nothing there that I had bought myself, except the jacket in the trash can. This wasn't my room; it was hers.

I took a shower, then changed into clean clothes. I kept expecting the local cops to kick down the door, but it didn't happen. They must have had their memories wiped, too. Neat trick. I opened my wallet and saw Annalise's debit card inside. Good. I was hungry again. At least I wouldn't have to sit in this room and starve.

I had the keys to the van, too. I considered driving it to a secluded spot and thoroughly searching all of Annalise's gear. She hadn't worn her ribbon-covered vest to the toy plant this morning, so she must have stashed it somewhere.

And there was the matter of her spell book. I knew she had one, but I didn't know where she kept it. Would it be nearby, so she could create more ribbons as needed? Or would it be hidden away somewhere back in Seattle, in a safe-deposit box, or buried beneath a concrete floor, or sealed in a crate and sunk in Elliott Bay?

Or it could be stashed in the back of the van.

I didn't believe it. Annalise wasn't careless enough to leave it lying around.

And while I didn't know much about this society of hers, I knew they had rules about their books: reading another peer's book was a killing offense. If I did find the book in the van, it would be because Annalise had left it there to tempt me. It would be the perfect excuse for her to break my neck.

Inside the night table was a phone book. Hammer Bay was small enough that the white and yellow pages were combined into one book, but no one with the last name of Hammer was listed. Figured. That would have been too easy.

I left the motel and walked past the van without peeking inside. I was too hungry for games. I went to the office and asked the nervous manager where I could get a bite to eat. He recommended a place.

It was only a couple of blocks down the road. I strolled over to it. The misty drizzle had lessened, but the heavy clouds still obscured the sun and dimmed the town. It was only about six in the evening, which meant I had another two hours of sunlight, at least. The thought lifted my spirits.

The place was a bar, but that was fine with me. I went inside and sat on a stool.

After a few moments, my eyes adjusted to the darkness. The bar ran the length of one wall, with a wait station near the door. The rest of the room was divided into booths. There were no dartboards or pool tables. There was no jukebox. The place was pretty empty. An elderly man sat at the bar, head bowed over his tumbler. Three men sat at the other end of the room, arguing in the relative privacy of a booth.

The bartender approached me. She was tall and lean, with glossy black hair that hung long past her shoulders and dark eyes that suggested she was at least partly Hispanic. Her long face had a no-nonsense friendliness that I liked immediately. "I didn't see you come in," she said. "What can I get you?"

I glanced down at her left hand. She wore two rings. Oh, well. "Let's start with a beer and a glass of water."

"That's fine," she said. "What kind of beer?"

"What do you recommend?"

"We have a terrific Elephant Stout on tap."

That sounded like an up-sell if I'd ever heard one, but what the hell, Annalise was buying. "Sounds great," I told her. She went back to the taps, and I looked around.

The older man looked over blearily and then turned back to his drink. He wore a modest suit that bulged at the middle, and he had carefully combed his hair over his bald spot.

Victim, I immediately thought. I could have rolled him for his wallet if I was desperate for chump change. A couple years back I'd have rolled him for his car keys, then driven his car straight to the chop shop.

That chapter was closed now. I didn't steal cars anymore.

I killed people. People like Carol the receptionist.

I wondered what was going to happen to the bodies of those women. Was it a crime scene now, with police tape, coroners, and witnesses who couldn't remember a thing? Or had those dead women been erased from the memories of everyone around them? I imagined the surviving office workers moving like automatons as they carried the corpses away. Or worse, walking past them like they weren't there, the same way people ignored the black streaks.

A gray-haired woman walked into the bar. She had a sensible work-and-church vibe that made her seem instantly out of place. She went over to the old man with the comb-over and set some papers on the bar beside him. They exchanged terms of endearment in a tone that suggested it was a habit for them and little more. The man tapped the papers. "What's this?"

"Financial papers and a birthday card for Paul," she said.

For a moment he looked as if he was going to ask for details, but instead he shrugged and picked up the pen. When he got to the card, he said: "Ten years old already? Is he coming home this summer?"

The woman sighed. "His scholarship covers a summer program in Atlanta, and he's going."

The man sighed, too, and signed the card.

As the woman walked out of the bar, the three men in the booth burst out laughing. They sounded loud, raw, and somewhat drunk. One called another a "fucking moron."

The bartender was just about to place my beer in front of me. She turned toward them, bared her teeth, and said: "Keep it down or take it somewhere else!" She didn't have to raise her voice.

They quieted down. The bartender set the beer in front of me, then served up a big glass of ice with a splash of water. "Sorry about that. Sometimes it's like a chimp house in here."

"I like noisy chimps. You know where they are. It's the quiet chimps you have to watch out for."

She smiled at me. "I'm Sara," she said.

"Ray."

"New in town?"

"Absolutely."

"I guess you came to apply at the toy plant?"

I shrugged. "Everyone keeps suggesting that."

"Well, don't," a man behind me said.

One of the three men from the back booth had come to the bar with an empty pitcher. Sara took it from him without comment and began filling it from the cheap end of the tap.

He was tall and rangy with a small scarecrow's head, and he stood closer to me than he needed to. I guess he wanted to look down on me while we talked.

"You're the first one to suggest I stay away," I said. "Something wrong with the company?"

"Not a thing," the scarecrow said. "I just don't want to see some stranger blow into town and take something that belongs to a local." Sara set the pitcher in front of him. "Thanks, little lollipop. If you get tired of these two, I have some prime lap space reserved for you back at the booth."

"Boy, you are one word away from being tossed out like trash. Don't make me call the Dubois brothers."

Brothers? Thinking back to the cops I'd seen at Harlan's shooting, they certainly could have been brothers, with Emmett the oldest. I filed that information away.

The scarecrow winked and sauntered back to the booth.

Sara grimaced. "I ought to ban them for good."

"Is this your place?"

"Yep," she said. She absentmindedly twisted the rings on her left ring finger. "Ever since Stan died."

"How long ago?"

"Nearly two years now," she said. "He was a good man. We worked hard. But lately the whole town's been going to hell."

"Why? It sounds like there's lots of work up at the toy factory. My boss and I were up at the offices this morning." I watched Sara and the old man closely. Neither reacted to that last statement at all. Neither said, *This morning? When all those women burned to death?* Apparently, neither knew about it, hours after it had happened. "They bring a lot of jobs here, don't they?" I continued. "Shouldn't the town be thriving?"

She shrugged.

"We're a timber town," the victim at the end of the bar said. "We're not a toy town."

"How do you mean?"

"A job isn't just a job," he said. His voice was thick and his words slow. Sara stayed close to him, listening just as closely as I was.

"A job is an identity," the man continued. "You don't put down a chainsaw and then pick up a sewing machine. Making doll clothes isn't the same as clearing trees. If you switch from one job to the other, you turn into a different person." He stumbled over that last word, but he was at least making sense.

"Why don't you guys cut timber anymore?"

"Lots of reasons," the man said. "The main one is that

we've cut pretty extensively on our land already. There just aren't that many trees out there worth harvesting anymore, where we can get them."

"And there's the environmentalists," Sara put in.

"That's right. Charlie Junior knew what to do about them. So did his father. But the latest Hammer doesn't care about any of that."

"To be fair," Sara put in, "Junior had let the whole thing slide the last ten years or so."

"It was his health, I think. When times got tough, he had breakdowns—"

"More like seizures," Sara said.

"Yeah, seizures. He worked like crazy to get through tough times, and he paid the price. But for the last ten years or so, he had the tough times without the working like crazy."

"Not that you can blame the man. He would fall on the ground and thrash like a flounder in a boat."

"Really," I said, just to contribute something.

"Yes," the man said. "Charlie Three seems to have inherited the family condition."

"And he's a helluva success, too," Sara said.

"I'll give him that," the man said. "Now, Cabot has a clean bill of health. No seizures, near as anyone can see, but he did get the family timber business, and it's sinking fast." The old guy slid off his stool and moved closer to me. "My name's Bill Terril. What's yours?"

"Ray Lilly," I said. We shook hands.

"Lilly, huh? That's kind of a girly name."

"Sure is," I said. "I'm the delicate type."

Bill chuckled as he looked me over. "I'll bet."

"So, this Charlie Three," I said, "he live in town?"

Sara and Bill were instantly suspicious. "Why do you ask?" Sara said.

"Whoa. It was just a question."

"We're pretty protective of our own around here,"

Sara said. "Especially of the Hammers. We look out for them. I don't know a body in this town who wouldn't. So, again: Why do you ask?"

I shrugged. "I dunno. Rich guy, little town. It sounds like he could live wherever."

"Nope," Bill said. "The Hammers created this town, and they stick by it."

I wondered how deep and widespread the support for the Hammer family extended. If Charles Hammer's memory wasn't wiped after this morning's fight—and I'd have bet it wouldn't be—he'd have gone into hiding. He might be tough to find without local help. I needed a way to drive a wedge between our target and the town.

Amazing, really, how quickly I'd gone over to Annalise's side.

"Huh." I didn't know what else to say. "So who's Cabot? Another one of the Hammers?" I asked.

"He . . ." Bill paused. He thought about how he wanted to answer.

Sara chimed in. "He's Charlie Junior's little brother. See, this town was founded by their grandfather, also named Cabot. He came out here with a crew of men and started cutting trees. He decided that the little Chimilchuk Inlet ought to be larger. He dredged it, widened it, and called it Hammer Bay.

"He had a lot of people rushing here to find work. Built the town right up. He ran a tight ship. He owned the newspaper, the grocery, the speakeasies, all of it. If he could have paid everyone in company scrip, he would have."

"But he was fair," Bill interrupted. "Everyone respected him."

"None of them were fair," Sara said. "None of them. All they cared about was themselves and what they'd built. The only one who's any different is Charlie Three."

"Dammit!" Bill snapped. "Charlie Senior was a great

man! He brought down governors and senators, and gave jobs to men who needed them. Men like my father."

"Don't go all wacky on me, Bill," Sara said. She waved as though he was a puff of smoke she didn't want to smell. "Charlie Three is trying to put a foundation under this town. He could do it, too. We'd have decent incomes without having to worry about what happens when the trees are gone. Charlie Three is bringing us into the next century."

"I don't much like it."

"Well, you're pretty much the only one."

The old man laughed. "Ain't that the truth. Most of the people in this town won't even talk to me anymore. Criticizing Charlie Three around here is like badmouthing the pope in Vatican City, even though he ain't a patch on what came before."

"Don't talk to me about Senior and Junior," Sara said. "You know how hard they made things for Stan and his own father."

"I . . . I'm sorry, Sara." Bill swirled his drink around in his glass. "You know how much I liked Stan."

She patted his hand. "I know, Bill. You slow down on that stuff, okay?"

Bill lifted his glass and then set it down without drinking. "It's not that the older generations didn't have their quirks. Remember that Scottish thing? But it's this latest one that's . . . he gave up on the trees and started making toys. And he gave up the reins."

"What do you mean?" I asked.

"When you have a stagecoach," he said enthusiastically, as though he'd spent a good bit of time thinking about this analogy, "when you have a stagecoach, you hold on to the reins, right? You have to control things. But what happens if you drop the reins, huh?"

"You stop moving," I offered.

"No. The coach tips over and everything spills out. It's

ruined. Broken. The horses charge off in different directions, fight each other, eat each other. They tear each other apart, that's what happens. Someone has to have control."

Sara suppressed a smile. "Bill, I don't think horses eat other horses."

My beer glass was empty, and so was my water glass. I ordered refills and asked for a menu. Sara told me that they didn't serve food anymore. She was all alone. I was disappointed, but she offered to dial a local pizza joint. I ordered a medium pepperoni.

I turned to Bill. "I hope you like pepperoni. On me."

"Well!" he said, shuffling back to his stool beside me. "That's fine. Just fine."

"You're welcome to have a slice, too," I said to Sara.

"I'll pass. I don't eat cheese." She lifted a tray of dirty glasses and carried them into the back.

"She's a good woman," Bill told me, keeping his voice low. "There's lots of fellas in town who'd like to get next to her. Especially since she got herself this bar."

I tried to picture myself standing behind the bar pulling beers, or frying burgers in the back. It was a nice idea, but it wasn't going to happen. "Is that so?"

"Her husband was a good man, too. Older than her. He hired her to wait tables and then a year later gave her a ring and a half-ownership in the bar."

"What happened to him?" I asked.

"Nothing she did," Bill said quickly. "He was killed by dogs."

"Did you say *dogs*?"

"A pack of dogs. And he ain't the only one. In the last six years or so, eight or ten local folks have been torn apart that way. Very mysterious."

"I don't get it. A pack of dogs? Are there feral dogs in the woods? Or does someone keep them?"

"There's no way to hide a pack of dogs in a small town like this one. Emmett Dubois tried to trap the dogs several times, but he never caught nothing. Me, I think they've had their vocal cords cut. That's why nobody ever heard them barking."

I remembered the wolf that had stood out in the middle of the street. "Are the cops in this town really all brothers?"

"Sure," Bill said. "And it was their own daddy who hired them for the job. It might seem strange to an out-of-towner, but being a cop is a family business in Hammer Bay. And it was never a problem while one of the Hammers was giving the orders."

"Does that mean it's a problem now?"

"Heh. Well . . ." Bill rubbed his face. I guessed he would rephrase that if he could.

"Let me put it another way: Are they good cops? Honest?"

Bill lowered his voice. "Emmett keeps a lid on things in this town. And on his brothers, too."

"So I should be careful, then?"

"Yes. Emmett is smart, and Sugar has always been a good kid. But don't be left alone with Wiley. Just be careful with him."

The pizza arrived. I paid for it with Annalise's card and offered Bill the first slice. He took it gladly. The conversation turned religious after that. Bill was sure I was a good Christian, and that the dog attacks were the work of Satan.

It went on that way for a while. The three of us talked about all sorts of things, and Sara accepted a slice after all. It was very friendly. I pried here and there about their personal lives but didn't learn much. Bill had one daughter and one grandson, Paul, who was at a boarding school in Georgia. Sara said she and Stan had never been blessed with kids. Of course. Bill started in on Charles Three again, but Sara told him to lay off.

After a while, the topic turned to me. Bill asked again

if I'd come to town to work at the toy plant. The scare-crow was standing at the bar, getting another pitcher. I decided it was time to try to drive that wedge between the town and the Hammers, so I told them why we had met with Able Katz that morning. "My boss wants Hammer Bay Toys to outsource some of its manufacturing to Africa. Sewing doll clothes, I think."

Sara looked as shocked as if I'd slapped her. "What? He'd never do that."

"It was only a first meeting," I said with a casual shrug. "So nothing was decided."

The scarecrow stared at me for a moment, then left the empty pitcher on the bar and went back to the booth.

"Sewing . . . Three of my aunts work in sewing. Aunt Casey needs that job to keep her house. We need those jobs here in town! Do you know how many of our older folks support themselves with a sewing machine now? What'll they do if the jobs go overseas?"

"People need jobs all over."

Sara collected my glass. "You know what, Ray? I don't want you in my place anymore."

The scarecrow and his two friends walked out the front door. They watched me silently as they passed. I didn't like that look.

I stood. Bill protested. "Aw, don't be that way, Sara. It's not his fault."

"It's all right, Bill," I said. "It was time I was leaving anyway. Sara, do you have a back door?"

She folded her arms across her chest. "Why?"

"Because I expect those three guys are waiting for me outside."

Bill struggled off his stool. "I'll go have a look-see."

"You stay right there, Bill," Sara said. "I'll check the parking lot if Ray here is feeling nervous."

She walked to the front door and went out. Bill lifted the lid of the pizza box. It was empty.

"Well," Bill said, "thanks for the grub and the company."

"It was my pleasure."

"Is . . . is it really true about Africa?"

"Times are harder there than they are here, Bill."

Sara came back in and told me that the parking lot was empty. So was the street.

She stood by the door. I walked across the room, matched her scowl with a smile, and went outside.

I had only taken three steps when I saw them leaning against a pickup truck. They smiled. The short one was holding a knife, and the other two were carrying tire irons. Scarecrow held a snub-nosed .38 in his off hand.

Behind me, I heard Sara close the door and throw the bolt.

CHAPTER SIX

"Hey, stranger," the knife holder said. "We're here to welcome you to Hammer Bay."

"Really?" I said. "Because I don't see a muffin basket. You wouldn't be lying to me, would you?" The bar blocked one side of the lot, and a cinder-block wall of the business next door blocked the other. There were no stairs, windows, or gaps that I could use to get away. Behind me was a chain-link fence with struts blocking my view of the other side. A Plymouth Reliant was parked up against it. If I was going to run, that was the way, but there was still that gun.

The one who had spoken was average height and wore large tinted glasses. The other was well under six feet and built like a fireplug; he held a beer in his off hand. Both were thick with muscle that comes with hard physical labor and the flab that comes with fried food. The short one wore a construction worker's helmet, and all three wore steel-toed work boots.

Glasses took a small box from his inside pocket. He lifted out a couple of tiny bundles wrapped in tissue or toilet paper and handed them to the others. Each man wet the bundle on his tongue, popped it into his mouth, and passed the beer back and forth to wash it down.

The short one nodded toward me. "Look at his tattoos. He's the one who set up Harlan for Emmett Dubois."

"Izzat right?" Glasses said, then threw the empty bottle at me. I ducked. It shattered against a fence pole behind me. "Well, well, well, now I'm double happy we waited for him."

The tall one bared his teeth and came toward me. He kept the barrel of the gun pointed at my stomach while he raised the tire iron. What was it with tire irons in this town?

"Don't you run from me," he said with all the practiced bullying of a wife beater. "Don't you run!"

I wished Annalise had let me keep my ghost knife.

He lifted the tire iron and swung for my head. I raised my left arm and caught the blow on my tattooed wrist.

It didn't hurt, but I did my damnedest not to show that. I cursed and clutched at my wrist as though he'd broken it.

The other two laughed. The tall guy wasn't in a mood to be entertained. "Harlan is my friend, and he's in the hospital because of you."

He swung the tire iron again. This time I caught the blow on my right arm. I made a small, strangled noise and cradled both arms against my chest.

The scarecrow sneered at me and dropped the revolver into his pocket.

Perfect. He stepped toward me and raised his tire iron again.

I laid a quick, right uppercut on the point of his jaw. He went limp and my left hand was in his jacket pocket before he hit the ground. I yanked the revolver free and fumbled it into the proper position. The scarecrow's tire iron clattered to the ground.

Glasses and the fireplug stepped back.

I pointed the gun at them. They froze in place.

"All right, kids. This doesn't have to get interesting. Let's make a deal. You never come near me again, and I won't kill you."

"Forget it," the tall guy said, struggling to his feet. "The gun's not loaded."

Glasses turned on him. "What do you mean, it's not loaded?" I wanted to know the same thing. "I told you what we needed to do."

The tall guy shrugged. "You're my friend, Wyatt, but . . . I left the bullets at home."

While they hashed that out, the fireplug grinned. He hefted his tire iron and stepped toward me.

I threw the gun onto the roof of the bar and jumped onto the trunk of the Reliant. Then I stepped onto the roof and leaped for the top of the fence. I hit it at waist level and rolled over the top. There was a Dumpster below me. I twisted and landed on it. I heard cloth tearing. I jumped to the ground and ran for the street, wondering if Annalise would spring for more clothes.

When I reached the street, I sprinted toward the left, away from the business district into a residential neighborhood.

I heard them shout behind me and kept running. I was confident I could take any one of them, especially with the protections Annalise had given me. But three was too many. Too easy for one of them to knife me in the armpit or smash in my skull while I was dealing with another.

So I ran. I passed one block, then another. As I started on the third, I looked back. All three were chasing me, and the tall one seemed to be gaining. That was fine. Wyatt and the fireplug were falling back, puffing and straining to keep up.

I rounded a corner and was suddenly sprinting right beside a police car. The fat officer sat behind the wheel drinking Mountain Dew from a two-liter bottle. The engine was off. He watched me run past but didn't reach for his keys or the radio. Great.

In the next block, I nearly stepped on a thick black streak on the sidewalk. I jolted to the side at the last minute, running into the street to go around it.

The beer and pizza began to weigh on me. I stopped beneath a streetlight and waited for the scarecrow.

He didn't keep me waiting long. And he wasn't stupid, either. He ran straight at me, then dodged to the side as he passed, swinging that tire iron.

I feinted a lunge at him, then stepped away from the swing. It missed.

The guy slapped his feet on the sidewalk as he tried to stop himself. I charged him. He turned and tried to leap back. With a weapon and a longer reach, I'm sure he was hoping to avoid a clinch.

He feinted a swing for my head, then went for my ribs. I barely managed to get my elbow in the path of the iron. It glanced off my arm without any harm but thumped into my hip. That one hurt.

I grabbed the tire iron as he tried to pull it away. My grip was stronger, and I ripped it from his hand and tossed it into the street. The scarecrow backed away into the streetlight, right where I wanted him.

I spared a glance at Wyatt and the fireplug. They were still half a block away, puffing toward us.

The scarecrow threw a solid left jab followed by a long, hard, circling right. Both were respectable efforts, although neither connected. I ducked under his right and landed a hard left against his floating ribs. I felt something crack.

He woofed and bent sideways. I threw a right into his midsection and slid a left hook over his shoulder against his jaw. He dropped.

I turned toward Wyatt and his remaining friend. We'd been standing in the light, and they had seen the whole show. They stopped running. After a second of indecision, they started walking away. I watched them go for a second or two, then went back to the man I'd just beaten.

I'd known guys who thought winning a fight was

cause for celebration. They'd laugh and cheer and spread around high fives. I didn't feel like cheering.

I took the guy's wallet while he was coming around. His driver's license said he was Floyd O'Marra. I also found thirty dollars inside. Good. Eventually, Annalise was going to want her plastic back. I decided to charge Floyd for the important life lessons I was teaching him. I pocketed the money.

"Damn," Floyd said, rousing himself. "Where am I?"

"Look around," I told him. "Tell me if you see anything familiar."

He looked up at me. "Oh, hell."

"How's Harlan doing, by the way?"

Floyd didn't quite know how to take that question. "He'll probably live." *No thanks to you* hung at the end of that sentence, unspoken but clear.

He started to sit up, but I shoved him back down. "Where do you work, Floyd?"

"Henstrick Construction."

"What kind of construction do you do? What do you build?"

"Whorehouses," he said, sneering a little.

"Is that so? Where can I find me a girl? All this exercise made me a little anxious."

"Outside of town," he said. "A couple hundred yards behind the bowling alley. The Curl Club. Ask for me and I'll get you a real warm welcome."

He tried to move away from me. I pushed him onto his back. "Do you want to help your buddy Wyatt?"

"He's my buddy, ain't he?"

"Do him a favor. Tell him to keep away from me. In fact, you and him should hop in your truck and take a little vacation. Vegas or something. Go have some fun. Because if I see any of you again, I'm going to spoil your whole fucking day."

Floyd had come around enough to start getting angry

again. He tried to roll away from me but winced at the pain in his ribs. He swore. "Next time I'm going to load that damn gun."

I couldn't take that lightly. I slugged him once on the nose. Not so hard that I'd break bones, but enough to make him taste blood. I held up his license. "Floyd O'Marra. 223 Cedar Lane. That sounds like a nice little neighborhood. Am I going to have to come to your house, Floyd? Am I going to have to burn it down? While you're sleeping there?"

He swore at me again. He was still feeling defiant.

Damn. Floyd just wasn't getting with the program. I couldn't let this guy go after he'd promised to kill me. I knew very well how easy it was to get shot.

I stomped on his hands, one after the other.

He howled. Lights started turning on in the houses around the block. I didn't care anymore. He swore at me some more, and each word was a half sob.

It wasn't a pretty thing. It wasn't a nice thing. But I couldn't have some guy running around after he'd threatened to shoot me. I'm not that brave.

I knelt beside him and lifted him off the ground. I knew it made his ribs hurt. I wanted him to hurt. I wanted him to get his thirty bucks' worth.

"Shut your mouth," I snarled at him. "In case you haven't figured it out yet, you're one word away from being a corpse, because the next thing I'll stomp on is your neck. Get it? Keep away from me. Next time I won't be such a sweetheart."

This time Floyd understood. He nodded frantically, his eyes closed. I dropped him onto the sidewalk and collected his tire iron.

I walked toward the bar. The police car was still parked in its spot, but I circled around the block to avoid passing it again. My hip felt tender where Floyd had hit me with the iron.

On the way back, I saw another black streak from across the street. Damn. The town was full of them.

I pushed open the door to the bar and strolled in like an old friend. Sara's mouth fell open. She backed toward the cash register, probably wishing she'd kept the door bolted. I dropped the tire iron on the bar. Loudly.

Bill was still sitting there. "Damn," he said. "Not a mark on him."

Sara lunged under the counter and pulled out a shotgun. The barrel was several inches too short to be legal. "Get out," she said.

"I don't care about you, Sara," I said. "I don't care what you've done. But I've come to Hammer Bay to do a job."

"Whatever," she said. "Get out."

She was scared, but not of me. I wasn't sure if that was a good thing or not. "Does Wyatt buy meth or does he make it himself?"

"What are you talking about?"

"Please. You can't tell me you don't know what's going on."

Bill chuckled. "Sure she can. She's a tough girl, but she's a little naïve."

I turned to Bill. "Which is it, then?"

"Wyatt buys it somewhere south of here, then sells it in the lot at his night job."

"Are the cops clueless or paid off?" I asked.

"Paid off, I bet," Bill said. "Considering."

"What night job?"

Bill laughed. "The Curl Club. He keeps it low-key, though. I don't think Henstrick has worked it all out yet."

"Wyatt isn't a customer there, is he?"

"No, he's a bouncer, like Floyd and Georgie. Most of her boys work the club when they're not working on job sites. Especially when times are hard."

"Who is this 'her' you mentioned?"

"Henstrick."

"Ah." I felt embarrassed to have to be told.

Sara was getting impatient and I was done. I backed toward the door. "Thanks, Bill."

He said he was glad to help. Sara asked me if what I'd said about Africa was true.

"Be sure to lock the door behind me." I left.

If I had played my hand right, Sara would begin asking around, spreading the rumor. Annalise was going to have to go after Charles Hammer again, and Hammer would know we were coming. I wondered how much it would take to truly isolate him.

A police car was parked across the street. Inside I saw the silhouette of the same fat officer I'd seen earlier.

I heard a clatter nearby. I turned toward the sound.

Something low and gray moved out from the side of the Dumpster. At first I thought it was a dog. Then I saw the tinge of red fur. It was the wolf from the night before.

It stared at me. The hairs on the back of my neck stood up.

The door to the bar opened. I whirled around and saw Bill limping toward me. He wore an eager, fevered expression.

"You're here for something, aren't you?" he asked.

I glanced back at the mouth of the parking lot. The wolf was gone. "Yeah. A couple beers and dinner."

"Sure, sure. I understand. Listen, have you talked to Pete Lemly yet?"

"Who's he?"

"Our local newspaper guy. He knows a lot of the local chess pieces, and how they like to move."

The police car across the street started up and pulled away. Bill glanced over at it, noticing it for the first time. His expression grew fearful. "Oh, Lord. I gotta get." He hustled back into the bar.

Apparently, I was not a person to be seen with.

I started walking. Two couples passed me headed for the bar. They walked close together as though huddling against the darkness, and when they laughed, their voices were too loud and full of strain.

I heard a woman scream. The couples heard it as well. They stood still, looking at one another as though waiting for someone else to make a decision.

I ran toward the sound. The woman, whoever she was, kept screaming. I sprinted around the corner and heard them following me.

About twenty yards ahead, I saw a woman standing on the far side of a Dodge Neon. Her face was lit by a fire in the car. She wore an expression of utter horror.

Then the fire went out. She staggered against a tree planted by the curb. A wave of wriggling silver shapes spilled out the back door, swarmed onto the nearest lawn, and burrowed into it.

I was just a few yards away when I felt that sudden *twinge* against my iron gate.

I slowed my pace. The woman brushed at her coat and then dragged a little girl from the backseat, urging her to hurry because it was already so late.

I stood ten yards away and watched her. Damn. Her child was gone, and she'd already forgotten. She noticed me and started to hurry. I had scared her.

The whole town was scaring me.

I walked around the block. By the time I reached the Neon, the woman and her child were gone. A black scorch mark on the sidewalk led toward the lawn, where the dirt was loose and shiny black in the streetlight. Another dead kid.

I walked toward the motel. At the last minute, I turned up the road and walked to the supermarket again. It took me an hour, but I eventually returned with a sack full of the last lean beef in the store. It was only four pounds, but if Annalise wasn't healed, it would be better than nothing. At least I didn't run into that cashier again.

As I walked across the parking lot, I noticed that the lights were on in her room. I went into my room next door, set the food on the table, and thumped lightly on the wall.

She knocked on my door within a few seconds. I let her in, then went into the bathroom to wash my face. I hate the feeling of dried sweat on my face.

"How are your hands?" I asked her.

"They're a little worse," she said. "Not too much worse, but they aren't good. I'm not sure what I should do."

Neither was I. I finished washing up and joined her in the other room. She was tearing the plastic off a skirt steak. Her hands were stiff and awkward.

"What about the rest of the Twenty Palace Society?" I asked.

She stopped and looked at me. "What about them?"

I knew I was about to tread on a sensitive spot, but it had to be said. "What if you called for help? You—"

"I don't need their help," she said evenly. "I don't need anything from anyone. I've been doing jobs like this since before you were born. Since before your father was born."

"Okay. Okay. I get it. You're a rock." I noticed that she had set my ghost knife on the table. I picked it up and started cutting the meat.

It felt good to have my ghost knife again.

Annalise ate all the meat I cut for her. When she was finished, she held up her hands and flexed them.

"Better?" I asked.

"Yes," she said. "But not healed. I've never had such a stubborn injury."

"We've pretty much bought out the local market."

"In the morning we'll try to find a butcher." She sighed. "The longer it's been dead, the less potent it is for me."

That kind of talk makes me nervous. Would she need to eat something alive soon? Maybe we should pick up a dozen oysters.

The door to my room slammed open. I threw myself to the floor. Someone shouted, "Police! Nobody move!"

Then I heard a gunshot.

"Luke! LUKE!" a man shouted. "Easy, now! Easy!"

I realized I was holding my ghost knife. I didn't want the cops to have it, so I set it on its edge and pushed it through the carpet. It disappeared into the floor.

"Nobody move!" someone else shouted. This voice was young. I wanted to glance at them, but I held myself completely still. I didn't need to see their faces. Not until they put away their weapons, anyway.

"Is anyone hurt?" the first voice asked. I recognized it as Emmett Dubois.

"I'm unhurt," Annalise said. Her voice was cool and relaxed.

"Good, good, now don't move."

The fat cop knelt on my back and cuffed me. I was hauled to my feet. Annalise stood beside me, her hands also cuffed behind her back.

"I'm sorry, Emmett," one of the cops said. He was the one with the seven-day beard. He'd apparently left his cigar in the car. I guessed this was Luke. "It's that *smell*."

"I know," Emmett said. His voice was soothing, an older brother talking to a younger. "We'll talk about it later."

They made us stand by the window while they tossed the place. They found my clothes but not the ghost knife. Emmett Dubois seemed pretty interested in all the meat wrappers, but he didn't ask us about it directly.

Then they took us to Annalise's room and let us watch

as they tossed it, too. She didn't seem to have brought anything of her own into the room.

Finally, we all watched as Luke and the red-haired cop searched the van. They threw everything onto the asphalt, even rolling out Annalise's dirt bike and searching under the seat, inside the exhaust pipes, gas tank, and handlebars.

A little man came out of the manager's office and watched. He crossed his arms and stood well back in the shadow of the door as though he was afraid to be seen.

They didn't find her vest of ribbons or her spell book. The only thing that seemed to interest Emmett was the satchel she'd brought to her meeting with Able Katz. He pulled the papers out, shuffled through them, and shoved them back.

If Annalise was bothered by the way they ransacked her stuff, she didn't show it.

"All right," Emmett finally said. "Let's load them up."

Luke came over to drag me into a waiting police car. The fat cop took Annalise. I saw him lean down and whisper something to her. I couldn't hear what he was saying, but I knew he wasn't offering her a private suite with cable TV. Not that Annalise seemed to be bothered by anything he said. They sat us in the back of the cars and drove us away.

I didn't like being in the back of a cop car again. It smelled bad. I had to sit against my handcuffs, and they hadn't even belted me in.

We drove north through the downtown, passing the parking lot where Wyatt had tried to ambush me. The police station was on a small side road at the edge of the water. Huge, irregular black rocks lay on all sides of the station and the tiny road leading to it.

We parked outside the station. Three Dodge Ram trucks were there, one gleaming black, one fire-engine red, and one painted gunmetal gray with flames on the sides.

They were tricked out with fog lights, chrome wheels, ski racks, and who knows what else. Beside them was a vintage Bentley, black, although I couldn't see enough of it to guess the year.

These were expensive cars, far above the level of the usual pickups and station wagons I'd seen around town or the dinged-up, rusted Celica parked at the far end of the lot.

They brought me inside but didn't process me. No fingerprints, nothing. Luke just walked me into the back and stuck me in a cell. Alone. He made me back up and stick my hands through the bars so he could uncuff me. He took his time about it.

"That girlfriend of yours isn't much of a looker," he said.

A chill ran down my back. I tried to turn to look at him, but he yanked the chain on my cuffs.

"She's got all them tattoos, though," he continued. "I'd guess she's a wild one. Am I right?"

I imagined Annalise backhanding Luke's head off his shoulders. "Watch your step with her."

Luke grabbed the back of my collar and slammed my head against the bars. My eyes filled with stars. I spun and fell against the metal bench. When I looked at him again, he had a nine-millimeter pointed at my head.

"A little caution might be a good idea right now, son. A little common sense, if you get my point."

I felt my head. There was no blood, but I'd have a fine lump in a couple of hours. And it hurt like a bastard.

Part of me wished he'd pull the trigger. I was sick of being chased, threatened, and left in the dark. A bullet, at least, would be a clean end.

"Common sense has never been my strong suit," I heard myself say.

Luke holstered his weapon. "Guess we'll have to work on that together," he said. He smiled at me and left.

I could, with a little concentration, summon my ghost knife, but I'd never tried it from farther than a few yards. I wondered if I could call it from all the way across town.

I closed my eyes and tried to shut out the pain in my head. The ghost knife had power, and that power recognized me. I didn't understand it any more than your average stickup man understands the chemical composition of the gunpowder in his nine-mil, but I knew how to make it work. I closed my eyes and concentrated.

I couldn't feel it. It was too far away.

Crap. With my ghost knife, I could have cut myself out of this cell in a few seconds. I planned to try again when my head cleared, but I wasn't hopeful.

The door opened and a woman walked into the hall. She looked past sixty, and she wasn't handling the years well. Her face was pale, and the pouches under her eyes were the color of storm clouds. Her hair looked as though she'd cut it herself without looking in a mirror. Her mouth moved ceaselessly: she licked her lips, chewed them, pursed them, twisted them into a frown. She carried a stack of files.

"You're the fellow who . . ." She broke off. I waited for her. "Why did you help Harlan Semple?"

I didn't say *Because my boss told me to.* Instead I said, "Is he somebody to you?"

"My nephew." She glanced at the door behind her. She didn't want to be caught talking to me.

"How is he? I wanted to visit him, but I haven't had time."

"He's stable now, after a bad night and day. They said you saved his life. Why did you do it? Did you know him?"

"No, I don't know him, and I'm not sure why I did it."

"Did he . . . did he say why he was doing what he was doing?"

"You mean shooting up the town?" She didn't flinch.

She just stared at me with the blank eyes of a hungry bird. "He said it was because of his daughters. He said he had two daughters, but they disappeared. He said kids have been disappearing from the whole town, but he's the only one who remembers."

She shook her head. "That poor, crazy-headed boy."

"Did he have two daughters?" I asked her.

"He didn't have anyone. His wife took up with . . . someone else after he was hurt. He was all by himself."

I didn't believe a word of it, but I was sure she believed it. She reached up and wearily wiped her eyes. I noticed a nasty scar on her hand.

"Is that a bite mark?" I asked. "A dog bite?"

She became flustered and started toward the exit.

"Wait a minute," I said. "Do you want to help your bosses?"

That stopped her. She glanced nervously at the door, then came back toward me.

I didn't get off the bench. I had to present this next bit carefully. She was obviously terrified of the Dubois brothers, and being so close to them every day meant she was probably desperate to keep them happy. She wouldn't pass on any information that might irritate Emmett or his boys.

"I don't care what you folks here get up to, understand?" I used a high voice and kept my head and shoulders as low as I could without breaking eye contact. She still stared at me dubiously. "Honestly, I don't care. The only thing I care about is avoiding trouble."

"You're not very good at it, though, are you?"

I smiled. "I'm trying. Listen, I'm just a driver. Annalise, my boss, is the one in charge. And she's rich. Very rich."

Her mouth twisted. "She doesn't look rich."

"She's eccentric, you know what I mean?"

She folded her arms. "Why are you telling me all this?"

"Just make sure your bosses know to be careful

around her. If something happens to her, her people will be all over Hammer Bay. Politicians, lawyers, state cops, private investigators, newspaper people, the whole works. They'll start talking to everyone in the town, auditing tax records, the whole deal. I've seen it happen."

"I still don't know why you're telling me," she said stubbornly. "Everyone here is completely professional. She doesn't have anything to worry about."

Of course she didn't have anything to worry about. But I didn't want to deal with the fallout if Annalise pinched off Luke Dubois's head.

"Come on, ma'am," I said. "Don't kid a kidder. Luke Dubois stood right outside this cell and made a crack about her. He needs to know."

"So you're trying to help him, too?"

"Luke Dubois burst into my motel room and shot the place up, then he banged my skull against these bars. I wouldn't piss on him if his hair was on fire. But I don't want to sit through another deposition, or give more statements to state cops and private eyes. I just want to get through the next couple of days without some damn catastrophe falling on my head."

She stared at me for a moment, then said: "I'll get Sugar." She left the room.

A few minutes later, she returned with the tall red-haired cop. He was all knobby muscles and bulging Adam's apple. His name tag said S. DUBOIS.

"Is there a problem, sir?" he asked, just like a real TV policeman.

I went through the whole spiel again, but it was a little more polished this time. Sugar listened without expression. Finally, he held up his hand. I stopped. "I'll be right back, sir," he said. Then he left the room.

The woman watched him as though she didn't know whether Sugar wanted her to follow or stay where she was, and that it was an important question. She decided to stay.

A minute later, Emmett came in. He looked relaxed, smiling like the host of a well-planned dinner party. "I understand there's a problem of some kind?" he said.

I went through it a third time, making it much shorter and much less emotional. I did my best to make it sound like Annalise was a land mine. I didn't want to sound like I was threatening anyone.

Emmett cut me off after I'd barely touched on the points I wanted to make. "Nothing is going to happen to her. This may not be the Ritz, but my brothers and I are professionals."

I rubbed the goose egg swelling on the back of my head. "Then there aren't any problems at all, I guess."

He looked at me. I looked at him. He didn't seem to like me much.

"I know who you are," Emmett said. I didn't answer. "Come along, Shireen." He led the others through the doorway and bolted the door from the other side. The lights switched off.

I lay back on the bench. It shouldn't have bothered me that Emmett Dubois knew me and my history. It was part of the public record. Anyone with an Internet connection and the correct spelling of my last name could dig up the newspaper articles in a few seconds.

But it did bother me. He knew about the time I'd served, the enemies I'd made, and the people who were dead because of me. I didn't know a thing about him, except that he was hiding something. I wasn't sure what it was, but it was all over his face.

I wondered, not for the first time, why he'd picked us up. My fight with Floyd was reason enough, but had Sara called him, too? And there was the incident at the toy company to consider.

Somehow, I doubted it was the latter. The further that morning's fight slipped into the past without comment, the more convinced I was that no one could remember it. The Dubois brothers didn't strike me as the souls of restraint—one of them would have said something. Also, Sara and Bill hadn't heard about it hours after it happened.

One person I expected to remember everything was Charlie Three. The fires at the toy offices tied him and his company to the burned kids, but how was he doing it and why? And according to Bill, the latest Hammer patriarch—although it was funny to call him that since he was barely older than I was—had cut the Dubois brothers loose. His father and grandfather had used the police to control the town, but they were on their own now.

And there were the seizures to consider, too. Bill said they ran in the family.

Actually, he'd said they came on when the patriarch was successful. That was something to talk about with Annalise, if I ever got the chance.

Had Hammer made a phone call and had us picked up? It was possible, but if I had a whole town under my thumb, I wouldn't have the cops bring my enemies to a cell. I'd have them run out of town or shot.

Of course, the Dubois brothers might march in like automatons and breathe fire on me, but I didn't expect it. They could find a better place to kill us than their cells.

Then again, maybe Hammer hadn't sicced the cops on us after all. Maybe Floyd and Emmett were bowling buddies, and I was going to get stomped by the rest of the league before morning.

It wasn't a pleasant thought, but I'd been around scary people before. I was a light sleeper, too, especially when people were thinking naughty thoughts about me.

I stayed awake a good long time. When a suspect falls

asleep quickly in a cell, cops see that as a sign of guilt. No one came to check on me, though, and eventually, I slept.

I heard the lock on my cell door clank open very quietly, and I was sitting up before I was even fully awake.

"Skittish, ain't he?" Luke Dubois smiled down at me. His fat brother stood beside him. It occurred to me that I'd never heard him speak. "Stand up and turn around," he said.

I did. He cuffed me and led me to an interrogation room. Emmett was waiting.

"Welcome, Mr. Lilly," Emmett said. "Have a seat. Wiley, set up the video, please."

Luke shoved me into a chair and left the room. Wiley, the fat cop that Bill had told me to be careful with, pulled a video camera out of a corner and set it on a tripod. The camcorder was a new model.

Emmett smiled at me as we waited. He had a pair of folders on the table in front of him, but he didn't open them.

Wiley started the camcorder, then sat in the corner. He pulled his gun from his holster and held it in his lap, staring at me as if he was trying to come up with a reason not to shoot me then and there.

Emmett recited the date for the benefit of the camera, then his name, Wiley's, and mine. I glanced at his watch. It was 3:15 in the morning. I wiped sleep out of my eyes. I needed to be alert.

"So, Mr. Lilly," Emmett said, smiling and leaning forward. "Tell me what you know about the murder of Karoly Lem."

CHAPTER SEVEN

"Uh, Carol E. Lem? Who's she?"

Emmett sighed as though I was being deliberately difficult.

"Are you stating, for the record, that you don't know a man named Karoly Lem?"

"Yes," I said.

"Are you sure that's the answer you want on the record?" Emmett asked.

"If I met some dude named Carol, I'd remember it."

Emmett chuckled. He slid the top folder to the side and opened the one on the bottom. "Karoly Lem," he read. "Born in Poland in 1962, moved to the U.S. with his family in 1980, became a naturalized American citizen in 1981. He lived in Portland for most of his life—"

"Is there going to be a test?" I interrupted.

"He came to Hammer Bay three weeks ago. He told Arlen, the manager at his motel, that he was scouting locations for Big 5 Sporting Goods. Six days ago, his body was found behind the library."

Emmett stared at me, waiting for my reaction. "Why are there so few children in Hammer Bay?" I asked. "I see lots of couples, lots of station wagons and plastic swing sets on people's lawns, but not many kids. Why is that?"

Emmett's eyes narrowed. He didn't seem to know what I was talking about. "Mr. Lem had been torn apart by some sort of wild animal." And yet, he'd called it a murder.

I knew better than to say the word *dog*. "Six days ago? You know, I have the most incredible alibi," I said. Wiley was still staring at me from the corner. My skin prickled where I imagined a bullet going in.

"I know you do," Emmett said. He opened the other folder. "You were still in jail, awaiting arraignment for . . . how many murders was it?"

That wasn't a question I felt any need to answer.

"Well, the number changed every time they found a new body, right? And the charges were dropped, weren't they?"

I didn't answer.

"In fact, some people were calling you a hero."

"I'm not a hero," I said, too quickly. A hero would have done more than kill a few predators. A hero would have saved his friend.

"Find any designer drugs in Hammer Bay, Mr. Lilly? Have you seen anything that can make the lame walk, and turn them into crazed killers, too?"

"Not yet."

"And your relationship to Mr. Lem?"

"I don't have one."

Emmett nodded at me. "I think we should take a break. Wiley."

Wiley shut off the camera. Emmett collected his folders and left the room. Wiley led me back to my cell.

It was still dark outside. Alone in the cell, I lay down on the bench and let myself drift off to sleep again.

I awoke to the sound of the cell being opened. This time it was Sugar Dubois letting me out. He didn't handcuff me. I glanced at the window and saw daylight.

"What . . ." Sugar said. He seemed almost shy. "Why did you have so many meat wrappers in your apartment?"

"I'm a collector," I said. "A rare cube steak can fetch a couple hundred bucks on eBay."

Sugar didn't think that was very funny. He led me out into the front offices. Annalise was already standing by the front door with Emmett. Shireen, Luke, and Wiley were nowhere in sight.

"You folks can go," Emmett said. "If you intend to leave town, let me know about it first. Understand?"

I looked at Annalise. She shrugged dismissively and walked toward the door. I heard Emmett make a low growl in his throat. He was used to being treated like a big shot.

I followed Annalise into the street. The Celica and the black and red trucks were gone. There was nothing to do but walk back to our rooms. My stomach grumbled, but food would have to wait. I wanted my ghost knife.

I noticed a silver Escalade parked on a side street near the station. It looked out of place, but I put it out of my mind. I had other things to think about.

"Did you know Karoly Lem?" I asked Annalise. She didn't answer. She was walking with her hands held out a little from her body. It wasn't a big change in her body language, but I noticed it. I spoke in a low voice. "Do you need a trip to the butcher shop?"

"Yes!" she hissed.

We walked quickly through town. "Why hasn't the meat cured you?" I asked her.

"I don't know. It always has in the past, but this time a little piece of pain remains, and I can't make it go away. The pain grows back."

"What should we do?"

She frowned up at me. That word *we* had just slipped out, but she didn't like it. "The longer a piece of meat has been dead, the less use it is to me. We need something as fresh as possible, and a lot of it."

A man walked toward us. He was dressed as a county electrical worker. I looked him in the eyes to catch his attention. "Excuse me," I said.

He checked us out. He didn't like the way I looked, but seeing Annalise beside me seemed to reassure him. "Yes?"

"We're not local—maybe that's obvious—but we're looking for a butcher shop. Is there one in town?"

"Well, I always go to the supermarket," he said.

"We've been there," I said.

"Okay. There is a place. It's expensive. It's at the other end of town just off Ocean Street. Look for a New Agey crystal and book shop and turn right. It's just a couple of doors down. You can't miss it."

"Thanks," I said.

I turned to Annalise. "That's just a couple of blocks past our motel. Do you want another ten pounds?"

"Twenty," she said.

We walked the length of Ocean, found the New Age bookstore, and walked up the side street. The butcher shop was closed and wouldn't open for another hour. At my suggestion, we walked back to Ocean and found a place to eat breakfast.

The silver Escalade now sat parked on the corner while we went into a seafood restaurant. I wasn't happy to see it again so much closer to us.

After we sat at a table, Annalise ordered for both of us. Apparently, we both wanted the fried-fish omelets, with a side of fish. After the waitress left, I excused myself.

I slipped out the back door of the restaurant. The alley smelled of old fish bones and was apparently home to a clan of feral cats. I made my way to the corner.

A quick trip up the side street showed me that the Escalade was still on the corner. Someone was sitting in the driver's seat. The engine was off, but the brake lights were on. Keeping a foot on the brake was a good driving habit, but it was bad for a stakeout.

I walked casually toward the vehicle. I would have

liked to have a hat to pull down low or a different jacket to put on, but I didn't. I hoped that being casual would cut it.

It didn't. When I was still a full car length away, the engine started and the car jolted into the street. I ran toward it, hoping for a glimpse of the driver, but the SUV squealed into traffic, turned a corner, and was gone.

So much for my ninja skills. I went back into the restaurant and joined Annalise at the table.

"Where have you been?" she asked. The waitress approached our table with our food.

"Checking out a car."

Annalise grunted. She took my plate, scraped the side order of fish and half of my omelet onto hers, then returned the rest to me. She used her hands cautiously, tenderly, but her expression was calm. I took her toast.

We ate slowly, killing time. We didn't talk. Annalise watched the street, so I bought the Seattle newspaper and scanned it for my name. There was nothing, thank God. While I read, Annalise ordered another plate of fish. I didn't ask if it helped.

Ten A.M. finally arrived. Annalise and I strolled over to the butcher shop and bought five whole beef tenderloins. The butcher wrapped them all up in one package. It weighed twenty-five pounds, and I carried it.

At the motel, Annalise stopped in at the manager's office. I followed.

The manager was the same nervous little guy I'd seen while the Dubois brothers were ransacking our things. He gaped at the big package wrapped in butcher paper on my shoulder, then opened his mouth to ask a question. Annalise didn't give him the chance.

"Have there been any messages for me?" she asked.

The manager looked down at his desk and shuffled some papers. He rubbed his nose and said: "Nothing. I'm sorry."

Annalise swore under her breath and turned toward the door. She was going to walk out.

"Hey," I said to her. She stopped and looked up at me. "You do know he's lying, right?"

She seemed startled. She turned back toward the manager. If he had kept his cool, he might have bluffed his way through it. Instead, he began to stammer and protest with all the sincerity of a hack politician.

"Now, hold on," he said. "I . . . I don't want to . . . um . . . want to be rude, but I . . ."

Annalise yanked the package of tenderloins from my hands and walked over to the counter. She lifted the beef over her head and slammed it down on the counter like a sledgehammer.

The wood cracked. Instead of a flat counter, it was now a sagging V shape. The manager screamed out, "Jesus!" as he leapt backward. Annalise tossed the slab of meat to me. It nearly knocked me on my rear end.

"You lied to me." Annalise's voice was quiet. I was standing behind her, but I knew the expression on her face very well. Annalise had a way of looking at people as if they were something small and disgusting and in need of stepping on.

The manager retreated toward the back wall. There was a door behind him, but he seemed to have forgotten it was there. If he had a weapon in the place, he'd forgotten about that, too.

"I . . . I . . ." was all he could say.

"Where is that message?" Annalise said. Her voice was rising. "It belongs to me."

"I don't have it," the manager squealed.

"Who does?" Annalise hissed. "Who took it? Was it Able Katz? Charles Hammer?"

"What? No!"

"It was Emmett Dubois," I said. The manager looked at me, his fear suddenly doubled. "The message was from a Polish guy who stayed here, right? And just before he was killed, Chief Dubois came by here and collected the note. Right? Or was it just after he was killed?"

"I can't tell you anything," the man said. "You don't understand."

"I understand," I assured him. "You're afraid for your life, right? How much are you paying Dubois every month?"

"I can't," he said. "I can't talk about it."

"Give me the figure. That's all I want. How much?"

He looked at Annalise. He was afraid of us, sure, but he *wanted* to tell. We all want to tell. We all want to air our grievances and spread our gossip. Dubois had scared him pretty well, but Annalise and I were all the excuse this little guy needed.

"A hundred dollars," he said.

"That's fine. Now, did Emmett collect that message from you before Mr. Lem was killed, or after?"

"You said the figure was all you wanted. You said—"

"It was all that I wanted. She"—I nodded toward Annalise—"wants something more."

He sighed. "Before," he said.

"That's what I thought," I told him. "Don't worry, no one needs to know that we heard it from you."

Annalise folded her arms across her chest. "What did the message say?"

"I didn't read it," the manager said, his voice nearly pleading. "I just put it in an envelope like the foreigner asked and set it aside for you. I didn't even know it was important until Emmett came by asking about it. I swear."

"That's fine," I said. "That's fine. Annalise, will we be moving to new digs?"

"No, we won't," she said.

I set the meat on the edge of the manager's desk. Red juices dripped through the torn butcher paper onto a stack of papers. "Well then," I said to the little guy, "It looks like you're stuck with us for a while. Let's go into the back."

He needed a little convincing, but eventually I led him through the door into his back office. As I suspected, he had a hidden camera at the front desk. I collected the VHS tape, wondering if the Dubois brothers were on one of these cassettes, too. A hidden stash of bribe videos would be good insurance, if he had the wit to play his cards right.

But we were here for the fire and the dead kids. We were here for Charlie Three. Dubois wasn't any of my business.

"Listen," I said as I tucked the videotape under my arm. "That message was important. More important than you realize, and you put a lot of people in danger by turning it over to Chief Dubois."

"What are you, then? FBI?"

"Of course not. And don't ask that question again. We're going to be staying here for a few more days, then we'll be moving on. Keep your head down and you'll be fine. Understand?"

We walked back out into the front office. He looked at his ruined desk and groaned. "What am I going to tell my wife?"

"Tell her that two disreputable-looking people came in here and lost their tempers," I said. "Try to stay as close to the truth as possible. You're not much of a liar."

Annalise and I went outside. She checked the van. Everything that the Dubois brothers had thrown into the parking lot had been carelessly thrown back inside.

We went into my room. I retrieved my ghost knife from the cut in the floor and pocketed it. It felt good.

I dropped the beef onto the table and unwrapped it. I cut a long strip of meat and then cut that into tiny slivers. Annalise started to pick them up with her fingers and gulp them down.

"How did you know Dubois had the message?"

Annalise asked. "And what difference does it make when he got it?"

"When the chief asked me about Karoly Lem, I figured he had something to do with you, even though I'd never heard of him before. He stayed at this motel, right?"

Annalise nodded while she chewed.

I kept the meat coming. "Not good. With all of us staying at the same place, it's too easy for someone like Dubois to connect us. Anyway, Lem is dead, and Dubois has to investigate, or at least make it look like he's investigating it."

"Do you think he killed Karoly?" she asked, her mouth full.

"I can't really tell, but I'd bet he did. What was Karoly here to do?"

She didn't answer me right away. She slid another piece of raw beef into her mouth and chewed.

I sighed. "I can guess, but it would be better if you just told me. Was he another one of your wooden men?"

"No," she answered quickly. "You're my wooden man. I've never had another."

"Okay," I said. I still didn't know what a wooden man was. "Then what was he doing? Casing the town?"

"Pretty much," she answered. "There aren't enough peers in the society to check out every strange report, so we have investigators who check things out. Hammer Bay . . ." She trailed off. Then she ate a piece of beef. With most people, you could let the silence play out and they'd eventually feel the need to fill it. But Annalise wasn't a people person. She was used to long silences.

"What about Hammer Bay?" I asked.

"We've investigated Hammer Bay before," she said. "We never found a reason to do an action, but we've had people here."

"What made you send them?"

"This time it was the success of the toy company. 'Toy

Company Breaks All the Rules to Succeed' was the head-line, I think. I have the clipping in the van." She lifted a hunk of beef and gulped it down. "We end up investigating a lot of that sort of thing—businesses that should fail but rake in tons of money instead. People who get rich quick. People who win lotteries."

"Lotteries? Really?"

She shrugged. "There are still a couple of luck spells floating around. They mostly don't work anymore, but when they do a lottery is usually involved."

A dozen questions presented themselves. Before I could choose one, she spoke up. "A hundred dollars doesn't sound like a lot of money. How did you know?"

"Something the cook at the diner said about all the different kinds of insurance he has to carry. And the Dubois brothers didn't buy those trucks on a small-town cop's salary. Besides, if they extort too much, eventually someone calls the state cops or the FBI. A hundred bucks is irritating, but not enough to fight the local bullies over. And if you're tapping twenty or thirty businesses, it adds up."

"I guess so."

"At Hammer Bay Toys, did you notice anything strange about the fire?" I asked.

"You mean aside from the fact that it shot out of the mouths of a bunch of middle-aged paper pushers?"

I laughed. This was practically a bonding moment. "Not just that. When the fire came near me, it felt like it had already happened. Do you know what I mean? It was like I was watching the fire right in front of my eyes, but at the same time the fire was something that had happened to me a long time ago. Kinda."

"Like you were feeling it and remembering it at the same time," Annalise said.

"Yes," I said. "I felt the same thing when I was standing next to the boy, Justin. It was as though the fire was reaching around the moment I was in and coming at me from the side."

Annalise stared at her hands and flexed them. She moved them pretty well, but she would have stopped eating if the pain was gone completely. "Not just in that moment. The fire seemed to strike at me in the past," she said. "It might have gone back and struck when I was just a kid, before Eli, before I had any of these protections."

I mentally filed the name Eli away. "It attacked you in the past to hurt you now? Is that even possible?"

She shrugged. "If it happened, it's possible."

"But then, wouldn't you have had this pain all of your life? Wouldn't you remember having chronic pain?"

She waved off my objections, tossed another piece of meat into her mouth, and spoke while she chewed. "I'm just guessing, but I'm not saying the fire burned me while I was a little girl at the butter churn. I'm saying it came at me from the past. Maybe the future. Not everything experiences space and time the way we do. Some predators can be pretty strange."

"Butter churn?"

"I'm older than I look, remember?"

I remembered. She looked to be about twenty-three or twenty-four years old. "Are we talking *Little House on the Prairie* old or Ye Knights of Olde old?"

She shook her head and looked away. "Just keep cutting." Her voice had a ghost of humor in it.

I wasn't sure what exactly had changed between us, but I was glad of it. Not just because I didn't want Annalise to kill me, although I'd be a liar if I said that didn't matter. The truth was that I wanted her on my side. She knew more about magic than I could ever guess, and she could handle herself.

She had power. I had to admit, I was drawn to that power. It was alluring. I wanted to be next to it, maybe leech off some of it for myself.

I tried to picture us in thirty years, when I was in my late fifties, still driving her around. Would she still look like she did now? I'd probably look like her father.

Unless she did for me whatever it took to make a person stay young . . .

No. I shook that thought away. Annalise wouldn't even tell me who she talked to on her cell phone. She certainly wasn't going to share the secret of her long life with me.

I was not going to spend my time daydreaming about something I would never get. That was poison.

And yet . . .

I looked at her again. She was so small. With her jacket off I could see her tattooed arms poking out of her short-sleeved shirt. They were so skinny that they made me queasy. She looked like she was wasting away. Her thin muscles rolled back and forth under her skin as she lifted a piece of beef to her mouth. Her elbows were like knots in a rope.

She had been scrawny from the first moment I saw her, but she looked worse now than ever. I wondered if her injury was burning the flesh off of her.

How long would she live with the pain in her hands? Would she have to go centuries like this, devouring a side of beef every day?

If the fire was coming at her from the future as well as the past, if it was always a second or two ahead of whatever cure she administered, she might never be free of it. Unless it killed her.

Annalise cleared her throat. "I'm going to tell you a story," she said.

CHAPTER EIGHT

"Okay," I said. I kept cutting meat, although it was nearly gone now.

"A long time ago, before most of the world was writing down its history, there was a powerful sorcerer. He was a primary, a dreamer, and his power was immense. I'm not much for history, so I don't remember his name. Let's call him Simon.

"Simon lived on a mountainside, in a huge palace. There were fertile fields all around, and Simon had a lot of villages and farmers working the land and paying him for the privilege. He wasn't a good man by today's standards, but for the time I suppose he was. And he protected his people.

"On the other side of a mountain range lived another sorcerer, Thomas. He wasn't a primary, but he still had a lot of power. And he summoned predators. Lots of them.

"At the time, the custom between sorcerers was live and let live, but Thomas was getting on Simon's nerves. His predators were killing Simon's villagers, turning them into vampires and other nasty shit, and stealing them away to work for him.

"Simon grew pretty annoyed, right? He sent a message to Thomas telling him to leave his lands and his people alone and get rid of his predators.

"Thomas, not surprisingly, refused. He said that he needed his predators for protection, and that he was doing nothing wrong himself. If some of his creatures roamed into Simon's lands to feed, there was nothing he could do about it.

"However, he did offer to leave the area, if he could take a copy of Simon's spell book with him.

"Simon immediately decided to kill Thomas."

I realized that she had stopped eating. I kept cutting and piling the meat on the butcher paper.

"So Simon gathered up a bunch of his spells and headed out. His lands were ruined and his people scattered. When he reached the edges of his enemy's lands, he began to fight.

"Now, Simon was powerful, but he couldn't get through. Before he could reach Thomas's palace, he was swarmed by predators: Floating Storms, Claw-in-Shadows, all sorts of things, not to mention his own villagers under the influence of Puppet Strings or transformed into vampires.

"He was driven back three times, each time expending more of his spells. He realized that he wasn't going to be able to take out Thomas this way, so he went into the forest and cut down a stand of poplar trees. Then he lashed the pieces of wood together. He put a spell on them to make them walk like men and swing their arms in a feeble imitation of an attack.

"When he had made enough, he sent them against Thomas's defenses. The predators swarmed them, destroying them wherever they found them.

"And in the confusion, Simon snuck into Thomas's palace and faced him one to one. Thomas didn't have a chance."

I had finished cutting the meat. It was there for Annalise whenever she wanted it. I wiped my ghost knife against the edge of the butcher paper. It didn't come very clean, but I didn't care. I dropped it, still wet with raw beef, onto the table.

I didn't look at her. I just stared at the pile of cut-up meat.

"Simon himself was never part of the Twenty Palace Society, but his student and heir was one of the founding members. And he shared the tactic of using wooden men with the rest of the peers. It's a tactic that has continued down through the centuries."

And that was the end.

Right about then, I thought, would have been the time for her to say, *Do you understand, Ray?* or *I'm sorry, Ray* or *But it doesn't have to be that way for you, Ray.*

She didn't say any of those things. She just picked up another piece of raw beef and started chewing.

"Excuse me," I said, and I went out of the room.

The fresh, salt air was bracing. *Stupid, stupid, stupid.* I must have been an idiot not to have seen it sooner.

The worst part was that I had volunteered. I'd asked to work for her. I hadn't understood at the time that it meant I would be a decoy, that I would be cannon fodder, but I had volunteered.

She had asked if I would be her wooden man, and I had said yes. She'd never explained what it meant. She had tricked me.

But of course, that was bullshit. I had been bluffing from the moment I met her and had pretended to know more than I did. And I had been lying to her in other ways as well, all to save my friend. If I was up to my neck, it was my own damn fault.

I was a decoy. Expendable. I had thrown my future away to save someone that I'd been forced to kill anyway. Damn.

I noticed the Escalade again, this time parked across the street. It would be harder to approach this time. I'd have to circle around two blocks to come up behind it, but what else did I have to do?

I went back into the motel room and asked Annalise if

she had a second scrap of wood with a magic-finder spell on it. She took it from her satchel and handed it to me without a word.

I held it up to the light by the window. It flared, all of the designs freezing in place and turning silver. Then it returned to its normal shade of black, with the designs slowly turning.

I touched the wood to the tattoos on the back of my hand. Annalise's magic made it glow with silver light, but after it acclimated to my touch, it returned to its normal slow churning. No powerful magic was close to us right now.

I picked up my ghost knife, rinsed it clean in the bathroom sink, and slipped it into my pocket.

I left Annalise in my room. I didn't have a way out the back, but I bet I could go through the manager's office to a back door, then an alley, then I could try to come up behind the Escalade again. This time I'd get close enough to check it for magic. If Charles Hammer was watching us, I suspected he'd make the scrap of wood pop like a string of firecrackers again.

I walked slowly toward the office, wondering what I could offer Annalise to get her to release me from my promise. If I took out Charles Hammer by myself, or found a permanent cure for her hands, or pieced together the whole story of what was happening in Hammer Bay, maybe she would let me go home, or promote me to tin man or something.

That pointless line of thought was interrupted by a white cargo van that rumbled into the parking lot. It was a Dodge, and it looked remarkably like Annalise's, except that it was newer and had a pair of battered ladders lashed to the top. The back door opened.

Floyd's fireplug friend crouched there. He pointed a snub-nosed .38 revolver at me. "Hey, there, jackrabbit," he said. "This one is loaded."

Two more guys crouched in the back of the van. My mind registered that they were there, but I couldn't look away from that damn gun.

"Your gun is drunk?" I said. My voice sounded much more calm than I felt.

"Get in. Someone wants to meet you."

I climbed into the van. They slammed the doors and my brain kicked in. They were all wearing construction boots. I looked directly at the fireplug. "Georgie," I said, "if Henstrick wanted to talk to me, she should have called. I would have liked a visit."

"Know my name, do you?" Georgie said. He smiled. "But you don't know everything."

The van bounced out of the parking lot. I glanced at the two other guys. Both held mean-looking hunting knives. If I knew everything, I wouldn't be in the back of this van.

"Get his wallet," Georgie said.

One of the other two, a trim ex-Marine type with dark bags under his eyes, placed the edge of his knife against the side of my neck. The third man sat well back out of everyone's way. The ex-Marine yanked my wallet out of my pocket.

"Raymond Milman Lilly," he read. "And here's Floyd's thirty bucks." He took the money out of my wallet and stuffed it into his breast pocket.

"Floyd is my bud," Georgie said. "I didn't like the way you left him."

"Really? Then why did you turn and walk away when I was beating his ass?"

Georgie didn't take my bait. "Conditions were unfavorable at the time. I like them better now."

"I'll bet you do."

The ex-Marine pulled the wood scrap out from my jacket pocket. We all looked at it. The design turned as slowly as ever. There was nothing magical about these fellows.

They stared, entranced. I tensed to spring at Georgie, but he sensed it, raised the gun, and leveled it at my face. "Be still," he said quietly.

"Whoa," the third man said, still entranced by the wood scrap. "That's cool."

The ex-Marine rubbed his finger along the design and yanked it back. "Tingles," he said. "How does it do that?"

"Trade secret," I told him. "We're trying to convince Hammer Bay Toys to manufacture and market them under their banner."

The ex-Marine shrugged and set it down next to me, apparently forgetting that I was being held at gunpoint. He pressed the blade more tightly against my neck as he jammed his hand into my jacket pockets.

"How we doing back there?" the driver called.

"We're fine," Georgie answered. "How far are we?"

"Halfway," the driver said. He turned sharply to the right. The ex-Marine lost his balance and his blade bit into my neck.

"Watch what you're doing," I snapped at him. He pulled the knife away slightly. I felt a thin trickle of blood on my collar, but I knew it wasn't serious.

"Sorry," the ex-Marine said. He pulled out my ghost knife and held it up. Everyone looked at it. It was just a sheet of notepaper covered with mailing tape and laminated. I could sense the power there, but none of them appeared to.

"What's this?" Georgie asked.

I held up my hand. "It's just a piece of paper," I said. "Toss it here."

I *reached* for the spell and called it to me. It shot out of the ex-Marine's hand, passing through a couple of his fingers on the way. As always, it passed through his living flesh as though he was not there.

The knife moved away from my throat. The ghost knife had done its work on the ex-Marine. I caught the spell and immediately threw it.

Georgie was taken by surprise, but not by much. The ghost knife went right where I wanted it to go, cutting through the top of his trigger assembly just as he began to squeeze it. The gun didn't go off, and a second later I heard the trigger clatter against the floor of the van.

In the time it took the broken trigger to fall, I called the spell back to me and slashed it through Georgie's leg. It cut a long slit in his pant leg, but the cut through his leg was bloodless.

I turned toward the ex-Marine. He was slumped and sagging, all the vitality drained out of him. For safety's sake, I slid the ghost knife through his arm one more time. It never seemed to matter where the ghost knife struck a living person—it always had the same effect.

Georgie and the ex-Marine slid to the floor as though they were fainting. The third man lunged at me, his hunting knife aimed at my throat.

I threw the ghost knife at him and batted at the knife with the protected part of my forearm. The spell disappeared into his chest. The strength went out of him, but there was still a lot of momentum behind that knife. I mistimed my block and felt the tip of the blade slice my unprotected upper arm.

The third man fell against me. I *reached* for the ghost knife again. If the spell went through the wall of a moving vehicle, I could be a block away from it very, very quickly. I wasn't about to leave my only real weapon behind.

"What the hell?" the driver said. I closed my eyes.

The ghost knife flew back into the van, cutting a slit in the wall and letting in a sliver of light.

The van swerved to the right and lurched to a stop. The third man fell on top of me, knocking me to the floor. I was pinned beneath him.

The driver climbed from his seat. I heard him open the glove compartment. I didn't try to free myself. I didn't have time. I switched the ghost knife from my pinned left arm to my free right arm. The driver turned toward me, gun in hand. It was another .38.

If I hadn't been lying under one of his friends, he would have had plenty of time to shoot me. We were at point-blank range, but he didn't have a clear shot. I threw my spell at him.

He tried to slap the ghost knife away but missed it. It entered just above his navel, and as soon as it disappeared I *reached* for it again. The spell boomeranged back to me, passing through the driver a second time. He collapsed.

I caught it. I'd never tried that trick before. I liked it.

I shoved the man off me and struggled to my knees. All four were still awake, but they were bleary-eyed and listless. I took both knives, Georgie's revolver, and the driver's, too. Both guns were identical to the one I'd taken from Floyd outside the bar. Maybe the construction workers in Hammer Bay bought in bulk.

Georgie looked up at me with glazed, pleasant eyes. "Sorry about the way I treated you," he said. "I don't know why I was so rude."

"Yeah, yeah," I said. The ghost knife didn't just take away their strength, it also cut out a person's rage and aggression. Temporarily.

I checked the cuts on my neck and left biceps. The one on my neck was barely a scratch. It had already stopped bleeding. The one on my arm would need a couple of stitches and had come way too close to my brachial artery.

I took their wallets. The four of them had a grand total of thirty-seven dollars on them. That's how it goes in the age of the debit card. I also took back the money Floyd "paid" me. I didn't bother with the IDs this time.

"All right, you clowns," I said to them. They all stared up at me with wet, docile eyes. I aimed the .38 at them. "Get on your knees beside the side door."

They did.

"Put your hands flat on the floor. Get them next to each other."

They pushed and nudged against one another, trying to position themselves.

"I'm sorry about all this," the ex-Marine said. "We were just—"

"Shut up," I said. I slid the ghost knife into my pocket and picked up the disabled revolver. I slid the cylinder release forward and dropped the rounds onto the floor. Then I picked up Annalise's scrap of wood and put it in my pocket. "Where are the keys?"

The driver spoke up. "In the ignition."

"What were you guys supposed to do with me?"

"Bring you to the Curl Club," the driver answered, "so Phyllis could talk to you."

"Phyllis?"

"Phyllis Henstrick. She runs the place, and Henstrick Construction."

"Why does she want to talk to me?"

"She didn't say," the driver answered. He crouched beside the others like a little lamb. All of them stared at the barrel of the pistol in my hand. They couldn't look away.

"I think," Georgie said, "that it had to do with a rumor she heard about Charles Hammer sending jobs overseas."

Of course, I thought. "Okay, boys," I said to them. My voice was low. "Live or die?"

Georgie understood right away. "Live," he said. The others agreed.

"Fine," I told them. "I'm only going to be in town for a couple of days, I hope, and I don't want to see any of you again. So I'm going to take out some insurance. Hold still. If any of you yank your hands away, I'm going to assume that means you've changed your answer."

I turned the revolver around and held it like a club.

"Please," the ex-Marine said. "Please don't."

"It's gonna hurt," I said, letting some of my anger show, "but not as bad as a bullet in the guts."

I slammed the butt of the revolver onto the backs of their hands, aiming for the knuckle of their index fingers.

It wasn't the smartest move, but the smartest move would have been to kill them all. I didn't want them shooting at me from a moving vehicle tomorrow. I had to take them out of the game somehow, and I had to teach them, and whoever pulled their strings, not to mess with me. Breaking their hands was gentle compared with what I should have done.

They cursed and whimpered like scolded boys. When it was done, I slid open the side door.

"School's out for the day," I said, and kicked Georgie through the open door.

He tumbled out onto the curb, and the other three scrambled after him on their knees and elbows. They crouched on the sidewalk, blinking in the drizzle, holding their arms across their chests just as I had outside Sara's bar. I slammed the door shut.

The keys were, in fact, in the ignition. I laid the guns in my lap, started the van, and pulled into traffic.

At the first red light, I picked up the driver's revolver. I took out my ghost knife and cut off the hammer, then sliced through the cylinder. I tossed it into the back of the van. Georgie's gun was already ruined.

I have my reasons for not liking guns.

On impulse, I opened the glove compartment and

peeked inside. My curiosity was rewarded with an envelope filled with five $50 bills.

Things were looking up.

My arm was bleeding pretty freely. It was annoying and I'd need to have it taken care of. I took the tourist map from my inside jacket pocket and consulted it. Looking around the neighborhood, I oriented myself to the two main roads in town. The hospital was behind me and to the east. I turned at a corner, then did it again.

I was a couple of blocks from the hospital when I saw a McDonald's. Half an omelet and toast hadn't held me, so I pulled into the drive-through. If I was going to wait in an emergency room, I might as well have lunch with me.

And wooden men don't have to worry about cholesterol.

I ordered the biggest, sloppiest burger they had, along with fries and a milk shake. In for a penny, in for a pound. As I pulled up to the pickup window, a pretty teenage girl with a splatter of pimples over her face leaned out the window.

"Hi, Uncle Ethan!" she said.

Then she saw my face. Her mouth dropped open, but she didn't say a word. "Hello yourself," I said. I paid her with Georgie's money. She gave me the food.

"That looks like my uncle's van," she said.

"Really? Weird," I said to her. I set the bag of food on the seat next to me and drove to the emergency room.

To my surprise, there were no other patients. To my further surprise, I didn't need stitches. The doctor cleaned the wound, glued it shut, and packed a bandage against it. It cost me three hundred dollars. Luckily, I hadn't bought two milk shakes. Uncle Ethan paid my bill for me, leaving about six dollars in my pocket. Easy come . . .

I thanked the emergency room staff and walked toward the exit to check on the van. Through the glass doors, I saw the Escalade slowly cruising through the parking lot. I stepped away from the glass. The SUV circled Uncle Ethan's van, then drove around the building.

I turned away from the doors and hustled through the hospital, moving as fast as I could without attracting attention. I had planned to visit Harlan Semple while I was here. That would have to wait.

I passed bare corridors with no doors. For a moment I felt lost, then I burst through some double doors and found myself in a storage room filled with plastic tubes in plastic bags, and IV stands. Feeling relieved, I broke into a sprint, running to the loading dock I knew had to be at the end of the hall.

There was a small panel van backed against the loading dock, and an eighteen-wheeler backing up beside it. A man in jeans and a polo shirt called out to me, telling me I wasn't supposed to be there, but I jumped off the loading dock and ran to the street beyond.

I reached the sidewalk. The street was nearly empty, and the Escalade was nowhere in sight. I was standing at the exit of the parking lot. Nothing there, either.

Wait. There it was. The Escalade pulled into view, then stopped, as if the driver was looking around. I ducked behind a tall hedge, bumping against the stop sign that controlled traffic entering the road.

The vehicle turned toward the exit and puttered toward the spot where I was hiding. I watched it through a break in the bushes, trying to get a glimpse of the driver. I couldn't. The overcast clouds reflected off the windshield, blocking my view. Still, I was sure it was Charles Hammer in there.

The Escalade pulled a little past the stop sign and paused on the sidewalk. I knew the driver would be watching the traffic to the left, so I stepped from my hiding spot, yanked open the passenger door, and hopped into the seat.

"Hello," I said.

The driver cried out in a high-pitched voice, and for a second, I thought Charles Hammer looked much shorter behind the wheel than he had in his offices.

Of course, it wasn't Charles behind the wheel. It was a well-dressed, dark-haired woman. She had broad, even, lovely features, hair that reached just below her ears. Her legs were thick with well-toned muscle. She looked to be about thirty.

And I had just jumped into her car like a carjacker.

"Oh!" she cried. "Oh, I . . . um . . ."

"Is there something you wanted to talk to me about?" I asked her.

She glanced at the cell phone holstered beside her car radio. "Do you want to call the police?" I asked. "Go ahead. I think that's a terrific idea."

"Look," she said, shrinking fearfully against the door, her hand inching toward the door release. "I'm sorry about following you around. You met with my brother, and—"

"Who's your brother?"

"Charles Hammer. At Hammer Bay Toys." I nodded. I could see the resemblance. "I wanted to talk to you—"

"Then why did you pull away when I approached you the first time?"

"I wasn't sure then. I just decided this morning."

She'd laid her hand on the door release, looking like she was ready to throw herself out of the car at any moment. I noticed a diamond tennis bracelet on her wrist. It was tasteful and worth more than Uncle Ethan's van. When she grimaced, I saw that her teeth were as white as pearls.

"Whatever," I said. I felt sour. I didn't want to terrify some woman. I didn't like the way she was looking at me. "Whoever you are, stop following me around. I don't like it."

I opened the door and slid out of the vehicle.

"Wait!" she called. I waited for her, both of my feet on the concrete and my hand on the door, ready to slam it shut.

"I'm sorry. I really do want to talk to you. I think you can help me. Would you meet me at this address in an hour?"

She held out a business card. I didn't take it. There was no point in getting distracted in my search for Charles Hammer.

Unless she was willing to help me.

"Please?"

I shrugged and took the card. She thanked me and apologized again. I shut the door. She pulled away.

I looked at the card. It read *Cynthia Hammer*. Below that was an address on Hammer Street. That was the right last name. I turned and walked back to the parking lot.

The fright I had given Cynthia Hammer had taken all the fun out of being a bastard. I returned to Uncle Ethan's van and tossed the keys on the floor by the brake pedal. I was tempted to wipe it down for fingerprints, but I noticed drops of blood on the driver's-side door and decided not to bother. Uncle Ethan, Georgie, and their two buddies should be turning up soon to have their hands worked on. They might as well find their ride waiting for them, even if they couldn't drive it home.

I walked around to the front of the hospital into the reception area. The very polite matron working there told me that visiting hours had just started. It was one in the afternoon. When I admitted that I was a friend of Harlan's, not a family member, she told me I would need permission from the family to visit.

She called a volunteer over and spoke to her in low tones. The volunteer then said, "Follow me, sir," in a shy voice. She led me to the elevator.

The inside of the elevator was stainless steel polished

as bright as a mirror. I saw my dirty, rumpled pants and bloody, torn shirt. I didn't like the way I looked.

The elevator doors opened, and the volunteer led me down a quiet hall to a little waiting area. Shireen sat alone, reading a tattered copy of *Redbook*. She was wearing a WSU Cougar sweatshirt.

The volunteer spoke to her in a voice barely louder than a whisper. "This gentleman would like to visit Harlan. Would that be all right?"

"Yes," Shireen said. She turned to me. "Maybe he'll talk to you. I'm his only family in the entire world, and he treats me like an enemy."

The volunteer had already started back toward the elevator. Shireen returned to her magazine. "Which room?" I asked.

She tossed her magazine onto the vinyl couch with an irritated sigh. "This way," she said.

She opened the door and stepped into Harlan's room. I heard a rasping voice before I saw him. He said, "Out," in a raw, strained voice.

"Someone is here to visit you," Shireen said. "Try to show him more courtesy than you've shown me."

Harlan lay in the bed. He had tubes in his nose, his arms, and his chest. He looked smaller, than I remembered him, but everyone looked smaller lying in a hospital bed. Everyone looked smaller without a gun, too.

Shireen pushed by me and shut the door behind her. I pulled up a chair and sat next to the bed.

Harlan looked pale and exhausted. He might have been getting good care, but no one was going to make him live if he didn't want to.

"Having a bad week?" I asked. Harlan made a wheezing sound that might have been laughter. He winced in pain. "Sorry, man," I said. "No more jokes. I promise."

He settled down. I went to the foot of his bed. There

was a chart hanging there, just like they show on TV, but I couldn't make heads or tails of it.

"How you doing?" Harlan rasped.

"How am I doing with my . . ." I almost said *investigation,* but that's a cop's word. I didn't want to say it. "I'm further along," I said, "but this town is a mess. And it's scary. But I've got nothing to lose."

And that was true. Harlan and I were both pretty close to death. Despite his injuries, I figured it was even money to see which of us would live longer.

"How long ago did this start?" I asked. "The kids, I mean."

Harlan held up his hand in a peace sign. Two.

"Two months?" I asked. He frowned. "Two years?!" He relaxed. I'd gotten it right.

Two years. Christ.

"Did something else happen around then? Something that seemed strange or . . ." Harlan's eyes grew dim. He was exhausted, and I had pushed him far enough. "Relax, dude," I said. "And hold on. I'm going to need to ask you more questions when you're better. I need your help, okay?"

He nodded faintly. I didn't really think he could help me much more, but I wanted to give him a reason to hold on. I stood and left him lying there, alone. I heard him struggling to breathe.

Shireen had company with her in the waiting room. Standing beside her was a short, fat man in a stained polo shirt and brown shorts that reached just below his hairy knees. He held a tape recorder in his hand. I disliked him on sight.

"Come on, Shireen," he said, his voice an annoying whine. "I'm going to find out . . ." Shireen's face was set in a scowl. She was not about to answer anyone's questions.

He glanced over at me, and his face lit up. He turned to me. "Hey! I've been trying to catch up with you for two days. I'm Peter Lemly with *The Mallet*. What's your connection with Harlan Semple? Is it true that you've come to town to outsource some of the Hammer Bay manufacturing jobs?"

I stared at him. He stared back, holding the tape recorder out. I leaned toward the microphone and said, very clearly, "You're just about as wide as you are tall, aren't you?"

He yanked back the recorder, but he didn't turn it off. He looked flustered and aggravated. "I know who you are," he said, trying to make it sound like a threat.

"So does she." I jerked my thumb at Shireen. "Now why don't you go away so I can express my sympathies in private."

"Are you a friend of the family, then?"

"Nope. Never met any of them before two days ago."

"What about the jobs at the toy factory?" he asked.

"I don't know what you're talking about." The rumor would work for us while it was a rumor. As soon as it appeared somewhere official, Able Katz could refute it and it would lose some of its power.

"Actually, I think you do. I'm the only media this town has, and I'm not going to be pushed around. I'm going to get some answers myself." He turned to Shireen. "Do you hear what I'm saying? I'm going to find out."

"I'm not going to talk to you, Peter." She wouldn't look at him. "I'm never going to talk to you. Now, excuse me, I think my visit is over."

She turned to leave. Peter started to follow her, but I stepped in his path.

"The lady wants to leave," I said. "Leave her be."

"So macho," he sneered. "So chivalrous. You have no idea who you're protecting."

"What story are you following?" If he had said *missing*

children, I would have swallowed my bile and bought him a drink. With my last six bucks.

"Town corruption," he said.

"You're after . . ." I let the sentence trail off. Lemly was eager to finish it for me.

"The Dubois brothers. And the mayor, too, if he's involved. And the town council. The whole town knows what's going on, but no one will stand up to Emmett Dubois. Except me."

"Good luck with that." Shireen had already entered the elevator at the end of the hall. The doors closed over her unhappy face. I turned away from my companion.

"Wait!" He grabbed my elbow. "What are you doing in town? What have you come here to do?"

"Good luck with your story," I said. "I hope you don't get anyone killed."

I turned my back on him and walked toward the elevator. He followed me, peppering me with questions. He wasn't very good at it.

The elevator opened again. I stepped inside and shoved Peter away from me. He didn't fall, but he did keep his distance while the doors closed.

I rode down the elevator, thinking about my own behavior in the last hour. I'd driven around in a stolen van, jumped into an SUV and menaced a woman, and shoved a guy in a hospital hallway.

I'd never been this reckless and aggressive, even back when I was part of Arne's crew. I knew the cause of it, of course. I was a dead man. I had agreed to be cannon fodder for Annalise's war. Despite her recent gestures of friendship, she had promised to see me dead, and it felt very, very close.

I laid my head against the cool stainless steel wall of the elevator. The best I could hope for was that I would be there when Annalise took down Charlie Three. I wanted to see her put an end to that bastard and avenge those children.

I didn't know when and how she would make her next move. Could she take out Charlie Three alone, injured as she was? What if she failed?

That pleasant thought was interrupted by the elevator doors opening. I walked into the lobby and asked the woman at the reception desk for directions to Hammer Street.

I got them. Of course Hammer Street wasn't on my tourist map, but it was near the toy factory, on the inland side of the plant, about as far south as the lighthouse.

I left Ethan's van where it was. Then I headed out onto the sidewalk, oriented myself, and started walking.

What I should have done was call Annalise. My destination was an address on Hammer Street—it could very well have been Charles's home. If I found him there, it would be best if she was with me. But she hadn't given me her cell phone number and I didn't want the motel manager to share my message with Emmett Dubois.

If Charles Hammer the Third really was at this address, was I going to kill him? Could I do it? It made me a little sick inside to think it, but I suspected the answer was yes.

Considering.

An even bigger question was whether Hammer would stay dead. That I didn't want to think about too much. I would take my shot at him, if I got one. If it didn't turn out well . . .

I *really* didn't want to think about that.

Of course, I wasn't exactly conducting myself like a sensible hitman. I'd just asked a hospital receptionist for directions to the victim's street, for God's sake.

Maybe I wouldn't have to kill Charles Hammer. Maybe I could find a better way.

I heard the sound of children screaming.

There was a long stretch of green grass on the corner ahead of me. Before I realized what I was doing, I was running toward it, ghost knife in hand.

Kids scattered in every direction, running off a junior-sized basketball court. On the asphalt, I could see a four-foot-high plume of fire with a little figure inside.

I ran into the street and sprinted toward the park. A hugely fat woman rushed toward the child, screaming. Then the flames sputtered out and the figure inside fell to pieces onto the asphalt.

I felt the twinge against my iron gate.

The fat woman stopped running. The few remaining children that hadn't disappeared also stopped. Parents began to call their kids back to the playground.

I reached the court. The fat woman turned and started walking back to the bench where the other parents were sitting. I was alone at the foul line.

As I'd seen with Justin Benton, this child had broken down into a mass of fat, silvery worms. They crawled across the asphalt court, shiny and revolting. Where they touched the ground, they left a trail of black soot.

I had no rational reason for what I did next. All I knew was that I had to destroy as many of those creatures as I could.

I swung the ghost knife at the trailing worms. Ordinarily, the mark would not hurt living things, but I suspected these were predators—creatures from the Empty Spaces, partly physical and partly magical. And the ghost knife cuts magic.

My spell slashed through the hindmost worm. There was a second's delay, then the worm split open and burst into flame.

I watched as the tiny creature was consumed by fire. Good. They could be destroyed.

I swung my ghost knife at another. Just before I made contact, a tiny cut appeared on its back and a tongue of flame erupted from it. I changed the direction of my attack just in time to avoid the fire, and my altered swing touched the worm in just the right spot to create the tiny cut I'd already seen.

I drew back from the fire. Damn. That time the wound had appeared before the ghost knife had connected. That meant something, I knew, but with my blood pounding in my ears, I couldn't work it out.

Both worms were still burning. I moved toward the side of the wriggling mass, striking at the tiny creatures at the edges. They flared and burned as I nicked them, but the flames never grew strong enough to combust the others. Maybe this spirit fire, as Annalise called it, didn't burn that way. It didn't matter. I crouched beside the mass, striking here and there, moving along its bulk away from the flames.

When the entire side was ablaze, I moved across the front, careful to avoid the tiny creatures as they crept forward. I imagined one of them leaping at me, burning me the way Annalise had been burned, but I kept up my attack.

Within seconds, the entire front of the mass was blazing. I began to work my way down the other side. The worms I had cut burned in the black streak behind the rest, and the creatures at the front crawled through the pyre of the others without apparent harm.

I crouched low and kept close, inflicting tiny nicks on the worms, watching for times when the little creatures flared up from my attacks before the attacks had actually landed.

We had gone ten feet. Then fifteen. Then twenty. Eventually, I stopped circling the mass. The spirit fire burned so fiercely at the edges and tail end that I couldn't get a clear shot there. I hopped to the front of the mass, dropping to my hands and knees directly in its path.

I struck at the worms as they tumbled through the wall

of flames at the front. I backed away. I was destroying the creatures, but the mass was still advancing. I couldn't stop it.

My feet touched grass. There were many fewer worms than there had been, maybe only 10 percent of the original mass, but I wasn't going to get them all. I cursed at them, swore at them as I killed them. Eventually, I had backed all the way onto the grass, and the first of the worms tumbled off the asphalt. Fewer than a dozen hit the soil and started tunneling, but that was still too many.

I jumped to my feet and rushed back onto the court. The worms had vanished beneath the earth, and I didn't like the idea that they might tunnel up from beneath me.

I looked at my ghost knife. There was no residue on it, no blood, no black soot, nothing. It was as clean as the day I'd made it. I slipped it into my pocket.

A long skipping rope lay on the basketball court with a discarded baseball cap beside it. The cap was lavender. It had been a little girl this time.

I looked at the streak. The northern edge of the court was not ten feet from the spot where the fire had started, but the worms had turned toward the southwest. They'd gone a long way, exposed to danger, to head in that direction.

I turned and looked along the path of the black streak. It pointed in the general direction of the Hammer Bay Toys plant. It headed toward Charles Hammer the Third.

At that moment, killing Charles Hammer seemed like the most important and most natural thing in the world.

CHAPTER NINE

I walked the rest of the way to Hammer Street in a daze. I kept trying to picture the face of the little girl that had just burned away, but all I saw was a rotating series of faces, all absurdly angelic. At that moment, I would have knifed Charles Hammer in a police station, in front of forty cops and a dozen TV-news cameras.

This was my mind-set when I finally reached Hammer Street. It was a single block long, curving westward with no sidewalks. I walked up the middle of the street. There were stone walls on either side of me, and thick black-berry vines growing over the top. The road sloped up-ward, and as I reached a cul-de-sac, I saw three houses.

The smallest sat on the north lot. It was made of brick and had pretty white balconies. The second house, on the southern lot, was made of mortared stone. It was low and wide, and was probably very modern forty years ago. Both were shuttered and dark.

The largest house occupied the western lot. It was made of wood and stood three stories tall. It had a nest of slanting roofs, mismatched balconies, and clusters of stone chimneys. On the southern side of the house, a tall, round tower loomed above the rest. It was the oldest of the houses, and it dominated the street. I turned around and saw the town of Hammer Bay laid out before me. Maybe the house was meant to dominate the town, too.

I checked Cynthia's card. Of course her address matched the large house.

I wondered if Annalise would be grateful if I killed Charlie Three myself, right now. I wondered if her hands would heal.

There were three cars parked in front. One was the silver Escalade. Beside it was a fifteen-year-old BMW, a good car and pricey when it was new, but it had suffered rust and salt corrosion and the damage had been allowed to spread. The third car was a blue Tercel. It was such an ordinary, unassuming car, it was nearly invisible beside the others.

The street was empty. There were lights upstairs at the large house, but everything seemed still. I assumed all three houses belonged to the Hammers, although I wasn't sure what gave me that impression. Maybe it was the way the street had been laid out for maximum privacy. Maybe it was that I didn't think anyone would share an address on Hammer Street in Hammer Bay with the Hammer family.

An instinct for caution made me approach the brick house first. I circled it, looking for an unblocked window. There wasn't one. The stone house, though, had a broken shutter on a back window. I peered in.

Nothing. No furnishings, no art on the walls, nothing. It was an empty shell. I went to the big house and rang the bell.

To my surprise, Cynthia answered. She looked aggravated, and several strands of her dark hair stuck out in random directions. "You're late," she said. Her tone wasn't friendly.

"Where's your brother?" I asked. The anger in my voice surprised me.

She ignored the question. "I'm afraid I'm a little busy right now. I'll have to ask you to wait in the library."

"Where's your brother?" I asked again. "Where's Charles?"

"I don't like the way you're asking that question."

I imagined myself throttling the answer out of her.

No. I turned away and stared back over the town. The cold, furious sense of purpose that had driven me across town began to fade. I was not going to start killing everyone between me and my target. Annalise would have, but I was not going that far.

"I'll wait in the library, then," I said to her.

She stepped backward to let me enter. "I don't like that you're late. I expect people to be punctual. I'm not a person who likes to wait for others." She sounded flustered and annoyed, and I wasn't sure if she was trying to put me in my place because I'd scared her in the car, or if something else was getting on her nerves and she was taking it out on me. Either way, I didn't care.

She led me into the library and shut the door. I looked out the window. I saw a wide green lawn with a winding white stone path laid across it. The sight was soothing.

I held up my hand. It was trembling. I wondered how I could find out the name of the little girl I had just seen killed. No one would remember her. No one would go looking for her. There would be nothing in the news. I could look for that fat lady, I guessed, under the assumption that it was her daughter, but what good would that do? She wouldn't remember her any better than anyone else. I could break into their house and search the place for a photo . . .

I laid my hands on the window frame and pressed my face against the glass. I was not going to break into that woman's house. That little girl was never going to be more to me than a small bonfire, seen at a distance. I didn't need her name.

There was a small door to my right. I ran to it and yanked it open. It was a bathroom, thank God. I would have hated to vomit into one of Cynthia's closets.

I washed my face and rinsed out my mouth. My emotions were back under control, and I felt better. I felt like myself again. I didn't want to be some angry hard-ass who bullied his way toward his enemies. I didn't want to be Annalise.

That gave me pause. How many dead bodies had Annalise seen? How many dead children, killed by some jackass with a spell book? No wonder she acted the way she did.

I heard a man and a woman start shouting at each other, and I headed toward the door. On the way, a small picture in a silver frame caught my attention. It was a black-and-white photo, taken a long time ago.

On the left side of the picture was a man in a dark waistcoat. His face bristled with white whiskers, and he had the satisfied look of a man who fed himself well. In the center was a tall, angular man in a long, road-worn coat with a walking stick in his hand. His hair was a little too long and needed combing, and he smiled out of the side of his mouth. He looked like a smooth talker and a bit of a con man, the sort of friend you keep for a lifetime but never, ever trust. Both wore hats and old-fashioned clothes. I guessed the picture was taken in the thirties.

On the right was a young girl in a pretty white dress. Her hair was bobbed, and her little shoes pointed slightly inward. I could see, at the lacy cuffs and collar of her dress, a faint spider's web of black lines. Tattoos. She had turned her solemn little face to look up at the con man, and I could see by her profile that she was Annalise.

I stared at the picture, dumbstruck. She looked eight or nine years younger than she looked now, but I was sure the picture was taken at least seventy years ago. Who was the man she was looking at? A second glance at him showed tattoos covering the back of his hand. I squinted at Annalise's face. She looked love-struck and slightly awed. Was this her teacher?

The shouting started again. I set the picture down,

opened the door, and went out into the hall. There were doors all around and voices were coming from behind one of them. I walked toward the sound.

"Now, Cabot," a man said. "There's no reason to be so upset. Cynthia didn't—"

"Don't tell me what she did!" a man shouted. I guessed it was Cabot. "I know what she did! I have eyes!"

"Well, here's a good idea for you," Cynthia snapped. "Use them."

"Things are going to come around again," Cabot said. "Things are going to be made right. You watch, and you *watch out*!"

I had almost reached the heavy oak door when it flew open. A man in his mid-fifties with a heavy paunch and a blotchy face stormed past me. His thick, dark hair was speckled with gray.

There was something in his expression that I didn't like. He looked like a man who didn't care anymore.

I watched him stomp off. His clothes had been expensive once, but the heels of his boots were worn away and his jeans were frayed at the bottom.

"I thought I told you to wait in the library." Cynthia had moved up next to me. She looked irritated. "Well?"

I heard the front door slam.

"I'm nosy."

She glared at me. After a moment, she said: "Come into my office. Please."

I followed her into a small room. The floors were hardwood, and a large desk dominated the far corner. The only adornments on the walls were a pair of kimonos set in wooden frames.

A fat little man sat on the couch, rubbing his face wearily. His long, graying hair hung over his shoulders. "That man exhausts me—"

"Frank," Cynthia cut in, "this is Raymond Lilly. Mr. Lilly, this is our mayor, Frank Farleton."

Frank lifted his face from his hands and looked up at me in surprise. He didn't look pleased to see me. "I know who you are. What are you doing here?"

I turned to Cynthia. "Call me Ray. I've seen the mayor before but didn't introduce myself. He was too upset about your brother's seizure. Isn't that right, Mayor Farleton?"

"What are you doing here, please?" he asked again. At least he was polite.

"She invited me. How long has Charles been having seizures?"

The mayor struggled off the couch. He had to huff vigorously to lift his bulk onto his feet. "What do you mean? Who invited you?"

I heard the front door slam again. No one else seemed to notice it. The office door was behind me to my left, the desk in front of me to the right. I backed against the wall and slid my hand into my pocket next to my ghost knife.

Cynthia strode behind her desk and offered me a strained smile. The mayor sat on the corner of her desk. "I don't think Frank means who invited you to my house. I think he means who invited you to Hammer Bay." Her pretty smile betrayed a touch of scorn. Her hands were shaking. She was having a bad day. "But," she continued, "you're here to answer my questions, not his. And if you don't feel like answering, all I have to do is call Emmett Dubois. Once I tell him you broke into my car and tried to take the keys—"

The office door burst inward and Cabot charged in. I was ready for him, but I was still too slow. He lifted his arm. He was holding a pistol.

Time seemed to slow down. Cabot aimed at Cynthia. His teeth were bared, his cheeks flushed red.

The mayor stepped in front of her, his arms spread wide, his fat cheeks puffed out in an almost comical way.

I swung the ghost knife at the gun. Cabot squeezed the trigger. The hammer drew back. I was too slow. The gun fired. A bare second later, the ghost knife swept through it, slicing it apart.

The mayor flinched as the bullet struck him just above the collarbone.

Cabot squeezed the trigger again, but the gun was already coming apart. It didn't fire. He turned toward me, his mouth opening in what I imagined would be angry protest. He looked at the remains of the gun in his hand in utter shock.

I slid the edge of the ghost knife into his chest and, before he had a chance to go slack, threw an overhand left. I was off-balance, but the punch landed just in front of his earlobe. Cabot dropped like a marionette with his strings cut.

I turned toward the others. The mayor was holding the top of his right shoulder with his bloody left hand. He stumbled away from Cynthia and looked at her. Then he collapsed onto the floor. The bullet appeared to have only grazed him, but he was bleeding profusely. His face looked pale.

Cynthia looked at me. Her mouth hung open in a little O, and her face was slack and pale.

I don't like guns. I stared down at the mayor for a moment too long, wishing the whole thing hadn't happened.

His face grew more pale by the second. Cynthia gaped at him.

"Call an ambulance," I said. Cynthia turned her empty gaze toward me. She seemed to be in a trance. "Right now!" I shouted.

She jumped and lunged for the phone on her desk. She wasn't used to being yelled at.

I grabbed an arm cover off the couch and knelt beside the mayor. I confirmed that the bullet had grazed him just above his collarbone, well away from the arteries in his neck. If he'd been less fat, it might have missed him altogether.

I wadded up the arm cover and pressed it against the wound. "Well, well," I said, trying to keep my tone light, "look what you've managed to do. This doesn't look too bad, though."

"It hurts," he said.

"Being a hero usually does."

"What? I'm not a hero. I wasn't thinking. I just—"

His face was getting paler. I grabbed a cushion off the couch and slid it under his feet. "Of course you didn't think," I said. "Who would jump in the path of a bullet if they were thinking?"

Cynthia spoke into the phone, asking for an ambulance. She spoke so quickly she was on the verge of babbling. I called her name to catch her attention, then told her to speak as calmly as she could. She took a deep, shuddering breath and recited her address into the phone. She told the operator on the other end that the mayor had been shot.

"I don't want to die," the mayor said. His voice was small and childlike. He squeezed his eyes shut, and I saw tears running down his face. "My wife . . ."

"I'm no doctor," I told him, "but I think you're going to be okay. Harlan was shot much worse than you, and he's recovering. Just try to take deep breaths and stay calm. The ambulance is on the way." The color came back into his face just a little.

Cynthia hung up the phone and stared down at the scene in utter befuddlement. "What happened to Uncle Cabot's gun?"

"Come over here and make yourself useful," I said. She circled around her desk and knelt beside the mayor. "Put your hands on this cloth and keep a steady pressure on the wound."

She looked at my bloody hands and balked.

"This man just took a bullet for you," I said. My voice was low and edged with anger. "Now do it."

She did.

The mayor looked up at her. "I'm sorry," he said. "I'm so embarrassed—"

Cynthia burst into tears.

I watched her for a moment, to make sure that she kept her hands on the wound. She did. The mayor began to comfort her, and his color definitely improved. It helped him to have someone to comfort.

Cabot lay in the doorway. I wiped my bloody hands on the front of his shirt, then began to pat him down. He didn't have another gun. He moaned and began to come around.

My ghost knife was in my pocket, although I didn't remember putting it away. I slid it through his hand. It wouldn't keep him unconscious, but it would make him docile.

I heard sirens. "You two sit tight," I said. "I'm going to open the front door." Cynthia and the mayor kept murmuring to each other. They didn't seem to hear me.

I dragged Cabot into the hall. Docile or not, I didn't want him waking up in the same room as them. Then I walked over and opened the front door.

The EMTs were already jogging up the steps, a stretcher in their hands. Behind them was Emmett Dubois, his hand on his holstered weapon. Emmett squinted the length of the hall and saw Cabot lying at the far end, his shirt smeared with blood. Cabot shifted his leg, barely on the edge of consciousness.

"He's right this way," I said to them, pointing to the open office door. They rushed past me.

When I turned around, I saw Emmett Dubois pointing his gun at me. "Turn around, put your hands behind your head, and drop to your knees."

"I'm getting sick of having guns pointed at me."

"Ain't that too bad." He pushed me onto my stomach and began twisting my arms behind me. Cynthia stepped out of the office and saw us.

"What are you doing?" she said. "He didn't hurt anyone. He *saved* us."

She told him what happened. Emmett uncuffed me and helped me to my feet. He offered a brief but insincere cop apology and made a beeline for Cabot. Cabot had come around enough to rub the side of his jaw. Emmett rolled him on his stomach and cuffed him. Cabot didn't resist.

Cynthia stepped close to me. Her hands were shaking. "I have to go to the hospital. Will you drive me? I don't think I can manage it right now."

"Sure," I told her.

The EMTs emerged with the mayor on a stretcher. They didn't seem to be in a hurry. Emmett dragged Cabot to his feet and led him toward the door.

"I'm sorry," Cabot said. "I'm sorry, everyone. I shouldn't have done that."

He went on and on like that. Hearing his meek, whining voice seemed to set Cynthia on edge, so I held her back to let the others get ahead. We stood on the front porch and watched them load the mayor into the back of the ambulance, and Cabot into the back of Emmett's police car. They started their engines but didn't turn on their sirens.

After they had disappeared around the corner, Cynthia turned toward me. "Do I look terrible?" she asked.

Her eyes were red and puffy from crying and her lip twisted down on one side as she fought back her tears. Her makeup was still perfect. "You can check yourself on the way. Do you have everything you need?"

"No, I'll be right back."

She rushed back into the house. I took the scrap of wood out of my pocket and laid it against the doorjamb.

Nothing. The design churned at its normal slow pace. The Hammer house was no different from any other. I looked at the other two on the cul-de-sac. If I were Charles Hammer the Third, heir to a timber fortune and owner of a wildly successful toy company, which would I live in? A tiny brick house or an empty stone one?

Neither, really. I started toward the brick house for no other reason than that it was slightly closer. I had only gotten a couple of steps when the door opened behind me.

"I'm ready. Let's go," Cynthia said.

She gave me the keys and I drove. She flipped down the passenger-side visor and studied her face. I tried not to pay too close attention as I wound my way through traffic, but I could see her hands trembling slightly.

"Are you all right?" I asked her.

"Yes. I think I'm going to be fine. What about you? Are you all right?"

The question surprised me. For a second I thought she'd known about me in the library toilet. *Hanging on,* I wanted to say. Then I realized she was talking about Cabot and the gun. "I'm fine. Maybe I'll freak out later, but I'm fine right now."

"You're not really going to freak out, are you?" she said. "You're just saying that to be nice." I shrugged, and she laid her hand on my arm. Just for a moment.

It was my turn to shiver. Damn, it had been a long time.

We reached the hospital. I was glad to see that Ethan's van was gone.

The receptionist told us that the mayor was in intensive care. Cynthia seemed to shrug this off, but I was confused. "I didn't think his wound was that serious," I said. "It looked like it just grazed him."

"Well . . ." The receptionist looked around and then began shuffling papers on her desk. She looked up at

Cynthia as though she was one of her supervisors. Maybe that's what it meant to be part of a founding family—everyone treats you like you're in charge. "I shouldn't have told you that much. HIPAA rules."

Cynthia leaned forward and said, "Look—"

"Is there someplace we can wait?" I interrupted. The receptionist called a volunteer, who led us to a waiting room on the third floor. We sat on a plastic couch beside a stack of bland supermarket magazines.

"His wife hates me," Cynthia said. "She hates me already. I just hope she doesn't take another swing at me. I wouldn't be surprised if she brought a hatchet. Good thing we're already in a hospital."

She went on and on like that. Cynthia rambled, mostly about how much Farleton's wife hated her. She didn't mention Cabot at all, and I didn't bring him up. Misery was pouring out of her, and I didn't want her to shut me out. Not when I needed her to point me toward her brother.

The door at the end of the hall opened, and Emmett Dubois entered. Trailing along behind him was a tall blond woman, probably just a year or two older than Cynthia. She was long-legged and wore way too much makeup on her lovely face. She looked utterly distraught.

Cynthia jumped up. "Miriam, I'm so sorry."

"I don't want to hear it," Miriam snapped. "I just want to see my husband."

Emmett stepped between them. "Let's find Frank's doctor. Would you come with me?"

Miriam shot a withering look at Cynthia, then followed the chief down the hall.

Peter Lemly rushed in. He was red-faced and sweating, and I could hear him panting from down the hall. He followed the chief and Miriam Farleton.

"Did you see that?" Cynthia said. "She hates me." I didn't say anything. "She's always hated me. Ever since high school. She was three years ahead and she dated Charles for a couple of weeks. He wouldn't turn his life over to Jesus, though, and he got tired of hearing her talk about it. He broke it off with her, and for some reason she blamed me. She thought I was making fun of her behind her back."

"Were you?" I asked, although I was pretty sure I knew the answer already.

"Hell, yeah. But Charles didn't care what I said. He never cared. He always had to do things his own way."

"Your brother sounds like an interesting guy."

She didn't take the bait. "I saw the way you were looking at her," she said.

I shrugged. "She and the mayor don't exactly look like a couple, do they?"

She laughed. "The whole town, men and women, felt the same way when they started going together. Frank was ten years older and even fatter than he is now—she's worked on his weight over the years. He's a good man, even if he's kind of a wimp." I didn't mention that a real wimp wouldn't have taken a bullet for her. "I think he'd be scooping ice cream in the back of a truck if he hadn't married her. She's the ambitious one. But they sure do seem to love each other," she said. "No one really understands it."

"Maybe he cast a spell on her."

She turned and looked at me. She was measuring me, trying to see if I had dropped the word *spell* casually or if I was hinting at something. The way she looked at me told me what I needed to know. I wondered what would happen if I laid Annalise's magic-detecting scrap of wood against her skin.

I shrugged. I wasn't ready to show my hand yet. She blinked and then shrugged, too. I wondered how much she knew about what was happening to the kids in town.

"Where's your brother?" I asked her. "I'd like to meet him."

She leaned back in her chair and looked at me sideways. "I'm supposed to be asking you questions, remember?" She had a half smile on her lovely face. It looked good on her, but it was too practiced. "I asked you to come to my house so I could shine a bright light in your face and pepper you with questions."

"Okay, but let's leave out the badge-wearing goons."

"I think we can go goonless for now."

We smiled at each other.

She asked me a couple of questions about Annalise's meeting with Able Katz. I answered with harmless lies. The questions she asked told me more about her than she realized. I figured she must not have friends in the company or any pull with her brother or she would already know the basics.

Emmett Dubois arrived. He told us that he would need statements from both of us. Strictly routine, he assured us. Cabot had already confessed.

This time, I wanted to put him off until I could talk to a lawyer. Maybe Annalise would hire one for me, but Cynthia turned to me and said: "Why don't you go first? I want to wait and explain things to . . . you know. Be nice to him, Emmett. He saved my life. Frank's, too."

"Of course I will, Cynthia," Emmett said.

We left the waiting area and walked into an empty room. Emmett set his folder and his hat on the bed, then took a tape recorder from his pocket.

"Do you mind if I tape this?"

"I guess that'll be all right."

He turned on the machine and recited his name, my name, the date, and other information. Then he asked me what happened.

I told him, with a couple of modifications. I didn't tell

him about the fire on the basketball court. I didn't tell him that I had gone there looking for Charles with the intent to kill him. I didn't tell him that I chunked into the toilet, and I didn't tell him that I'd cut the gun with the ghost knife.

I did say that the gun fell apart after it fired that first time. I said I felt lucky that I hadn't been killed, and that I personally didn't think I'd saved anyone's life. Cabot's gun was defective, and I coldcocked him. Even if I hadn't been there, I said, he couldn't have done more than he did.

We went over it again, this time focusing on why I was there, why Cynthia had invited me, and why I had gone. I had sensible answers for everything, and he didn't seem concerned.

It was the friendliest conversation I'd ever had with a cop. It made me a little nervous, but I did my best to smile and act friendly in return.

Finally, he shut the recorder off. "That jibes with what Cabot told me, although he claims that you broke the gun with your bare hands."

"Heh! Really? Weird. Someone should tell him guns are made of metal."

Emmett chuckled. "That's what I figured. We did take the gun into evidence, though. It was in a strange condition."

"How so?"

"It didn't explode, the way guns do when the barrel is jammed. It was sheared apart. Like it was cut."

"Is that unusual?" I asked, being careful to look him in the eyes—but not too closely—and not to touch my face.

"I've never seen a weapon fail that way. Never heard of it, either."

"Weird. And lucky."

He looked at me for a moment, then smiled. He was a

friendly guy today. "It sure was lucky." He began to gather his stuff. Then he stopped and looked at me again. He knew something he wasn't saying.

There was something else going on here. There was something I wasn't seeing.

And honestly, I didn't like being on such friendly terms with Emmett Dubois.

"Excuse me, Chief," I said. "Can I ask your opinion on something?"

"Okay. What is it?"

I opened my jacket wide, so that when I reached into it he would see there was no gun. I drew out the scrap of wood.

"This is a little something that I'm trying to sell to Hammer Bay Toys. I think it's a neat little trick."

I set the scrap of wood on the bed beside his folder. The design on the front continued its slow, implacable churning.

"Well, I'll be damned," he said. He looked down at the moving paint, obviously intrigued. Then he looked up at me. "May I?"

"By all means," I said.

Emmett picked up the scrap of wood. As soon as he touched it, the design went dark. A tiny flare appeared on the wood, and then a jet of black steam and iron-colored sparks erupted from the design.

The chief had a predator inside him.

Emmett dropped it and jumped back. He laid his hand on his weapon. "What the hell was that?"

"This," I said, "is a Geiger counter for magic." I picked it up. My tattoos and ghost knife made the design flare silver for a second. "You have some kind of nasty spell on you, Chief. What is it?"

He stared at me, his eyes wide. I stared back. Was he involved in the deaths of those children? Did he even know about them?

"Come on, Chief. Tell me what's going on here. What's happened to you? What's happened to your town?"

"Who are you? What are you doing in this town?"

"You already know who I am. You read all about what I did last fall. As for what I'm doing here, there's something wrong in this town. I'm here to fix it. Party's over, Chief. *We* know about you now."

He sniffled. I had spooked him. He wasn't used to that. "Maybe I should take you in—"

I laughed. "You don't have any idea *what I am,* do you? I'm not going anywhere with you this time. You're going to have to tread carefully."

It was a bluff, but I wasn't going to put myself at his mercy. He was infected and had to be destroyed. Once Annalise found out, she'd pinch his fat head off.

But was Emmett an underling? The secret source of Charlie Three's seizures? Or was he another victim?

Emmett glared at me and backed toward the door, his hand on his weapon. I just smiled at him. He left.

I sat for a moment, thinking about Cynthia, the mayor, and Cabot. Was Cynthia in on it with her brother and Emmett? Was Farleton in on it, too? Maybe Cabot was trying to put a stop to the deaths. It was something to think about.

I walked back to the waiting room. Cynthia was still sitting on the plastic couch. I was startled to see Annalise on the other side of the room, incongruous in her oversized fireman's jacket, steel-toed boots, and tattered pants. For one absurd moment, I thought she'd come to be treated for her burned hands.

Cynthia stood when she saw me. "Was he decent to you?"

"He was fine."

She rubbed her hands on her pants, looking uncomfortable. She wanted me to keep her company, but Annalise was already moving toward me. Cynthia sat again. Annalise took my elbow and led me down the hall out of earshot.

"What have you been doing?" she asked.

"Making enemies. Friends, too. The chief of—"

"That girl said you saved her life," Annalise interrupted. "Is that true? Who is she?"

It seemed funny that Annalise was calling Cynthia a girl. Cynthia looked to be six or eight years older, but looks can be deceiving. "Sure, it's true. And she's Cynthia Hammer, sister to Charles Hammer the Third. She's the one who was following us in the SUV."

Annalise glanced back at Cynthia, making sure she was still on the couch. "I want you to fuck her," she said. "Then find out everything you can, especially where her brother is. I can't track him down."

"You're a real class act, boss."

"Just do it. I have work to do in the morgue."

She turned on her heel and stalked away. I wondered again how many dead bodies she had seen, and how long it had taken her to become what she was.

And she hadn't even given me a chance to tell her about the predator in Emmett.

I ran into the hall, calling her name. She stopped and turned toward me. A passing nurse shushed me forcefully.

"What is it?" Annalise asked.

"Predator," I said, my voice low. She tensed and leaned toward me. I had her attention. "Inside Emmett Dubois. I don't know what it is, but I'd guess his brothers are infected, too."

"How do you know this?"

I removed the scrap of wood from the inside of my jacket. She frowned and took it from me.

"Did he see this?" she asked, holding up the slowly moving design.

"Yep."

Annalise nodded and pocketed the scrap of wood. "You have your next assignment," she said, and walked toward the elevators.

I went back to Cynthia. She was, apparently, my next assignment. Spending the night with her wasn't the worst thing that could happen, but I didn't like that Annalise had *ordered* me to do it. I didn't even like the idea that she would know. It was creepy. I sat a little farther away from Cynthia than I had before.

"Is that your wife?" Cynthia asked. "Your girlfriend?"

I was honestly confused for a moment. "Who?"

"That redhead. The one you were just talking to."

I laughed. "Sorry," I said. "But that's funny. She's actually my boss, and she hates my guts."

"Oh."

"It's complicated."

"Well," she said, "I'm glad she's not your girlfriend."

That was my cue to say something smooth. Before I could think of something, the door to Frank's room opened and Miriam stepped out.

"Are you Ray?" she asked me.

I stood. "I am. Is there something I can do?"

"He wants to talk to you." Her lips were pressed together in disapproval. She pointedly did not look at Cynthia.

I moved toward her and the door. "Is he well enough for that?"

"No, he isn't. The gunshot wound was minor, but he had a heart attack in the ambulance. The surgeon is on his way to the hospital now. But he insists on speaking to you."

"I'll be quick," I said, and went into the room. She shut the door behind me, remaining in the hall.

Frank lay in the hospital bed, tubes running out of his nose. Peter Lemly stood by the side of the bed, and another man stood beside him. He must have arrived during my interrogation, because I didn't recognize him. He was tall, straight, and serene, with graying hair carefully styled. He was the third of the four men who had met with Emmett Dubois beside the van when I saw Charles have a seizure. He turned toward me without meeting my gaze, and I saw that he was wearing a clerical collar.

It made sense for the reverend to be there. But I didn't understand why Lemly was in the room.

"We meet again," Frank said. His voice was hoarse and weak.

"Let's do it without the ambulance next time," I said. "Shouldn't you be resting?"

He gasped between breaths. "I wanted to thank you."

"Forget about it. Relax. You're going to undo all my hard work."

Miriam had entered the room just in time to catch that last word. She narrowed her eyes at me. No one else seemed to care. Ah, well, I'm the bane of respectable women everywhere.

"Anything I can do for you," the mayor said.

"When you're stronger, I want to talk about Hammer Bay."

"He needs his rest," Miriam said.

"Of course." I backed toward the door. I was trying to think of a way to compliment him, to tell him, in front of his wife and a reporter, that I thought he was a damn brave man, but he spoke before I could.

"Hammer Bay," he said. His voice was low and a little angry. "My town. So rotten and corrupt. It's time I did something about it."

Miriam glared at me. Peter Lemly lunged forward, his tape recorder in hand. "Would you repeat that, Uncle Frank?"

Miriam snatched up a clipboard and thumped Peter

on the top of his head. He wasn't deterred. The mayor began to say something else, but the reverend grabbed Peter's elbow and steered him out of the room after me. Within a couple of seconds, we were both out in the hall.

Cynthia was not sitting on the couch. She wasn't anywhere in the hall that I could see. Had she stepped out for a second, or had Miriam shooed her away while I was in Frank's room?

"Did you hear what the mayor just said?" Peter asked me. The door closed behind us. "Did you hear?"

"I heard that the mayor is your uncle," I said.

"Never mind that." He paced the hall. "The mayor is going to fight corruption in this town." He sounded excited, as though he was in a thirties gangster movie.

"Tell me about the town."

"It's pretty straightforward," he said. He was a guy who loved an audience. "The Hammers control the jobs. They're the first family around here, and they've always had a nose for the next thing. The next move to make. Until Cabot, that is.

"The Dubois brothers keep the peace, maybe a little too much. And lately they run a protection racket. I've been trying to get someone in town to go on the record about this, but no one will."

"Not since Stan, the bartender."

"How did you know about Stan Koch? He was supposed to bring me a bunch of records showing how much he'd been paying to Wiley Dubois over the years, but he was killed."

"Attacked by wild dogs."

"There really aren't a lot of dogs in town. Never have been. Someone gets a dog, it barks all night and all day, and within a couple of weeks it vanishes. That was a dull story to track down, let me tell you."

"The Hammers and the Dubois brothers. Is that it?"

"There's the reverend in there. Thomas Wilson. His

church is the largest in town. There is a small Catholic church behind the Bartells Pharmacy, and there are some folks who speak the language of the angels in living room services, but Wilson's is the biggest. He doesn't do much, though. He cares about souls, not works."

"Who else?"

"I guess Phyllis Henstrick. She runs the vice, and some of the jobs, too. When business is good, her boys build and fix. When it's bad they get a little something from the whorehouse. A whorehouse is pretty recession-proof. That's pretty much everyone."

"What about drugs? There are always drugs."

"Sure, there's a little weed to be had here and there. No one much cares about that. Everything else, the Dubois brothers have some trick where they hunt them down."

"They take them over?"

"Actually, no. Their mama had a little trouble with pills back in the day. Mama's little helper, if you know what I mean. She cracked up their car, killing herself and their little sister. They don't much like drugs. When someone goes into the woods with a trailer to start up a meth lab, they don't come back. They just disappear, and Emmett drops by to give their friends little warnings. You know what I mean?"

"Subtle things, under the guise of investigating the disappearance, right?"

"You *do* know what I mean. So, is Hammer Bay Toys moving its manufacturing overseas?"

"If I wanted to talk to Charles Hammer the Third after business hours, where would I find him?"

"Probably at his home."

"And where's that?"

"Oh, no. We're protective of our patrons around here, Mr. Lilly. You're going to have a hard time with those sorts of questions."

"What if I ask about his seizures?"

"The Hammer family, er, *condition* is a private affair, which means the whole town knows about it. Not that there's anything to tell. Now, is Hammer Bay Toys moving its manufacturing overseas?"

"No comment."

"Oh, come on! I just laid out the whole town for you, and you don't pay me back?

"I have something for you. How much do you know about the shooting at the Hammer place?"

"Cabot took a shot at his niece after they argued about the family business. He hit Frank instead. You coldcocked him and saved them both."

"Not quite true," I said. "The truth is, the mayor saw the gun and stepped in front of Cynthia, protecting her. He stepped in the path of the bullet without even thinking about his own safety. Sure, I slugged Cabot, but I was standing right next to him when he came in. I don't think he even realized I was there. And I didn't really save anyone; Cabot's gun came apart after one shot. Frank is the real hero."

"Is this true?"

"Ask Cynthia."

"Don't think I won't. What else?"

"First, don't put anything in the paper about the mayor and Emmett Dubois. Not yet. Give Frank a chance to recover and prepare for the fight."

"He's had three terms to prepare for a fight."

"If you publish too soon—"

"I hear you. Anything else?"

"Leave town. Go to Seattle and sign on with a big daily. Or a weekly. But go. This town is dead already."

"So it's true, then? The jobs are going to China?"

"I'm not kidding. It's time to leave Hammer Bay while you still can."

"*Pft.*" He waved me off. "I'm not giving up on my town."

The door to Frank's room opened and Rev. Wilson stepped out. He managed to look down at us without actually looking at us. "I wonder if it would be possible," he said, his tone stuffy and superior, "for you to converse elsewhere. These rooms are not soundproof, you know."

Peter wedged his bulk between the reverend and me. "Are you going to support the mayor in his fight against corruption?"

"The mayor is in a terribly weakened condition. He won't be fighting anything or anyone for quite a while. It would be irresponsible for you to claim otherwise." He turned to me, glancing at me briefly before turning his eyes to the side. "And why are you still here?"

That was a good question. I walked away while Peter tried to get a statement from the reverend about what he was already calling the mayor's "new initiative."

I walked to the elevator. Beside it was a hospital directory, which told me that the morgue was in the basement. I entered the elevator and pressed the button. Cynthia hadn't returned, so I decided to stick close to my boss.

Why was Annalise in the morgue? I hoped it had something to do with Karoly Lem. I didn't want to go down there and see the corpse of someone I knew.

The basement was practically a ghost town. I wandered through the halls, looking for a sign that would point the way. Eventually, I found one. I followed the arrows.

I expected gray paint on the walls and rows of metal tables with bodies lying on them. I was glad to be wrong. What I found was a small reception desk in a little waiting room. Annalise stood beside the desk, filling in a form on a clipboard with her sharp, jagged writing. Her face was pale and her thin lips were white. She had a sheen of sweat on her forehead. Opposite her was a morose-looking woman with nothing to do but watch.

"Someone will contact you about the body," Annalise said as she handed over the clipboard. The woman accepted it and slunk through the door behind the desk. She was gone.

Annalise hefted a blue canvas bag from the edge of the counter. She winced. Then she turned to me.

"What's in there?" I asked.

"Karoly's things. What are you doing here? I gave you a job to do."

"While I was looking for a club to hit her over the head with, she slipped away. I'll have to drag her back to my cave some other time."

She scowled at me. I saw something in her expression I hadn't seen before. She looked vulnerable.

"Hey," I said. "Are you okay?"

"I'm fine."

"Don't lie to me," I said, amazed that I was genuinely worried. "How bad are your hands?"

She walked around me toward the doors, stuck her hands into the handles, and sucked air through her teeth. She was hurting. Bad.

I pulled the doors open for her. She didn't like receiving my help, but she didn't have a choice.

We walked up the hall together, turned a few corners, and pushed through a couple of doors. I had no idea where we were going. I decided to change the subject. "Did you find out what Karoly's message was?"

"I have his laptop in here," she said. "I'll read through it when we get back to the room."

"They let you have his laptop?"

"They searched it and didn't find anything. Who picked you up in the van?"

"Saw that, did you? Thanks for getting me out of

trouble, boss. They worked for a player I haven't met yet: Henstrick, the woman who runs a construction firm and a brothel."

"Oh, yeah? Well, stick with the job I already gave you."

"I didn't say I . . . forget it." She stared at the floor as we walked. I wondered how well she knew Karoly, and how hard she was going to grieve for him, if at all. "While I was in the Hammers' house, I saw a picture—"

"I have an idea," she interrupted. "Go to the parking garage and get the van. I'll wait out front for you."

The look she gave me was angry and dangerous. Her face was paler and more sunken than before. I backed off. She held out the blue canvas bag, and I took it, being careful not to brush it up against her injured hands. She stalked away.

My life would become a lot easier if she were killed here in Hammer Bay. At least, I assumed it would. Maybe, when a peer in the society died, her wooden man was killed, too, like a pharaoh's slaves. Maybe the wooden man was reassigned to another peer, or traded around like a punk.

Or maybe they were cut loose. Maybe they were told to go away and not come back.

It sounded thin, but even so I didn't want anything to happen to Annalise. She hated me and would probably engineer my death, but the power she had was fascinating.

And I liked her.

Christ, I needed to get laid.

She hit a metal panel on the wall with her elbow, and the double doors in front of her opened. She stepped through, and the doors closed behind her.

I hustled back up the hall and reentered the morgue. I wanted a look at that clipboard Annalise had filled out. I wanted to see if it had an address on it, or a phone number. I wanted anything that I could use to track down some information on her or the Twenty Palace Society.

The reception area was empty. I rang the little bell on the counter. No one came. I rang again. I was all alone with the cracked plastic chairs and the slowly ticking clock.

I set the canvas bag on the floor. I'd seen the woman carry Annalise's clipboard into the back, but that didn't mean she hadn't brought it out again. I leaned over the counter and searched. There was an outdated computer, a steaming cup of coffee, a small collection of Pez dispensers, and a big framed picture of some sort of picnic. There was no form clipboard.

I vaulted over the counter and shoved the chair under the desk. There were file drawers below, but I didn't go for them yet. I figured that I'd have better odds in the back, and I had to do this quickly, before Annalise noticed the delay.

I laid my hand against the door. If there were metal tables and corpses on the other side of this door, I hoped they'd be covered with a nice, big cloth.

I pushed the door open.

The first thing I thought was: *That body should be on a table, not the floor.* Then I noticed a pool of blood slowly creeping toward me.

It was the morgue attendant, of course. Her throat was a raw, red mess, but her face looked utterly peaceful.

There were, indeed, tables in here. Two of them had sheet-covered bodies on top. I saw a phone on the wall and decided not to use it.

I couldn't see the clipboard anywhere.

On a table in the corner of the room I saw a pile of dark blue clothes set beside a pair of shiny black shoes.

There was a holster and pistol on top of the pile. Cop clothes.

The blood had almost touched my shoe. I stepped back.

From somewhere in the room I heard a low growl.

CHAPTER TEN

I jumped backward, pulling the door behind me. I caught a glimpse of something large and low rushing at me. It struck the door hard, slamming it shut.

The door banged open again, and I fell backward onto the desk. The swinging door revealed a wolf, its hackles raised, teeth bared, red eyes glaring at me. This one was black, tinged with gray, and bigger than the reddish one I'd seen on the street. Or maybe it seemed that way because it was looking at me like I was lunch.

I snatched the steaming cup of coffee off the counter. The wolf moved toward me, and I threw the coffee, splashing some onto my hand. Damn, it was hot. The black liquid struck the creature across the face. It let out a high-pitched whine and drew back.

I rolled the chair forward, ramming the wolf while it was off balance and knocking it back into the morgue.

I grabbed the door handle. There was no lock on this side. I reached around and slammed my palm on the handle on the other side. Something clicked. I hoped it was a lock.

The wolf found its feet and twisted in my direction. I leaped backward, pulling the door behind me. I saw long white teeth straining toward me, and then the door was shut.

I vaulted back over the counter and landed on the canvas bag. I slipped and fell on my backside. Hard. Damn. I was going to be eaten alive because I was a clumsy idiot.

I grabbed the cloth bag, rolled to my feet, and rushed into the hall. I didn't expect the locked door to hold for long, and I was pretty damn sure that was not an ordinary animal. In fact, I was pretty damn sure it was Emmett Dubois.

I could have run after Annalise, but the wolf might have followed me through a hospital filled with patients and staff. I wasn't that ruthless yet. I wasn't Annalise. I ran in the other direction, toward what I hoped was the parking lot behind the hospital.

I pushed through the double doors and sprinted down an empty hallway. There were no doors on either side, but there was a turn up ahead. I saw an exit sign and bluish light shining there. I ran faster.

I was halfway down the hall when I heard the double doors open behind me. Over my shoulder I saw the wolf padding toward me. Its teeth were bared and its tongue hung out. Its eyes glowed, for God's sake, even in the harsh fluorescent lights.

The wolf paused about a third of the way down the hall. It seemed to be showing me more of its teeth. Was that a smile? Whatever his doubts about me during my interview, I was running from him now. He'd called my bluff and he knew it.

I turned the corner, headed for the exit. The fire doors leading to the parking lot were right in front of me. They were chained shut.

I was trapped. Or, I was supposed to be trapped.

I took out my ghost knife and cut the chain. Its weight pulled it to the floor with a loud rattle. I pushed open one of the doors and slid the ghost knife through the other one, just beside the latch.

I heard the clatter of sharp nails on linoleum. The wolf was losing me, and he knew it. I slipped through the door and slammed it behind me, then slid the ghost knife through it right next to the latch.

The wolf rammed the push bar on the other side of the door. The latch mechanism I had just cut made a grinding noise but didn't open. Thank God.

I backed away. The doors would hold for a little while, until Emmett finally hit them hard enough to bust the latch or decided to go back for his uniform and gun.

Emmett Dubois was a werewolf.

I ran to the far end of the lot where the van was parked, then drove to the front of the building. Annalise was waiting at the curb, scowling at me as I approached. Had I just said that I liked her? I decided it was time to stop being stupid and start hating her again.

I opened the door for her. She climbed in. She didn't put on her seat belt. "What took you so long?"

I was not in the mood to share information. If she wanted something from me, she was going to have to give something. "Tell me about the last time you were in Hammer Bay. Tell me about the last time you met with the Hammer family, and about the tall man with the walking stick."

She didn't answer. She looked at me closely for nearly a minute. I realized that I was still breathing hard, and my hands were shaking. The adrenaline had not left my system yet.

I began to get uncomfortable.

Finally she said in a low voice: "The tall man with the walking stick was named Eli Warren. He was a peer in the society."

"Were you his wooden, um . . ."

"No," she said. "I was his apprentice. And his toy."

Saying that cost her something. I could hear it in her voice. But I pushed. "Where is he now?"

"I killed him," she said. "He betrayed the society. He sold spells, then used the society to hunt down his customers. I figured out his game and told the society. They told me to kill him. I did. As a reward, they gave me his spell book."

"Do you think the spells we're facing here came from Eli's book? Could he have sold them to the Hammer family way back when?"

"I don't know. Each spell book is unique. Even if they contain the same spells—and most have at least a couple of spells in common—the marks are never identical. But the society excised a lot of Eli's book before they passed it on to me. I certainly don't have a spell that would make people around me breathe spirit fire. But he and I did come here, just before I puzzled out his scam."

"Do you have a spell that could turn a person into a werewolf?"

"That's a pretty specific question. The answer is no, but I do have a spell that makes my sense of smell as keen as a wolf's for a short while. To track people. I never use it, though. Now I ask why you ask."

"While I was getting the van just now, I was stalked by a wolf. Right down in the morgue. The woman you were talking to was dead. Her throat was torn out."

Annalise's eyes narrowed. She didn't say anything.

"I think it was Emmett Dubois," I said.

"How certain are you?"

"Well, not terribly certain. I saw what looked like a police uniform on a table near the body, all neatly folded, and I did just make an enemy of him. And the magic detector went nuts when I touched it to him."

"But you didn't see him change? He didn't say, 'I'm going to change into a wolf and rip your heart out'?"

"No. Does he have to?"

"No," she said. "We can kill him anyway just to be safe. But if he's carrying spells or infected with a predator, we should watch him to see if he's not alone."

I nodded. "Thanks for trusting me."

"You're earning it," she said. "And you're useful. But remember whose side you're on."

We stopped at the supermarket again and bought more beef, a roll of aluminum foil, and a leg of lamb. This time, Annalise came inside with me and picked the cuts she wanted. As we were walking back to the van, I asked: "Is the pain getting bad?"

"You don't understand."

"Okay. Very bad? What if we got you some painkillers? Even something as lame as ibuprofen ought to help."

"You don't understand," she said again. "I'm dying."

I stopped and stared at her. "What do you mean?"

"Inside the van," she said.

We climbed in, and I shut the door.

"There's a spell called golem flesh, right? It's a protective spell, like our tattoos, only better. For some reason, it shows up in almost all the spell books. No one is sure why, but pretty much everyone gets it."

I wasn't sure what she was talking about. How did spells "show up" in books? But this wasn't the time to interrupt.

"When Eli first recruited me, he laid these tattoos on my skin. I wasn't his wooden man, but . . ." Her voice trailed off. "When I was my own person again," she continued, "I cast golem flesh on myself. As I said, nearly everyone in the society has it. It protects your whole body, not just the parts that are marked, and you can still feel things."

She paused. I knew what she meant. The tattoos on my chest and arms were numb. The enchanted skin in those areas couldn't feel anything—not pain, not cold, not heat, not a human touch. And Annalise was, as far as I'd seen, nearly covered with them.

"You just have to eat meat to survive. That's the trade-off. Any kind will do, and the less cooked the meat is, the more recently you've killed it, the better."

"And the meat will heal you," I prompted.

"When I'm injured, the meat tries to heal me. That's all it does. Nothing I've eaten has sustained me. I'm eating and eating—"

"And the food is going to a wound you can't heal."

"And I'm starving."

Most people could go weeks without food, but Annalise wasn't most people, and this was not regular food. "How long?" I asked.

"I don't know."

I started the engine and pulled into traffic. I wanted to reach out and lay a hand on her shoulder, to comfort her somehow, but it didn't feel right. Despite the fact that she had begun to trust me, there was still a gulf between us. There was a gulf between her and the world.

"What do we do, boss?" I asked.

"Finish the job," she said. "Afterward, we may know enough to heal me. If not, I'll go to the society and see if they can help."

"Why not go to the society right now? Why wait?"

She shook her head and would say nothing more on the subject. Conversation ended.

We reached the motel. I suggested that we move to a new motel, or at least change our rooms. She turned that idea down. She'd searched all over for Charles Hammer and come up with nothing. No one in town would talk to her. She was in pain. She was tired of searching for our targets. Maybe, if we stayed put, they'd come to us.

That didn't strike me as the most sensible idea in the world, but I wasn't in charge.

We went into her room. She picked through the things in Karoly's bag. It was mostly mundane personal effects, unless the ballpoint pen was enchanted to shoot fireballs, or the comb could turn french fries into hundred-dollar bills. It didn't seem likely, though; I couldn't see a sigil on any of them.

She took out the laptop and plugged it in. I didn't know much about computers. I'd had a PlayStation before I did my time, but I never had much use for the spreadsheets, email, or the Internet.

Annalise didn't look like an expert either. She pecked at the keys with one finger. After a minute or so, she picked up a teddy bear wearing a shirt that read WE MISS YOU, DAD! and popped its head off.

Some sort of computer plug stuck out of its neck. Annalise connected it to the back of the laptop. It looked as though its head was stuck inside the computer, and I couldn't help but smile. I'd bet Emmett Dubois hadn't found *that*.

I took out the meat and started slicing it up. I was pretty good at it by now. I also took out the box of plastic forks and began spearing little pieces of meat on the forks and setting them on a piece of aluminum foil beside her.

Annalise took out her cell phone and pressed a speed-dial number. She held the phone to her ear. "Karoly is dead," she said after a moment. "I have his drive, but not his password."

She took a bite of meat while she listened to whoever was on the other end of the line. *Click click tap tap*. The room began to feel stuffy.

"Got it," she said. "Thanks." She shut her phone and began scrolling through files on her screen.

I finally finished cutting the meat. I arranged it into a pile, then went into the bathroom to wash my hands and the ghost knife. When I returned, she was still staring at the screen. I sat opposite her and speared pieces of meat with the forks.

The quiet began to make me antsy. "Find anything?"

"Nothing useful," she said. She took another bite of meat and laid the empty fork down. I picked it up and stabbed it into a new piece, then set it beside her. I was beginning to feel like a manservant. This was not exactly the straight job I'd envisioned when I got out of prison.

I decided to earn more of her trust. "I still have your plastic, you know."

She didn't look up from the screen. "I know." She continued staring at the screen. I should have brought a book.

Annalise looked at her watch. "It's getting late. Why don't you get some food? I may be at this all night."

I lunged out of the chair and went out. It was still daylight, but my stomach was grumbling. I went into the office and smiled at the woman behind the desk. She scowled at me. Apparently, the other manager told her all about us. She gave me directions to a bookstore in town.

I drove out there and bought a detective novel, then drove across town and ordered my pad thai. I was tempted to eat in the restaurant window and read my book. We were stirring up the town, trying to see what would float to the top. I should be visible for that, just to see what shook out. But I didn't like leaving Annalise alone, not if she was dying. I ordered takeout.

I drove back to the motel, and as far as I could tell, no one was following me. No one had staked out the motel either. After checking in on Annalise, I went to my room, ate, read three chapters, then fell asleep.

I dreamed about fire all night.

I awoke to a thumping on my door. It was Cynthia, and she looked terrified.

"I'm sorry to bother you. I'm sorry," she said, glancing back toward the street nervously. Everything cast long shadows; it was very early, probably no more than an hour past dawn. "But I don't have anyone else to turn to."

"Er, come in." I stepped away from the door to let her in. I had fallen asleep wearing my pants, but I didn't have a shirt on. I could feel Cynthia watching me as I dug out a clean one.

I retreated to the bathroom to wash my face. I used cold water. I was sure she hadn't dropped by for a quick roll in the sheets.

When I returned, I gestured for her to sit at the table. I sat at the foot of the bed. After a moment's hesitation, she lowered herself into the chair. She was wearing a long-sleeved, chocolate-brown dress that just reached her knees, white stockings, and little, flat-soled brown shoes. Simple, but she looked very good.

I made a point of looking at her eyes. "What's the problem?"

"It's Cabot," she said. "Emmett let him out of prison this morning."

"Ah, shit. Who told you this?"

"Does it matter?"

"I asked, didn't I?"

She looked at the floor. "I'm sorry, I—"

"Hold on," I said. "I didn't mean to snap at you." I noticed the tiny coffeemaker on the table beside her. "Hey, do you want a cup of probably terrible coffee?" I stood.

She jumped out of her chair. "I'll get it. I need something to keep me busy."

She went into the bathroom to fill the pot, and I went to the window and peered around the edge of the curtain. Cynthia's silver SUV was parked beside the manager's office, but everything else looked the same.

She came out of the bathroom with a pot full of water, poured grounds into the filter, and filled the brewer halfway.

"Why don't you fill it up," I said. "I'm going to need it."

"You don't have enough coffee. Too much water and you get bitter coffee."

I shrugged and sat on the foot of the bed again. I thought all coffee was bitter. What did I know?

"Where did you get those tattoos?" she asked. "Behind bars?"

There was something in the artificially casual tone of her voice that I didn't trust. "No. After."

"So you have been to jail."

"Yep. Prison, too."

She looked at me, trying to decide if that was a joke. She was still undecided when she started the coffeemaker.

"Why . . . what did you . . ."

I decided to help her out. "What did I do to get sent to prison?"

"Um, yeah."

"You have an awful lot of questions for me all of a sudden. Or are these the questions you meant to ask me yesterday?"

"Well, I came here to see you, so—"

"You can go if you want. The door's right there. But don't think I'm going to answer a lot of questions if you won't answer mine. Who told you that Emmett released Cabot this morning?"

"Okay. That's fair." She set the two cups on the table. The coffeemaker had stopped brewing, but I could see liquid still dripping into the pot. "It was Sugar Dubois."

"Why did he do that?"

"He didn't say, but we were in high school together. We knew each other a little, and he was always nice. Deferential, even, like some boys get when they have a crush."

"He warned you because he had a crush on you in high school? Is there more to it than that?"

"Not to the crush. We never dated or anything. He was too far below me then. Don't make that face. It was high school. You know what that was like."

Actually, I didn't. I never stayed in school for more than a couple of weeks at a time, although I'd gotten my GED in prison. Not that I was going to tell Cynthia that. "High school is over. Is he making a move on you right now?" It made sense, if the Dubois brothers wanted to consolidate power in the town.

"Ugh. I think he knows better."

Okay. I'll bet he did. "Do you think Emmett put him up to it?"

"Why do you ask that?"

"Questions with questions." Before she could apologize, I said: "It seems strange to me that he'd go against his own brother because of a schoolyard crush."

"I don't think it's that simple. Sugar loves his brothers, but he's always wanted to be a cop. Actually, I think he always wanted to be a cop on TV, and I don't think the setup his brother has here in Hammer Bay is what he had in mind. He has to accept some of what they do—they're his brothers—but letting Cabot go when he might take another shot at me . . . I think they went just a little too far this time."

I didn't say anything to that. Emmett turned into a wolf and tore people's throats out, and I suspected his brothers were the same. Setting Cabot free was small potatoes for them.

I wasn't sure what play Emmett was making by setting Cabot loose. Was he hoping Cabot would take another shot at Cynthia, or was he trying to keep things as chaotic as possible, just as I was?

Cynthia passed me a coffee cup. She'd filled it while I wasn't paying attention. I took a sip. It wasn't bitter. How about that? There's a right way to do things after all.

"That's what I think, anyway," Cynthia said. She sipped her coffee and winced. It was obviously below her standards. To me, it was wonderful. "Now, how about you?"

I shrugged. "I went to prison because I was in a fight."

"That must have been some fight."

"Actually, it wasn't much of a fight at all. And it's not something I'm proud of."

"I'll drop it."

"Thanks. Why were you arguing with Cabot yesterday?"

"That doesn't really matter, does it?"

I sighed. I took a long sip of coffee and savored it. It took a few moments of silence for her to take the hint.

"We were arguing about the family business, if you think that's important. Charles inherited the timber company from Dad, but he wasn't interested in it. Uncle Cabot rounded up some capital and bought it. Charles used the money to start the toy company, which everyone thought was nuts, but it's Cabot who's going bankrupt and Charles who's thriving."

"So . . . what? Cabot felt cheated?"

"He wanted more financing from Charles to take some of the pressure off. And he wanted Charles to . . ." She paused, searching for the correct phrase. She had suddenly become very careful with what she said. "Charles has access to some resources that Cabot wanted to use. Advice, really. Cabot wasn't sure which way to jump."

That rang a bell. I couldn't quite remember why, but I'd heard something like that before. "Charles wouldn't help him."

"I'm not sure why, but no, he wouldn't. Charles wouldn't even meet with him. Uncle Cabot began to get really intense about it. I guess he was in more trouble than anyone realized."

"And he came to you, because?"

"He wanted me to help him with Charles. I don't know what he expected. I don't own any part of Charles's company, and I barely see him myself anymore."

"What do you live on?"

"Trust fund," she said carelessly. "The interest is more than I need, so I invested some instead of blowing it. I'm doing pretty well right now."

"Does Cabot know that?"

"Hell no, and don't tell him, either. I'm not throwing my money down his rat hole."

"So he thinks Charles has all the money. And you don't have any pull with your brother. Did you explain that to him?"

"Sure, but he didn't believe me."

I shrugged. "Neither do I."

"Excuse me?" She sounded irritated.

"People shoot each other for all kinds of stupid reasons. I mean, really stupid. I bunked with a guy who shot his brother-in-law over who deserved the biggest piece of chicken. But what you're describing is all wrong. If Cabot was going to shoot anyone, it would be Charles, for refusing to help him. Why would he pop one off at you? Charles is in town, right? I'll bet Cabot knows where to find him. So, either he knows you have a good-sized nest egg, or there's something else going on."

"He must know about the nest egg," she said, a little too quickly. Her voice sounded shaky, but I didn't ease up on her.

"I still don't believe you. Let's cut the bullshit. Cabot wanted to use you against your brother. He had a plan, and he made an offer to you—I don't know, more money or control of the toy company or something, right? He wanted you to help him with a hostile takeover."

"That's for publicly traded companies. Hammer Bay Toys is privately owned."

"Fine. I don't know a thing about high finance. In that case, he wanted you to have your brother declared incompetent."

Cynthia blinked. Bingo.

"Right. Charles has been having seizures. Has he been to a doctor? I'd guess not. He's too busy with his company, and he brushes off anyone who asks about them."

"Who told you about his seizures?"

"Everyone knows. I saw one the night Harlan Semple shot up downtown. What did Cabot promise? You file commitment papers on your brother, and he'd support you? You'd get control of the toy company and he'd get an infusion of cash? Or you'd sell the company and split the proceeds? And Charles would get the medical care he'd need. I'll bet he told you this was the best thing for Charles."

She stared at me. The look on her face told me that I wouldn't be doing the job Annalise had given me anytime soon. "Okay. Yes. That's the pitch he made, basically."

I didn't push that *basically*. I suspected that Cabot knew about Charles's spell book and that he wanted it for himself.

But did Cynthia know about it? And if so, how much? I couldn't be sure, and I didn't want to push too hard and shut her down. She'd just been shot at, and I could see the fear in her. Besides, I had more important things to worry about.

"Where's your brother?"

"What does that have to do with my uncle?"

"Questions with questions," I said.

"Tough shit," she snapped. Her anger put some strength back into her voice. "What does it have to do with Uncle Cabot?"

I shrugged and drained the rest of my coffee. It made me hungry. "Nothing. My boss and I want to meet with him."

"About what?"

Fine. I set the cup down. "Why are you here, telling me about your uncle?"

Suddenly, she wouldn't look at me. "I'm afraid . . . I think he might come after me again. I can't ask Emmett for help. Or Sugar, either. Not now. I want . . . I need someone to help me."

Damn. She wanted me to kill him.

CHAPTER ELEVEN

"And how exactly am I supposed to do that?"

"I don't know," she said, still not looking at me. She knew very well what she wanted, but she wouldn't say it.

"Why don't you leave town? You could be in Sea-Tac in less than three hours. From there, you could go anywhere in the world. I hear New York is nice in the spring."

"I can't leave my brother."

"The brother you never see? Please. Tell this story to Able Katz. He strikes me as a smart guy. He'll square things with the Dubois brothers. He could help more than I could. But neither one of us is going to commit murder for you."

The word *murder* didn't make her flinch. "I have money."

"So buy a gun. I'll bet you can afford a nice one."

"I'm sorry I bothered you." She stood and turned toward the door.

"I didn't say I wouldn't help you. Just that I wouldn't kill him for you. What if I talked to him? Maybe I could make him back off." And maybe I could get him to tell me where Charles the Third was hiding.

"Would you do that?" she asked.

"Sure." I couldn't help smiling. "In exchange, all you have to do is show me how to make a good cup of coffee."

We went out of the room. The shadows were a bit

shorter and the air noticeably warmer. Cynthia took out
her car keys, but I wanted to stop in and tell Annalise
where I was going, and also to make sure she didn't
need me.

I knocked. She told me to come in.

She was in the same position she'd been in the night
before. She looked a little paler, and her eyes looked wa-
tery. Her bedcovers were rumpled, so I knew she'd had
some sleep. Or at least had tried.

"Any luck?" I asked.

"I opened his files. Understanding them is something
else."

"What do you mean?" I slipped into the room, and
she turned the screen toward me.

"Have a look."

I squinted at the screen. "Is that some kind of code?"

"It's Polish. Karoly made his notes in his native language. Which I should have expected, but damn. I'm going to ask for English-speaking investigators from now
on."

"Well, it answers one of my questions, at least."

"What's that?" she asked.

"Why didn't Emmett know about your investigation
as soon as we hit town? I'm not sure what was in the
note Emmett took—"

"The note isn't on here. I checked. He must have written it by hand."

"I thought so. We didn't find a printer in his stuff."

"I'm uploading the files to the society. Someone there
will translate and prioritize them."

"That's cool. Can I see them when they come back?"

She stared at me a moment. "Maybe. It depends on
what—"

The door opened. Cynthia stepped inside and shut
the door behind her. She stood as close to the door as she

could without being on the other side of it. "I'm sorry," she said. "I didn't feel safe out there alone."

I turned to Annalise. "Emmett let Cabot out of his cell. I'm going to go have a talk with him. Cabot, I mean."

She looked me in the eyes. There was something in her look that I didn't understand, but it seemed to be full of meaning. It unsettled me. It was as if I was becoming something she hadn't expected.

Or maybe she was trying to tell me to go get laid.

"Do you need anything before I go?"

"No," Annalise said. "Leave the van, in case I need to run out for something."

"Understood." We left. In the parking lot, Cynthia turned to me. "I thought you said your boss hates you. She doesn't look like she hates you."

"I know," I said. "Ain't that something?"

I thought about Annalise, sitting listless when Cynthia opened the door. Was she dying? Was I watching her die?

I realized Cynthia was talking to me. "Whoa. Back up and start over please," I said "I was somewhere else."

She looked at me like *Are you serious?* "I said that my uncle is probably at his office by now. He goes there every day, no matter what."

"Let's try there first. But I expect he'll stay at home. Does he live in one of the other houses on Hammer Street?"

"Uncle Cabot? No. He has a studio apartment in town now."

That surprised me, but I didn't say anything. We drove downtown, and Cynthia turned up a narrow side street. She parked. "That's it."

She pointed toward a run-down warehouse. I had to look at it twice to notice the HAMMER BAY TIMBER sign above the door. The outside was made of rough, unpainted wood. The walls had warped from the damp. This was a company that had fallen on hard times.

I opened the door.

"What should I do?" Cynthia asked.

"Go have breakfast. Or lunch. Or a cup of coffee. Park a block away from wherever you end up. I'll come and find you."

She told me where she'd be. I stepped out.

"Wait! What if something happens . . . if you don't show up?"

"New York is nice in the spring." I shut the door and she drove away.

I walked around the building first. I didn't see anything except a back door beside an empty Dumpster, some tall weeds, and a high, dirty window with a pale light shining inside.

A gentle drizzle began to fall. I tried the back door, but it was locked. My ghost knife was in my pocket, so that wasn't an obstacle for me, but I didn't cut my way in. I walked along the other side of the building, ducking under the fire escape and running my hand along the rough wood.

I reached the front door. The warehouse loading ramp was just a step up from the ground. I peered into the windows, but they were too dirty, and the inside too dark, for me to see anything.

I felt a twinge below my collarbone. Another kid was gone. I looked around, trying to find the source of the feeling, but of course I couldn't see anything. It could have happened anywhere in town. I gritted my teeth and pulled on the door. It was unlocked, and it creaked as I opened it.

The floor groaned as I walked on it. Enough light shone through the dirty windows that I managed to cross the floor without breaking my nose against a wooden post or tripping over the odd piece of furniture.

There was a flight of stairs against the side wall, and dim light shining from the top. I climbed them, and they groaned under every step. I took out my ghost knife—I wanted to be ready for anything.

"I can't pay you!" someone shouted from the top of the stairs. "Whoever you are, I don't have your money!"

I'd heard that shout yesterday. It belonged to Cabot.

I reached the top of the stairs. There was no doorway; the stairs simply opened into his office. I could smell the sour stink of old cigarette smoke.

Cabot was sitting at his desk with his head down on the blotter, a cigarette burning in an ashtray beside him. He didn't look up. If I had been sent there to kill him, I could have put a bullet into the top of his head and been gone again with no trouble.

I looked around. The floorboards were warped, and the walls seemed to be buckling with age. A huge map of the Olympic Peninsula was tacked to the wall. It was yellowed and curled at the edges.

"Go away," Cabot said again. He still hadn't looked up. "I don't have anything to give you."

"Don't be so sure," I said.

He started and looked up at me. His eyes widened with shock, he yanked open a desk drawer and stuck his hand inside.

"HEY!" I shouted. My voice boomed inside the room. Cabot was startled and froze in place. "If I wanted to kill you, you'd be dead already. Leave the gun in the drawer. You've been stupid enough with guns as it is."

I walked toward the desk, pulled a chair around, and sat opposite him. "You should have locked the front door," I told him. "What will you do if Peter Lemly comes here for a story? What if the mayor's wife decides to pay you a visit?"

"Christ. Frank. I didn't want anything to happen to him. I like Frank."

"Oh, shut up. Every jackass that shoots the wrong guy talks that way. It makes me sick."

He looked sheepish. He had the same thick dark hair as Cynthia and Charles, but it was shot through with gray. His chin was weak, and rimmed with folds of fat. His eyes were large with dark circles. He was just as run-down and creaky as this building, and just as depressing.

His hand was still in his desk drawer. He began to slowly move it, still searching for that gun.

I lunged out of my seat and slammed the drawer on his hand. Then I grabbed the top edge of the drawer and yanked it out of the desk. It flew backward and smashed the corner of his window before falling. Papers and pens scattered to the floor, but I focused on the heavy clunk of a handgun.

Another pistol. Cabot started toward it, but I shoved him back with all my strength. He fell against the chair and crumpled into the corner.

I picked up the handgun. It was a .45, and a little old-fashioned. Pulling back the slide, I saw that it was loaded but hadn't been cleaned recently. Sloppy. Everything about this guy was sloppy.

"Go sit down," I told him.

He moved like a little kid being sent to the corner, but he did it. "Who are you? What do you want?" he asked.

It was a relief to find someone who did not already know my whole history. "Just a guy doing a favor for a friend. What are you going to do, Cabot?"

"Nothing," he said. "I'm going to go to jail. And I'm going to go bankrupt. I'll probably have to sell the house on Whidbey and . . ." He was withdrawing into himself as he talked.

"Cabot," I said again. He looked at me. "What are you going to do about Cynthia? About Charles? How many more guns do you have?"

"Oh," he said. "Will you apologize to Cynthia for

me? I'd been drinking, and I was desperate, and . . . and I was worried about Charles—"

I laughed. "So worried that you shot at his sister?"

"Charles is sick," he said resentfully.

"How sick?"

"He's got a tumor or something. He's lost a ton of weight—have you seen him recently?"

I thought about the tall, slender, dark-haired guy I'd seen at the Hammer Bay Toy office. I nodded.

"Well, he used to be fat. Big, porky fat, like a Samoan or something. But he's just melted away. And he's been having seizures."

"What? Like epilepsy?" I pretended not to know anything. I wanted to see what he would tell me.

"Don't know. He hasn't been to a doctor as far as I can tell. We have the same doctor—the whole family does—and I know Charles hasn't been to him. And he hasn't left town, either, so he hasn't been to see anyone else."

"How long has this been going on?"

"About two years, I guess. It started right around the same time as . . ."

"As what?"

Cabot rubbed his nose. "As, um, the play-offs. We were watching the NBA finals, and he fell down in the bathroom. He wouldn't let us take him to County. I think that was the first time. He looked surprised and kind of shocked, like it hadn't happened before."

"Is that why you tried to have him declared incompetent?"

"If he's seriously sick," Cabot said, his gaze sullen and his face stubborn, "he needs to see a doctor."

"And if you get a couple bucks out of the deal, that's just a happy side effect, right?"

"That's not how it is."

"If you say so."

My needling got a rise out of him. He leaned toward

me, his voice getting higher and more petulant. "You don't know what you're talking about! You're not even a part of this family!"

"Thank God for that. I didn't bring my Kevlar."

He opened and closed his little fish mouth several times, then the wind went out of him. He sagged against the back of his chair.

"How do they do it?" he said. "My brother always knew just the right thing to do. He always made the right move. It was like he knew just what would happen. I've never been able to do that. I just follow my nose and try to do the smart thing, but I have no idea where it will lead."

"You wouldn't make much of a chess player," I said.

"I suck at chess. Is that the secret? Chess?"

"I wouldn't know."

"It doesn't matter now. I've been sitting here, trying to decide if I should kill myself. I don't think I have the guts for it."

"Good. Prison is bad, but you can survive it."

"God. At least I wouldn't have to look at this anymore." He shifted some papers on his desk and pulled out a slender newspaper. It was a copy of *The Mallet*. The headline at the top read CABOT HAMMER ARRESTED FOR ATTEMPTED MURDER!

I took it from him and scanned the front page. It was a special edition, run especially to cover this story. The article was written by Peter Lemly and told the same basic story that Cynthia had been spreading. Cabot and Cynthia had a big argument; Cabot tried to shoot her but struck the mayor instead when he shielded her. Cabot was then subdued by a "visiting businessman." For a few moments I was peeved that some other guy had gotten credit for what I did. Then I realized I was the businessman.

"Did you know," Cabot started, talking to me like a

friend—didn't the guy have any friends?—"my brother could make people do what he wanted. My father, too."

"*Make* how?"

"It wasn't like he voodooed their minds or anything. And he never blackmailed them, as far as I could tell. He just wanted something and other people wanted him to have it. When he bid on a plot of forest, whoever was handling the parcel awarded it to him. It was like he made them want what he wanted them to want. He just bent them to his will, without any effort at all. And he always knew how to handle people. He knew how to use the Dubois brothers, and when to hold them off. He could play Reverend Wilson like a radio."

I twisted that around in my head until I sorted all the wants. "Isn't Charles the Third doing the same thing with his toy company? Isn't he putting out products that people are snapping up?" I remembered what Able Katz had told us: Hammer's toys weren't supposed to be a huge hit, but they were. I could have gone further, talking about the way the local townsfolk defended him like he was their king, but I wanted to see Cabot's reaction.

"Yeah. Yeah, I guess so. You know what's funny? I never would have pegged little Charlie to be the tycoon type. Now he's this reclusive business genius, spending all his time hiding in the tower, but I never thought he had it in him. He was such a fat, dorky little kid."

I remembered the high, round room I'd seen at the top of the Hammers' house. That must have been the tower. If I'd known, I would have slipped out of the library and confronted him. I made a mental note to tell Annalise about it. "Fat kids grow up," I said.

"No, no, I don't mean it like that. He wasn't just fat. He was lazy and stupid. He never got a joke unless you explained it to him. Kids bullied him on the playground. He was that kind of kid. He used to talk about helping the poor or saving the whales, but he never had more than a vague idea how to go about it, and he never . . . okay. Once, he decided that he was going to help some of the older folks in town. You know, retired lumber workers and their wives, they get sick or property taxes go up, and it's trouble.

"So little Charlie decided to start a food drive. He must have been fourteen or so, and he's as big as a whale. Everyone jokes that he's going to be eating half the food himself, though not to his face, of course. But most people like the idea and chip in. We stored the food right downstairs in this building. It was quite a stack—I was surprised by how much support the kid got.

"But Charlie lost interest as soon as it started to be successful. He spent his afternoons playing video games on the couch while the cans and stuff collected dust.

"In the end, I distributed it myself. Those folks were really grateful to get the deliveries, and a couple of them asked when there would be another. I had to tell them that I thought it was a one-shot deal. They were pretty disappointed. Poor folks. Stuck in this town. This fucked-up town.

"So, I didn't think the kid had a successful company in him. But he's just as good at it as his father."

"Why didn't you continue the drive yourself?"

"What's that?"

"The food drive. If it helped so many people, why didn't you take over?"

"Well . . . that's not the point I wanted to make."

"I understand your point. Your nephew was this big loser who suddenly turned into a successful guy, and you didn't."

"Well, not that I'm a loser . . . wait. Scratch that. I *am* a loser. I've always been one. But I've had my family to back me up. Until now. Crap."

"What changed for him? What changed for your nephew?"

I didn't expect him to say *Must be that spell book his daddy gave him,* but I hoped for something more than this extended bout of self-pity. Instead, he said: "God only knows. My kids certainly don't have it."

He was wearing a wedding ring. "You're divorced?" I asked.

"No. No, I'm still married to their mother. We love each other very much."

I wasn't interested in that. "How many kids do you have?"

"Four. Ages eight through fifteen."

"Cynthia said you live in a studio apartment."

"Well, yeah, I do, but they don't. They live on Whidbey Island."

"Is that right?" I asked. Cabot shifted in his chair uncomfortably. He didn't like the way I was looking at him. If he'd known what I was thinking, he'd be even less pleased. "When did this happen?"

"A couple years back after school ended. My wife has never been happy here, so I bought her a place up there. Everyone is transitioning nicely."

"Why do they live so far from you?" I asked. I was pretty sure I already knew the answer.

He scratched at his chin. "They have a good school district there." He shuffled some papers on his desk. "I want my kids to grow up in the best environment possible."

I leaned forward. A dangerous spark of anger had caught in my belly. "Cabot, you want to know what you should never do? You should never lie to me. Especially when I have this gun in my pocket."

He blinked a couple of times. "I don't know what you're talking about."

"*This town. This fucked-up town,*" I mimicked. "Charles the Third has his first seizure, that you know of, in what—April? May? And a couple weeks later you ship your kids to the other side of the mountain."

"Well—"

"While your company is gasping for its last breath."

"Okay—"

"You bought your wife a little place on Whidbey Island, where the real estate costs—"

"All right! All right! That's not the whole story."

"Tell me the whole story."

I could see that he wanted to tell me to get lost. He glanced at the pocket of my jacket. I still had the gun, and I had slugged him unconscious once already. "It's for their own safety," he said. "I have enemies in town—"

I slammed my hand down on his desk and jumped from the chair. I stood over him, and he stared up at me with wide, startled deer's eyes.

I could see it in those eyes. He knew about the kids. He knew about the fires. He remembered them.

Two years it had been going on, and he hadn't done a thing except move his own family to a safe place.

"I think . . ." I didn't know what I was going to say. It was like I had another person inside me, making all my decisions for me. "I think I'm going to kill you."

"What?" His eyes grew wider.

"I've got the gun. I'll lay the newspaper in front of you and put a bullet into your head. Everyone will think it was suicide."

"Now, wait a minute—"

"You wait a minute. You're spreading bullshit like it's sweet butter, and you think I should sit here and gulp it down?"

He lunged for me. I punched him in the throat.

He fell back against his chair, choking and gasping for air. I could have killed him with that punch, but I'd pulled back at the last moment. Had I pulled back enough, though?

"Don't—" Cabot wheezed at me. I figured that if he could talk, he would live. I was a little disappointed.

"That's just the start of what I'm going to do to you if you lie to me again." Cabot looked up at me and I saw it in his face. He was ready to tell me everything. "Tell me about the kids."

"There . . ." His voice was hoarse. He took a deep, shuddering breath. "There isn't much to tell."

"Tell me anyway."

"One day, my youngest came home early from school crying. She said that one of the kids in her class caught fire and burned to death, right before her eyes. This was the middle of May." He paused to rub his throat and take another deep breath. "I thought she was playing a game, but she insisted it was true. Her friend Carrie had caught fire while sitting at her desk.

"I went to her teacher and spoke with her in the classroom. One of the desks in the back of the room was scorched black, and there was a black trail leading out of the room and down the hall. The teacher acted like she couldn't see the scorch mark. She claimed that the desk had been empty all year long, and that there was no student named Carrie in her class.

"I'd met Carrie. She'd come over for playdates. There was a drawing on the wall signed with her name, in scrawling Crayola letters. The teacher couldn't see the black marks, couldn't see the drawing, and didn't remember the little girl.

"I thought she was crazy. I went to the school board, but they told me the same things the teacher had, and asked me if I had seen a doctor lately.

"Well, I went to Carrie's house to speak to her parents. Neither one of them could remember their own daughter. It was as though I'd had this memory of a little girl with bobbed red hair inserted into my brain. And my daughter's brain, too.

"It wasn't the last time it happened. Two weeks later, my kids started telling me that their friends were disappearing, and no one remembered them. Finally, I brought my lunch to the school and sat in my car, watching the playground. In the week I sat there, I saw two kids burn up. The other kids would freak out when it started, and then, when it was over, go back to playing as if nothing had happened."

"What about the worms?"

"I don't know. I don't know what they are, or what they mean. But I was freaking out, so I sent my wife and kids away, hoping they'd be safe. So far, they are."

"Are you so sure about that? What if you had five kids before, but you just can't remember one?"

"Do you think I haven't thought about that? But I'm sure. I'm sure."

I didn't like the sound of that. "That's it? That's all you did about those kids? You talked to a couple people?"

"That's all I could do! I talked to Emmett and Frank and Reverend Wilson. They looked at me like I was losing my mind. My kids were getting into fights in school because people thought we were going nuts. All we could do was to wait for it to blow over. What else was I supposed to do?"

Something, I wanted to say, but I held my tongue. "And you swear you don't know anything about those worms?"

"Nothing. I don't know what they are. How do you know about this? Everyone else forgets all this."

I wished Annalise had left me her scrap of wood. I would have liked to know if Cabot was infected, enchanted, or brain-damaged like Harlan. "Stand up."

He pushed his chair back and stood.

"Empty your pockets."

He began to turn them out, dumping everything inside them onto the desktop. Wallet, key ring, gas receipt, bottle opener . . . all very bland and boring. But none of it looked like magic to me.

I leveled the gun on him. "Strip," I said. "Start with the shirt."

He started to grumble, but he did it. He unbuttoned his shirt and hung it over the back of the chair. As he turned, I saw a tattoo on his back.

"Hold it," I said. I turned him toward me. Well, well. There, tattooed on his back, was an iron gate. It was identical to mine.

"Where did you get this?" I asked.

"My father put it there when I was a baby. He put it onto all my kids, too, before he died."

"Why?"

"I don't know. It's supposed to be some kind of good luck. It bugs me sometimes, though."

I thought about the twinge I'd felt outside the building just a couple of minutes ago. "When does it bug you?"

"Every couple of days, I guess. It feels like someone pokes it with a stick or something."

"Did it bug you when you saw that little kid catch fire?"

"Well . . ." He hesitated. I knew he was going to lay out another lie. "It's possible, I guess. I don't remember."

"What about when Charles had his seizure?"

"How long is this conversation going to take?"

"We're getting to the important stuff right now. What about Charles?"

"Nothing that I remember." If he was lying, he was getting better at it.

"Where's the book?"

"What book?"

"The book! *The* book!"

"I don't know what book you're talking about!"

I shoved him over the desk and slammed his head against the blotter. He started to resist, but I placed the barrel of the gun against the back of his head. I hoped no one was going to walk in at that moment.

"Please!" he said. "You're not really going to do it, are you? You're not really going to kill me?"

"What do you think about all those burned-up kids?"

"I think it's horrible. I have nightmares—"

"But not so horrible that you kept trying to stop it."

"What was I supposed to do? People thought I was crazy! I'm a Hammer—I can't be the town joke!"

That was almost it. That last sentence almost made me squeeze the trigger. I wasn't even angry anymore. I just felt cold and bitter. Cabot seemed like a dirty little mess that needed to be wiped up. All I had to do was squeeze the trigger.

"Please," he said simply.

I pulled him off the desk and shoved him into the chair. "You have a chance to live, if you really want it."

"I want it! I do!"

"We'll see. Where's the book?"

"I don't know about any book! I swear!"

He made it sound like the truth, but I wasn't convinced. "Wrong answer. Let me explain something, Cabot. I'm here to put a stop to these fires, and I don't care who I have to step on to do it. If you're not going to answer, you're in my way."

"But I really don't know. I swear."

"Tell me about your father and the thing he put on your back."

"I was just a baby! I don't remember that!"

"What about your own kids? You weren't a baby then, were you?"

"He took each of them for one night. He sent Carla and me away. In the morning, they had this mark on their backs. Carla didn't like it, but I told her to stuff it. It's family tradition, and I was afraid we wouldn't get a penny out of him otherwise."

"What about the Dubois brothers?"

"What about them? They certainly don't have any book. I'm not even sure they can read."

This was getting nowhere. I took the ghost knife from my pocket.

"What are you doing?" Cabot asked.

"Hold still." I slid the ghost knife through Cabot's arm. He collapsed, struck the wooden floor hard, and began whimpering. Then he curled up into a ball.

"Please," he said in a half-choked whimper. "Please please please please."

I'd seen the ghost knife take away people's vitality and hostility, but I'd never seen a reaction like this. I'd meant to make Cabot more docile to get honest answers out of him. Instead, I'd cut away his bravery and uncapped his fear. I'd broken him.

The ghost knife was a spell I'd cast. My first. It was a part of me, and there was still a lot I didn't understand about it.

"The book. Who has it?"

"I don't know! I swear I swear I swear I swear—"

"Enough." He shut up.

What was I going to do with this guy? He'd recover if I left him, but was I allowed to leave him? What if he was also carrying a predator, like Emmett Dubois? What about his iron gate?

I didn't know what Annalise would do with him if she caught him. I didn't know if carrying a spell, even one he didn't cast himself, was reason enough to murder him. If it was, his whole family would die, too.

Could I do that? Could I tell Annalise about Cabot's iron gate, and the iron gates on his kids, knowing it meant she might hunt them down and kill them? Hell, she might make me kill them, as a kind of initiation.

Or should I keep my mouth shut, let them walk away, and betray Annalise again?

I looked down at Cabot. He didn't look dangerous, but I couldn't leave that spell active. What if Annalise laid her scrap of wood on him? I reached down and slid the ghost knife through the iron gate.

The mark burst in a shower of black steam. Cabot bucked, kicking the desk. Papers fluttered to the floor.

I felt something go out of him as the spell came apart. It was like a third person in the room had walked out and I hadn't noticed its presence until it was gone.

Cabot moaned and wept, laying his face against the floor. He looked miserable and pathetic, but I wasn't done with him yet. I had to make sure he didn't have any more spells on him.

I pocketed the gun and dragged him out from behind the desk. He didn't resist. I wasn't sure he could resist, even if he'd had the guts for it. All he did was cover his face with his hands and plead in a voice so small that I couldn't make out anything he said.

There were guys I'd met in prison who would have gone stiff as a rod to see a man break down that way, but it made me feel queasy. Still, I had to be sure there were no more spells on him. Annalise would want to know.

I rolled him over. I slid the ghost knife through the top front of his pants, cutting the belt and zipper wide open. Then I grabbed his pant cuffs and pulled.

I *really* hoped no one would walk in on us now.

I studied him long enough to confirm that there were no other marks on him. I kicked his pants to him.

"Humiliating, isn't it?" I said. "Some guys would be so furious at being treated like this that they'd get themselves a gun and come after me for revenge. Don't be that stupid. Understand?" He nodded. "I want a couple things. First, tell me where the book is. And don't lie. If you lie, I'll know."

"I swear," he said in a pathetic voice. "Please, I swear I would never lie to you. I don't know. Maybe Cynthia has it—"

"Second, keep away from Cynthia."

Cabot shut up and nodded. His eyes were as big as saucers.

"Third, you aren't protected anymore. I don't know when the next kid is going to die, but I do know you're going to start forgetting them soon. Maybe you'll be happy to forget. But don't forget this: I don't want to see you again.

"Last, get out of town. Don't go back to your apartment. Just get in your car and go to Whidbey. Tomorrow, go see a lawyer, but tonight go be with your kids. You may still end up dead or in prison, but at least you'll get to see them."

That was it. I couldn't look at him anymore. I couldn't look at what I'd done to him. I backed away, quickly scanning the room. I didn't want to leave anything behind. I didn't want to come back here ever again.

I walked to the stairs and went down. They creaked and groaned. I could hear Cabot behind me, quietly weeping to himself. The ghost knife had destroyed him in a way I'd never seen before. I took it out and looked at it in the semidarkness of the stairs. I could feel the power in it, and I could feel that power was partly mine, but only partly. How would it feel to have the spells on my body destroyed?

More important, what would Annalise think of what I'd done? We were here to destroy predators and steal spell books. Spells were too powerful to circulate out in the world. The scorched black earth all over Hammer Bay was proof enough of that.

The only exception, as far as I could tell, was the Twenty Palace Society. From talking to Annalise, I knew they had strict rules about the use of their magic, and if they were a little too ruthless with it, it was only out of fear and a desire to protect us all.

Even so, I felt like a hypocrite. I'd done a lot of stupid things in my life. Who's to say that it was okay for me to walk around with spells all over me, but Cabot couldn't? And who says the Twenty Palace Society should be the ones who decide?

I walked across the wooden floor toward the door. I was going to tell Annalise about Cabot and his kids. If she decided they had to die, or if that was some sort of rule for the Twenty Palace Society, so be it. Maybe I would be the one to do the deed. It would serve me right.

I hoped we could let them go, though. Cabot didn't have any spell book. I was sure of that now. I would just have to ask Cynthia next. And Charles the Third.

I stepped through the doorway into the dim daylight. Four men were standing on the curb. They pointed snub-nosed .38s at me.

"That's him," someone said. Another man was standing behind the first four. His hands were wrapped in casts. It was Floyd.

I didn't recognize the others. I realized that I should have been afraid, but my adrenaline glands had apparently not gotten the danger message yet.

The door to the warehouse was still open behind me.

"Don't do it," one of the men said. "Hear me out first."

He was medium height and built like a decathlete. He had a thick mustache and goatee, but his head was shaved. Finally, I'd met the fourth man who had spoken with Dubois, Charles Hammer, and the mayor when Harlan had been shot.

His expression told me what I wanted to know most: he wasn't jumpy, wasn't nervous, wasn't uncomfortable. He would kill me if he had to, and then he'd go on with his day. I shrugged. "Okay. What do you have to say?"

"Our boss is interested in you. She would like to invite you to have lunch with her."

His expression was cold. All four guns were still pointed at me.

"I accept."

CHAPTER TWELVE

This time we rode in a Chevy Sport van. It had plenty of space for the goons to sit around me and keep me covered.

Floyd sat in the front passenger seat. The guy who extended the invitation sat on the bench behind me. Another sat beside me, and the last two were on the seat in front of me. They twisted around to aim their revolvers at me.

The one beside me held his gun too close to my arm. I could have wrestled him for it, if he didn't have three armed friends backing him up.

"Bobby?" the one next to me said.

"Do it now," the man behind me answered. "And don't use my name, dipshit."

I looked at the guy beside me. I'd known dozens of guys just like him inside, and the one thing I couldn't do was show them my fear. "Why can't you use his name but he can use yours?"

If the guy took offense, he hid it well. He pocketed his gun and started to search me. He did a pretty terrible job of it, even if he did manage to find everything useful I had on me. He took Cabot's gun, my wallet, Annalise's keys, and my ghost knife and handed each one back to Bobby.

"What's this?" Bobby asked me, holding the ghost knife over the back of the seat so I could see it.

"My good-luck charm."

"Yeah? What's this squiggle?"

"My doctor's signature. I copy it when I'm forging a prescription."

"Not funny. Give me the real answer."

"Okay. Really, it's the last signature Kurt Cobain ever gave. He died the day after he signed it."

"Whoa," one of the guys in front of me said. He was a scrawny black guy with bad teeth. "I want to see that."

I couldn't help it. I laughed.

"Shut up up there. It's nobody's signature. And it sure ain't no good-luck charm, otherwise you wouldn't be here."

"You just wait." I winked at the scrawny guy in front of me and sat tight. As long as I didn't make a break for it, I figured I'd live long enough to eat lunch.

I sat quietly and watched the town pass by. I could feel the ghost knife behind me. I knew I could call it, but this wasn't the time.

We approached the supermarket. I told the driver I wanted to stop in and pick up a bottle of wine—I hated to show up at someone's house empty-handed. He slowed at the entrance to the parking lot, unsure if he should stop. Bobby cursed at him and told him to pass it by.

I didn't laugh this time, but I did smile. The guys were liking me less and less all the time. Bobby, unseen in the backseat, griped and mumbled about the amateurs he had to deal with.

"Don't be an idiot, *Bobby*," I said. The vehicle was suddenly silent. "Professional criminals are the stupidest people in the world. I know. I've been one of them."

We drove the rest of the way to the Curl Club in silence.

The first thing I saw when we approached the club was a high wall. It looked freshly painted. Tall, flowerless stalks had been planted along the cinder block. I wondered what sort of plant it was.

We pulled up to the wrought-iron gate. The driver lifted a remote control, pressed a button, and the doors slid apart.

Inside, I saw a big lot with a line of cars along the far wall, parked out of sight of the road. The club itself was off to the right, nestled into the side of the hill. It was four stories high, and judging by the long windows, the bottom floor was some sort of auditorium.

To the left, there was a smaller building, only two stories, with a loading dock in the front. Finally, at the far end of the lot sat a little cottage. It had a little weather vane on the top and a mailbox in front. A homey little sign above the door said simply OFFICE.

We didn't drive to the office, as I expected. We pulled right up to the double doors in front of the big building. A small sign above the door said CURL CLUB. It, too, was freshly painted. The rest of the guys began to pile out, momentarily forgetting that they were supposed to be threatening me. I felt the barrel of Bobby's gun tap the back of my head, so I climbed out of the van like a good boy.

"Watch him," Bobby snapped. Two of the gunmen turned their weapons on me again. Floyd smirked like a kid who was going to see his big brother get a spanking. The Kurt Cobain fan opened the doors. Bobby stayed behind me.

The sport van pulled away. I turned to watch it go, thinking about that remote control. I felt a hand shove into my back. "Move." I did.

We walked into the building. The first thing I noticed was that the main floor was even bigger than I'd thought. Not only was the ceiling twenty feet above me, but the floor was sunken.

"Come on," Floyd said. He was still smirking.

We descended the stairs. The room was done up like a

bumpkin's idea of a casino, but done on a budget. The wallpaper and carpets were whorehouse red, which was appropriate, I suppose. I saw a pair of roulette wheels, a handful of craps tables, and a lot of blackjack tables. In the corners were a couple of lonely, neglected-looking slot machines. Judging by the number of customers, business was slow. Maybe these were just the all-day die-hard gamblers.

Against the far wall was a mezzanine with green felt tables. Poker, I guessed. At the end of the mezzanine I saw a fire door marked EXIT.

We turned left and walked across the floor toward a flight of stairs. The boys accompanying me were relaxed, and I didn't do anything to spoil their mood.

We climbed the stairs. One of the men was gasping for breath by the time we reached the hallway at the top. The corridor seemed to run the length of the building, with several doors on the left side but only one on the right. At the far end, a second flight continued up. The Cobain fan rapped on the first door on the left, and someone inside threw the latch. The door opened.

We all walked into a little restaurant. At first I thought it was a bar, but this place had no booths and no dark corners anywhere. At the back I could see a little stage with a brass pole.

Only a single table was occupied. Bobby and I walked toward it, but the others hung back by the door. Seated at the table was a young woman of about twenty, slightly plump, with dull yellow hair, black eyebrows, and pale skin. She smiled at me with painted lips, and her gaze was intense and slightly intimidating. She was plain-looking at best, but she had an aura of furious vitality.

Beside her, a woman of about seventy, with dyed-red hair piled on top of her head and a shapeless dress over her shapeless body, sat slightly hunched. She stared up at me with narrow, suspicious eyes, picked up a long, white cigarette, and took a deep puff.

I assumed I was looking at Phyllis Henstrick.

"This is him," Bobby said.

"Thank you, Bobby," the old woman said. Her voice was raw from years of smoking. "Have a seat." I wasn't sure which of us she was talking to. Bobby pulled out a chair for himself and pointed at the one he wanted me to take. We both sat at the table. She didn't object.

She watched me for a couple of seconds. The silence dragged out. "Thank you for coming," she said finally.

"Thank you for inviting me so politely."

"You're welcome." She was so deadpan I couldn't tell if she was being sarcastic or if she really was unaware that I'd been brought here at gunpoint. She stuck the cigarette between her lips and sucked on it. Bleh. I'd only spent a couple of seconds with her and I wanted to get away. "We have a lot to talk about," she said, "but it's a little early for lunch. Maybe you'd like to go up-stairs. Tiffany can show you the way, and keep you company for a while, if you're feeling a little tense."

I looked at Tiffany. She still had that dangerous glint in her eyes. It had been a long time for me, so of course I was tempted, but the ugly old woman took an ugly puff on her ugly cigarette, and I found the common sense to resist. "I'll pass. Sorry, Tiffany. I'm sure you're very good at your work."

"Not your type, eh?" the old woman said. "I don't have any boys on the premises."

"I'd turn down anything you offered me, except a ride into town. Or breakfast."

She turned to Bobby. "Would you ask Arlo to fix us some turkey sandwiches? And cole slaw." She turned to me. "Do you like cole slaw?"

"Not really."

"Bag of chips for him." She turned to me again. "Do

you have any food allergies? You aren't going to fall over dead if you bite a tomato, are you?"

"Well, I do prefer my arsenic on the side, thanks."

She chuckled and waved Bobby off. He stuck his hand in his pocket, presumably where he had stuck his gun, and gave me a nasty look. He was leaving me alone with this woman, and he didn't want me to try anything stupid.

The old woman stared at me again. "Poison is a little too hifalutin for us, I'm afraid. We don't go into that fancy stuff. Too easy to screw up."

"Uh-huh."

"You did a real number on Floyd and some of my other boys."

"Floyd can't take a hint."

"Well, that's the God's honest truth. But Floyd is a workingman, too. He has a nut to make, just like everyone else. How is he supposed to pay his bills while he can't work?"

"Since he was hurt doing a favor for Wyatt, Wyatt ought to give him a cut from his meth money. If Wyatt doesn't take care of his people, he's not going to have them for long."

She blinked. It was a small thing, but I'd surprised her. She covered it up well, though.

"I know all about taking care of people. The folks in Hammer Bay look out for each other. We need each other. If one of us gets into trouble, all of us suffer."

"Is that why the Dubois brothers are shaking down the local businesses for protection money? Is that why you're running a casino? To help the good folks of Hammer Bay?"

"Emmett and I don't get in each other's way. That's how it has to be. And this place does help the community."

"By taking their money?"

Bobby returned to the table. He sat beside us without comment, his hand still in his pocket.

"And the money from people in Sequim, Port Angeles, and Port Townsend, too. Most of the boys who work here are on my construction crews. When there's a boom time, the boys practice their trades: wiring offices, patching roofs, hanging Sheetrock. Frankly, during a boom this place is a pain in the ass. We're understaffed and too busy. But during a bust this place keeps bread on the table for a lot of local men."

"You convinced me. You're a town hero."

"I'm not a hero, smart-ass. I'm an employer. Communities need employers, no matter what you think of the business they do. When my husband passed, God rest his soul, this place was falling apart. No one was building. No one was playing the cards. The whores were walking petri dishes. You know what it's like to sit in a room with a bunch of whores no one wants to touch? It's depressing. They're not typically great at the art of conversation. No offense, Tiff."

Tiffany shrugged. She was still watching me. She looked like she wanted something from me.

"I turned this place around. Me. I rehired the men my husband, God rest his soul, turned out onto the street, along with a few Cabot let go, too. Do you know how I was able to do all that?"

"Do I have to guess until the food arrives?"

She ignored that, bulling on with her little speech. "Because of Charlie Hammer. Little Charles Hammer the Third opened up a plant and a big office and started putting people to work. Those paychecks went into home repairs and new builds. In other words, to me. And I put a bunch of that money into the pockets of my boys. So you'll understand if I get a little squirrelly when some prick blows into town and threatens to ruin things."

"Am I the prick?" I asked. "I hope so, because I was waiting for you to get to my part in this."

"You had a meeting with Charles. Now your little girlfriend is stalking him, trying to follow him around. I know. You can't keep secrets in a town like this."

I laughed. I couldn't help it. I laughed right in her face.

"What's so funny?" she asked. "I know all the secrets around here. I know the mayor's, the reverend's, the chief's—"

"You know Emmett Dubois's secret?" I asked. I wondered if she meant that he was a shape-shifter, or that he liked to have Tiffany dress him in a diaper and spank him.

"I told you he leaves me alone, didn't I?"

"If you know his secret," I said, "you know he should be stopped."

"If by 'stopped' you mean 'killed,' I'm not sure I can. I have a basketful of questions about him still, and I'm not sure I could take him out clean."

Tiffany turned her gaze on Phyllis as if she was about to volunteer for the job. Phyllis spoke to her as if she could read her mind. "Now, Tiff, I don't want you or Bobby or anyone else going near Emmett Dubois. You're good people, but you're not tall enough to ride that ride."

"Yes, ma'am," Tiffany said. Bobby sat quietly, serenely confident that he could do whatever Phyllis asked of him.

I shifted in my seat. My stomach grumbled. "So you know how he manages to take out his enemies with a pack of dogs when he doesn't actually have a pack of dogs."

She eyed me keenly. "I do. It's pretty obvious to anyone willing to believe. It's that willingness that most people can't manage."

I smiled at her. "I'm willing. For good reason."

"Then I suppose you noticed the plants surrounding the wall out front?"

"I saw them, but I'm no botanist. Wait a minute. Are they wolfsbane?" The old woman nodded. I almost laughed again but I held it back. "Maybe we could help each other. We seem to have a common enemy."

"That doesn't make us friends. I want to know why you're interested in Charles Hammer. Until we get that straight, you're nothing."

A man in kitchen whites entered with a tray. He set a plate with a turkey sandwich and an ice cream scoop of soggy cole slaw next to Phyllis. He set a second plate next to me. The sandwich was identical, but I had a tiny pile of supermarket potato chips. We each received a tall glass of iced tea.

Phyllis gestured at the food. "Tuck in, Nothing."

We picked up our sandwiches. Mine was as dry as plasterboard and just as flavorful. It didn't matter. I hadn't eaten all day. The tea tasted like sour water, so I didn't have more than a sip.

While I chewed, I thought about Phyllis. She was loyal to Hammer, and she had a lot of muscle and cash. One of her men probably had a brother-in-law who worked night security at Hammer Bay Toys, or a wife who worked in his office. She probably also had blackmail material on half the town. She was connected, and I had to figure a way to turn her to our side.

I finished half the sandwich and felt full, but I ate a chip just to keep busy. Phyllis was still working at her sandwich. She reminded me of a bear I'd seen on a nature show—it was tearing into a picnic, hunched over, holding a balled-up pizza in its claws and ducking its head to tear off bites.

I looked over at Tiffany just to have something more pleasant to look at. She stared at me with a creepy insect expression. I got the impression that she was imagining herself having great fun with me, but not in a way I'd especially enjoy.

"So," Phyllis said, then swallowed a lump of dough

and meat. "Why did you meet with Able Katz at the toy offices?"

"I thought the whole town knew that by now."

"I want to hear it from you."

"My boss owns a factory in Africa that could handle some of the manufacturing work."

"Outsourcing."

"Sure. I hope you're not *surprised,* Phyllis." I tried to sound worldly, which I wasn't. "That's how the game is played."

She slapped her hand down on the table. "This isn't a game!"

"And it's his company, not yours. Maybe he started it as a charity, but I don't think he's going to keep doing that forever. His margins are too thin—"

"His company is a success. It's turning a profit, because of our work."

I didn't disagree, and I noticed that she had thrown herself in with the old ladies who were sewing Eagle Rider outfits. "And his ideas. Hard work he can get anywhere."

"He turned you down, didn't he?"

"Able Katz turned us down, on standing orders from Charles. He also agreed to meet with us again. The door's not shut. They're turning a profit now, but everything is boom and bust, just like you said. What happens when they hit a bust period? According to Able, they're overdue. And if they don't sign with us, it'll be someone in Malaysia or the Philippines. In fact, there's a prison in China—"

"Prisoners!" She slammed her hand down on the table, making the plates jump.

I ate another chip while she fumed. I had no idea if anything I'd said made sense. It was a jumble of news stories I'd heard mortared together with bullshit. It seemed to be having the desired effect, though.

I leaned closer to her. "That's not the end of it." I waited a moment for her mind to clear. When I had her full attention again, I continued. "You know what Emmett Dubois is." I paused again, making sure that she kept up with me. "Well, near as I can figure, Charles Hammer is something worse."

"What is this? What bullshit is this?"

I was losing her, but I had to risk it. "How do you think he's been so successful? Even Able Katz doesn't understand it. You remember when I said every business has a boom and bust? Katz knows that Hammer Bay Toys should have had a bust by now. Even a little one. But they haven't."

"Where is this going?"

"The guy is making his success happen *another way,* and the whole town is paying the price."

Bobby was looking at me like I was old fish. I couldn't read the look in Tiffany's eyes at all. Phyllis was squinting suspiciously at me again. "What price is this supposed to be?"

I sat back in my chair. "Where are the kids? Where are the kids in your town? The school yards are empty. The parks, too."

Bobby turned to Phyllis. "This dude is out of his mind."

I watched Phyllis's face. "Imagine what they'd say if you told them about the Dubois brothers."

Phyllis kept staring at me. "Are you saying he's made everyone sterile or something?"

"Worse. I'm saying the kids were here, but now they're gone and no one can remember them. How many girls do you have who have kids? It seems like it should be a pretty common thing for working girls to have a couple of kids. How many do?"

"We look after our girls here," she said. Her jaw was

thrust forward, stubbornly refusing to acknowledge what I was saying, but her eyes looked troubled.

"What about your boys? How many of them are married with kids?"

"There's Ty, and Thomas, and, uh, Richard."

"That's it? Ty, Thomas, and Richard? Three guys out of how many? And how many of those men drive station wagons or minivans—cars no guy would own if he wasn't a father? Your future is almost gone, and you don't even realize it."

Tiffany turned toward Phyllis. "I don't like what he's saying." She stood and circled the table toward me. I tensed, putting both feet on the floor.

Bobby slipped his hand into his pocket. I stayed put.

Tiffany bent over me and patted my face. Her hands were soft but clumsy. She smelled like baby powder. "You must have been having a bad dream or something." She tilted my face up and looked into my eyes. She had the stare of a praying mantis. After a few seconds, she saw what she wanted to see and went back to her chair.

"Do you see those men behind you?" Phyllis asked. I turned and looked at them. "Any one of them," she continued, "would put a bullet in your head if I asked them to." Behind me, Bobby coughed. "We could drop your body in the rain forest. No one would find you. No one's found any of them."

I turned back to her. "Killing people is easy," I said. "It doesn't impress me. What would impress me is if you could wake up and see what's going on."

"All that talking must have left you parched," Tiffany said. "Why—"

"Tiff," Phyllis said sharply. "The boys over there are getting bored. Why don't you talk to them for a while?"

Tiffany looked a little stung as she retreated toward the door. I didn't pay much attention.

"So," Phyllis said, "How is it that you can blow into town and see what's going on, but we can't?"

I couldn't tell her anything about Annalise or the spells she'd put on me. "Willingness to believe," I said. It was the wrong moment to play coy with her, but I didn't have a choice. Annalise was already unhappy that I'd showed the scrap of wood to Emmett Dubois. I didn't want to repeat the mistake.

"What about your lady friend?"

"Never mind her."

Phyllis turned to Bobby, "Speaking of which, they're late."

Bobby took out a cell phone and started to dial.

Oh no.

Phyllis looked at me. "We'll ask her when she gets here."

"You didn't send men after her, did you? You didn't give them guns or anything?"

"Don't break a sweat, kid, I told them not to hurt her."

I didn't know whether to laugh or cry. The salty chips had made me thirsty; I took a swallow of iced tea just to bide my time. So much for recruiting Henstrick. I felt a little dizzy.

"No answer," Bobby said.

"Don't bother," I said. "They're dead."

Phyllis glared at me. "What do you mean, dead?"

"I mean, if you sent men to strong-arm my boss the way they've been trying to strong-arm me—with guns and knives and bad manners—they are dead. *Thirty* men couldn't kidnap my boss. Get it? If you want to talk to her, visit her yourself or send someone to ask politely."

My head started to feel light. The lights went dim. I suddenly felt very tired.

"Dammit," I heard Phyllis say. Her voice sounded

far away. "Send someone after them. Find out what's going on."

Then, darkness. My last thought was that I was helpless now. They could do anything they wanted to me. I took that thought into oblivion.

CHAPTER THIRTEEN

I awoke suddenly. I was sitting up, leaning against a pile of pillows. My hands were bound.

I'd been handcuffed to the post of a bed. I rolled off the mattress. I didn't want to think about who had been on it before.

Each of my wrists had a handcuff of its own. One end was locked on me; the other end was locked tightly around the thinnest spot in the post, which was about the width of my two thumbs. It looked like a hack setup, but after ten minutes of trying I still hadn't managed to free myself. So much for hack.

The room was slightly more homey than a hospital room but slightly less homey than a Best Western. The wallpaper, curtains, and bedcovers were decorated with a dense, multicolored pattern that reminded me of a counter at a diner, like they were designed to hide stains.

A big LED clock on the bedside stand told me the time was 8:45. There were no windows anywhere, so I couldn't tell if it was morning or evening. I was hungry again. Damn.

No one had left any saws or key rings nearby. I wanted my ghost knife. I closed my eyes and *reached* for it, searching for the slightest tickle that would tell me it was close. Nothing. If I survived this, I'd have to practice sensing the ghost knife from farther and farther away.

I wrapped my arms around the post, stood on the box

spring, and laid my shoulder into it, using my weight to try to break it off. No good. A better plan would have been to kick the top of the post, but that would have made noise. I didn't want to let people know that I'd woken up.

I lay back on the bed, set my heels on the top of the post, and grabbed the chain of the cuffs. Then I pressed with my feet, holding myself in place with the cuffs. I had leverage, but the strain on my wrists prevented me from using my full strength.

I heard a key turn in the lock. I redoubled my efforts, gritting my teeth against the pain, but I didn't hear the slightest sound of cracking wood.

The door opened. A voice said, "You were right. He's up."

"Hear hear," a woman said. "Stop that right now."

I let my feet drop to the ground and stood. A man and a woman approached me. They were in their late forties and looked as average as any supermarket shopper. He was balding and walked with a plump shuffle. She was heavily done up and carefully balanced on high heels.

She carried a tray with a platter of fish and chips on it. "Here you go, dear. You've been up here a couple hours, and I'm sure you're hun—"

I kicked the platter out of her hands. Greasy fish and dark vinegar splashed onto the ceiling and wallpaper opposite us. "Go fuck yourself."

The woman stepped back. "Well!"

The man became indignant. "You have some nerve," he said, huffing out his cheeks.

"Try it!" I shouted at him, my voice rebounding off the walls of the room. They were taken aback by how quickly things had escalated. "Even with my hands cuffed I'll stomp you."

The woman laid a hand on the man's shoulder. Her long, fake nails dug into his shoulder.

I shut my eyes, closing out as much of the rest of the world as I could. I *felt* for the ghost knife. Nothing. The supermarket shoppers weren't carrying it. They turned and left.

I rolled back onto the bed and returned to working on the post. The encounter with the shoppers had fired my anger, and I strained even harder, but I couldn't crack the damn wood. If they already knew I was awake, there was no reason to keep quiet. I lay on my back and started kicking the top of the post.

Kick kick kick. I wasn't being secretive or clever about it. I wasn't in the mood for either. Tools would have been great, but I didn't have any. If I could have tipped the bed on its side, I would have laid my weight against the frame and broken the post that way, but I couldn't move my hands far enough to get decent leverage on the whole bed. So I kicked and kicked, letting my anger block some of the pain as the cuffs dug into my wrists.

Finally, I heard wood crack. I began to kick frantically then, until the wood splintered enough that the post bent at an angle.

I rolled to my feet and put my shoulder against it, breaking it off. I was free.

I lifted the broken hunk of wood. The empty ends of the handcuffs swung free.

The lock on the door clicked and the door opened. Bobby entered. He held a .38 in his hand. "You've been making a lot of noise up here."

"Quietly waiting to be killed is too hifalutin for me."

He didn't seem to remember the reference, and I didn't care. He waved at me with the gun, encouraging me to follow him. I tossed the broken post aside and followed him into the hall. There were three more men waiting out there, along with Tiffany.

She was looking at me like a hungry dog eyeing a steak.

I knew right then, from the look on their faces, that they were taking me away to kill me.

"We found our boys," Bobby said.

"The ones you sent for my boss?"

"They were friends of mine."

I wanted to tell him that was the price of playing gangster, but there was no point. "Next time you want to talk to her, be sure to use the magic word."

"I think we'll send her a different sort of message."

I looked at the other men. They had guns but didn't look happy to be there. They weren't gunmen; they were carpenters or Sheetrockers or whatever. They looked like guys with an unpleasant job to do and they looked like they wanted to get it over with.

Bobby twisted my arms behind my back and clamped the empty ends of the handcuffs onto my wrists. I'd never been double-cuffed before. I guessed they were a little nervous about me.

There were doors along both sides of the hall. The carpet was deep red with faint brown stains.

Bobby turned to the fattest of them. "Bring the van around to the back."

"I hope that's not your personal van," I said to his retreating back. "Bloodstains don't come out."

Tiffany's expression was still, but her eyes were wide with wonder. "I want to do it. Is that all right? I brought my knife. I want to do it." She sounded a little breathless.

"Shut up," Bobby said. He wasn't taking any pleasure in this, but he was being professional about it.

"I'll make it quick, if you want," she said, and glanced back at me. "I can do it whatever way you want."

"Fine," Bobby said. "Just shut up about it."

We started walking down the hall. Tiffany was ahead of me on the left, leading the way. Her stride was measured and careful, as though she was hyperaware of herself and her surroundings. Bobby was behind me again, this time on my left as well. A young, clear-eyed kid who seemed barely out of high school was behind me on the right. In front of me on the right was the same tubby, middle-aged guy who had searched me in the Chevy van. I wondered if he was still carrying my things. I also wondered why I was cooperating with my killers.

I stopped walking and turned around. The kid nearly bumped into me. Bobby lifted his gun and pointed it at my heart. "Keep going," he said.

The kid followed Bobby's lead. He pointed his gun at my chest, although he was still much closer to me than he should have been.

I closed my eyes. I could *feel* the ghost knife behind me.

"Why should I make this easy for you?" I asked.

If Bobby had been smart, he would have lied. He would have told me that he didn't *really* want to kill me, that he was going to let me go if I promised to disappear so completely that his boss never found out. But he'd seen too many movies. "Because if you don't," he said, "you're going to hurt. A lot."

I *reached* for my spell. The ghost knife slid out of the chubby man's pocket and landed in my hand. At the same moment, I heard Tubby sigh and stagger. It must have passed through part of him on the way to me.

I looked at the ceiling. They did, too. I cut the handcuff chain with my ghost knife. My hands were free.

The next part happened very fast.

I swept my left hand upward as quickly as possible and struck the kid's gun arm, batting it aside. The gun went off, but the barrel was pointing past me. I heard the boom of the shot and felt the rush of air as it passed my shoulder.

At the same time, I threw the ghost knife at Bobby's gun. Again, I was too slow. Bobby squeezed the trigger.

I felt the pressure of the bullet striking my chest, but there was no pain. *He killed me*, I thought. *Shouldn't it hurt if he killed me?*

Hot gas billowed over my neck, and a burning speck struck beside my Adam's apple. The spot where he'd shot me didn't hurt. I didn't feel anything there. There would be no wound, either, if Annalise's tattoos had held. I didn't look down to check.

The ghost knife slid through Bobby's gun, cutting it in two, then vanished into his chest. I heard him gasp.

My back was still exposed, and I'd left the kid too long. I lunged at him, punching him on the side of the head and ripping the weapon from his hand. I grabbed the back of his head, spinning him between me and Tubby and Tiffany.

I didn't have to worry. Tiffany was frozen in place; whatever she'd imagined would happen, this wasn't it. And Tubby was on his knees, a bloody gunshot wound in his chest. Then he fell onto his back. He wasn't going to get up again.

I don't remember a lot about the next few seconds. There was a feeling of tremendous pressure inside my skull. I know I didn't shoot the kid's gun. I know Tiffany was much quicker with her knife than I'd expected, and I hit her too hard on the side of her face.

What I do remember is standing over Bobby, Tiffany, and the other two and slicing the kid's bloody gun in two. One of Bobby's teeth was still wedged in the barrel.

I'd broken their bones, but at least they'd live. They were better off than Tubby. It took every ounce of willpower I had to keep from vomiting all over them.

Doors all along the hallway swung open and heads poked out. Geniuses. They hear gunshots and rush toward them. The peeping face nearest to me was Rev. Wilson.

I stepped around the bodies on the floor to the dead man. He had forgotten to shave that morning. I took Cabot's gun from him and pocketed it. I also took back my wallet and keys.

After a moment of indecision, Wilson rushed toward me. He was wearing long black pants but no shirt. "What is happening here?" He looked me in the eye for the first time.

"These guys need an ambulance," I said. "But I'm afraid this guy is gone." I was talking too fast. I wanted to be cool and collected, but I felt anything but.

"Why did you—" Wilson began.

I heard a commotion behind me. Three more men had appeared at the far end of the hall. They rushed toward me, guns in hand. One held a walkie-talkie to his mouth.

"Help them," I said, and rushed past him. Another man rounded the corner of the hall ahead of me.

The door nearest to me was the one Rev. Wilson had come out of. I ducked inside and locked the door. I had a gun, but I didn't want to use it. There were too many people around, and I wasn't some badass hitman. Also, I had already gotten more lucky than I deserved. If Bobby had aimed at my head instead of my heart . . .

A woman was standing next to me. She was stark naked and unashamed. I guessed she was about forty-five, with long, auburn hair and a simple, honest face. Wilson had good taste.

"What's going on out there?" she asked.

"General naughtiness."

She reached toward my chest and tugged at the bullet hole in my shirt. It was scorched with powder burns. "I see that," she said.

For a moment I thought she would panic just as I was about to. "I don't want trouble—"

"Of course not. Come this way." She led me through the room into a second, smaller room. She was very calm.

"Bobby and the boys have been getting worse and worse over the last few years. They used to be working guys protecting their own. Lately they've been acting like thugs."

There was a second door, next to a window that showed the forest slope behind. It was the way out. She took a key ring from a hook. "Not everyone wants to come in through the casino. We have a couple of rooms with a back door."

She unlocked the door and swung it open. The sun had gone down, but there was still a little light in the sky. I stepped out onto a metal staircase. There was a little carport four stories down.

I turned toward the naked woman. "Thank you."

A shot ricocheted off the metal stairs. I didn't see where it came from, and I didn't hang around to find out. I pushed my way back inside and shut the door. I heard the faint sound of construction boots running up the metal steps.

Damn. So much for sneaking out the back.

I ran back into the bedroom. The knob rattled but didn't turn. Someone's meaty fist pounded on the door.

"Keep out!" the woman yelled. "He's got a gun!"

For a moment, I thought that she could see it in my jacket pocket, but then I realized that she was just buying time. She came close to me and said in a low voice, "The cops—"

"They won't be on my side," I said. "Get over in that corner. Get as low as you can."

She did. Someone was still pounding on the door. They'd be inside in just a minute or two, as soon as someone with a key turned up.

I leapt to the other side of the bed and knelt on the floor. I jabbed the ghost knife into the floor, holding it by the barest corner so it would reach as far as possible, then I slid it along the floor, cutting a rough circle.

The circle didn't drop through to the floor below. I heard jangling keys on the other side of the hall door. "What are you doing over there?" the woman whispered. I wished I knew her name.

They'd be inside in a moment. I could have taken Cabot's gun from my pocket, but I didn't. Instead, I jumped onto the circle I'd just cut. I heard the lock disengage.

Wood splintered, and I fell through the floor.

I fell about ten feet and struck a tiled floor. My knees jarred, and I rolled to the side. It hurt, but I'd managed not to twist my ankle.

I rolled against something soft. It was a big, soft pile of sheets and bedcovers, and I missed it by two feet. There was a smear of red blood on several of the sheets, and it took me a second to realize that it had come from me. My hands were covered in blood.

I was in a laundry room. Three big industrial washers and dryers stood against the outside wall. There were no windows.

"Sweet sainted Mary!" A tiny old woman with a thick brogue stared at me. I stood and ran past her toward the door.

"Keep away from the hole," I told her. "Men with guns are going to be coming through in a moment."

I ran past the dryers and saw that they ran on natural gas. I stopped. The gas line joined the machines at the top. I yanked open the dryer doors, shutting off the flames. Then I traced the gas line along the ceiling to where it disappeared into the wall. There was a shutoff valve there. I cut it out.

The old woman gaped at me.

"Gosh," I said to her. "You have a gas leak. Better tell those boys upstairs with the guns."

I saw shadows move in the space above the hole. I turned and ran through the double doors. The old woman was shouting something, but I didn't know who she was shouting at. I just hoped she had the sense to pull the fire alarm.

I recognized this hallway. Beyond the opposite wall was the little restaurant where Phyllis had drugged me. I ran toward the stairs. I would rather have avoided the casino, but that didn't seem possible.

Two men came up the stairs. One of them was Floyd. He pointed at me with his bandaged hands, and the guy next to him lifted his weapon.

I ducked to the side as the gun boomed. I didn't feel the bullet hit me, but there wasn't a lot of cover in the hallway.

There was a door next to me. I yanked it open and dove inside. Another shot boomed, and something tugged at my pant leg. I didn't feel any pain.

I was in a linen closet. Neat stacks of folded sheets lined the walls around me. I pulled the door shut, and the darkness gave my animal brain a moment's comfort, tricking it into thinking I was hiding.

I knew the wall in front of me led to the outside world, but it was also three stories from the ground. I wouldn't make that jump.

I lay down and cut another hole in the floor. This time, I angled the ghost knife outward so that it wouldn't catch.

Gunshots tore through the closet door. The sound was terrifyingly close, and splinters rained down on my back. I cursed and resisted the urge to draw Cabot's gun and shoot back. That would be a losing game for me.

I finished the cut, and the section of floor fell away. At the same moment, the fire alarm went off.

I looked down through the hole. As I'd hoped, I was just above the mezzanine. I slipped through the hole and landed on one of the poker tables.

The fire alarm was clanging loudly, and everyone stood

around and looked at one another. No one wanted to be the first to head for the exit. Hadn't they heard the gunshots?

I jumped off the table, pushing aside a man in a UPS uniform who had a nice stack of chips beside him. I glanced over at the long flight of stairs. Rev. Wilson, still without his shirt, led several men toward the exit. They were carrying Bobby, Tiffany, and the dead chubby guy and walked straight across the floor in full view.

I turned toward the exit I'd seen earlier. There was one man standing there. He wasn't looking at me and didn't seem to have seen me come through the hole in the ceiling. I rushed toward him, taking out Cabot's gun to get his attention.

When he did turn toward me, he looked unhappy. For a second I thought he would jump the rail.

"Hold still," I snapped at him. "Give me your gun."

He gave me his .38. Henstrick must have bought them in bulk. "Hey, man—"

"Shut up and get these people out of the building. There's a gas leak. Hurry!"

I pushed past him and went through the doorway. The night was no darker than it had been two minutes ago. I started down the metal stairs, just as exposed as I was before, but as I'd hoped, there were no shots. The trip was shorter, too.

It would have been nice to lose myself in a crowd of people fleeing the fire alarm, but the patrons were too slow and I wasn't going to wait around for them. I ran along the back of the building, away from the gate. I needed a vehicle to get away, and a remote to open the fence. I could cut my way through the fence or the wall, but fleeing on foot would be suicide.

I ran around the building and spotted the sport van, still parked in the same spot. The gate was closed. They'd open it for the ambulance and fire truck, but I didn't want to wait. I sprinted for the van, cut a hole in the driver's window, and unlocked it.

Someone shouted, "There he is!"

Cynthia's Escalade backed toward me. "Get in!" she yelled, and the passenger door swung open.

I looked back at the minivan. The remote sat on the dashboard. I grabbed it and jumped into the open Escalade.

Cynthia gunned the engine. The door swung closed on my ankle. I cursed at the sharp pain and pointed the remote through the windshield. There was only one button. I pressed it.

A gunshot shattered the back window. Cynthia screamed and ducked her head. Out of habit, she slammed on the brakes, but before I could say anything she hit the accelerator. The gate slowly rolled open. The parking lot was long, and whoever was shooting was going to have plenty of time to get a bead on us.

I slid closer to Cynthia and draped my arm over her. With my forearm hanging beside her head and neck, my tattoos would provide her some protection, but not a lot.

A bullet punched through the front of the driver's side window and snapped a hole in the windshield. Cynthia cried out just a little. The gate slid farther open. I thought it would be wide enough for us to clear, but I wasn't certain. I saw a woman running toward the opening. Her course put her in line with our bumper. Cynthia eased off the gas pedal, as though she was afraid to hit her. Something struck the back of my chair, passing inches from my ribs.

I slammed my palm on the horn. The blare made the woman look at us with a startled, furious expression, then jump aside.

More glass shattered, and I heard bullets punching holes in the SUV. Cynthia ducked low, barely peeking over the dashboard. She spit out a stream of curses. I would have cursed, too, if I could have unclenched my teeth. Instead I held on to the dashboard, hating guns, hating Phyllis Henstrick, hating Annalise and everyone who had led me into this mess, including myself.

Just as I thought the barrage had gone on too long, and that our luck couldn't hold anymore, we were through the gate. Cynthia wrenched the wheel to the side and we skidded along the road. The bullets stopped.

An ambulance with flashing lights and blaring sirens raced at us. Cynthia swerved and slammed on the brakes, and the ambulance roared by. I turned around. Through the shattered back window, I could see a few people running through the open gate.

"Oh my God," Cynthia said, her voice shaky. "Oh my God."

I still had the remote in my hand. If I pressed it, the ambulance might have trouble getting the injured people out, but Henstrick's amateur gunmen might be delayed long enough for me to get away. I didn't press the button.

"Keep it together," I said. My voice sounded loud in my ears. "Keep going. People are coming through the gates."

She turned the car and gunned the engine. We roared up the asphalt road, passing the supermarket. Cynthia bared her teeth. She had tears on her cheeks.

There was a red light up ahead. She wasn't slowing down. "Light! Light!" I shouted. I leaned over and stomped on the brake pedal. The Escalade skidded to a halt.

A woman in a Volvo station wagon loaded with groceries was waiting to pull out of the supermarket lot. She gaped up at the bullet-ridden SUV.

The light changed, and Cynthia eased into the intersection, carefully turning the wheel with shaking hands.

She checked her speedometer several times. She drove like it was her first time behind the wheel. The car rattled and clanked.

"What should I do?" she asked me.

"Drive to your house."

She did. We got out of the car and walked around it. There were two holes in the windshield. I hadn't noticed the second, even though it must have happened right in front of me.

Three of the bullet holes were clustered low on the driver's door. Those must have passed under our seats. Four more were sprayed across the back panel, two very close to the back left tire. Someone had tried to shoot it out. There were two more bullet holes in the front fender. Judging by the way her engine had sounded on the way home, I suspected her engine block had gone the way of the dodo.

"You're bleeding!" Cynthia said. She touched my shoulder blade. I felt a tiny sting. I had no idea how I'd gotten hurt. "Come inside."

She led me toward her front door. I looked up at the round tower room at the top of the house. Cabot had said that Charles spent all his time at the tower now. I wondered if he was up there, and what I would do if I found him.

Cynthia led me up the stairs to a large bathroom in the back. While I sat on the edge of the tub, she took a box of Band-Aids and a squeeze tube of disinfectant from the medicine cabinet. She took off my jacket, felt the weight in one of the pockets, and reached inside.

"You had a gun the whole time? Why didn't you shoot back?"

"Someone might have gotten killed."

We started laughing. It was a release for her, I knew, but my own laughter only increased the pressure building inside of me. I thought about Bobby's tooth, and the chubby guy lying dead on the floor. I thought about the way Tiffany's face seemed to *give* when I hit her. I kept laughing, but the sound of it scared me. I was alive. I wanted to shout the word at the tile ceiling just to hear it bounce around me. *Alive.*

I clenched my teeth and forced myself to be quiet. I shouldn't have been laughing, because whatever I was feeling at the moment, it wasn't happiness. Hammer Bay was full of people doing terrible things for the best reasons. It made me furious. I made me feel dark and low to the ground and ready to kill. This town was making me into something ugly and dangerous. I had to get away, but I knew I couldn't. Not without setting things right.

Of course, Annalise and I were here to kill whoever we had to kill to stop the magic and save the kids in Hammer Bay. I was here to do terrible things for the best of reasons, too. I hated this town, but I knew it was a mirror image of myself.

I didn't like it. I didn't have to like it. I was here to be vicious, to beat, kill, or humiliate anyone I had to, and I wasn't going to stop until all the magic had been expunged from this place and things were set right. And God help me, I was finally ready to do it. I was ready to go as far as I had to go to get the job done.

Cynthia told me to take off my shirt. I did. She dabbed at my shoulder blade with a wad of tissues. "This isn't bad at all. It's barely a scratch." I didn't answer. "They were terrible shots, weren't they?"

"Most people are."

"No one has ever . . . do you think they knew it was me? Do you think they were trying to shoot me?"

I understood. She probably had the only Escalade in town, and most people would recognize it.

"No," I told her. "If they had realized it was you, I don't think they would have shot at us. Henstrick is still loyal to your family. I think they were just all worked up and not thinking straight. In fact, I think you should expect a call and an apology from Henstrick."

I could feel her rubbing something onto my shoulder blade. It stung. Her hair brushed my shoulder, and goose bumps ran across my back.

"Do you go there often?" I had a hard time keeping the suspicion out of my voice.

"No. After I dropped you off at Uncle Cabot's office, I didn't go for a cup of coffee like you said. I didn't realize how I would feel when I saw you go into that building alone—for me—and I couldn't just go off and eat a banana muffin or something while you risked your life. So I stayed close just in case. I don't know what I was going to do, exactly, but I hated feeling like a coward.

"So, I was parked down the street when you came out. I saw those men grab you outside the office, and I recognized Bobby, of course. I followed you to the casino and lost two grand at the blackjack table waiting for you to turn up."

That made sense, and I was grateful that she'd come for me. "The gun is Cabot's," I told her. "He was planning to shoot himself, but I convinced him to get out of town."

"Thank you," she said in a quiet voice.

"You saved my life tonight."

"We're even, then." She taped a gauze pad onto my shoulder blade. It felt like a big pad, but the scratch didn't hurt much. I wondered again if her brother was in the house somewhere. She patted my shoulder with a dismissive finality. "All done."

I stood. She was very close to me, and she seemed so small. Her hands were still trembling. I took her hand and held it in mine. I still felt a sickening rage inside. It took all the self-control I had to touch her gently. "Thank you."

We held hands for a moment. She felt warm and soft and impossibly fragile. I could have squeezed that hand and broken it to mash. The thought terrified me. I was as gentle as I could be.

She let my hand go, and it fell to my side. She stared up at me. Her brown eyes seemed to have turned black. "What next?" she asked.

"What's in that round room at the top of the house?"

"That's my bedroom."

"Take me there."

She hesitated for a moment. It was just a moment. She looked up into my eyes, then took my hand and led me to the stairs. I carried my shirt and jacket.

We entered the round room. It was tastefully decorated, I guess, with a lot of muted green pastels. Every surface had at least one candle and, for some reason, a stuffed rabbit.

Charles Hammer wasn't here. As far as I could tell, he had never been in this room. I was vaguely disappointed as I laid my jacket and shirt on a chair. I was absolutely ready to shoot him dead. I didn't know if I'd ever find myself feeling so ready to kill someone again.

Cynthia stood a few feet from me. "This is it," she said, as if waiting to see if I approved of her inner sanctum.

I wasn't going to kill Charles Hammer today. "Take off your clothes," I said.

She did. I took mine off at the same time.

I saw what I knew I'd see. She had a tattoo on her shoulder blade right where Cabot had his. She had an iron gate, too.

She knew what had happened to all those kids. What was still happening.

She lunged at me and we kissed. We were wild and desperate. I was still filled with rage, but I tried as hard as I could to keep it from her. I liked her.

Even though she had known all along. She had known. She had known. She had known. She had known. . . .

We made our way to the bed. It was good to feel alive. It was good to touch someone. It was good to feel like a human animal, to smell and taste and hear and see someone close.

She responded to me more powerfully than any woman ever had before, but I could not stop thinking about those dead children, about the flames, about the pale, gray worms, and that she knew all about it. It made me furious and sick at the same moment that we were grasping at life.

When my own release finally came, my mind was full of images of murder, and there was no pleasure in it at all.

CHAPTER FOURTEEN

I woke up without realizing I'd fallen asleep. The gray sunlight was shining on my face, and the bed jostled slightly.

Cynthia was sitting on the other side of the bed with her back to me. She was wrapped in the top sheet. I could see the iron gate on her back. The thing that had made me sick with anger last night now seemed like another unfortunate fact of life in Hammer Bay. Who was I to judge Cynthia? Or anyone? I was not exactly pure myself.

I reached out to her and touched her shoulder. She let me, but she didn't respond. She didn't seem angry or resentful. She simply didn't react. I took my hand away.

"Last night was powerful," she said in a low voice. "It was wild and strange and very powerful, but I don't think I'm going to want to do that again. Not ever. It was good. It was great, in fact, but it scared me, too. I don't want to visit that place again."

"I understand," I told her.

"Are you sure?" she asked.

She turned toward me. The look on her face made me ashamed. I wished I could start over again, more gently this time, but her expression said it all. Never again. "I'm sure."

"Do you want some coffee?"

I nodded. She stood and dropped the sheet. I watched her put on pair of jeans and a T-shirt. I couldn't help imagining her on the floor, screaming, as black steam jetted from the iron gate on her back. She told me that she would wait for me downstairs and left.

Alone, I covered my face with my hands. I couldn't see or hear anything. I looked inside myself and didn't recognize what I saw.

I stood and dressed in the clothes I'd tossed onto the floor. My shirt still smelled of gunpowder, and there was a powder-burned hole in the center.

I followed the smell of coffee downstairs. Cynthia stood by the bubbling coffee machine with her phone to her ear. The clock on the wall said it was just after 11 A.M.

She hung up the phone. "You were right," she said. "Phyllis left me a message asking if I was all right and saying she was sorry her people were so stupid. She offered to pay for any damages."

"I thought as much."

"What about you? Is she going to come after you? I could call her and tell her to leave you alone."

"Thanks, but it's better if you don't get mixed up in that any more than you already have."

"God, I nearly got shot last night. It doesn't seem real."

"It will when your next car-insurance bill comes."

She laughed. I was glad to hear it. We stood beside the counter, about three feet from each other. We didn't touch.

"How do you like your coffee?" she asked.

"I'll have it however you're having it. I don't care."

"Soy sauce and horseradish, coming up."

This time we both laughed. She set our cups on the table, and we sat. I took a sip. It was very dark and very sweet. I liked it.

"So," she said to me. "You never did tell me why you met with Able Katz."

"Tell me about the seizures," I said. "Have you ever had them?"

The remnants of her smile faded away. She stirred her coffee. "Is it like that?"

"Like what?"

"Am I supposed to give you dirt on my family? On my own brother?"

"I think you misread me."

"It's just a toy company, for Christ's sake—"

"I don't give a damn about the toy company. I don't care about that."

"You don't care about a multimillion-dollar contract for your boss? Isn't that why you came to town?"

"No, it isn't. And you should know better than that." She didn't respond. "There are strange things happening in town, aren't there? People being attacked by mysterious packs of dogs, for instance?"

I let her think about that for a minute. She stared at me, trying to guess how much I knew. "Why are you asking about Charles's seizures? You think it has something to do with the people who have been mauled?"

"I won't know until I ask."

"Well, it doesn't," she said. She took another sip. "My father had them, and his father, too. Charles has them worse than Pop, but it's a family thing."

"Do you have them?"

"Not so far," she said. "It's always a possibility, though. Charles's episodes didn't start until two years ago. My dad never had them as a kid, either, according to Uncle Cabot. Scary thought, huh?" She didn't look up from her coffee when she said it and she didn't look scared.

"I've been having a lot of scary thoughts lately. What about the dogs?"

"It . . . I don't know. I wish I did. I'd tell Emmett if I knew who was using those dogs. It's a horrible, horrible way to go. I get shivers just thinking about it."

I didn't believe her. I wanted her to be on my side in this, and not only because of the help she could give me, and I certainly didn't want to fight with her. "Are you sure you don't know anything? Maybe there's something about the killings that you would mention if you had a little time to think about it. Something funny about each one."

"Like what?"

"Like, did these people have enemies in common? Did they die at the same time of day, or at the same sort of place? Anything in common? Anything unusual?"

"Stanley Koch died in the alley behind his bar. Wilma Semple ran off the road up the highway. That was just a car wreck, though, although they said a cougar got to her before the ambulance did. Henry the grocer was mauled on his loading dock along with his night custodian, a man named Johnson, I think."

"What's the town gossip?"

"When Wilma died, everyone thought it was Harlan. She had just divorced him and taken up with another man. And Stan had just barred him from his place for a month for bad behavior. But Harlan didn't even know Henry. He did all his shopping at the Safeway."

"Did Wilma own a business in town?"

"No, she didn't."

"Then who had she taken up with?"

"Luke Dubois."

"So you know the Dubois brothers are behind this."

"Lots of people think so. Only a couple will say it out loud. Luke had been after Wilma for years, though. He was pretty torn up when she was killed."

"You think she found out something that she wasn't supposed to?"

"Like what? That the cops in this town extort protection money? The whole town knows that."

"I mean, that the Dubois brothers are werewolves."

She flinched. "What?" She was honestly surprised. I was relieved to see it.

"Werewolves."

"Are you joking?"

"Phyllis Henstrick said it was obvious to anyone willing to believe."

She stared off into space for a minute or two, holding the cup halfway to her lips. I took a sip, enjoying the warmth in my belly. It felt good to sit here with her like this. I tried to imagine myself sitting here day after day, talking to Cynthia while we shared coffee. I thought it would be a good life.

It was never going to happen. Not while Annalise was around, and not while Charles still had his "seizures."

"Is that true?" she asked.

"I think it is."

"What should we do about it?"

"*We* aren't going to do a thing about it."

"Okay, then. What are *you* going to do about it?"

"I'm going to cure them, if I can."

It was the truth, but it wasn't the whole truth. As far as I knew, the only cure was the most permanent one.

"Wow." That was all she said. "There's so much ugliness in the world."

I looked down at the table. Some of that ugliness came from me, and it was only going to get worse. "Tell me about the kids."

The color drained from her face. She didn't answer. She just gaped at me.

"Tell me about the kids in Hammer Bay who have been burning to death. Yeah, I know about it. I have the same tattoo you do. It twinges whenever Charles has a seizure, just like yours. Tell me about them."

"I . . ." She wouldn't look at me. She wouldn't speak.

I reached out and gently took her hand. Whether that made her feel comforted, trapped, or both, I couldn't say.

"What do you want me to say?"

"Everything," I said. "Start wherever you have to, but I want everything."

She pulled her hand away, lifted her cup, and drained it.

"My best friend ever since I was six was Daphne. We went through grade school together, high school, everything. She's divorced now. Her ex is a creep, but she had the most wonderful little girl. She was bold and adventurous—she drove Daph crazy. Daphne couldn't keep up with her, but I loved that little girl, and I knew she'd grow up to be someone wonderful.

"One day I met Daphne for lunch, and she didn't have her little girl with her. I asked if she'd found a sitter, and Daphne said her dogs could play in the backyard just fine. Her dogs. I asked who was looking after her daughter, and she said, 'Who?' Just like that. 'Who?' As if her little girl had never existed.

"Then she started talking about leaving Hammer Bay. What did she have to keep her here, besides a best friend? She had no roots, no family. She was gonna pursue her dreams while she was young enough to do it.

"Eventually, we got into a fight about it. Believe me, that little girl was worth more than any dream anyone has ever had. It was an ugly fight, and some of the people in the diner who knew us butted in. They kept telling me that Daphne didn't have a daughter, that she'd never had one."

Cynthia's hands were trembling. She pressed them against the table. "Daphne started worrying about me. She thought I was having a psychotic break or something. She brought me to her apartment to convince me that she'd never had a kid. She walked me through the rooms, saying, 'See? No one lives here but me.' And all I could see were these little toys on the floor and Golden Books on the shelves."

Her voice caught in her throat. She took a deep,

quavering breath. "Daphne left town a couple weeks later. I should have gone, too, but I couldn't. By then, I'd seen it with my own eyes." She stopped talking. She looked down at her empty cup. "There was a baby in a baby carriage . . ."

She stopped again. She had said enough.

I stood and refilled our cups. I brought the sugar to the table. She scooped and stirred but didn't look at me. After a few minutes, I asked: "What did you do about it?"

"I hired a private investigator. I told him that something strange was happening to the children in town. He thought I was crazy, but he was happy to take my money. He searched around, interviewed people, the whole thing. Emmett scared him away after a week. All I got out of it was a bill and a useless report."

"Why do you think you can remember and no one else can?"

"My tattoo. Isn't that what you already said?"

"I'm just making sure we're having the same conversation. Cabot said you got it from your grandfather."

"Why do you think he would put it there? So that we would know when something went wrong? If that's so, I don't think I've been much use—"

"I don't think that's why. I think it's there to protect you and the rest of the family from that fire. Your grandfather was playing with dangerous magic, and he took pains to protect his own in case things got out of control."

"I . . ." She couldn't finish that sentence, and she couldn't look me in the eye. "I don't want to believe that."

"But you do."

"Yeah, I guess I do. I don't have a choice anymore, do I?"

An idea occurred to me. "You're the one who gave the boarding school scholarship to Bill Terril's grandson, aren't you?"

She shrugged. "I started the scholarship after the private investigator flopped. Well, after the relocation assistance flopped, too."

"Hold on. Start over for me, please."

She sighed and sipped her coffee. "The investigator was a waste of time. I didn't know what to do. I knew people had to get their kids out of Hammer Bay, but how was I supposed to convince them to go? The truth sure as hell wasn't going to do it.

"I started a relocation fund. I offered ten grand to any family with kids who wanted to move out of town. Only fourteen families signed on. This was right as Charlie's toy company was taking off, and people thought I was trying to sabotage him. I got a lot of nasty looks, not to mention gentle lectures from concerned townspeople.

"It wasn't enough, though. The kids . . . it was still happening. So I started a scholarship fund for boarding schools across the country. I wasn't prepared for how popular that one was. I wrote checks for eighty-seven kids to go to Oregon, Massachusetts, even Canada. It's not easy to find spots for that many kids."

I remembered the empty house just next door to this one. "That sounds expensive."

She still wouldn't look up at me. "Not all of my assets are liquid. I had to scramble for some of that money, sure, but I could do more, if people were willing or if I knew what to do. I wish . . ."

"What? Tell me."

"Before Daphne left town, I convinced her . . . actually, I paid her to get one of these." She pointed to the iron gate on her shoulder. "I paid extra to have it copied exactly. *Exactly.* Daph didn't like it, but she had already enrolled at the University of Washington and needed money. She was already leaving me."

I knew where this was heading. "But it didn't work."

"No."

There was more to casting a spell than tracing a couple of lines. If she didn't know that, she didn't have the spell book Annalise and I wanted to find. Hell, she might not even know it existed.

I was glad of that.

"What else could I do?" she asked. "I stay here because my family built this town. I own a good chunk of it. These families only stay because the toy factory gives them jobs. I'd firebomb the factory—hell, the whole town, if I had to—but Charlie . . ." She let her voice trail off.

"What? What did Charlie do?"

"He said he could fix it."

That gave me goose bumps. "What do you mean?"

"He said he could turn the kids back into kids. He said he could cure them. He told me not to worry, that he was going to take care of it and that I didn't need to give everything away to stop . . . He said a lot of things about this town and our family. But he told me to leave it to him, that he could undo it. I believe him. Do you think he can do it?"

I suddenly felt sick. Could Charlie Three undo the transformations that had struck the town's children? If so, I'd made sure the little girl on the basketball court could never come back. If so, I'd killed her. "I don't know."

"Well, you can cure the Dubois brothers, can't you? Maybe Charlie can cure all those kids."

My fear and nausea turned into a hard little knot. I'd once tried to cure people of the predators inside them. I'd failed in the ugliest way I could imagine.

I looked into her eyes. Her face was full of hope that her problems were going to be fixed by someone else—someone with the power and authority to set things right. Mingled with that hope was the fear that she was passing the buck. I wished there was something I could do for her. "Maybe."

"You don't believe it, do you?"

"I won't know what to believe until I talk to your brother." She glanced at the phone on the wall. I shook my head. "Face-to-face.

"Do you think this is his fault? I know you do. You're not that good a liar. But it's not his fault. It can't be. He would never do something like this."

"Cynthia, his company logo has fire on it."

"That's not . . . when he was a kid, he had nightmares all the time about a burning wheel, and it . . . he'd wake up screaming from them." She stopped talking and looked all over the table as if she expected to find a persuasive argument lying on it. "Can I tell you another story? About Charles?"

Hammer Bay seemed to be made of stories. "Go ahead."

"Charles wasn't the kind of kid to have a lot of friends, okay? He was a good kid, mostly, but it just didn't work out for him. He did have the latest, most expensive toys, though, so a lot of kids wanted to play with him. See what I mean?"

"Yeah."

"So he had these dreams, okay? And he and a couple of the kids who played with him got the idea to roll these old car tires down the hill behind our house so they'd bounce into the trees. Being a kid and kinda dumb, Charles tried to impress everyone. He put something flammable on them—I never found out what—and set a couple on fire before he rolled it down into the woods.

"I don't know if it was because of his dreams or if he was just being a dumb kid like every dumb kid, but he started a huge fire. Three families lost their homes, and Charles cried and cried. After that night, he became very sensitive to his place in this family. He understands what it means to be a Hammer in Hammer Bay. He put that burning wheel into the company logo to remind himself of his responsibilities. He would never do something to hurt the people in this town again. It just isn't in him."

"What if he thought he was doing more good than harm?"

She opened her mouth to respond, but no words came out. Her expression went far away for a moment, as if she was remembering something. When she looked at me again, she seemed less sure of herself. "He would never do something like this."

"Cynthia, what if you're wrong?"

She laid her hand over her mouth and her eyes brimmed with tears. I did not offer kind words or a gentle touch. There's no way to comfort a person who suspects someone they love is a killer. Her secret fear had been spoken aloud, and she needed to face the naked truth of it. Or maybe I'm just a bastard.

"Is that really what's happened?" she asked.

"I'm not sure yet. But I want you to help me put a stop to this."

She nodded. I was glad. If there was anyone who could get me close to Charles, it was her. I hoped she was ready.

The newspaper was lying on the table. I noticed the headline: TIME I DO SOMETHING ABOUT IT. The subhead read: HERO MAYOR VOWS TO TAKE ON CORRUPTION IN HAMMER BAY!

"Oh, hell. That idiot!" I stood without thinking about it. "Have you read this?"

"No, I never read it. Why?"

I handed the paper to her. She glanced at the headline, then skimmed through the article. "I don't understand. *Frank Farleton* is going to 'do something' about Emmett? From his hospital bed?"

"I need Reverend Wilson's phone number." I rushed to the phone and held it in my hand.

"The phone book is right in there." Cynthia pointed at a drawer beside my hip. I pulled out the thin directory and flipped it open to W. There was only one Wilson in Hammer Bay: Wilson, Thomas. I called him.

The phone was answered by a woman who sounded elderly, probably his secretary. She seemed to be terribly upset. "He's busy right now. He can't come to the phone."

"It's an emergency. A real emergency."

She sighed. She probably thought I was tempted by drink or that I was coveting my neighbor's car. "Who should I tell him is calling?"

"Tell him it's Raymond Lilly."

I heard the phone clatter onto a desk. The wait seemed interminable.

"Hello?" he said.

"Reverend, it's Ray Lilly. Listen—"

"Martha told me you didn't really hold a gun on her. In fact, she was surprised when I told her you had one." It took me a moment to remember what he was talking about. "You should know," Wilson continued in a slow, mopey tone, "that I'm composing my letter of resignation right now. It's for the best, I think. I love her, but my congregation—"

"Hey!" I shouted into the phone. "Reverend, I don't care. Understand? Don't tell me about it, because it doesn't matter. Have you seen today's paper?"

"Uh . . . well, no, I haven't."

"The mayor's life is in danger. Do you hear me? The mayor is going to die, if he isn't dead already. You can save him. Are you listening?"

I wished I could read his face. His voice was flat and steady as he said: "I am."

"This is what you're going to do. You're going to call four members of your congregation who own guns.

They should be people with courage and faith in a reward in the next life, understand? Also, make sure none of them work for Phyllis Henstrick. You're going to send them to the hospital. Tell them to walk in the front door with their weapons in plain view. They are to walk all the way to the mayor's room. Two of them will stay inside the room and two will stay in the hall outside the door."

"I don't understand why—"

"You just told me, Reverend, that you're listening. Are you still listening?"

"Okay. I am."

"Get those people in position. No one, and I mean no one, is to go into the mayor's room with a weapon."

"Emmett Dubois is going to take a statement from Frank this afternoon—"

"Emmett is at the top of the list. If he tries to enter that room with his gun, your people are to shoot him. Understand me? This isn't a joke. No one who works for Henstrick should get in to see him, either."

I heard him rustle paper on his end of the line. "Lord preserve us," he said in a low voice. "Peter Lemly has thrown a rock at the beehive. But can't we just have Frank taken to another hospital? Emmett is—"

"We're going to have him moved, yes, but that's going to take time."

"But guns in a hospital . . ."

"Reverend, listen to me. Last night, you could have gone out that back door. You could have slipped away from all that trouble and run. You didn't. You stepped up and took charge. This is another opportunity for you. Dubois, Hammer, and Henstrick have been running this town into a shit hole; it's time for you to step up and take your place. Hammer Bay needs you, and to hell with that letter you're writing. That's just another secret back door."

It was a corny pitch, but I could hear Wilson's breathing change. I had him hooked. I just needed him to follow through.

"You're right," he said. "Of course, you're right. I'll make some calls."

We hung up.

Cynthia gaped at the newspaper. "I should have realized right away—"

I took the paper from her. "Do you have another car?" I asked. "One that doesn't have bullets in the engine block?"

"Of course."

The other car turned out to be an Audi TT. It was smaller than I would have liked, but I didn't have a lot of choice.

Cynthia revved the engine. I slid the passenger seat back as far as it would go and climbed in beside her. I still had Cabot's gun in my pocket.

"Where to?" she asked.

"The mayor's house. You know where it is, right?"

She threw the car into gear and sped into town.

At the first red light, she turned to me. "Can I ask a stupid question?"

"Sure. I'll bet I have a stupid answer."

"Shouldn't Wilson's people have silver bullets?"

"Christ, I hope not."

"You don't know? What if they shoot Emmett and nothing happens? Won't Emmett kill them?"

"I'm hoping Emmett won't go that far into the open, but people do unexpected things when they feel cornered."

"What about the silver? Do we have to have it?"

"I don't know. And I'll bet Emmett doesn't know, either."

The light turned green, and Cynthia peeled into the intersection. "What do you mean?"

"He's probably never been shot with a regular bullet. I'm sure he knows all about the silver bullets and full moons and stuff, but that's the movies. I don't think he'd trust his life to something he saw in an old movie. I'm willing to bet he doesn't know if he's bulletproof."

"Not know? How could he not know?"

"You've had a tattoo on your back your whole life. What can you tell me about it?"

"Um, it's magic?"

"What's the spell called? What does it do? Where did it come from?"

"Okay. I don't know anything about it, except that it hurts when Charles has his seizures. But do you think Emmett is the same way? Just doing what he's doing in the dark?"

"We'll see."

Cynthia swerved her car suddenly and slammed on the brakes. We skidded to a stop next to the curb. There were a lot of cars parked behind us.

"Frank and Miriam's house is a couple doors back."

We climbed from the car and walked toward a modest two-story house with a tidy flower garden in the front. The bay window was blocked by cream-colored drapes. It looked like a little old lady's house. The car in the driveway was a huge Yukon that someone had painted tangerine orange.

I walked to the front door and rang the bell. Beside me, Cynthia sighed. "I'm not looking forward to this."

The door swung open, and I found myself looking down at a little woman with steel-gray hair and a pair of cheap, safety-goggle sunglasses over her regular glasses. She shifted her position to bar my way.

Cynthia leaned toward her. "We need to speak to Miriam right away."

"Who is it, Cassie?" a woman called. Cassie took one look at me and started to close the door.

I hit it with my fist, thumping it open.

I walked into the living room. Miriam Farleton sat on a little chair at the far end of the room. Seated all around here were seven old women, all dressed in what looked like their Sunday clothes. Cassie, at the door, made eight. Miriam's eyes were red from crying, but her cheeks were dry. I guessed these were friends who'd come by to comfort her. Not one of them was less than thirty years her senior.

The ladies gasped as I bulled into the room, which was full of lace, delicate furniture, and little ceramic figurines. I was afraid to touch anything—I might have put a grubby manprint on it. "I'm sorry to barge in this way," I said, "but there isn't a lot of time."

She didn't respond. The woman sitting next to her struggled to her feet. She was a stocky little lady, and her hands were large and strong. She stepped between the mayor's wife and me. "I don't think you were invited here today," she said, glaring at Cynthia. "Either of you."

I tried to talk past her, acutely aware of the bullet hole in my shirt. "Have you seen today's paper? I think your husband is in danger."

"Threats, is it?" the stocky woman said. "If you don't leave right now, I'm going to call—"

"Who?" Cynthia asked. "Emmett Dubois? Emmett is going to kill Frank if you don't let us help!"

This time the gasp from the room was followed by a lot of whispering. Great. The whole town would know what was going on by dinnertime. I turned to Miriam again and held up the newspaper. "Can we please talk privately?"

Miriam stood. "Yes."

"Miriam," the woman said, "you shouldn't be alone with strangers right now."

"Why don't you join us, Arlene," Miriam said. "If that's all right?" I nodded. Arlene and Miriam led us through a swinging door.

The kitchen was pastel blue and decorated with duckling wallpaper. I wondered if there was a room somewhere in this house for Frank.

I showed the headline to Miriam and Arlene. "This," I said, "is essentially a declaration of war against Henstrick and the Dubois brothers. Lemly put your husband's neck in the guillotine. Yours, too."

Miriam held the paper, skimming over the story. "Oh, Peter," she said. She looked tired.

"What do you aim to do?" Arlene asked. I suddenly recognized her. She was the one who'd given Bill Terril a birthday card to sign in Sara's bar—she had a grandchild at boarding school in Georgia. Small town.

"Reverend Wilson is already putting people outside Frank's room to protect him, but that's a short-term solution. We need to get him out of town to a place where they can't find him. And we need to do it secretly."

I glanced at the doorway. Miriam and Arlene followed my glance and understood. Arlene patted Miriam's hand and started toward the door. "I'll shut down the rumor mill for a little while. I'll be right back." She stepped through the door way.

Miriam looked me in the eyes. "Why don't we call the state police," she said quickly, "or the FBI?"

Call the cops, I thought. It wasn't an idea that came to me naturally. "We will," I assured her, "but that's the long-term solution. They're a bureaucracy and they move too slowly. Let's get your husband to safety first, then worry about who to tell."

"He'll go to prison, you know," Miriam said. I could hear Arlene reading the riot act in the next room, but I couldn't make out what she was saying. "Emmett opened an account in Frank's name in Oregon. He's been putting money in it every month, as though it was a payoff. Frank and I didn't even know until Emmett sat us down and showed us a bank statement. He made it look like Frank is part of the whole thing. The FBI is going to go after my husband just as hard as they go after Emmett."

There was a loud boom from the living room, followed by a crash of breaking glass. I charged through the double doors, almost knocking Arlene to the carpet.

The big bay window that looked out into the garden was shattered. The rod had fallen, and the drapes lay in tatters on the carpet. A woman sitting on the couch clutched at her shoulder. Blood seeped through her fingers. Another woman held her hand against the back of her head. I realized that people were screaming and that some of those screams were actually squealing tires.

Cynthia ran to the window. I pulled her away.

Arlene was examining the woman with the cut on her head. I went to the woman with a bleeding shoulder. "This isn't too bad," Arlene said casually, as though she'd seen much worse. "But we'll still need to go to the emergency room."

"This too," I said. The woman I was examining stared at the bullet hole in my shirt and the tattoos beneath it. "Is anyone else hurt?"

I didn't get an answer. I heard a door open. Two or three of the women, Miriam included, pushed through the doorway into the front yard.

"No!" I shouted at them. "Stay inside!"

They didn't listen. So much for my leadership skills. I turned to Cynthia. "Organize a ride to the emergency room for these two. We have someplace to go first."

I ran out into the yard. Miriam and her three friends stared up the street, trying to see who had fired at them.

As I came near them, I saw a long white van drive up from the other direction. The black barrel of a shotgun protruded from the back window. It pointed at Miriam.

I shouted at them to get down, but she and her friends simply stared at the van in bewilderment. They were as still as paper targets.

I was too far away from the van to use my ghost knife, but Cabot's gun was still in my pocket. I jammed my hand inside and wrenched it up. The hammer caught on my jacket, tangling the gun.

I had already lost my chance. The shotgun had her in its sights. She was not going to survive.

But the weapon never fired. The van passed us, then squealed away down the road.

I couldn't figure it out. Was this just a warning, or had someone lost their nerve? I hoped it was the latter; it would restore my faith in humanity a little to know that there were people out there who couldn't shoot a bunch of women in cold blood.

I dropped the gun back into my pocket and ran to Miriam. She looked shocked.

"He didn't shoot," she said, sounding amazed. "I looked right into the barrel of that gun and I prayed it wouldn't hurt too much, but—"

"Would you get back inside, please?" I couldn't keep the annoyance out of my voice.

That startled her. She and the other women turned and bustled back to the house. I watched for the return of the van and saw something small rolling in the street. I ran toward it, keeping an eye out for vehicles.

It was a yellow hard hat. The name "benny" was written in all lowercase letters on the inside lining. I sprinted back into the house.

Arlene was organizing the others into their cars. She had a brisk honesty that I liked. "These two will be all right," she told me as I entered. "Vera is going to drive them to the hospital to be checked up, but I think they're more frightened than anything."

"What's that?" Cynthia asked.

"I found it in the street. It must have come from the van."

A little woman I hadn't spoken to yet grabbed my wrist and looked at the lining. "That belongs to my little brother, Benjamin."

There was a general expression of astonishment. Arlene came over to us. "Vera, do you think he shot at us?"

Vera scowled down at the hard hat. "He's always losing things. I knew he was in debt to that damn casino, but I never thought he'd go this far, or that Phyllis would ask him to."

"We don't know who was behind that shooting," I said, "so don't start rumors. Now let's go. Vera, you're taking the injured to the hospital, right? Cynthia and I will take Mrs. Farleton there in a bit. We have a stop to make."

"I'm going with you," Arlene said. She had a stubborn look in her eye.

"There isn't room," I told her.

"My car can squeeze in four," Cynthia said.

"I know," I told her.

"I'm going," Arlene said.

"She is, or I'm not," Miriam said.

I threw my hands into the air. How could I argue with these people?

I took the gun from my pocket. One of the women gasped, and I felt a little twist of nausea at her fear. I led Vera and the other women to Vera's station wagon, where they all squeezed in beside one another. As they pulled away, I imagined Luke Dubois sneaking through Miriam's back door and killing them all while I was out front. I ran back to the house and found them waiting for me.

I stood facing Miriam. I had her full attention. "Your husband seems like a good man. Do you love him?"

"I do."

"What about all this?" I waved at the house, the furnishings, everything. "Do you love all this, too? Because it's time to choose."

"What do you mean?"

"It's time for you and your husband to get out. You're going to have to leave a lot behind. Artwork, knick-knacks, all sorts of stuff."

"I can do that," she said. "Staring down the barrel of a shotgun clarifies things."

"Get your financial stuff," I said. "Bank records, credit-card papers, mortgage papers, insurance stuff, whatever. And get photo albums and old love letters, too. Everything else you should leave behind. Expect it to be burned to the ground before you get back."

She nodded and hurried up the stairs. Arlene started to follow her, but I caught her arm. "I have two questions for you: Do you have a reliable car? And if so, can she borrow it? They can't run away in a tangerine Yukon."

"Yes," Arlene said. "Yes, of course." She went off to help Miriam.

Cynthia and I stood in the living room. She smiled at me and squeezed my hand. I took a deep breath and relaxed. I was glad that she was helping me. I hoped that I wouldn't have to cut the iron gate off of her, or worse.

Within five minutes, Miriam came back downstairs with a banker's box in her arms. On top of that was an old leather-bound Bible. "I'm ready."

"We'll put them in the back of Arlene's car. Arlene, we'll meet you at the hospital. Ready?"

We went out the front door and loaded up the back of Arlene's Forester. While Miriam pushed the box into place, Arlene tapped my elbow. "Who are you?"

"Raymond Lilly."

"That doesn't really answer my question."

"I'm aware of that." Miriam shut the hatch. "Go quickly, please."

Arlene climbed in behind the wheel and pulled away. I made Miriam get into the backseat of the Audi and stay low. I felt silly rushing around like movie spies, but being shot at changes things.

"Where to now?" Cynthia asked.

"We need Annalise."

"Your place, then." She pulled away from the curb, and we drove quietly for a few blocks.

Miriam broke the silence. "Do you think Phyllis tried to have me killed?"

"I'm not convinced it was her. The hard hat was a little too obvious. And from what I've seen, her guys all carry the same snub-nosed .38."

"I heard she got a deal on them because she bought in bulk," Cynthia said. "She's a real cheapskate."

"But it was her sort of van," Miriam said. "And I'm sure some of her men have guns of their own at home."

I knew how easily a vehicle could be stolen. "It's pointless to speculate. What matters is that we get you and your husband to safety."

Five minutes later we had arrived at the motel. My room had been tossed and all of my clothes torn to shreds. I would have to make do with the bullet-hole shirt for a while longer. My detective novel had been destroyed, too. Bastards. Now I wouldn't find out who the killer was.

Annalise's room was empty, but it had also been tossed, and everything in it torn apart. Miriam peered over my shoulder into the room. "Mercy," she said. "Do you think something has happened to her?"

"I'm not worried about her," I said. "I'm worried about us."

The van was gone, too. I wished she had given me a

damn cell number I could use. I needed her, and I had no idea where she was or what she was up to.

Cynthia tugged on my sleeve. "Are we done here?"

I could have asked the manager where she'd gone, but I didn't trust him to give an honest answer.

I was on my own.

CHAPTER FIFTEEN

"Here," I said. Cynthia pulled into a parking lot. "Leave the engine running," I said. "I'll run up and run back."

"What are you planning to do?" Miriam asked.

"If you see trouble, peel out of here without me, understand?"

Cynthia nodded. She and Miriam began scanning the street. I turned and ran into the building that contained the offices of *The Mallet* and Peter Lemly.

In the lobby, I scanned the directory. There was an actuarial on the second floor and marriage counselors on the third. The fourth was the editorial offices of *The Mallet*.

The elevator looked slow and confined to me, so I took the stairs, vaulting up them as quickly as I could. I nearly knocked over a middle-aged couple coming down from the third floor. I mumbled an apology and squeezed past them.

At the top of the stairs I saw the door for *The Mallet*, est. 1909. It wasn't locked, and I let myself inside. There were three doors along a short hallway. The farthest door was marked EDITORIAL. I put my hand on the knob and hesitated. The air was very still. Peter wasn't here, and I wanted to sprint back down to the car. Instead, I opened the door.

I immediately smelled blood. I walked toward the desk and window at the far side of the room. There was a pair of fresh blood splashes on the glass, and the desk had been knocked crooked.

Peter was behind the desk, mostly. His arm lay in the far corner, his hand still clutching a nine-millimeter. His head lay a few feet away beside a single spent bullet casing. I wondered if he had managed to hit his target.

I backed out of the room, wrapped my hand in my shirttail, and pulled the door closed, then wiped my fingerprints from the knob. I did the same to the knob on the door to the stairs.

I ran down the stairs, out the door, then hopped into Cynthia's car. "Any trouble?" I asked her.

"No. You?"

"Oh, yes. Peter Lemly is dead."

"Oh, shit," Cynthia said.

"Shouldn't we call someone?" Miriam asked.

"Like who? The cops are probably the ones who killed him."

"An ambulance, of course. What if he's just badly hurt?"

I turned around and looked in her eyes. "Miriam," I said. "He's very, very dead."

She snapped her mouth shut and stared out the window. Cynthia raced through town and pulled into the county hospital lot. She parked as close to Arlene's car as possible.

Within five minutes, we were all walking down the hallway toward Frank's room.

Just outside his door, I saw a tiny, bald black man of about seventy. The top of his head came up to the bullet hole in my shirt, and he wore huge, black-framed rectangular glasses that make his eyes look like apricots. He held a long, black rifle in both hands.

Across the hall, a bird-thin woman of about sixty sat on the same padded bench Cynthia and I had sat on the day before. She held a World War II–era carbine across her lap.

The tiny man thrust out his chin and slid his finger over the trigger. "Stop right there, young man," he said in a high, nasal voice. "You stop there."

"Lord in heaven, Roger," the thin woman said. "Can't you see that they have Miriam with them?"

He squinted at us through his gigantic goggles, then scowled. Letting people into the room must have felt like a loss of much-loved authority.

I glanced at the far end of the hall. Two hospital security guards leaned against a door. They were watching Roger and us but were obviously unwilling to approach closer.

At that moment, Arlene pushed past the guards, with Rev. Wilson and a doctor close behind. Miriam, Arlene, and the doctor bent their heads together for a conference. The doctor's voice was low but emphatic. He was unhappy about something, and I was pretty sure I knew what it was.

Rev. Wilson turned toward me but kept his gaze pointed off to my right. "Emmett was here just a few minutes ago, but he's gone now."

"He wouldn't surrender his weapon," Roger announced. "Or submit to a search."

"And he smelled funny," the bird woman said.

I imagined he would, if he hadn't had time to wash off Peter's blood. "What about his brothers?"

"There's been no sign of them," Wilson said.

I remembered the spent casing by Peter's body. I went to the doctor, who was objecting most strenuously to something. "Hey, Doc," I interrupted. "Have any of the town police been admitted to the emergency room today?"

"I'm a cardiologist."

"Don't be annoying, please. If one of them came into

the ER, the whole hospital would have heard about it, right?"

The doctor obviously wanted to continue his argument with Miriam, but she was paying attention to me. He sighed. "Right, and no."

I hoped Peter had missed with his shot. "Thanks. Now run along and get us a wheelchair, would you? We're taking the mayor out of here." He blinked at me as he tried to generate a suitably outraged reply.

I heard a low growl behind me.

I turned. Luke Dubois stood by the door we had just come in. Standing next to him was a wolf.

Shit. Too slow. If only I hadn't stopped for Peter Lemly, I might have gotten them away in time.

"Everyone stand where you are," Luke said, looking pleased with himself.

The other wolves I had seen in Hammer Boy had been tinged with red or gray fur. The one beside Luke was black, and it was big. I remembered Wiley's dark mop of hair, and knew this one was him.

"Not protecting your secret anymore, Luke?" I said. "It must hurt to have killed Wilma over something you're just throwing away now."

Luke was startled, but he didn't break down in tears or anything. "I didn't . . . I would have never . . . we don't have to be afraid," he said, turning the subject toward something he wanted to talk about. "All this time we thought we had to be afraid, but we don't. And we're not giving away our secret. Not today, at least."

That wasn't good. We were in for a bloodbath. "Roger," I said, keeping my voice low, "shoot that damn wolf."

The gun went off almost before I finished the sentence. It was brutally loud in the tiled hallway, and despite myself, I flinched.

A bloody hole appeared dead center on the black

wolf's head. Roger was a good shot. As I watched, the hole closed over. The wolf barely staggered.

"You see?" Luke said. "All this time we've been afraid, and we didn't have to."

Damn. Peter *had* shot one of them. We needed silver, and they knew it.

I heard screams behind me. A red wolf had knocked down one of the security guards and was tearing apart his forearm. The grayish wolf had already gone for the throat of the second man, who struggled weakly against the attack, red blood squirting onto the tile floor.

"Get into the room!" I shouted.

Cynthia barreled into the door. I heard her shouting at someone inside not to shoot her.

Roger worked the bolt of his rifle. His face was set, as though he was trying to work out a complicated puzzle.

The gray wolf charged us. The birdlike woman stepped toward it and lifted her rifle. There was another shot, but the wolf leaped on her, knocking her to the floor. It sank its fangs into her neck just below her ear. She didn't get a chance to scream.

Roger grunted. The black wolf had landed on him. I kicked it in the ribs just as it snapped at his throat. Roger's gun went off. Luke, still standing at the end of the hall, collapsed backward onto the tile floor. The wolf tore into Roger's throat.

I rushed at Miriam. The red wolf came at her first. Arlene and Rev. Wilson both lunged at the creature. Wilson and the wolf went down. The reverend was not going to last long.

Arlene grabbed Miriam and shoved her toward the door to Frank's room. They collided with me. Rather than fight my way around them toward the reverend I let myself be pushed into the room. I ran when Rev. Wilson, the guards, Roger, and the old lady could not, and I was glad to do it.

I slammed the door shut and threw my shoulder against it. There was no lock. Someone slid a chair under the doorknob. I looked up and saw that it was the cardiologist. I hadn't seen him enter the room, but here he was, holding the door with me.

"What's going on?" he asked me, his voice low and breathless. "What is that officer doing with those dogs?"

"Killing us, if he gets the chance."

I turned and looked around the room. Frank was lying on his bed, tubes up his nose. Standing beside him were a fat middle-aged man with rake-thin arms and a fat elderly man with a handlebar mustache. Both were carrying identical doughboy-era rifles. Along with them were Cynthia, Miriam, and Arlene. Miriam was fussing over Arlene's hand, but the rest were looking at me.

"Is everyone all right over there?"

"It's Arlene," Miriam said. "She's been bitten pretty badly."

"You have a patient, Doc."

Cynthia fetched a rubber doorstop from the corner and kicked it beneath the closed door. Blood started to flow under the door. "I saw what happened when the old guy shot the wolf. It wasn't hurt at all."

"I know."

"We need some kind of silver weapons, don't we? Silver bullets or something?"

"I don't know. I wasn't planning to fight them. That's why we were running away. But I don't know if silver will work."

"What happened out there?" the man with the mustache asked. He looked like he wanted to throw his gun down and run. The middle-aged man was even more spooked. "Where's Roger and Binky?"

"They're both dead," Arlene snapped. "So is Reverend Wilson."

"What?" Mustache said. "How—"

Everyone began talking at once, in high, panicked tones.

I felt someone try the handle. Someone pushed. Someone strong. I pushed back. I could hear sounds coming from the other side of the door, but I couldn't make them out.

"Hey!" I shouted at them. "Be quiet!" No effect. Everyone was still badgering Arlene for explanations. Frank began to look pale. Miriam rushed to him. "Shut up!" I shouted at them, but all I did was add to the noise.

From the other side of the door, a wolf howled. Then two, then a third. Everyone in the room fell silent.

"All right in there," Luke Dubois said. He didn't sound like a man who had just been shot. He sounded happy. "What say we talk terms?"

"Sure thing," I said. "Let everyone in this room leave unharmed, and I won't rain hellfire on your ass."

Luke chuckled. "Hellfire, huh? You didn't look like you had much hellfire on hand when you were scurrying into that hospital room. You looked like you had a load in your pants."

"You don't know who I am," I said.

"Don't care, neither. Not anymore."

"That's because you're stupid." I took the ghost knife out and threw it through the door. It cut a slit in the wood and passed through. I heard Luke grunt. Something metallic fell onto the tiled floor. I *reached* for the ghost knife. It flew back to me, cutting a second slit through the wooden door and landing in my hand.

"What . . ." Luke's voice was small and frightened. "What was that?" I knew the ghost knife had taken the fight out of him. Hopefully, it would give him pause, too.

"That was just the start. That was small magic for small potatoes like you. Where did you get this trick for shape-shifting, Luke? Straight from the Hammer family,

I'll bet. I'll bet the first Cabot gave it to your grandfather, and he's passed it down over the years. I'm right, aren't I? Didn't you ever wonder where he learned the trick?"

"He's rich," Luke said, as if that explained everything.

"Please. He got his magic from the same place I got mine. From the same book, in fact. But he only taught the Dubois family that one trick, right? He only gave you that one spell. And you didn't even know enough about it to be sure the magic protected you. Not until Peter Lemly unloaded a round into one of you."

I just kept talking, hoping to stall him. I didn't know what to stall him for, but it was all I had.

"So what? What does that have to do with you?"

Cynthia came up to me and held out her hand. "This was all I could find," she whispered. She had a delicate silver chain in her palm. I took it. I hoped it would do some good.

"Damn, Luke," I said, "you fellas have been stumbling around in the dark for years. And now, when you finally realize what you have, you blow it by killing Karoly and Lemly, and now going after the mayor. You drew too much attention to yourselves. Now we're here to take the magic back."

"We're just protecting our own interests," he said, his voice almost complaining. "This is our territory."

I waved at the two fat men while Luke kept talking. They approached me timidly. Rake-Thin Arms was about to ask a question, but I held my finger to my lips. I gestured for them to throw their weight against the door. They did.

I ran to the window. We were on the fourth floor—too damn high to jump. But there was a ledge. I took out my ghost knife and cut a large hole in the window, as large as I could make it. Then I turned to Cynthia and the doctor. "Out onto the ledge," I whispered.

Cynthia didn't hesitate. She stepped through the window and climbed out. The ledge was only six inches wide, and there was nothing but parking lot below, but she inched her way along.

The doctor followed her after a moment's hesitation. Frank didn't have the strength for that kind of climbing, and Miriam wasn't going to leave him. Arlene wasn't going to leave Miriam.

I went back to the door and shoved the fat guys aside. "Go," I whispered. Whatever Luke had been saying, he was done saying it. I laid my arms against the door and braced myself, for whatever that was worth. I looked over my shoulder.

The two fat guys rushed toward the window. Mustache looked out at the ledge, then turned back to me. I could see he wasn't going to risk it. Rake-Thin shoved him aside.

"You have two choices, Luke," I shouted through the door. "You can stay in Hammer Bay and be hunted like animals, or you can run for it. Rio is nice, I'm told. I'd think that would be a good place for a murderer to lie low."

"No," Luke said. I could hear courage in his voice. Damn. He was recovering from the ghost knife too quickly. "I don't think so. I've been to Rio."

The door seemed to explode right in front of me. Splinters of wood struck my face. I felt a dead pressure against the tattoos on my stomach. Gunshot.

I fell backward. Splinters fell around me in slow motion. I fell in slow motion, too. I knew a second gunshot was coming, but it seemed to take a long time.

Then it boomed. I hit the floor and rolled to the side. A third shot slammed past me. Then a fourth. Mustache dove for the ground. Rake-Thin Arms toppled through the window like a sack of flour and vanished. Miriam screamed as more shots blasted through the wood. At first I thought she was screaming over the death of the middle-aged fat guy, but then I noticed a single round bullet hole just above Frank's right eye.

Arlene grabbed Miriam and dragged her to the floor. Mustache crawled toward me, holding the rifle.

Boom boom boom. The barrage seemed to be endless, although I'd guess there were no more than ten or twelve shots. When it ended, the door was Swiss cheese. I heard Luke eject a clip and replace it. He racked the slide.

I expected him to say something before he started shooting again, but he just jammed his pistol into one of the holes in the door and started shooting.

The barrel of the gun was only a couple of feet above me. I slashed at it with the ghost knife. The trigger fell free and landed with a *ting* on the floor outside.

Luke drew back the weapon and cursed. He kicked at the door and broke open a section with several bullet holes. His foot got stuck in the hole.

Mustache shot him through the ankle. Luke cursed violently as he yanked at his foot. Mustache and I saw the wound heal in seconds.

"Jesus wept," Mustache said. "What do we do now?"

I had an idea. "Gimme."

Mustache handed me the rifle. I took the silver chain from my pocket and cut it in half. Then I cut the halves as well. Might as well try it.

Luke pulled his foot free, and the black muzzle of a wolf jammed through the hole in the door. The wolf snarled and snapped at me, throwing itself against the splintering wood, forcing itself into the room.

I dropped a piece of chain down the barrel of the rifle. I held the shoulder stock low and the muzzle up, so the chain wouldn't slide out.

The black wolf lunged at me. Saliva splashed against my face. The creature's jaws gaped.

I jammed the rifle barrel down the wolf's throat, as deep as it would go. Then I tilted it up. I heard the chain slide down the barrel.

The wolf yelped. It froze in place for just a moment, its eyes widening, then started to pull back.

Before I could even think about it, the ghost knife flew into my hand. I slashed it across the wolf's throat. The gun fell backward and so did I.

The wolf tried to scream, but a solid inch of gun barrel was stuck in the back of its throat. It tried to retch. It wrenched itself back through the broken door and fell to the floor, shuddering.

"What do you know?" I said quietly. "It worked." The gun barrel was cut at a slant now. I felt a twinge of guilt at ruining what looked to be a family heirloom.

I tried to slide a second piece of chain into the barrel, but my hands were shaking too badly. Mustache reached over my shoulder and held the weapon steady.

My thanks were drowned out by howls from the hallway. Luke called Wiley's name. I glanced through the hole in the door and caught a glimpse of pale, blubbery flesh. Wiley had turned back into a human. Damn, it *was* like the movies.

I slid another length of chain down the barrel. "I'm sorry about the gun," I said.

"Forget the gun, boy," Mustache answered. "Just don't let those bastards in here."

"Fair enough." I slashed the ghost knife through the barrel, cutting it at a sharp angle. Then I shaved the leading edge until it came to a rough point. It wasn't as sharp as a spear, but it might do the job if I put my back into it.

Mustache gaped at me, the end of his rifle, and the ghost knife in turn. "What—"

"Don't ask," I said. "National security."

His mouth snapped shut. I glanced over at Arlene and

Miriam, who were still crouching on the floor. Arlene's face was blank with terror, but Miriam, holding her dead husband's hand, looked at me with deep suspicion.

The Dubois brothers were still making a racket in the hall. I heard a slapping sound as Luke tried to revive his brother.

"I guess you have reason to be afraid again, huh, Luke?" I felt dizzy and manic. It felt good to have a weapon, even a hack one. A swatch of gray-flecked fur moved past the hole. I knelt and leaned toward it. A chance to kill Emmett was too good to miss.

A section of door burst open, and Luke's arm smashed through the damaged wood. Before I could react, he ripped the rifle out of my hands.

Shit. I rolled back on my heels and started to stand, and I bumped into Mustache's big soft belly. I reached for the rifle stock, but Luke ripped it through the broken door.

The ruined door splintered apart, and a flash of red and black burst into the room. I threw myself at it, feeling a chunk of wood strike my ear as I lunged. The wolf stumbled coming through the door, giving me the split second I needed.

Someone from the other side of the door shouted: "Sugar! Don't!" It wasn't Luke's voice. It was Emmett.

I landed on its back, plunging the ghost knife into the back of its head.

The wolf faltered but didn't go down, even with my full weight on it. I caught the ghost knife in my teeth, freeing my hands. I wrapped my arms around the wolf's neck.

It tried to turn itself around to snap at me, but I held on, refusing to let it turn. It tried to wriggle backward out of my grip, but I swung my legs against its hind legs, knocking it to the floor. It took every ounce of strength I had, and I knew I couldn't hold it for long.

I dipped my head, jabbing the ghost knife into the wolf's back. It weakened, but only a little. Its feet scrabbled against the floor, twisting its body away from me and threatening to steal my only leverage. I started to lose my hold on him.

"My God!" Mustache shouted from behind me. "They're cutting him wide open!" I had no idea what he was talking about.

The ghost knife wasn't working. The Dubois brothers had a greater resistance to my spell than anyone I'd ever met. I knew I couldn't stay in this position for long—the wolf would eventually scramble out from under me and I'd have no way to hold those teeth at bay any longer. I needed a plan.

The only idea that came to me was the open window. The fall wouldn't kill Sugar, I figured, but it would put some distance between us. Maybe I could get Miriam, Arlene, and Mustache to a safe place in the time it took the wolf to come at me again.

But I had no way of gaining my feet without losing my hold.

Then I felt something. It was a sensation of power, somewhat like Annalise's iron-gate spell when I first stole it from her so many months ago. I felt it just under my chest, in the wolf's back. I lowered my head and slashed the ghost knife toward it.

The fur on the wolf's back suddenly erupted in a jet of black steam and sparks. The wolf howled, and I felt the steam scald my left shoulder and neck. I tried to hold on, but the pain was too much. I shoved the wolf away from me.

It staggered back. It had blurred and become indistinct, as though some parts of it were appearing out of or receding into a fog. It was as if I was looking at two superimposed versions of the same being. The wolf was fading, and the man was reappearing.

The paws became hands. The fur became skin. The snout became Sugar's face. The magic was still pouring out of him in iron-gray sparks and jets of black steam.

I lunged at him, grabbed him by the arm, and rushed him toward the window. Arlene and Miriam had to pull their legs back as we passed. Sugar had difficulty keeping up with me, but he was dazed enough to try.

We reached the window, and I heaved him through it.

He was still changing as he vanished below the sill. I didn't hear him scream.

Mustache elbowed past me and looked out the window. "Sweet Jesus," he said, "please have mercy on this sinner, as you have mercy on all of us sinners."

I backed away from him. I didn't want to see Sugar's body, and I didn't want to pray for his salvation. I wasn't that good a person.

"Sugar!" Emmett yelled. "Sugar!"

"He's waiting for you outside," I said nastily. "In the parking lot."

I heard retreating steps. They were going. Thank God.

"We did it," I said.

"You did it, son." Mustache clapped me on the shoulder. "Good work."

I looked over at Frank. He was stretched out on his bed with the single bullet hole in his forehead. It didn't seem like good work to me. I felt like a screwup of the first order. If I'd skipped a visit to Peter Lemly's house, if I'd looked at the newspaper sooner, if I'd been more forceful when I'd told Lemly to hold off on the story, I might have saved Frank's life, and the lives of the others, too.

"What did I just see?" Miriam said. She struggled off the floor and helped Arlene up, too. "What was that? Was that Sugar Dubois?"

"I think we know what we saw," Arlene said. "I just have a hard time believing it."

I rushed to the window and looked out along the ledge. Cynthia and the doctor were not there. I looked down at the parking lot, but I saw only the bodies of Mr. Rake-Thin Arms and Sugar Dubois. Had Cynthia gotten away? I hoped so. I hoped I wouldn't see her again. I hoped she would go far away from here, and that I'd never have to cut the iron gate off of her, or use her to hunt and kill her brother.

Miriam approached me. She pulled the front of my shirttail, exposing two more bullet holes across my stomach. One was so low that it was almost below my tattoos—that bullet could have shattered my hip.

I also noticed that my right forearm was bloody. I glanced down and saw that wooden splinters from the door had jabbed through my skin on the inside of my arm. The cuts were few and shallow; I'd hurt myself worse shaving. Still, I was surprised that I hadn't even felt it. I began to pluck the splinters out.

"Are you one of them?" Miriam asked me. Her face was flushed and her eyes were wild. "Are you cursed?"

"I can't do what they did," I told her.

"But are you cursed? Have you sold your soul, the way they did?"

Mustache laid his hand on her arm. "Miriam, he just fought for us—"

"Be quiet, Walt! I have to know." She waited for my answer.

My adrenaline high was wearing off, and I felt shaky and exhausted. I was tempted to tell her what she could do with herself, but I'd promised to help her and I'd failed. If Walt could pray for the souls of the people who had just tried to tear him apart, I could at least comfort her with lies.

I'd spent enough time in a cell with a reformed preacher to know generally what to say. "I can't tell you very much," I told her. "I swore an oath not to. I was a sinner, like everyone, and I'm still a sinner, but an angel with a flaming sword and a crown of light appeared to me, and . . . I can't tell you more. I shouldn't even have said—"

She laid her hand on my arm. "Thank you."

"You should get out of town now."

Someone banged on the door. "What's going on in there? Open up!"

I spun toward the door, but it was only more hospital security guards peeping at us through the broken door. I moved toward it to unlock it, but Arlene grabbed my elbow.

"What about me?" she asked. "One of them bit me. Does that mean . . . am I going to become one of them?"

She looked at me as if I was an expert. I knew how it felt to want to *know* but not have answers.

But I didn't have any answers for her. Silver had hurt one, yes, but that didn't mean these were Hollywood-style werewolves. For all I knew, the Dubois brothers could change into ten different animals, not just wolves.

"I can't answer that," I told her. "I'm sorry. I honestly don't know."

Arlene turned to Miriam. "I can't go with you, dear. I can't go anywhere until I know."

Miriam clutched at Arlene's injured hand. Arlene winced, but Miriam was too rattled to notice.

I turned to Mustache. "Walt, is it?" He nodded. "I need you to drive Miriam out of town. You're going to take Arlene's car because it's already packed."

Miriam turned back to the hospital bed. "Frank . . ."

"I'm sorry," I said to her. "I'm sorry I didn't do better."

"My father hated him," she said. "Said he was a weakling. He even said it to Frank's face once. But he was such a sweet man, and so funny. He always knew how to make me laugh. Lord, how can I leave him like this?"

She moved toward Frank's body, but I caught hold of

her and steered her toward Walt. "Take her now. Right away."

Arlene pressed the keys into Walt's hand. "Don't worry," Walt said. "This sort of trouble can be cleared up pretty quickly. Then we'll get you back to see about your Frank."

Someone had finally brought keys for the door. Security guards unlocked it and swung it open, peering carefully around the doorjamb as if afraid we might start shooting at them.

The hall was full of blood and bodies. Wiley Dubois was gone. Had they taken his body away, or had he survived the silver I had jammed down his throat?

"They cut him open," Walt said to me. "Emmett and Luke cut Wiley open like he was a fish and dug that bit of silver out of him. I guess the fat son of a somethin' must have survived."

"Guess so." I gently shoved the others toward the door, and we all walked into the hall. "Don't look at them," I said. "Just keep going." Something heavy banged against my hip. I still had Cabot's gun in my pocket. I'd forgotten all about it.

"Hold it right there," a man said. He stepped through the bodies to bar our way. He was wearing a cheap suit and a name tag that identified him as head of security. "You're all going to have to wait for the police."

Miriam started laughing. It was a frightening sound.

Arlene stepped up to the man in the suit. "It was the police who did all this."

A young woman in a doctor's jacket came around the edge of the hallway and moved toward the bodies. She knelt down and began checking Rev. Wilson for life signs. She didn't look like she expected to find any.

"What are you saying?"

Arlene stepped up close to the head of security and read his name carefully. "Listen to me, Mr. Arnold

Reyes. Luke Dubois just killed the mayor, and several of the people who tried to stop him. We're going to take the mayor's wife out of town until the FBI, state police, or an angry mob does something about the Dubois brothers. Hopefully, it will be something brutal that leaves them in lots of tiny pieces. And if you try to contact Emmett, or if you get in our way, you're going to be very glad that you're already in a hospital."

Mr. Arnold Reyes let Walt and Miriam pass. "Who's going to explain this?"

The young doctor stood. "They're all dead," she said. I gestured toward Arlene's hand. The doctor bent over the injury and studied it carefully with gloved hands. "This will need to be bandaged, but no stitches, I should think."

I looked up. Cynthia was standing beside me. The cardiologist was right beside her. He looked rattled. Cynthia was pale. I let out a deep, relieved sigh. They'd found a safe way inside after all.

"This dude is going to explain it all," I said to Arnold Reyes and waved to the cardiologist. "Come here, hero. You get to tell everyone what happened."

"But I don't know what happened." The tall doctor looked like he wanted to flee down the stairs and never come back.

"Did you recognize the cop that was here?"

"Um, yes."

"Did you hear him say what he came for?"

"The mayor."

"You're the spokesman. I'm going to see that these other people get to a safe place." I took Cynthia's arm and started to lead them away.

"Where's Frank?" Cynthia asked.

I shook my head at her, and she stepped back. "I'm going to stay here. That doctor isn't going to be able to explain it all."

"All right," I said. "Don't say anything that will sound crazy."

She smiled at me. She looked terribly fragile. "Give me some credit. I'm going to want to see you again later. My place?"

I nodded to her, then started to push Walt and Miriam through the doors. Arlene trailed behind, with the doctor holding her hand. No one spoke.

At the doors to the parking lot, the doctor made Arlene go to the ER. I led Walt and Miriam outside.

"I'm sorry," I said as Miriam was about to get in the car.

She threw her arms around my neck. I could feel her tears smearing on my face. "Lord bless you," she said.

They got into the car and drove away.

I walked back to the ER and watched Arlene get bandaged up. She filled out some paperwork, and then it was time to go. As we walked toward the parking lot, I looked through the glass doors and saw Annalise's van parked out there. Annalise stood beside it, waiting for me.

"Now what?" Arlene asked me.

"Call a friend and ask for a ride home."

I walked through the doors into the gray afternoon. Arlene followed closely behind. "No," she said. "I can't go home and wait. It would kill me. I have to know."

I didn't respond. We approached Annalise.

She stared at me as we approached. "You've been raising quite a ruckus, I hear."

"You could have joined in if I had a way to contact you. A cell phone number or something."

She shrugged. "You seem to have come through okay without me."

"People died." She didn't respond. She didn't even blink. "And the bad guys got away."

"How many bad guys?" she asked. "What kind?"

"Three, maybe four. Remember when I said I wasn't sure if Emmett was a werewolf or if he was alone? I'm sure now, and I'm sure about all three of his brothers. I may even have killed one or two of them."

"Really?" Annalise glanced at Arlene, measuring her expression.

"Yep. What about you? Have you found *him*? Did some of Henstrick's people visit you?"

"No, and yes."

"What happened to Henstrick's men?"

"They had a car accident. A terrible, terrible accident. None of them survived."

"Okay. What's next?"

"I've never killed werewolves before. That sounds like fun."

CHAPTER SIXTEEN

Annalise pulled open the passenger door and climbed in. I walked around to the driver's side.

"I'm coming with you," Arlene said in her most commanding tone.

"No, you're not." Annalise's voice didn't carry a lot of power the way Arlene's did, but there was a dangerous undercurrent to it that I doubted Arlene would recognize.

"I am," Arlene said. "I need to. There are some things I have to know."

Annalise had not yet closed the door. Arlene climbed onto the footrest and stepped up much too close. Maybe someone else would have been uncomfortable, would have yielded, but Annalise's girlish little voice just got very low. "Step back."

"Arlene," I said. "Get down. You don't know what you're doing." Reluctantly, she stepped back onto the parking lot. "Boss, she could be useful."

Annalise snorted. "How?"

"I can find them," Arlene said. "Emmett keeps the others close. They've never left the house they grew up in."

"What if the Dubois brothers aren't at the station? She could direct us to their house."

"So could a phone book."

Arlene smirked. "They're unlisted. You—"

"Fine," Annalise said. "But she's your baggage, Ray.

You have to haul her around, and it's on you if she gets killed."

Annalise slammed the van door. Arlene huffed indignantly and began to walk around the front of the van.

I went to meet her. "Don't annoy my boss."

"She certainly seems to be short on manners."

"You're not listening. Emmett Dubois is nothing compared to the woman in that van. She's not going to show either of us any respect, and if you can't handle that, you can go back to organizing the cleanup at church socials."

"I . . . I understand." Arlene looked toward the ground.

"Climb in," I said. "You'll have to stand between the seats. We're not set up for hitchhikers."

She did. I strapped myself in behind the wheel and started the engine. "Where to first, boss?"

"Let's try their home. If you injured them, they might go to ground."

"North," Arlene said immediately. "They live on the north end of town, about three blocks east of the station."

I pulled out of the parking lot slowly. Even so, Arlene winced as she used her injured hand to stabilize herself. On the way, we passed a knot of people attending to a body on the sidewalk. It was Rake-Thin Arms, who had been shot and fallen out the window. I wondered if I would ever learn his name.

Sugar Dubois was nowhere in sight.

After a few minutes of driving, Arlene turned to us. "Can I ask a question?"

Annalise didn't answer. "Okay," I said. I had a question of my own to ask, but I wasn't going to do it in front of Arlene.

"If one of them bit me, does that mean I'm going to . . ."

She'd already asked me this question. I didn't know if

Annalise was going to answer or not. After a few moments of silence, I said: "Annalise? Is she going to become a predator?"

Annalise turned and looked at Arlene. "If I knew for certain that you would, you'd already be dead."

"The silver hurt them," I said. "Regular bullets didn't do anything. And one of them had a sigil on his back. He turned into a human when I broke it."

Annalise didn't respond.

"Please," Arlene pleaded. Her voice was small. "Can't you tell me anything?"

Annalise turned and looked at her. "I can tell you this: if you're one of them, I'll make it quick, because Ray seems to like you. There's nothing more you need to know."

That was the end of that conversation.

We pulled up to the Dubois brothers' house a few minutes later. It was a large wood-frame house with a long front yard and a high chain-link fence around it. Behind the house, the ground sloped upward into wild terrain.

Arlene pointed to it. "Their grandfather bought that house. The men have always shared it. When you marry one Dubois brother, you marry them all. Not that any of them are married at the moment. Luke's first wife never left the house until she'd boozed herself to death. That was years ago, before Wilma. Emmett's wife—well, she disappeared one day with her kids. If anyone is there, it's one of the brothers."

Annalise opened her door and stepped out of the van. "Boss?" I called. "Do you need me, boss?"

"I doubt it." She slammed the door shut and walked toward the front gate.

"I brought this," Arlene said, holding up a slender letter opener. The blade was silver. "I stole it off the desk at the emergency room. Shouldn't I give this to her, just in case?"

I turned back to Annalise. She unzipped the front of her jacket, then stepped up to the padlocked gate. She grabbed the chain link and tore it off the frame. Beside me, Arlene gasped. Annalise shook her hands at her sides. They must have hurt her very much. She stepped through the gap and walked casually toward the front door.

"She doesn't need it," I said. "We'll keep it in case one of the brothers makes a break for it."

Annalise kicked the front door down. She entered the darkness of the house.

While we waited, Arlene laid the flat side of the letter opener against her wrist. I could see that the edge was pretty dull, but that wasn't surprising. Silver was not a metal for weapons. The tip seemed sharp enough, though.

Arlene lifted the blade from her arm. Welts had begun to form. She looked at me. "Are you going to tell her?"

"I have to," I said.

"Good." She held up the opener and stared at it. "I can't do it myself, you understand. That's a terrible sin."

"Under the circumstances—"

"It's a sin," she said with finality. "I won't let my last act in this world be a sin."

"If you could choose, how would you want it?" I asked. I knew Annalise could take Arlene's life quickly and simply.

Arlene stared at the silver blade. "Fighting. I want to go down fighting." Then she knelt on the dirty floor of the van and began to pray.

A few minutes later, Annalise emerged from the house. She walked down the front path and climbed back into the van. "They weren't there, but we already knew that."

"Then why did you go in?" Arlene asked.

I glanced at the house and saw orange firelight flickering in one of the windows. If there was a spell or spell book hidden there, it would soon be ashes. I started the engine and pulled away. "The police station, then."

"Don't you think they would want to find a doctor for Sugar?" Arlene asked.

"They were already at a hospital," I said. "They could have charged into the emergency room with their guns drawn and gotten whatever they wanted. I don't think they want doctors or drugs or stitches. I think they want their magic."

We drove the remaining two blocks in silence. All three pickup trucks were parked in front of the station, along with the Bentley and two police cars. One of the patrol cars was parked at an angle, as though it had skidded to a halt. The blinds on all the windows were closed.

I drove around the corner and parked a full block away. "What's the plan?"

Annalise glanced at Arlene, then turned to me. Her expression was unreadable. "You're my wooden man. I'll go around the back and wait for you to draw their attention. When you have, I go in through the back door and start doing my work. If you survive, that's nice, too."

"You know what would be nice?" I said. "Some gloves. I'd like some latex gloves or something. My fingerprints are already on file with the police. If I do survive, I don't want to spend the rest—"

"If you needed gloves, I'd have given them to you already," she said.

"What about me?" Arlene asked.

Annalise glanced down at the welts on Arlene's forearm. "I'll take care of you later." She got out of the van.

Arlene gripped my shoulder. "I'm coming with you. Is that okay?"

It wasn't, but I couldn't find it in myself to tell her so. "Come on," I told her. Guess I wasn't going to die alone today.

We climbed out of the van and walked down the block, passing the diner Annalise and I had eaten in that first night. The windows were still covered with cardboard, but the waitress spotted us anyway and came outside. "Aunt Arlene, what's going on? I heard there was a gunfight at the hospital, and Emmett and the boys just screeched into the station like they were starring in an action movie. Do you know what's going on?"

Arlene turned to her. "Emmett Dubois killed me," she said.

The waitress stepped back in surprise. "What? What do you mean?"

"He's killed a lot of people," Arlene said. Her voice was flat. I looked at her gray hair and wrinkled skin—she had looked about sixty when I first met her, but she seemed much older at the moment. I wondered if she'd led a good life, and if I would be ready to end my life at her age, or at any age. "He's been bleeding this town dry. Someone has to end it. And end him."

"What do you mean he's killed you?" the waitress asked. "Has he poisoned you?"

"Yes," Arlene said. "That's it exactly."

The waitress stepped forward. "Aunt Arlene—"

"Don't." Arlene waved her niece away. "I have something I need to do."

She and I walked the rest of the way toward the station. I told her to stand at the corner of the wall, beside the stairs, then I circled around behind the trucks. The red one was full of garbage and fast-food wrappers, so I broke into the black one.

With the ghost knife, I cracked the ignition lock and started the truck. I raced the engine loudly, threw it into reverse, and backed out of the spot.

The blinds rippled, and I stood on the brakes, making the tires chirp.

The front door flew open, and Luke lunged out, his face twisted with anger. Obviously, this was his truck. He lifted his revolver and aimed it at me.

I ducked beneath the dashboard, but I didn't hear any shots. Maybe he loved his truck too much to shoot at it.

Emmett yelled at him, and although his voice was faint, I distinctly heard him say, ". . . your own brother." I peeked over the dash and saw him go back into the building.

Obviously, I needed to do more to catch their attention. I threw the truck into drive.

The door flew open again, and Luke shoved Shireen into the daylight. She looked terrified. He pointed a revolver at her head, and she cringed and sank to the ground.

And began to change. Shireen seemed to recede from me, while a strange, hairy *thing* became visible. It was long and ungainly, with spindly, crooked legs and clawed fingers and toes. Its head was round and bristling with fur, and it had a short snout filled with brutally long teeth.

It stepped forward into the daylight, its gaze locked on me. It had its orders, and it was pretty clear who it was supposed to kill.

It moved toward the steps. It was clumsy on its spindly legs, but those teeth looked vicious. It went down on all fours, but that appeared to be even more awkward than walking upright, so it grabbed the railing instead.

Poor Shireen.

I revved the engine and shot forward. On her crooked legs, Shireen stumbled at the bottom of the stairs. The pickup slammed into her with its full force.

The air bag went off in my face, and I felt the truck bounce backward. The air bag deflated, and I threw open the door.

Shireen's arm and legs were shattered, and her rib cage

was crushed. Before my eyes, her broken bones righted themselves with loud pops and cracks. She moaned and whimpered.

Maybe I could get into that red truck after all and park it on her.

Shireen growled at me. Her transformed legs weren't built for standing or walking upright, and she stood awkwardly. Steadying herself on the crumpled, hissing hood of Luke's truck, she lunged for me.

I ran around the back of the truck. Shireen followed me, growling and snarling. I held my ghost knife close to my chest and crossed my left forearm across my throat. The tattoos on my arm didn't cover enough flesh to truly protect me, but I had nothing else. I didn't know if her bite would carry the same curse as the Dubois brothers', and I didn't want to find out.

She lunged at me again. I leaped to my left. She tried to change direction and follow, but stumbled. Her flailing right arm tore through my sleeve. I backed away and circled her, and she turned to follow me.

I glanced up at the police station. No one was watching us. So far, I wasn't much of a distraction for Annalise's attack. I wondered if Luke and Emmett were trying to save Sugar's life in there.

Shireen snapped at me, then faked a little lunge. I jumped straight back, just to keep her honest. I looked over her shoulder and saw Arlene charging silently at Shireen's back, her silver letter opener high over her head. She wasn't moving quickly, but she was putting everything she had into the charge.

Arlene's foot scraped against the asphalt. Shireen hopped away and turned toward the sound. Arlene, still ten yards away, didn't slow her charge.

Shireen bent low, letting her hands touch the ground, then leaped forward, snapping her jaws on Arlene's wrist. The old woman screamed. The opener fell from her hand and bounced down Shireen's back. Shireen flinched when it touched her, then wrenched her whole body to the side. Blood spurted from Arlene's arm. She lost her footing and went down. Shireen caught hold of Arlene's hair with one spindly claw and released her wrist, then turned her fangs to the old woman's throat.

I heard screams from somewhere nearby. Someone was watching.

I forced myself to look away from Arlene's bloody murder and searched for the silver blade. It couldn't have fallen far, but I didn't see it anywhere. I dropped to my hands and knees and spotted it under Luke's truck. I scrambled between the back wheels. The truck was tricked out to have a high clearance, but I still had to scrape my belly through oil and antifreeze to reach the opener. I crawled to it, trying to be as quiet as I could. Arlene was dead already, I knew. Wooden man or not, I didn't want to be next.

I closed my hand on it, feeling the slipperiness of the antifreeze and oil on the wooden handle. At the same moment, Shireen stuck her head under the carriage of the truck and snarled at me.

I felt something grab at my jacket and begin to pull me out from under the car. Shireen had caught the gun in my pocket, which I had forgotten about again.

I slashed and felt the opener strike bone. Shireen yelped and let go of me. I slid away from her, not that it would do me much good. She could be on the far side of the truck before I could. She could even grab hold of my feet and drag me into the daylight. Then the best I could do would be to kill her just as she was killing me.

But she didn't do that. She came right back at me the same way, and this time she led with her face. Her mouth was open, and I could see blood smeared into her fur.

She was moving slowly. I held the letter opener tightly

but didn't attack. She was presenting such an easy target, I figured there had to be some sort of trick.

But she didn't lash out at me. She kept creeping forward, getting closer and closer. It was almost as if she was daring me to strike—or she wanted me to. I couldn't let the opportunity pass. I stabbed her, plunging the silver blade deep into her eye.

She shuddered. I pushed the blade in as far as it would go. She collapsed and fell still.

I slid away from her. I wanted that letter opener, but I didn't want to take it out of her just yet. She became indistinct and Shireen's human face returned.

I rolled out from under the truck as slapping footsteps grew louder. Three townspeople had rushed over to us and stood around the bodies of the two women, gaping. I ran around the back of the truck and shouldered a man out of the way. It took me a moment to realize that he was the cook from the diner.

"Everyone get out of here," I said. I tried to sound commanding, but fear and adrenaline make my voice squeak.

"She changed," the cook said. Shireen still lay half under the truck, her torn clothes partly covering her wrinkled flesh. She looked very human and frail. I tried not to think about that. "Did I really see that? Did I really see her change?"

"Nope," I said. The two young women standing beside the cook stared aghast at the ruined bodies at their feet. "Now get away."

I pulled Shireen out from under the car. Her head bobbled as it dragged across the ground. The handle of the letter opener scraped the asphalt. I felt a powerful urge to retch.

"You shouldn't do that," the cook said. I took the letter opener from the body and forced myself to stare into the bloody ruin that used to be her eye. It didn't seem to be healing the way her broken limbs had. She was dead.

I moved away and knelt beside Arlene. She lay still and cooling on the asphalt, but the ragged tears in her throat and arm were slowly joining together. She was dead but healing.

It seemed unfair that she had wanted to go out fighting but now wouldn't be able to. In just a minute more, she would be awake, and talking about how she wanted to die rather than become a second Shireen.

I slid the blade of the letter opener between her ribs. Her wounds stopped knitting closed, but she didn't groan or sigh.

Behind me, I heard a door open. I turned to see Wiley Dubois step out of the police station, a shotgun in his hand.

No time for squeamishness. I ripped the letter opener out of Arlene, then threw my shoulder into the nearest of the two women. They both stumbled away from me. I ducked toward the back of the truck. "RUN!" I shouted.

The shotgun boomed as I hit the ground. The cook called out to Jesus, then beat a quick retreat. The two young women were already way ahead of him.

I scrambled to my feet and raced toward the other side of the truck. I heard the terrible clicks of the shotgun being pumped and dove behind the truck bed. Then came another boom, and I felt fire scrape along the back of my left calf.

I hit the ground and rolled. For a moment I was sure that the bottom half of my leg was gone, but that was just my imagination running wild. I had caught a couple of pieces of buckshot in my calf muscle.

I immediately peeked over the back of the truck and saw Wiley huffing down the front steps, heading for the narrow space between Luke's wrecked truck and the damaged station wall. He pumped the shotgun again.

I held the ghost knife in one hand and the letter opener in the other. The gun in my pocket was useless. Damn. I didn't have many choices left. I could run away and be shot in my unprotected back. I could backpedal and get shot in the legs or the face. I certainly couldn't hide.

All I could do was charge him. Charge at a man with a shotgun, and hope I could get close enough to stab him before he killed or crippled me.

I took a deep breath. This is what a wooden man does. He plays decoy and he dies.

I stood. Wiley lifted the shotgun to his shoulder.

From inside the station came the sound of gunshots and a scream. Wiley turned toward the sound, and so did I. It was a man's voice, high-pitched with panic. The scream was cut off with a strangled sound, and Emmett shouted Luke's name. The gunshots continued, a dozen over the course of a few seconds.

The window shattered, and something the size of a soccer ball flew through it. It smashed into the windshield of Luke's car. Wiley gaped at it for a second, then hustled up the stairs toward the front door. He had bigger problems than me.

There was another flurry of gunfire from inside the station.

I rushed to the front of the truck, but I already knew what had broken the windshield. It was Luke's head.

Annalise had started her attack.

I couldn't resist one more look at Luke. Thankfully, his face was not much in view, but it suddenly became indistinct. It was vanishing right before my eyes. Damn. I should have stabbed it with the letter opener.

There were more gunshots from inside the station. Ducking below the windows, I ran toward the stairs. I saw a flare of green light, and Emmett began screaming "No no no!" at the top of his lungs. I burst through the door.

The desks we had walked past on our first visit had been smashed and knocked aside. Just beside the door, a pile of scorched black bones lay on the tile floor.

Annalise stood in the center of the room, her fireman's jacket wide open, ribbons hanging from her vest. Luke Dubois's headless corpse lay at her feet.

But his head was starting to appear on his shoulders. His head was coming back.

"This is amazing," Annalise said to me. "I've never seen anything like it. Look at the fat one."

I looked down at Wiley again. Raw meat was growing on his bones. It was repulsive. "Jesus," I said. "Everything about these guys makes me sick."

"No more," Emmett said. He stepped out of his office, a pistol at his side. The slide was back; he'd already emptied it. "Please, no more. We'll leave town and never come back. We have money we can pay. Anything. Just let me take my brothers away from here."

"The spell," Annalise said. "I want it."

"Wha . . . what do you mean?" Emmett said.

"Ray, do that one." She nodded at Wiley's corpse.

There was nothing much of him to stab with the letter opener, so I swept the ghost knife through the same place on his shoulder where Sugar had been marked with a sigil. The space where the spell would have been suddenly erupted with a jet of black steam.

Wiley's body stopped regenerating. The gory mess inside his rib cage sagged and began to spread out across the floor. I hopped away from him.

"Oh my God, Wiley." Emmett's voice was small. I felt a twinge of sympathy. Then I remembered the dead woman in the morgue, and all the bodies at the hospital, and my sympathy shriveled into cold hatred. He didn't have the right to grieve.

"You're right, Ray," Annalise said. "These guys are repulsive. Do the rest."

"No!" Luke yelled. "Don't do it!" He was alive again.

Annalise put her foot on Luke's back, holding him down. "I already did it," she said to him, "and I may do it again if you don't shut up."

I crossed the room and slipped the ghost knife through Luke's shoulder. There was another jet of steam and Luke screamed.

Emmett let his empty pistol fall to the floor. "We did some good here, too." His voice was feeble and small. "We protected the town, too."

I didn't care, and neither did Annalise. I walked toward him, being careful not to get between them. I cut his spell with the ghost knife, and he collapsed to the floor in agony. I didn't watch this time. I walked over to Sugar.

He was lying on the floor in the middle of a spell circle. Compared with the other circles I'd seen, this one was surprisingly simple. It was not drawn or painted on the floor, it was just a hoop of silver wire. There were no other marks or designs that I could see.

Sugar was in bad shape. His arms and legs were broken, and I could see where his skull had cracked and swollen. He looked like he was in terrible pain. His shirt had been cut open, and there was a new sigil on his chest. He wasn't healing, though. He didn't seem to be changing at all.

That seemed important, although I wasn't sure why.

I cut the silver hoop with the ghost knife. There was no rush of power or bolt of black steam. I moved toward Sugar and bent to cut the sigil.

"Don't!" Emmett pleaded. "Please. He'll die without it."

Annalise snorted in irritation and moved her foot to Luke's skull. Luke let out a little shriek.

"Boss, wait!" She did. I turned to Emmett. "Give me the spell, and tell me everything you know about it. Where it came from and who gave it to you. All of it."

Emmett looked nervously toward Annalise. He reached into his jacket pocket and took out an index card inside a plastic sleeve. He held it out to me. His hand trembled.

"Toss it." He did. I glanced at it. There was a complicated design on one side of it, and a four-line rhyming poem on the other.

"My father gave it to me." Emmett said. "He got it from the original Cabot Hammer, the man who founded this town, a long time ago. I don't know much more than that, except that I'm supposed to say the words while the person getting the spell sits in the hoop and looks at the other side of the card. That's the only copy, too. My father told me to never try to copy it.

"We didn't kill people every full moon or anything. It didn't work like that. We—"

Annalise stamped down on Luke's skull. At the same moment, I slid the ghost knife through the sigil on Sugar's chest. The magic rushed out of it, and his tortured breathing stopped.

Emmett's shoulders sagged. All the fight was gone from him. "Do it. Just go ahead."

Annalise looked me in the eyes. "Ray."

My turn at bat. I took Cabot's gun out of my pocket and pointed it at the back of Emmett's head.

In the movies, you often hear actors say it's hard to kill someone. They'll say it's the hardest thing in the world. Well, that's bullshit. Prison is full of people who thought murder was some kind of achievement—I lived with some of them.

And most of those guys wish they could take it back, because the truth is, the only thing a person needs to commit murder is a moment when they don't care about the consequences, when they don't think about what they're doing and what it means.

Most people spend their whole lives without thinking what it means.

I couldn't do that. I had done too much time and had too much conscience. I'd shot my best friend when I was just a boy, and I'd hated guns ever since. I knew exactly what would happen. I knew exactly what it would mean.

I squeezed the trigger anyway.

CHAPTER SEVENTEEN

Emmett's corpse looked just the way I expected it to look. So did the room around me. So did Annalise.

I saw a flannel shirt hanging on a coatrack and used it to wipe down Cabot's gun. I tossed the gun onto the floor. It thunked as it landed. I wasn't worried about Cabot, though.

Everyone in town had seen me. There was no way I was going to avoid prison this time. I was a cop killer. He was a corrupt cop and a killer himself, but that wouldn't matter once the manhunt began.

But what choice did I have? I couldn't let him walk free. What if he had another copy of the spell somewhere? What if he went looking for more magic? He would just move somewhere else and start killing again.

With some difficulty, Annalise pulled a red ribbon off her vest and dropped it onto a stuffed chair. It burst into flame. She kicked over a desk, scattering a stack of papers onto the flames. The fire was already licking at the painted walls. Soon the station would be lit by orange firelight, just like the Dubois home.

I returned Annalise's debit card. I didn't want anything of hers, especially not her money.

"Stop moping," she said. "You did something useful here, even if the work makes you feel dirty."

"Let's just go."

I followed her toward the door. A small, framed photo hung on the wall, and while I didn't want to look at it, I couldn't turn away. It showed Emmett with his arm around Charles the Third. The youngest Hammer was about thirteen and tall for his age, but he was carrying an extra hundred pounds of flab. An older man with Charles's narrow face and unruly black hair flipped burgers on a gleaming barbecue. That must have been Charles the Second, Charles Junior.

While the fire grew behind me, I leaned close to the picture. The elder Hammer was the only one not smiling—his face was worn and sagging, his eyes rimmed with dark circles. He was a man with regrets. In the background, I could see the huge windows of an expensive modern house and a smooth, curved gray stone wall like the base of a castle.

The firelight cast flickering shadows over the photo. The flames had reached the ceiling. Annalise stood by the front door, waiting for me silently. Time to go.

We walked outside. The storm clouds had blown away, and I could see blue sky and sunshine for the first time in days.

A crowd of people stood across the street. The van was parked around the corner. We walked toward them.

"Next time, I'll park closer."

"Good idea. You look like a mess."

I pulled at my shirt. It was torn, sopping wet, and it stank of gunpowder and antifreeze. "I needed more than four changes of clothes, I think."

"I didn't think you'd live through that many. Are you going to vomit?"

"Oh, yes," I said to her. "But not right away, I think."

As we neared the crowd, the cook approached me nervously. I must have been quite a sight. "What's happening?" he asked. "What's going on in this town?"

"The Dubois brothers killed Reverend Wilson."

There were gasps of astonishment from the crowd. "What?" the cook said. "You can't be serious."

"Go away," I told him. We pushed through the crowd and headed up the block. No one tried to stop us. "Charles Hammer is next, right, boss?"

"He would be, if I knew where to find him. That's all I've been doing is looking for him. He hasn't been home or at his office since we were there last, and Karoly's notes don't tell me anything."

"Are your hands any better?"

"No," she said. "They're worse. I expect I won't be able to use them at all by tomorrow. They feel like they're burning, and I can barely bend my fingers."

We reached the van. I opened the door for her and helped her in, not bothering with the seat belt. I climbed in behind the wheel and started the engine. "We could stop off at the butcher again—"

"Don't bother," she said. "The last time it barely helped at all, and I don't want to spend all day on it. It's a waste of time."

"And your stomach?"

"I'm starving." She didn't look at me. She just stared ahead. "I feel a little weak and disoriented, to tell the truth. I'm going to have to rely on you a little more than I would normally. Can I do that?"

"Yes," I said. "I just killed a cop in cold blood for you. If that doesn't prove I'm on your side . . ."

Right then I felt like vomiting. Thankfully, I hadn't eaten in hours.

I pulled out of the parking space. I didn't have anywhere to go, but I didn't want to be near the scene of the fight any longer. I didn't know where I was going, so I just drove.

Hammer Bay was pretty in the sunlight. I thought of all the people who were not going to see this sunshine, from the woman in the hospital morgue to the reverend to Sugar Dubois, and I felt a twist of cold anger. I tried to aim it at Charles Hammer, or his grandfather, or Eli Warren, who had brought the spells to this town in the first place, but in truth, I was angry at everything, including myself. The world seemed to be full of killers and those who stood by and did nothing about them. I suddenly wished I was one of those who stood by.

"If I don't survive," she said, "I don't want you to go after Charles Hammer by yourself."

"Why not?" I sounded a little indignant, but she ignored it.

"Because he's too big for you, and I don't want him getting a close look at the spells you're carrying. If things go wrong, head out of town. One of the peers will track you down and debrief you."

"I'll be in jail by then, right? Will the society get me out again?"

She shrugged. She was dying, and she didn't much care whether I went to jail or not. I'd have probably felt the same way.

I drove toward Cynthia's house, glad that it was my left calf that was throbbing, not the one I drove with. Maybe we could get Charles's location out of her. Something was nagging at me. There was something I should have remembered but couldn't quite recall.

"You don't think he left Hammer Bay, do you?"

"I hope not," Annalise said. "I don't think so. He started this whole thing for his company and his town. I don't think he'd cut and run."

I nodded. Cynthia had refused to leave, too. "What about a boat or something? He's rich enough to have one."

"He does. Karoly's notes told me which one. I sank it last night. He wasn't there."

Then I remembered. "Cabot said that Charles has been spending all his time hiding in the tower."

"There's a high, round room at their house."

"That's what I thought, too, but no dice. That's his sister's bedroom."

She didn't react to that. "Did the sister tell you where he is?"

"She wouldn't. Not her own brother." This was the point where I could have told Annalise about Cynthia's iron gate, but we had more important things to discuss. "I want to ask her one more time."

Annalise didn't say anything after that. I wondered what she would do to force an answer out of Cynthia. Had I saved Cynthia's life so my boss could kill her?

Then it hit me—the gray stone wall in Emmett's photo, Cabot's remark that Charles had been hiding in the tower . . .

I switched off the turn signal and kept going south.

We passed out of the business district. I looked toward the ocean and saw the sunlight sparkle on the water. It was a beautiful sight.

And there, naked in the sunlight, was the lighthouse. Except that with no mist or fog around it, it didn't look like a lighthouse at all.

I pulled over and shut off the engine. "Where's that bad map?"

We searched the glove compartment and the spaces under the seats before I remembered that I had looked at the map in Ethan's minivan. I found it in the inside pocket of my jacket, folded up into a tiny square. I unfolded it. The lighthouse was marked with a number four. I turned the map over and found the entry for number four.

"What's all this about?" Annalise asked.

"A lighthouse that isn't a lighthouse," I said. "Here it is: 'In 1949, Charles Hammer the First bought a castle in Scotland and had it shipped to Hammer Bay, where it was rebuilt stone by stone. Sixteen years later, an earthquake toppled all but the southernmost tower, which still stands today.' "

I stared at the tower. It didn't have the battlements that I saw in old movies. It was slightly crooked, but it was a tower. This was the "Scottish thing" Bill had mentioned.

"That's where he is."

Annalise nodded. "Let's finish this job."

"Boss," I said. I wasn't sure how to say what I wanted to say next, so I just blurted it out. "Do you think there's a way to turn those worms back into kids? Do you think they can be cured?"

She did not like that question. "Anything is possible, Ray."

I thought that, if I'd asked her if we could fly a candy-cane rocket to Jupiter, she would have given me the exact same answer in the exact same tone. "Boss, I had to ask."

"I know you did." That was all she had to say.

I drove to the waterfront and parked behind a seafood restaurant. The southward road turned east, away from the cliff and the ocean, leaving an unpaved driveway to go the last two blocks toward the edge of town. We walked toward it, seeing little more than a tumble of black volcanic rocks ahead. And the tower.

It stood alone, well away from the rest of town and a dozen yards from the edge of the cliff. At the base, I could make out a low, modern house, with huge windows along each wall. And there was a broad asphalt platform where a person could turn a car around. I couldn't see a driveway connecting it to the town, and I couldn't see the ruins of the rest of the castle.

"There," Annalise said. She nodded toward a pair of Dumpsters a few doors down. The driveway to the tower was hidden behind them.

We walked quickly back to the van. I pulled out of

the parking lot and drove toward that driveway. We passed three identical burgundy Crown Victorias, but I chalked them up to someone's desire to keep up with the Joneses.

The gravel road was barred by a long gate. I stopped, climbed out, and cut off the lock with my ghost knife. The gate swung wide open. I drove down the sloping driveway and parked the van at the end. No one was going to be driving out of here unless they tipped the van onto the rocks, which, frankly, was not all that unlikely.

I climbed out and opened Annalise's door. We walked toward the house. It was much larger up close than it had seemed from the parking lot. The windows were all two stories tall. And none of the shades were drawn.

Something was wrong.

I slipped over to the garage and peeked into the window. Inside was the same elegant black S-class Mercedes I'd seen parked outside the toy factory door. It was a couple of years old. There were no other cars in sight.

"This isn't right," I said to Annalise.

She was too short to look in the window and didn't bother to try. "What do you mean?" she asked.

"There's a Mercedes in there. Charles Hammer drives a Prius."

"He's rich." She moved toward the front door.

Not right. Not right. Not right. I took the ghost knife from my pocket and threw it, cutting the phone line.

I was about to cut through the locks on the front door when Annalise clumsily turned the knob and pushed. The door swung open. It was unlocked.

We entered. Golden sunlight filled the room. I could see storm clouds down at the edge of the horizon, but the sunlit waters were beautiful.

I shut the door and noticed something hanging beside the hinges. It was a long, double-edged knife. The blade appeared to be made of silver. I suspected it was there on the off chance that the Dubois brothers turned on their masters. I took it off the hook and held it in my off hand.

I followed Annalise toward the far end of the room. There was a flat-screen TV hung on the wall and a very low couch facing it. The coffee table was littered with a dozen empty cans of beef stew, bread crumbs, and torn-open baguette wrappers. It looked as though someone had holed up here, but then why were the shades wide open?

"Through here," Annalise said. She kicked open a door and entered another long room. I followed her.

This room had plush carpeting. All the shades were drawn, and the air was thick. At the far end, about twenty feet away, was a long wooden desk. Heavy drapes hung just behind it.

The high leather chair behind the desk was turned away from us. It moved slightly. I saw the sleeve of a dark suit jacket on the armrest.

"Charles Hammer the Third," Annalise said, with the tone of a judge passing sentence. She pulled a ribbon from her vest. "You—"

"That's not Charles Hammer," I said. "That's Able Katz."

Able Katz swung the chair around. He looked quite smug.

The drapes fluttered, and four men stepped out. They were built like boxers, wore the brown uniforms of a private security force, and held Uzis in their hands.

A door to the side opened, and six more guards rushed into the room. They fanned out along the wall to our left.

"There are two more waiting for you by the front door," Able said. "So don't try to run that way."

I noticed a webcam on the desk, beside the computer. Charlie Three was watching us, but from where? I dropped the silver knife into my pocket.

"Oh, no," Able said. "Not your pocket, young man. That's not good enough. You'll have to toss that weapon away from you, onto the floor. In fact, please dispose of all your weapons that way." He smirked at us.

Annalise reached up and tugged a fistful of ribbons off her vest.

"Wait," I whispered to her. "They're just guys doing a job."

"Their job is to let a child killer go free."

"That's nonsense!" Able barked. "Charles has done nothing of the sort. You two are the ones who have been tearing this town apart."

I kept my focus on Annalise. "Emmett was a killer, but these guys were hired to protect someone. They aren't evil."

She turned to me. "Of course they're not evil," she said. "I'm the one who's evil."

The phone on the desk rang.

Everyone seemed startled except for Able. He answered it. "Yes, Charles?" He listened. "I will." He pressed the button on the handset and turned the phone to us.

"Can you hear me?"

It was Charles Hammer, talking over the speaker-phone.

"Yes," I said. Annalise looked impatient, but I wanted to hear him out.

"Let me explain myself," the voice said, "and I hope we can avoid any unpleasantness. I really, really would like to avoid violence, if that's possible. More than anything."

I watched the guards. Hammer could have been delaying us until the state police arrived, or even more guards, but I doubted it. He had ten armed men in the room with us, and two more, if Able was to be believed, by the exit. "I'm listening."

"Able," the voice said. "Do you trust me? Some of

what we're going to say will sound bad, and these people may make accusations against me that I don't deserve. I want you to understand—"

"There's no need for that, Charles," Able said. "I trust you."

"Great." Charles took a deep breath as though he was about to cliff dive for the first time. "First I want to explain—"

"Want want want," I snapped. "Don't tell me what you want. What about the kids you killed?"

"I never killed any kids! The missing children are still alive, and I can get them back. I've been searching for a way to get them back."

"Looking through your book, huh? The one Eli Warren sold to your great-grandfather?"

"How did you— It doesn't matter. Yes, I'm looking for a way to get them back. It's the number-one priority for me. The children are the next generation of Hammer Bay."

I laughed at him. "You're not running for office, are you?"

"Sneer if you want," the voice said, "but everything I've done is to help the people of this town. I've worked hard to bring jobs and dignity back to Hammer Bay."

"And you had help," Annalise said.

"Yes." There was a pause. "I did have help. A consultant, of a sort. A fortune-teller."

"The same one your father had, and your grandfather."

"My great-grandfather, too. 'Use it sparingly,' my father told me, but there were so many things I didn't know. And the people . . ."

He kept talking. He sounded very much like the weary activist, so burdened with the tasks ahead of him and so impressed with his own motives and ideals.

But something had struck me. *Fortune-teller,* he'd said.

What if he was not just looking into the future? What if the magic he was using was actually controlling the future?

It made sense if he was using magic that let him step outside of time in some way. Annalise's burned hands kept coming back, no matter what she did to treat them. The Dubois brothers could heal anything, even brutal, mangling death. Maybe they were simply backing up in time, to a point before they were injured. Maybe that's why the new sigil on Sugar Dubois couldn't heal his injuries the way his brothers had been healed. It could not restore him to a time before it was in place.

As for the Hammer family, I had assumed that the seizures they suffered during hard times, and the smart moves they had made to turn things around, had come from visions of the future. But what if they were more than visions? What if he was *making* good things happen?

How else to explain a successful line of toys about Marie Antoinette, for God's sake?

I tried to picture the power of a spell that could control whole populations of people. I couldn't. How could he be so strong that he forced people to love his products? How could he force people to forget the people they loved most?

Then it dawned on me. He wasn't doing it. His "consultant" was.

Goose bumps ran down my back. Annalise was right. This was completely out of my league.

I looked at Annalise. She was scowling at me. "Have you been paying attention to this crap?" Charlie Three was talking about siting a plastics factory.

"His great-grandfather summoned a predator out of the Empty Spaces, right?" I said. "And this dick has been communing with it somehow, using it to draw in customers for his fucking *toys*. And *it's* been taking the children for some reason, probably to eat them."

"That's what I figure, too," she said. "And I'll bet it was this predator that controlled those women in his office"—she held up her hands—"burning them all to protect him. *He* doesn't have the power or the guts for a move like that."

I turned to Able Katz. "Do you remember what happened after our meeting at your office?"

"What meeting?" he said, sounding irritated. "I've never seen either of you before in my life." Charles was droning on, but I was focused on Able. It was true. Just as I'd suspected, he couldn't remember meeting us any more than Doug and Meg Benton could remember their dead kids. The predator was controlling people.

"Why hasn't the predator run amuck? Why hasn't it tried to kill everyone on the planet?"

"It's probably bound somehow. Eli must have helped them summon and bind it."

"That was a long time ago. Do you think it's likely to get free?"

She looked back at Able Katz, who was scowling at us. He must have thought we should pay more attention to his boss's speech. "It's already free enough to kill."

I thought of the way the children had fallen apart when they burned. They'd turned into little worms and crawled off to the southwest. To here, in fact, or somewhere close to here. I wondered if the predator was feeding on those worms.

Hammer started talking about median home prices, and I couldn't take it anymore. "Shut up!" I snapped. "You want to avoid violence? I'll make you an offer. Send your guards away. Turn over to us all copies of the book Eli Warren sold to your great-grandfather. Take us to your so-called consultant."

"But," the voice said, "the company can't continue without my, um, consultant."

"The company isn't going to continue," I said. "And neither are you. There's too much blood on your hands."

"I can find those kids again!"

I turned to the guards. "Hear that? I'm talking about missing children, and he's worried about his company. Is that who you're trying to protect?"

"Don't bother," Able said. "These men are not going to turn against us. They're professionals. That's why I hired them. They do their jobs."

Annalise turned to me. "And you had better do your job."

She dropped the fistful of green ribbons onto the carpet, then grabbed my arm. She winced while she did it.

The ribbons struck the carpet and flared into green fire. Flames engulfed my legs, but I didn't feel any pain. Several of the guards gaped at us in shock, and one cried out. They thought we were burning ourselves alive.

The fire crawled up our bodies and billowed outward. As soon as the flames reached above her head, Annalise charged forward.

Able Katz's expression went slack. He stood and inhaled deeply.

The tinny voice on the speakerphone shouted, *"No! No! No!"*

Annalise slapped the desk to the side. It smashed a window and tore the drape from the rod. The desk and drape fell outside and crashed to the rocks below.

The four guards who had been flanking Able opened fire on Annalise, drowning out Hammer's voice.

Annalise slammed into Able, knocking him into the wall with a sickening thunk. Blood-red fire blasted from his mouth, igniting the wooden beams in the ceiling. He had been about to breathe dragon breath on us, just like the officer workers at Hammer Bay Toys.

I dropped low into Annalise's green fire and rolled toward the far wall. The guns made an incredible racket in the enclosed room. I felt something zip past me. It must have been a ricochet off Annalise's invulnerable body.

I lifted myself into a crouch. The green flames were spreading toward me, and the six guards along the wall bolted toward the door they had entered through. Good. Let them run. At least they'd live.

One of them turned and saw me. He raised his weapon.

Without thinking, I threw the ghost knife at him. One of his partners bumped him in the rush to get to the door, and another stepped briefly into his line of fire. Then the ghost knife struck him over the heart.

The guard collapsed onto the carpet. The man behind him tripped over him and fell into the doorway, blocking it. The green flames reached them, and they disappeared within the fire. I could hear their screams.

I summoned my ghost knife. It flew into my hand. Of course I had killed them. Damn.

The door behind me opened. I spun, catching a quick glimpse of the two men entering through the doorway we had just used. Both held their Uzis at the ready. I threw the ghost knife again and ducked into the flames, throwing myself flat on the floor.

The bullets zipped above me. Then I heard a bang, as if one of the Uzis had jammed and backfired, and the two men cried out. All gunfire in the room stopped. Just then, the green fire evaporated. I looked around the room. The two guards who had entered behind us were smoking skeletons. One of the submachine guns in their hands had burst open.

"You did good," Annalise said, her back to me. The room seemed strangely quiet after all the gunfire, but there was a terrible stench of burned plastic and roasted flesh in the air.

"It doesn't feel like good," I said. I glanced over to where she had been fighting. The other four guards were also smoking bones. So was Able Katz.

I should have been sick, but I had already passed that point. Maybe if there had been one body, or two, I could have puked my guts out and cried like a little girl, but these were too much. It didn't seem real.

"At least for them, it was quick." Annalise turned toward me. Her right eye was gone. She had only an empty socket there. Just below that empty socket, in her cheekbone, was a second bullet hole.

"Holy . . . !" I shouted. I backed away from her. She had two bullets in her head, with no exit wounds, but she was walking around as if nothing had happened. What the hell was she? Was she even alive?

"I know," she said. "It sucks when this happens." She reached up and gingerly touched her face with her stiff, inflamed hand. One of her fingers slipped into her ruined eye socket.

That did it. I heaved a thin, acid stream onto the carpet.

"Oh, knock it off," she snapped. "You're not the one who got shot. Let's go."

She charged through the doorway, kicking the smoking bones out of her way.

Holy God, what was I doing here? What was she?

I was about to follow her, but I couldn't. I couldn't step over the bones of the men we'd just killed.

"What are you waiting for?" she snapped at me.

I didn't answer. I couldn't help picturing the guards' wives and children, their mothers and fathers.

The smashed-up computer lay in a heap beside one of the bodies. I strode over to it and lifted the webcam. The little red light was still on, but I didn't know if it was still sending images.

"This is your fault," I said to the camera. "You put these people here. You asked them to die for you. You—"

Something smashed the camera out of my hand. It was a scorched human skull.

"For God's sake!" Annalise hissed. "This is why you'll never be more than a wooden man, Ray. You're too fucking soft. Don't talk to the targets. Don't taunt them. Don't be their fucking friends. It just makes things harder. Be a fucking professional. Treat them like objects." She held up the skull and waved it in front of my face. "They're glass figurines, Ray, and nothing more— some are very pretty, some not so much. But it's your job to break some of those figurines, and you can never tell right away which ones that'll be."

I stepped away from the skull. "Don't—"

She stepped toward me, and for a moment I thought she was going to rub the blackened bone against my face. "Does this bother you? Get over it. This is what we do. We make corpses. And maybe, if we make enough of them . . ."

She broke off. Her hand was shaking. She let the skull fall to the floor and cradled her hand against her chest. Her pain must have been intense. She scowled at the floor. I saw anger in her expression, and resentment, too. And regret.

The overhead sprinkler system turned on. I looked up to see water dousing the flames Able had blasted onto the ceiling. Annalise and I stood in the downpour while brilliant sunlight shone through the broken window.

"Boss—"

"Could you kill a priest, Ray? Could you kill a priest who only wanted to help terminally ill children? Could you kill a mother who was trying to protect her kids? Could you kill a five-year-old girl whose only crime is that some idiot adult cast a spell on her? I could. I've done all those things."

"Annalise—"

"You're good at this, Ray. You're good at this job. And the society needs good people, more than ever. But you're useless if you stop right before the finish line to moralize. We have a planet full of people to save. Get it? If someone gets between you and your target, there's a planet full of people who will die if you can't bring yourself to do your job."

She clamped her mouth shut and turned away. I had the impression that she had a lot more to say, but she had to hold it back. She sealed it all off with anger.

Suddenly Annalise seemed very human to me, despite the grotesque injuries to her face. And she was right. If we stopped now, more little kids were going to die. Charles Hammer needed killing.

She marched into the hall. "Come on. We have to search the house." I bent and touched one of the unfired Uzis. It was, as expected, cool to the touch. I lifted it and draped the strap over my neck. It was a weapon, but it didn't make me feel any more confident about the coming fight.

I followed her into the hallway. There were three doors along the far side. I charged into the first one. It was an empty bathroom. Annalise opened the next. It was a laundry room and pantry. Farther down the hall was the kitchen, complete with gas range and walk-in fridge. Beyond that was a set of stairs leading to the second floor.

The upstairs was just a single room, broken up by a couple of support columns. There was a small cluster of exercise equipment, some bookshelves, some closets, a terrace with a monstrous charcoal grill, and an open futon against the far wall.

"This way," Annalise said. She kicked open a door. It led to a ten-foot-long covered causeway that connected to the entrance of the tower. We strode across it, looking down at the jagged black rocks twenty feet below.

The tower was made of gray stone blocks. It was dark inside, with only a single electric light burning above.

Annalise sprinted up the wooden stairs. I followed as closely as I could with my injured leg. She seemed to have forgotten that I was supposed to be her decoy.

We ran up the spiraling stairs, never pausing at the landings or glancing out the windows. Annalise tugged a ribbon free, but I couldn't see what it was. My shoe was filling with blood, and I started to fall behind.

Annalise finally reached the ladder at the top of the stairs. She climbed up, threw her shoulder into the trapdoor above us, and broke through it.

She flinched, turning her face down toward me. There was the boom of a shotgun. Annalise's head snapped back, and I knew she had taken the blast in the side of her face. The ribbon fell from her fingers, and she sagged toward me for a moment. I heard the gunman rack a new shell into the shotgun.

Instead of falling off the ladder and through the center of the tower, Annalise stood up straight again. She was still fighting.

"No!" someone shouted in disbelief. "No!"

Annalise was halfway through the trap. She covered her face as another blast struck. This time, she had braced herself and didn't even flinch.

Whoever was up there racked the shotgun once more. Annalise climbed out of the trapdoor. I was right behind her.

Charles Hammer backed toward the other end of the room. Annalise ran at him. He aimed the shotgun low, blasting at her feet. Her legs went out from under her, and she fell onto her hands. I heard her hiss in pain.

I gained the tower room. I saw books all around me, and another silver hoop in the middle of the room. This one was bent and twisted into a variety of strange sigils. On the other side of that hoop stood Charles Hammer. He looked like a sick man. His skin was sallow, his hair was greasy, and he had bags under his eyes. The room smelled like old socks and gunpowder.

Annalise stood. I slipped my ghost knife between my teeth and lifted the Uzi. No sense in being fancy about it.

Hammer's eyes rolled back into his head. His mouth dropped open and he took a deep breath. My iron gate twinged painfully. It felt as though someone had reached under my skin and made a fist.

I squeezed the trigger. Nothing happened. It felt stuck. I squeezed it as hard as I could, but the weapon still wouldn't fire. I realized that the safety had to be on, but I had no idea where the safety was.

Charles blasted a column of fire from his mouth. Annalise threw herself at me, knocking me back through the trapdoor. I fell off the ladder just as the flames engulfed Annalise from head to toe.

I heard her scream. I was screaming, too. I tumbled down the stairs, wrenching my arm against the railing as I yanked myself to a stop. My legs dangled over the edge, with the long, long drop through the tower below them.

I pulled myself onto the steps, untangling the gun as I did. The fire still blasted over the top of the stairs. There was no way to enter the room above without charging straight through the flames. I held up the gun, found what looked like the safety, and flipped it. My iron gate throbbed.

Then the jet of flames stopped. I heard a sick, choking noise. What the hell, I thought. I charged up the stairs, screaming.

Everything in the room was charred and blackened. The acrid stink of smoke burned my nose and eyes. I couldn't see Annalise anywhere. Hammer stumbled back against the tower window, clutching at his throat.

The inside of his mouth was as black as the room

around me. The fire had cooked him as it came out. But as I watched, his lips turned pink, and his mouth and throat healed as quickly as Arlene's ravaged throat had.

I shot him.

I tried to fire a short burst up the center of his body, from crotch to forehead, but the Uzi kicked like crazy, and the trail of bullets tore through his shoulder instead. Charles Hammer the Third stumbled back and fell out the tower window.

I ran across the room, feeling the burned wood wobble dangerously under my feet. I reached the window before he struck the rocks below. I saw him hit. Hard. He was still.

I noticed a piece of silver wire set into the windowsill. It ran from the hoop on the floor out the window and then down the side of the tower. I wondered what was at the other end. I also wondered when my iron gate was going to stop throbbing.

Then I saw Hammer lift his arm. Damn. The gun and the rocks hadn't finished him. He wasn't dead.

I turned back to the trapdoor, wondering if Annalise had managed to leap out a window, too, when I saw her. I had run right past her without recognizing her.

She was burned. Her skin and clothes were blackened and shriveled. She was not burned down to her bones, she was too tough for that, but her mouth gaped wide and her little hands were curled into fists. She held them as though she was about to knock my head off. She was absolutely still. She was gone.

CHAPTER EIGHTEEN

I knelt beside her and touched her face. Her skin crumpled like burned paper, and hot grease scorched my fingertips.

Damn damn damn. I wanted her back.

I ran down the tower stairs. I didn't know how much time I had before he healed himself, but I knew it wasn't much. My mind was racing, wondering why Annalise had deliberately sacrificed her life for mine, wondering whether the ghost knife or the silver blade I'd taken from behind the door would do the job the Uzi couldn't, whether my iron gate would ever stop hurting, and whether the pain from my iron gate meant that more kids were burning to death even as I ran after their killer.

I reached the bottom of the stairs.

Through the thick Plexi enclosure around the causeway, I saw Charles Hammer struggling across the huge black rocks. Then I noticed the tumble of broken gray stones among the volcanic black. That was where the rest of the castle had collapsed.

There was a twenty-foot drop below the causeway, and I knew I couldn't jump down onto the jagged black rocks. I slid the ghost knife through the Plexi, cutting out a section that was eight feet by five feet. It fell across the rocks.

I lowered myself out the hole and dropped onto the plastic. It bowed under my weight but didn't snap. I scrambled across it and out onto the rocks.

Hammer was a good thirty yards ahead of me. He seemed to be heading southeast, although I couldn't imagine where he was running. The town was to the northeast; if he wanted help or protection from the people of Hammer Bay, he was headed the wrong way. As far as I could tell, the only thing to the southeast was forest and mountain.

I kept after him, my ghost knife between my teeth, silver knife in my pocket, and the Uzi banging against my knee as I leaped from rock to rock. I considered dumping the gun. It had already proven less than useful, but I couldn't bring myself to do it. I needed all the weapons I could get.

Annalise had told me not to go after Hammer by myself. She had said he was too much for me. She was probably right. But I had just touched her burned face. I couldn't let that go. I couldn't run away.

I focused on the rocks, trying to increase my speed to shut off my thoughts. Now wasn't the time to think about my boss. Now was the time to figure out what Charles Hammer had become, where his silver wire led, and how hard I was going to kill him.

I looked up from the rocks I'd been navigating. Hammer had vanished. Cursing furiously, I tried to rush toward the spot where I'd seen him last. I hoped he had entered a cave or fallen down a well. If he had turned invisible or something, I really was out of my league, and I was headed in the wrong direction.

But I kept going forward, hopping from rock to rock, occasionally looking up to see if he had reappeared from behind some low hill of stones.

I jumped over a rock and stumbled across a flat pile of stones. It was a collapsed wall, and I could see a piece of gray, pitted wooden furniture jutting out from behind the rocks. Beside it was a small pile of broken crockery. I was standing on the collapsed castle.

I hopped the last few rocks to the spot where Hammer had vanished. Nothing. I couldn't see a thing there, except for a strip of faded red cloth and a smashed grandfather clock that had spent decades exposed to the weather. I looked all around. If he had turned invisible, he could come right up behind me and burn me to a cinder before I even knew he was there.

I noticed an open spot between two of the rocks. I leaped toward it.

And there it was. I was standing at the top of a stone stairwell that led down into the earth.

I leaped onto the stairs and started down. After about ten feet, the smooth gray stone walls became jagged cave. It quickly became very dark, and I didn't have any sort of light. Again I was reminded of Annalise's warning, and again I shut it out. She had just saved my life. I wasn't going to let this guy go.

I slowed a bit. The light became more dim. I could still see, but not well. How much farther?

I reached the bottom of the stairs. There were two tunnels, one off to my left, another to the right. I listened for the sound of Hammer's footsteps, but I couldn't hear anything except the ocean.

Damn. Which way? One tunnel went almost directly south, the other went west-northwest. The latter led toward a section of the collapsed building; the former led away from it. There were good reasons for choosing either.

I noticed a glimmer on the wall. It was the silver wire. It ran just below the ceiling and vanished into the darkness of the northwest tunnel. I reached up and ran my fingers over it, feeling the rusted *U* of iron that held it in place against the stone.

I followed it. As I moved into the darkness, I put the ghost knife into my pocket and slung the gun over my back. I trailed my left hand along the wire, making sure that it didn't turn down some unseen tunnel or vanish into a rock wall. I held my right hand in front of me and stumbled down the cave.

The floor was about as flat and smooth as a path in the forest, which was better than I expected. I wasn't sure if it was man-made or not. I had no way to know; I was just grateful that I didn't have to climb over jagged rocks in the dark.

The ground sloped upward, then turned downward again. Before I went below the edge of the slope, I turned around and looked at the entrance to the tunnel behind me. The golden sunlight of the afternoon still glowed there. I turned around and went down into the dark.

Moving through that tunnel was slow work. It annoyed me that I couldn't hear anything but ocean sounds echoing off the stone. I wanted to hear footsteps or the sounds of Hammer cursing as he bumped his head in the dark. I wanted evidence that I was on the right path.

I followed the tunnel as it curved to the right, then to the left, and sloped down. I thought I might be somewhere under the house, but it was pointless to try to map my progress. I just kept my hand on the wire and continued.

I suddenly stepped in hot water. I yelped in fear and jumped backward, striking my head against something. I listened carefully. The ocean sounds were very loud.

I stepped forward. The water sloshed over my shoe and retreated, then washed up again. *This* was the ocean. The waves were washing back and forth along the tunnel. I waded into it for a couple of steps, getting wet up to my knees. Why was the water so hot? Maybe there was some sort of volcano nearby.

I waded out farther. The water was hot, but it wasn't scalding. I told myself that some people spend a lot of money to submerge themselves in swirling hot water. The tunnel angled down and I quickly reached the point where it went under the water.

Damn. Had Hammer really gone this way? I didn't want to drown down here in the dark, but this was where the silver wire led. I also hated the idea of letting Hammer go because I didn't have the nerve to follow him. I took a deep breath, then another, then I ducked my head under the water and pulled myself along the rocks through the tunnel.

I didn't open my eyes. What was the point when I couldn't see anything out of the water, either? But I remembered all those little gray worms. I imagined them all around, trying to wriggle under my skin.

I tried to clear my mind. Too much imagination was not in my best interests right now. I kept moving, pulling myself along the bottom of the tunnel. My chest grew tight. If I didn't find air, I was going to have to turn around very soon.

No. I was not going to turn around. I was going to reach the far side or I was going to drown here and rot. If Charles Hammer came this way, so could I.

Unless Hammer had magic that let him see in the dark and breathe underwater. Or unless he took the south tunnel, because this one had been blocked by the collapsing castle.

I didn't want to think about that, because it was already too late to turn back.

My lungs were burning. I held on even though I knew it was too late. I had gone too far. I had gambled and lost.

I reached for the next rock, but it wasn't there. I panicked, letting air bubble out of my mouth. Then I found a handhold a little farther away.

The cave was sloping upward again. I pulled myself along the rocks, praying that I wouldn't slam my head against a stone and drown myself.

I broke the surface and took a gulp of stale, heavy air. It stank of salt and steam, and I didn't get enough oxygen out of it. I clung to the rocks, desperately sucking in air.

After a minute or so, my heart stopped racing and the spots stopped dancing in front of my eyes. The air was close here, but it wasn't going to kill me.

And I saw a light. There was a very faint light coming from somewhere above me.

I laughed aloud. Light. Just seeing it up there gave me strength.

The cave was vertical here. I grabbed the nearest rock and began to climb. The rocks were wet and slick, but I moved slowly and steadily toward the light.

Partway up, I caught the Uzi strap on a rock. I had a sudden chill thinking about what would have happened if it had caught while I was under the water.

I reached the top of the wall and crawled over the lip. Ahead, I could see the bend in the cave. Light was coming from somewhere around that bend, and I crawled to it. The air was fresher here, but it was also thick with steam. I stood. The roof was too low for me, but I hunched along, going farther and farther upslope. There, against the wall and spattered with mud, was the tarnished silver wire.

I followed the bend in the tunnel, checking my pockets for the ghost knife and the silver knife. They were both there. I tilted the Uzi this way and that, draining as much of the water out of it as I could.

The tunnel exit was narrow. I peered through it. Below me was a broad cavern made of volcanic rock. A thin stream of water ebbing back and forth along the far wall and clouds of steam billowed against the roof, just above my head. The whole place was lit by a bright, flickering source of light from somewhere to the left.

I squeezed through the opening into the cavern. Charles Hammer was not in sight. There was a second cavern to the left. Maybe he had already gone toward the source of the firelight.

Beside me a path ran along the upper edge of the cavern, but there didn't seem to be any way down except by free climbing the cavern wall or flying. I wasn't about to do either.

At that moment, I heard a pained grunt echo against the rocks. I stepped back into the narrow opening behind me. Charles Hammer climbed through a small opening in the far right wall of the cavern, then ran along a wooden walkway. He went straight for the second cavern on the left.

The bastard had taken the other path. He must have gone the long way around because he thought the way I went was impassable.

It was too far to shoot accurately with a submachine gun, even if I thought it would do some good. And he was definitely too far for me to throw the ghost knife.

I started along the high ledge, trying my best to match his pace. He was quick though, and the ledge was slick and precarious. Even with the shortcut I had taken, he was still ahead of me.

My biggest advantage was that he hadn't seen me yet. I lifted the gun and rushed ahead. Hammer reached the opening into the second cavern.

I came to the end of the path. Below me was a long flight of stone stairs chiseled into the wall. I started down. I could hear Hammer's sneakers thumping against the wooden boards.

After about fifteen feet, I came to a break in the wall. It was a little window into the second cavern. I looked through.

I saw it.

Not very long ago I used a stolen spell to reveal the predators that move through the Empty Spaces, searching for worlds full of life like our own. They were strange creatures made of stone or color or motion—terrifyingly alien creatures living in a terrifyingly alien environment. What I saw through that opening in the cavern wall gave me chills. I was looking down at one of those predators.

It was a huge wheel of fire, maybe 150 feet tall and partially submerged in a pool of ocean water. Steam billowed up around it, filling the cavern and dripping down the walls.

Charles Hammer approached the creature. From within the wheel, a huge flaming eye opened up and looked down at him.

I ducked down below the opening and held my breath. Goose bumps ran up and down my whole body. It was alive. The wheel of fire was alive and it was here, on Earth. I peeked through the opening again and saw what I'd expected to see—a thick circle of shining silver surrounded it. The silver was inscribed with sigils, and it was untarnished. From where I stood, it looked clean and new. I noticed the silver wire running through the opening, down the cavern wall, and toward the silver ring. By squinting, I could see where it connected. I jerked my hand away from the wire. What if the wheel could sense me touching it, the way a spider could sense movement on its web?

Christ, what was I supposed to do about this? I slid to the steps, ducking down out of sight. This was the source of Hammer's power, and I was sure it had been here for decades.

I took out my ghost knife and held it up. It was just a piece of laminated paper. What good would it be against that massive wheel of fire? The silver knife wouldn't be much better. And that assumed that I had the nerve to cross the silver ring that held it in place. What if attacking it also set if free?

Annalise was right. I was completely out of my league. *They love to be summoned, but they hate to be held in place.* I peeked through the opening again. I couldn't see any sign of anger in that massive eye. I couldn't see any malevolence, just a tremendous power and tremendous *otherness.*

Charles Hammer stood before the ring, his arms raised above his head. He was shouting to it, imploring it the way a man might plead with a cruel god, but the echoes in the cavern garbled his words so thoroughly that I couldn't understand them.

I felt a sudden spasm in the iron gate on my chest, the most powerful one yet. I could feel waves of power flowing out of the wheel of fire, pressing hard against me.

On the cavern floor, Hammer had fallen to the wooden walkway. He writhed in agony, clutching at the same spot on his back where Cynthia had her iron gate. Then, suddenly, he relaxed, rolled onto his knees, and pressed his forehead against the boards. I might have thought he was praying if he hadn't been shuddering with gasps and sobs.

Something began to rain down from the ceiling, dropping through the steam and landing around Hammer. At first, I thought the roof was caving in, but the objects were small and the shower ended quickly.

Hammer looked around him as the fallen objects began to move, then he lifted his arms in helpless misery.

I realized what the falling objects were. Another kid had burned to death, and these were the gray worms created by the fire.

The worms scuttled across the uneven stone floor toward the far side of the cavern. I craned my neck and looked at the spot where they were heading.

There, I saw a second wheel lying on its side.

This one was not made of fire. It was simply a mass of

wriggling worms in the shape of a wheel. It was much smaller than the burning wheel, and it was not surrounded by a silver ring. The worms crawled and wriggled in a clockwise direction, giving the impression that the wheel was slowly turning.

It was a child. The wheel of fire was using the bodies of the children of Hammer Bay to create a second wheel, one not held in place by a magical binding.

Hammer turned back to the burning wheel, pleading with it some more. The fiery eye did not react, did not seem angry. It just stared at him implacably.

There was no way those worms were ever, ever going to be turned back into human children.

Hammer kicked at a section of wood, flipping it over. Underneath was another silver hoop, very much like the one in his tower. He stepped into it.

My iron gate flared white hot. The world went dark.

I woke up slowly. I don't know how long I had lain there on the stone steps, but I hadn't soiled my shorts, and I wasn't dying of thirst. It couldn't have been longer than a couple hours, although it might have been only a few seconds. I jumped up and looked through the opening in the wall.

Hammer was out of the hoop, crawling across the rocky floor of the cavern toward the baby wheel. Gray worms clung to his clothes and hair as he laboriously scuttled from one jagged rock to the next. He moved dreamily, as though he was sleepwalking.

He reached the edge of a long slab beside the smaller wheel. Now that he was next to it, I had some sense of its scale. It was at least forty feet in diameter.

Hammer plucked the worms off of his clothes and hair and tossed them onto the wheel. Then he stood among the rocks and lifted his head as though taking a deep breath.

He was about to breathe fire onto the baby wheel. He was about to ignite it.

The Uzi was in my hand before I realized what I was doing. It didn't matter anymore that I was too far away. I had to try something. I couldn't let a living wheel of fire get loose on the world, and I had no other way to stop him.

I fired a short burst that chipped the rocks twenty feet short of where Hammer was. I adjusted my aim and tried again. This time I hit the small wheel itself, to no apparent effect.

I felt the monstrous wheel turn its attention to me. Waves of power washed over me. My iron gate burned and throbbed. I didn't dare look at the predator. I didn't have the guts.

A jet of fire erupted from Charles Hammer's mouth and sprayed over the baby wheel.

I unloaded on him. Bullets spattered against the slab he was standing on, and miraculously, one struck his ankle.

His foot flopped inward like a broken chicken neck, and he fell hard, sliding down among the rocks. The jet of fire from his mouth roared upward toward the ceiling, igniting nothing.

Fires sputtered along the baby wheel, but they quickly died out. Hammer was going to have to try again. I saw him clutching at his throat.

I threw the empty gun away and sprinted down the steps. I had taken out Carol the receptionist by venting the flames as she was breathing them. Maybe I could do the same to Hammer, or maybe I could stab him with the letter opener in my pocket. Either way, I needed to be closer to him to do it.

I leaped down the steps at breakneck speed, ghost knife in hand, my bloody calf aching. If I fell, if I didn't stop him in time, I'd be dead, and so would a lot of other people. I tried to avoid a fall.

At the bottom of the stairs I leapt across a fissure onto the wooden walkway. It broke underneath me. My foot slid down the side of a rock and jammed painfully between two stones. The broken plank flew upward and wedged itself against the inside of my thigh. Nothing was broken or sprained, but by the time I freed myself from the mess, Hammer had regained the lip of the slab. His ankle and throat looked completely healed.

He was fifty feet away, too far for me to throw the ghost knife. I'd failed.

He took a deep breath.

An idea came to me. If I could call the ghost knife toward me, maybe I could control it in other ways, too.

I looked down at the spell in my hand and imagined it going through Charles Hammer's throat.

A jet of flame shot from Hammer's mouth.

I glared at the tattered spell in my hand and willed it to move.

It shot from my palm and zipped across the cavern for Charles Hammer's back.

Hammer turned his head back and forth, playing the fire over the baby wheel. Spurts of flame began to shoot up from the wriggling worms. Hammer turned far enough so that part of his face was visible, and I saw his agony.

The ghost knife struck the back of his neck. A jet of flame burst out of the cut like steam escaping a ruptured pipe. Flames engulfed his head, and the jet of fire lost pressure, falling short of the baby wheel. It hadn't ignited.

His whole head burning, Hammer fell backward. He did not scream, although I imagined he very much wanted to.

I sprinted along the causeway. The huge wheel stared down at me. As I ran past the silver wire, the pain in my iron gate grew. It was reaching out to me, trying to destroy me. Only Annalise's spell held it at bay.

I leaped off the walkway and started bounding across the rocks. The pain eased as I put some distance between the silver wire and me. I reached the slab where Hammer had been standing.

He was lying on his back, wedged between two stones. As I watched, his skin turned from scorched and blackened to pink and healthy. I thought how much I wished Annalise could do the same, and I hated him all the more.

"Oh, God," he gasped, as though he'd been holding his breath. "No more."

"What a fantastic idea," I said. I slid down the slab of stone and landed on his chest with both knees. I pulled the silver letter opener from my pocket.

"No!" Hammer screamed. He struggled, his arms flailing and batting at me, his legs scrabbling against the stones. I grabbed his arms and held them down.

His eyes rolled back in his head. He took a deep breath.

I jammed the silver blade under his chin into his brain.

He bucked twice. No jet of fire came out of him. He fell still and silent. He was dead.

I stood, leaving the letter opener in place. He didn't heal and he didn't wake up. I had guessed correctly. The wheel couldn't exert its power over him while he had the silver inside him.

At least, I hoped it couldn't. The silver ring that enclosed the wheel of fire was not enough to keep its immense power in check. I didn't know how long the knife would hold him.

I could have turned him over and destroyed his iron gate but decided against it. What would that have accomplished except to allow the wheel to erase his memory?

I looked up at it. I felt very small beside that terrible creature.

"Can you understand me?" I said. *Don't talk to the*

targets, Annalise had told me, but I couldn't resist. "Can you understand? Can you see the future? Can you control it?"

/Yes./

It was not a sound, it was a pressure against my iron gate and my mind at the same time. I felt sick and small, like an ant who sees a boot moving above him.

"Can you make me do what you want, the way you controlled all those parents and toy shoppers?"

There was no answer this time. I took that as a no.

I walked across the rocks toward the hoop Hammer had stood in. It was connected to the main ring by a second silver wire.

"What do I have to do to get you to control the future for me? Do I have to be inside the silver hoop?"

/Yes./

"Well, then," I said, "that's some sad luck for you, you great big bitch."

I held up my hand. My ghost knife flew into it like a bird returning to its nest. I bent down and cut the silver wire that connected the wheel's binding circle to the hoop, then I cut the other wire that led through the tunnel to the tower. I didn't see any more wires.

Immediately, the pressure against my iron gate eased. I had isolated the wheel, partially reducing the power it could bring to bear on the world outside its silver ring. Hopefully, with the wire cut and the silver blade wedged in Hammer's body, the predator wouldn't be able to heal him again.

I climbed back over the rocks to the baby wheel. Tiny worms wriggled sluggishly in a circle. It was not ready to be born. Maybe our attack on Charles Hammer had rushed the birth process, forcing the wheel to turn the spirit fire on it before it was ready. It didn't matter now.

I held out the ghost knife, letting the crawling worms cut themselves on the edge of the spell. The worms broke apart, falling to the stones like windblown ash. I yanked my hand away from the tiny gouts of flame that erupted. Thankfully, the fire did not spread.

I felt a great, mournful wail wash through me. It was not something I could hear, but it seemed to fill me nonetheless. I was murdering the wheel's unborn child, and it couldn't do anything but watch.

It took a while to finish the job. There were thousands of worms, but I could kill four or five with a quick swipe of my arm. I could have struck more, but I didn't want to throw my spell in case the wheel could catch it somehow, and I didn't want to let the little worms touch my skin.

I felt the predator behind me trying to exert its will over me. It didn't work. Cutting the wires had limited the amount of power it could use outside the ring. Still, the iron gate on my chest throbbed and ached.

The baby wheel shrank as I killed it. Eventually, it was reduced to the point that the inner hole vanished and it became a disk. When that happened, the remaining worms fell apart and died on the stones around me.

I was hungry. I was thirsty. I wanted to get the hell away from Hammer Bay. I didn't know how far I would have to drive before the sigil on my chest stopped throbbing, but I was willing to gas up and find out.

The wheel of fire looming above me really was out of my league. I didn't even want to look at it. I'd collect Charles Hammer's spell book, if I could find it, and let a peer in the society figure out what to do about the wheel. Someone needed to destroy it, but that someone wasn't going to be me.

I climbed over the rocks toward the wooden walkway.

Charles Hammer was gone.

I cursed and turned toward the hoop. He wasn't there, either. I'd already broken the connection between the hoop and the wheel of fire.

I scanned the entire cave. He wasn't anywhere nearby.

I hopped to the walkway, trying to pretend the wheel of fire was not looming above me, watching my every move, and sprinted toward the outer cavern. I didn't know how long ago Hammer had come to and fled, but I expected him to leave by the same long tunnel. I climbed up the stone stairs. I was going for the shortcut again.

The trip back seemed surprisingly quick. Maybe it was because I was so focused on chasing Hammer, or maybe it was because I knew what lay ahead, but in no time at all I was climbing back into daylight.

There was a tiny drop of blood on the top step. I didn't need to look for a second. I didn't need a blood trail to track him. He would be at the house or at the cars. Either he was collecting his things or he'd had gotten them already and was running.

I leaped over the rocks toward the house, angling for the asphalt parking lot and garage on the eastern side. I didn't see any lights or movement through the house windows. That was bad. If he was already gone, I was never going to catch him. I didn't know anyone willing to hand me leads on him, I didn't have any idea what other properties he owned, and I didn't have any damn money. Once the tank of gas in the van ran out, I was stranded.

If Hammer managed to get to an airport, I was never going to catch him later. Maybe someone in the society could, but I had no way of contacting them. It was on me or no one.

I finally reached the asphalt parking lot and climbed up onto the flat ground.

There was a tiny drop of blood on the ground beside the garage. The van was still parked in the mouth of the driveway. Hammer hadn't driven out. I went past the garage and raced to the house.

The smell of burned flesh hit me hard. I held the ghost knife close to my chest as I crept through the house.

Nothing seemed to be changed as far as I could tell. I moved through the rooms, past the piles of bones, up the stairs, and across the causeway.

I heard nothing. I didn't see any movement.

I stepped onto the landing. The wooden stairs spiraled above me. There was another drop of blood on the first step.

He'd come this way, obviously. Unless the blood was mine. Was he still up there with Annalise's corpse?

I heard soft fabric rustling. It was my only warning. I threw myself sideways.

Bullets streamed through the doorway. Hammer had come up behind me and fired a good long volley at me. I crouched on the stairs, hearing the shots ricochet inside the cylindrical tower. I covered my face with my tattooed forearms and waited. A ricochet tugged at the sleeve of my shirt, but that was as close as he got.

Finally, the shots finished. I knew he had more guns out there if he had the stomach to rummage through the bodies for them. If he had the nerve, he could charge in here and put a nasty end to me.

"You bastard!" he shouted, his voice high and desperate. "You can't kill me, and if I see you again, I'm going to burn you alive. I can still feel the power of the Great Wheel inside me. It's still inside me and you can't take it away!"

I moaned. "Call an ambulance," I said, trying to sound wounded and helpless. I held the ghost knife ready. "Please." Maybe, if I could lure him closer . . .

"Hah! Fuck you!"

I heard his footsteps as he ran away. I heard bones clacking. Then he was gone.

I peeked into the causeway. Nothing. I ran into the house. Bones had been scattered around the hall. The front door was standing open. I ran toward it.

Hammer was sprinting across the asphalt, holding a

book in his left hand and a set of keys in his right. An Uzi hung on his back, bouncing around near his kidneys. In a just world, the gun would have gone off, blowing out his midsection and the family jewels, ending the line. It didn't happen. He ran around the van, leaping onto the rocks to go around it.

Keys. Dammit, that's why the bones were spread around the hall. He must have taken a set of keys from one of the guards.

That's when I remembered the three Crown Victorias parked on the street.

I ran back into the house, kicked the bones aside, and grabbed two of the Uzis. Whatever Hammer had, I wanted double. I looped both of their straps around my neck. Offering a silent apology to the unburied dead, I ran out of the house, climbed into the van, and started it up.

It took a moment to turn the van around in the parking lot, then I raced up the driveway and fishtailed across the gravel road, wishing I had more acceleration. A vehicle that didn't handle like a refrigerator box would have been nice, too.

I swerved out onto the street just as one of the Crown Vics screeched out of its parking space and took off down the main road. I stomped on the accelerator, hoping to T-bone it and trap Hammer inside, but it had already passed me. I caught a quick glimpse of him behind the wheel, his eyes wild and his neck covered with gleaming red blood.

My heart sank as I watched the vehicle accelerate down the block. There was no way I could keep up with him. Still, I pulled the shoulder harness over me and clicked it into place. I was going to ram him, if I got the chance.

A soccer ball bounced out from between two cars, and Hammer slammed on the brakes. He slowly drove around it, then sped up toward the corner. I roared after him and chased him through Hammer Bay. He crept through stop signs and red lights, blaring his horn, screeching to a halt when he came too close to another car. This was his town. He was not going to break anything in it—at least, not where anyone would see.

I managed to clip his taillight when he braked for a woman on a bicycle, but it wasn't enough to stop him. He raced past the supermarket, past the hospital, past the last biker bar at the edge of town, then he crested a hill and vanished onto the highway.

If I couldn't keep up with him in town, I was never going to be able to follow him on the winding highway.

I rumbled up the crest in the hill. Hammer was pulling away. I picked up the Uzi with my left hand and leaned it out the window. I didn't have any other choice now, and there were no innocent bystanders to worry about.

I fired on him, trying to keep my shots low, near the tires. My aim was crap and the gun bucked like crazy. His back windshield shattered, and he swerved as he ducked below the dash. I punched holes in the trunk, for whatever good that did.

The magazine ran dry. I was reaching for the second one when Hammer, still ducking below the dashboard, swerved across the center line. A pickup truck loaded with gardening equipment rounded the curve ahead, heading straight for him. The driver blared his horn.

The vehicles swerved away from each other. The pickup slid onto the shoulder of the road and rumbled through the gravel. Hammer overcorrected, angling across the road and over the shoulder. He hit the brakes too late and smashed into a tree.

The pickup driver slowed to a stop, and so did I. I saw Hammer's air bag deflate back against the steering wheel. Hammer was hurt, but I knew he wasn't out of commission. I tossed away the empty gun and climbed from the driver's seat.

"Did you see what happened?" the pickup driver said, not really looking at me. "He swerved right into my lane!"

He rushed toward Hammer's car, intent on helping him. Hammer shoved open his door and stumbled out of the car. He was holding the Uzi. The pickup driver stopped suddenly about ten feet away and said something like "Whoa, friend . . ."

Hammer pointed the weapon at me. I fired.

He blossomed with bullet holes and fell back against the car. He lay still. The driver fled back to his truck like a perfectly sensible person.

I rushed over to Hammer and took his gun away. The bullet wounds were already healing, but slowly. Without the silver wire, the connection between the man and the predator must have been faint.

Using the ghost knife, I sliced off his clothes. I found an iron gate on his shoulder, just where it had been on Cynthia and Cabot. I cut through it, letting the black steam and gray sparks arc into the air.

There was another sigil on his stomach. It was a circle with flames at the four cardinal points and a single eye at the center. This one didn't look like a tattoo, though. It looked, and felt, like a tumor that had grown under his skin. I slashed the ghost knife through this one, too. There were no jets of steam or sparks, but Hammer's bullet wounds stopped sealing over.

As an experiment, I slid the corner of the ghost knife through his wrist. His skin split apart as if I was using a scalpel. He was dead.

The pickup truck raced away. I climbed into the Crown Vic and found an old leather-bound journal. It fell open to a page that read "To Call and Bind a Great Wheel, Which Will Grant You Favorable Outcomes."

On impulse, I pulled out Charlie Three's wallet. I found five hundred-dollar bills and ten twenties. I took them all. This had been a valuable lesson for him.

I tucked the book under my arm and went back to the van.

CHAPTER NINETEEN

I drove back into town. I should have dumped the van, stolen a car, and made a run for it, but I doubted I would get far. Half the town had seen me at the casino, the hospital, the police station, and during the car chase through town. The FBI or the state police were probably already looking for me.

Besides, I had no choice. Charles Hammer might have left another copy of his spell book in his tower. I had to finish Annalise's work and burn it down.

I drove through town without incident. Traffic still seemed lighter than it had. Most of the people must have been on the north side of town, where two columns of black smoke rose toward the sky. I pulled into Hammer's driveway without attracting any apparent attention. There were no police cars waiting for me, and no one seemed to have come to the house. The front door was still wide open.

I went inside and let myself onto the terrace. There was no lighter fluid beside the barbecue, but there was a long lighter, a bag of charcoal, and a charcoal chimney. That would do. I tore some pages off Charles's kitchen calendar and squirted olive oil on them. Then I put the paper on the bottom of the chimney and the coals in the top.

I'd almost forgotten about the sprinklers. I followed the sprinkler pipes along the ceiling to the place where they joined the main water system beneath the kitchen sink, and turned the valve all the way off.

Then I stood and opened the fridge. I was hungry, sure, but I had another thought nagging at me.

On the bottom shelf of the fridge, Charles had left three porterhouse steaks. I carried them along with the lighter and chimney to the tower.

I set the lighter and chimney on the landing inside the door. Then I sprinted up the stairs with the steaks in hand.

Annalise was still there. One look at her and I knew my idea was crazy and useless. I opened the first package and, with the ghost knife, cut a long strip from the steak. Annalise's mouth was wide open in a frozen scream. I stuffed the piece of meat into her throat.

I did it again and again. If I was crazy, I was crazy. Maybe they would put me in a nice, uncomfortable psych ward when they finally nabbed me.

As I finished the second piece of meat, I felt something in the back of Annalise's throat move.

She breathed on me.

She still looked dead. Her skin was charred and blackened, her face shriveled, her eyes empty sockets.

I put my hand back up to her mouth. I could swear I felt a faint breath. Unless I had lost my mind.

I cut up the third steak as quickly as I could, jamming it down her throat. When it was gone, I picked her up, getting greasy ash all over my ruined shirt, and carried her down the stairs and out of the house. I opened the back of the van and laid her down as gently as I could.

Then I ran back into the house, lit the charcoal chimney, and set it on the landing beside the stairs. Soon it would be hot enough to ignite the wood.

I ran into the kitchen and disabled the electric pilot light on the gas stove, then turned all the burners on full. In the front room, I tipped the overstuffed couch against the wall and lit a pile of magazines beneath it.

The magazines would light the couch, which would ignite the wall, which would still be burning when the gas reached it.

All of this took three minutes at most, but it seemed like forever. I finally ran back to the van and raced out of the driveway. There was always the possibility that someone would go to the house and be hurt or killed when the gas main went, but that didn't seem likely. Hammer liked his privacy, and the town gave it to him.

I drove through town again, pulled into the supermarket lot and parked beside the Dumpster, where the van wouldn't be visible from the road. My clothes were a mess.

People in the supermarket gave me some strange stares, but I limped as quickly as I could and paid with Hammer's cash. I bought another leg of lamb and forty pounds of pot roast.

Once back in the van, I started the engine. I didn't have any capacity for planning left. All I had was a buzzing, jangling urge to flee town.

I heard a loud *thoom* as I pulled out of the parking lot. A quick glance toward the water showed a heavy black cloud where Hammer's tower was supposed to be. People around me screamed or jumped into their cars to race toward the fire.

I turned the other way and drove out of town.

Several miles down the road, I came to the same empty lot where Annalise and I had confronted the Benton family. I pulled in and parked behind the abandoned stall.

I climbed into the back. Annalise was still breathing, but more faintly than before. Feeling her breath gave me chills. It was like feeling the breath of a ghost.

I opened the first package of pot roast. Just a few days before, I would have left her to burn in the tower, or I would have pitched her into the woods behind me and been glad to be rid of her.

Not anymore.

For the next hour, I sliced off strips of meat and fed them to her. She lived.

ACKNOWLEDGMENTS

First, I'd like to thank Ted Elliott, Terry Rossio, and all the regulars at the Wordplayer.com forums, most especially Bill Martell. I would never have learned how to put a story together without that site.

And thanks also go to Caitlin Blasdell and Betsy Mitchell for giving so much of their care, expertise, and precious, precious time to this book.

Finally, the largest share of my gratitude goes to my wife, MaryAnn, who believed in me when believing in me didn't make a bit of sense. This book wouldn't exist without her.

Here is an excerpt from *Game of Cages*, the
next book in the Twenty Palaces series
by Harry Connolly

COMING SOON
FROM DEL REY BOOKS

CHAPTER ONE

It was three days before Christmas, and I was not in prison. I couldn't understand why I was free. I hadn't hidden my face during the job in Hammer Bay. I hadn't used a fake name. I honestly hadn't expected to survive.

I had, though. The list of crimes I'd committed there included breaking and entering, arson, assault, and murder. And what could I have said in my defense? That the people I'd killed really deserved it?

Washington State executes criminals by lethal injection, and that first night in my own bed, I imagined I was lying on a prison cot in a room with a glass wall, a needle in my arm.

That hadn't happened. Instead, I'd met with an attorney the society hired, kept my mouth shut, stood in at least a dozen lineups, and waited for the fingerprint and DNA analysis to come back. When it did, they let me go. Maybe I'd only dreamed about the people I'd killed.

So, months later, I was wearing my white supermarket polo shirt, stocking an endcap with gift cards for other stores. It was nearly nine at night and I had just started my shift. I liked the late shift. It gave me something to do when the restlessness became hard to take.

At the front of the store, a woman was questioning the manager, Harvey. He gestured toward me. At first, I figured her for another detective. Even though the last press release about me had stated I'd been the victim of identity theft and the police were searching for other suspects, detectives still dropped by my work and home at random times to take another run at me. They weren't fooled. They knew.

But she didn't have a cop's body language. She wore casual gray office clothes and sensible work shoes, an outfit so ordinary I barely noticed it. She moved briskly toward me, clutching a huge bag. Harvey followed.

She was tall and broad in the hips with long, delicate hands, large eyes, and a pointed chin. Her skin color suggested she had both black and white parentage, which in this country made her black, even though her coloring was pretty much brown. "You're Ray Lilly, aren't you?" she asked.

"Who's asking?"

"My name is Catherine Little. I'm a friend of your mother's."

That last sentence hit me like a punch in the gut. The last time I'd seen my mother, I was fourteen years old and headed into juvie. She was not someone I thought about. Ever. "Who are you again?"

"I'm Catherine. I work with your mother. I'm a friend of hers. She asked me to contact you."

"Where is she?" I peered into the parking lot, but it was pitch-dark outside.

"Okay. This is the hard part. Your mom's in the hospital. She's had some . . . issues the last few days. She asked for you."

I laid my hand on the gift cards on the cart beside me. They toppled over, ruining the neat little stacks I'd been working with. I began to tidy them absentmindedly. "When?"

Catherine laid her hand on my elbow. "Right now," she said. "It has to be right now."

Something about the way she said it was off. I looked at her again. There was a look of urgency on her face, but there was something else there, too. Something calculated.

This woman didn't know my mother. I knew it then as clearly as if she were wearing a sandwich board sign that read I AM LYING TO YOU.

Her expression changed. My face must have given me away, because she didn't look quite so sympathetic, but she still had a look of urgency. "We have to hurry," she said.

Harvey laid his hand on my shoulder like a friendly uncle. "Ray, go get your coat. I'll clock you out."

I told Catherine I'd meet her out front and went into the break room. She had to be with the Twenty Palace Society; there was no one else who would want me. I had been dreading the day they would contact me again. Dreading it and wishing for it.

I grabbed my flannel jacket and hurried outside without speaking to or looking at anyone. I could feel my co-workers watching me. Just the thought of talking to Harvey—or anyone else—about my mom, even if it was just a bullshit cover story, made me want to quit on the spot.

Catherine waited behind the wheel of an Acura sedan, one of the most stolen cars in the country. I sat in the passenger seat and buckled up. She had a sweet GPS setup and some electronic equipment I didn't recognize. I squinted at a narrow slot with a number pad on the side—I could have sworn it was a tiny fax machine. While I had been living the straight life, cars had moved on and left me behind. She pulled into the street.

"I'm sorry," she said. "That really hit you hard, didn't it? They told me to contact you that way. I didn't realize . . . Sorry."

She seemed sincere if a little standoffish. "Who's 'they'?" I asked, just to be sure. "Who are you?"

"My name is Catherine. Really. 'They' are the Twenty Palace Society. We have an emergency and I need help. You're the only other member in this part of the country at the moment."

My scalp tingled. It was true.

Part of me was furious that they'd dangled my mother in front of me like bait, but at the same time, I wanted to lunge across the hand brake and hug her.

Finally. Finally! The society had come for me. It was like a jolt to the base of my spine. *Finally, something worth living for.*

"Are you okay?" she asked warily.

"I'm okay." I did my best to keep my voice neutral but I didn't succeed all that well. Christ, she'd even said I was a *member* of the society. I belonged. "We need to go by my place."

There were no tattoos peeking from the cuffs of her sleeves or the collar of her shirt. She had no sigils on her clothes or the interior of the car. No visible magic. She might have had something hidden, of course. I was tempted to rummage through her pockets to search for spells.

She drove to my place without asking for my address. My hand was trembling and I gripped my leg to hide the adrenaline rush. I'd thought about the society often over the last seven months. Aside from the attorney, and a visit from an old guy with a brush mustache who'd debriefed me about Hammer Bay, I'd heard nothing from them, not even gotten a call from Annalise letting me know how she was. I had been telling myself I wanted to be cut loose. I had been telling myself I wanted to be forgotten.

But now they had come for me again and every traffic light and Christmas decoration seemed saturated with color. In fact, all my senses seemed to have been turned up to ten. I felt alive again, and I was grateful for it.

At my aunt's house, I had Catherine drive around to the back. I climbed the stairs to my mother-in-law apartment above the garage and let myself in. I went to the bookshelf and pulled a slip of paper from between two yard-sale hardcovers. It had been sealed with mailing tape and had laminate over that. A sigil had been drawn on one side.

My ghost knife. It was the only spell I had, except for the protective tattoos on my chest and forearms. They didn't count, though; the ghost knife was a spell I'd created myself, and I could feel it as if it were a part of me.

I slipped it into my jacket pocket and looked around. What else did I need? I had my wallet and keys and even, for the first time in my life, a credit card. Should I pack clean underwear and a change of clothes?

Catherine honked. No time for that, I guessed. I rushed into the bathroom and grabbed my toothbrush. Then I wrote a quick note to my aunt to tell her I'd be gone for a while and please not to worry. Catherine honked again before I was done. I carried it down the stairs and annoyed Catherine further by running toward the back door of the house. I stuck the note on the backside of the wreath on the screen door, rattling it in the frame.

The inner door suddenly swung inward. Aunt Theresa was there, looking up at me. "Ray?" She wore a knit cap over her wispy gray hair and a bright red and green scarf around her neck. Cold. She was always cold. It was one of the many things about her that made me worry.

"Oh! I thought this was movie night. I was leaving you a note." She must have come to see who was honking.

She popped open the screen door and took the note with fingers bent sideways from arthritis. "Movie night is tomorrow, dear." She opened the note and read it. The note didn't mention my mother—that was

Catherine's cover story, not mine, and I wasn't going to lie to my aunt about her little sister.

I glanced at the room behind her, expecting to see Uncle Karl in his badge and blue uniform, scowling at me. He wasn't there.

Aunt Theresa looked up at me. "Will you be back for Christmas?"

The way she said it startled me. Of course I had gifts to give her and Karl, but I hadn't expected her to care if I . . . I felt like an idiot.

"I hope so," I said, and meant it.

She shuffled forward and hugged me. I hugged her back. She knew a little about what I did. Not about the society itself, and not enough to get into trouble, but enough to worry. "Be careful."

We let go. I backed down the stairs and hurried to Catherine's car. I should have said something reassuring to Aunt Theresa, but it was too late now. Time to go.

I climbed into the Acura and belted up. My adrenaline was up and I couldn't help but smile. Catherine didn't like that smile. "Do you have everything now?"

The ghost knife in my pocket felt like a live wire. "Yep."

She rumbled through the alley and pulled into the street. I thought it would be best to let her tell me what was going on when she was ready, but after driving in silence for four blocks, I couldn't hold back.

"What's the emergency?"

"Well . . ." she said, and then fell silent while she negotiated a busy intersection. Her body language had changed again—she was irritated. I wasn't sure why; didn't it make sense for me to stop at home before I went on a job?

"Well," she said again, "earlier today we found out there's going to be an auction. Tonight. In fact, it might be taking place right now, although I hope not. I went an hour out of my way to pick you up, so you better be worth it."

This was a sudden change in tone. I wondered where it had come from. "I'll do my best," I said, but that made her scowl and blow air out of her nose. "What's being auctioned?"

"A predator."

That was the answer I didn't want to hear. Predators are weird supernatural creatures out of the Empty Spaces. I'd seen two so far, along with the pile of corpses they left behind. "Do you know what kind?"

"What kind?" She seemed to think this was an idiotic question, but I had no idea why. "No. I don't know what kind."

"Okay." I was careful not to snap at her.

"Who are you?" she asked. She looked me up and down. I didn't feel a lot of friendliness coming from her.

"I'm Ray Lilly," I answered, keeping my tone neutral. "Remember? You just pulled me out of work."

"I know your name," she said, leaving out the word *dumbass,* but implying it anyway. "What were you doing at that supermarket? What are you doing in that apartment?"

"Working. Living."

"That's not cover for a mission? Okay. What I want to know is who you are in the society. Because you are definitely not a peer. Are you an apprentice? An ally?"

"I'm not any of those things," I said. "I'm Annalise Powliss' wooden man."

She exhaled sharply, then laughed to herself a little. "For God's sake," she said. After a few seconds more, she pulled into a Pizza Hut parking lot. She didn't turn off the engine. "All right," she said, and I could tell by her tone that I wouldn't like what she was about to say. "Somebody fucked up. You shouldn't be here, not with me, and I shouldn't have been sent a fucking hour out of my way to pick up a fucking wooden man, not on a supposedly emergency job. What's the point in having you along? I don't need you and I don't want you. Hell, I don't even like looking at you, knowing what you are.

"So here's the deal: you keep quiet and do what I say, or you get out right now. I have a long night's work ahead of me, and I don't need you getting in my way. So which is it going to be? Because if following orders is going to be too much for you, you need to be out of my car and have yourself a nice day."

She stared at me, waiting for a response. It had been a while since anyone had spoken to me like that. If Catherine had been a guy . . .

Not that using my fists had ever turned out well for me. Old habits don't just die hard, they make living hard, too. "You must be part of the diplomatic wing of the society."

She sat back, rolled her eyes, and sighed. "What the hell did I do to deserve this?"

"I'll tell you what you did," I answered. "You talked to me like I ran over your dog. Whatever your problem is, it has nothing to do with me."

"Oh no?" She turned the key, shutting off the engine. "Bad enough to have a peer or an ally along. Then I would spend all my time praying the collateral damage didn't hit me. But every wooden man I've ever met was either a stone-skulled thug, terminally ill, or a terminally ill stone-skulled thug." She made sure to look me straight in the eye as she said it. She had guts. I would have liked her if she wasn't so obnoxious. "Which are you?"

"Well, I'm not terminally ill."

She frowned. I'd lived down to her expectations. "Well that's just dandy."

"If you order me to get out of your car," I said, "I'll hop out right here. I'm not going to ride with someone who doesn't want me. But that's the only way I'm getting out. When the friendly guy from the society turns up to debrief me, I'm not going to tell him I *chose* not to go. Understand?"

She turned away from me. The society had kept me out of jail, somehow. I had no idea what would happen if I refused to take a job. Would they kill me? Would they lift whatever spell kept the cops off my front door? I had exactly one person handy that I could ask, and she was trying to kick me out of her car.

Pizza delivery guys carried red cases across the lot. They didn't seem happy about the way we were parked. I wondered how much they made a month.

"All right, then," Catherine said, "we go on the job and you take your orders from me."

"That ain't going to happen, either," I told her. As Annalise's wooden man—I went when she said "go" and I did when she said "do"—but that didn't mean I was going to take orders from everyone in the society. Not unless Annalise told me to. "If you have a good idea, I'll be happy to go along with it. If not, then not. That's the only deal you're going to get. If that's not good enough, *you* can explain why you gave the boot to the guy the society sent you an hour out of your way to pick up."

She chewed on that for a while, then pulled into the street and drove onto the highway onramp. We weren't talking, apparently, but I could bear it. At least she didn't want to kill me.